EMBRACE THE WIND

Embrace the Wind

An Historical Novel of the American West

Susan Denning

No Limit Press

No Limit Press
PO Box 1094
White House Station, NJ 08889
Email address: embracethewindnlp@gmail.com
Website: www.nolimitpress.com

ISBN 978-0-692-82352-1
Printed in the USA

Typesetting services by BOOKOW.COM

This book is dedicated to my mother, Frances, a strong, resourceful woman who, like Aislynn, did the best she could with what she had.

Preface

Embrace the Wind is a work of historical fiction. By definition, the story is invented and built around a historic period. I was blessed to have stumbled upon an eventful time in the West, 1867–1871. The story, which begins in Far Away Home and concludes in Embrace the Wind, straddles the end of the old frontier and the beginning of the modern West. It was a time and a place where women's roles were changing. In the raw and untamed West, they lived with lawlessness and violence. However, they bravely took risks, challenged convention and created a new social order.

Many of Aislynn's experiences are based on actual events reported by frontier women. They were revealed in books, diaries, letters and contemporary newspapers. I believe Aislynn is true to her time. This novel reflects the real triumphs and tragedies of these courageous pioneers. Personalities, dialogue and scenes involving historic figures are all imagined. Dates, times and locations have been altered to fit the flow of Aislynn's story. After all, this is a work of fiction.

Acknowledgments

I want to thank all the wonderful people who helped make this book possible:

To my incredibly dedicated husband, TD, it is hard to find the words. (Yes, I wrote that!) No matter what crazy thing I want to do in life and no matter what challenges we face, you never waver. I love you and am grateful for you every day.

Thank you to our son, Tim. You have been patient, supportive and understanding through this journey, which has spanned most of your young life. I love you, too.

There are several people who deserve a very special thank you: Geoff Woodland is a fabulous writer, an honest critic and one of my biggest supporters. Although Geoff lives half a world away, he always seems to be willing to answer my cries for help regardless of the time zone challenges.

A special thanks to Bridgette Laramie, an amazing publisher, who has patiently guided and encouraged me through this entire process.

Diane Moody, who despite being a busy, prolific author has been very generous with her time and advice.

And to Sheila Garry Avery, who has stuck with me through each book: reading, editing, making valuable suggestions and honest assessments. You truly are a strong woman.

To my editors and pre-readers—Cyndi, Fritzi, Kyle, Jean Marie, Sebastian, Derbigny, Arlene, Lisa, Carol, Brenda,

Barbara, Duggee, Anne, Kristin, Linda, Rachel, Chrissy, Sandy, Jacqi, Ann, Deb, Carol, Bev, Dorothy, Shayna, Sebastian and Lorrie.

And to Geoffrey Dodson of wyomingtalesandtrails.com, who graciously shared information and the cover photo- 16th Street, Cheyenne- 1869 by A.J. Russell.

I am also grateful to the Wyoming State Library. I started my research into life in 1870s Cheyenne at the Library of Congress, an extraordinary resource for any writer. The knowledgeable librarians shared copies of The Wyoming Tribune and the Cheyenne Daily Reader. After a few days, one of the librarians showed me the most useful website, The Wyoming Newspaper Project. The Wyoming State Library has entered all the newspapers from the territorial period through the present online. This enabled me to read every issue of these newspapers from the day Aislynn arrives in 1870 until the chapters end in 1871. The events found in these historical documents are the basis for the storyline of Embrace the Wind.

The staffs at the State Law Library and the Warren Museum answered my questions and gave me valuable guidance. I am particularly indebted to the Wyoming State Archive staff, specifically Carl Hallberg and Larry K. Brown. I emailed them questions for years, and they graciously assisted me.

Thank you all. I am most grateful.

CHAPTER 1

May 1870

"Excuse me, Mrs. Maher," the conductor began as he bowed politely. "May I assist you with your overhead luggage? A little lady like you can't reach that high."

"Yes, thank you," she murmured, while thinking, *If only I were a lady.* Aislynn sat erect, her hands resting in her lap, trying to look like the proper widow. In the elegant Ladies Coach, with its prim, green silk seats and the clean smell of lemon oil rising from the black walnut walls, it was easy to appear respectable. However, beneath the black crepe, her shame festered.

Slowly stuttering toward the station, the train jerked forward and back, rocked side to side and jumped every time the iron wheels clicked over a seam in the iron rails. Coal smoke from the locomotive, dust from the prairie and tiny flies rushed in when the conductor opened the door. Aislynn waved her black-gloved hand before her nose and mouth, warding off the vexation.

When the brakes screeched the train to a halt, the conductor appeared at her side. He extended his elbow over the vacant seat next to hers. "Please take my arm, and I'll walk you to the door. You can wait there while I collect the steps."

The warm, dry wind grazed Aislynn's cheeks as she stood above the platform in the railcar doorway. Below, a chaotic scene unfolded. To her left, gray smoke rose from greasy cook fires while vendors hawked food. Two large women wearing stained aprons and straggly hair argued over the noise of the throng. At the center of the platform, a two-story sandstone station with the words *UNION PACIFIC RAILROAD* boldly carved over heavy wooden doors dominated the scene. A flood of people flowed in and out. Freight wagons crowded the building on two sides, all eager to get close to the train and its treasures. Near the station's doorway, a weather-beaten Indian hunched under a dingy blanket extended an empty hand. To Aislynn's right, a gang of scruffy, rowdy men swarmed a boxcar and deposited a ramp at its door. Her eyes caught a slice of Cheyenne beyond the station. A small parade of low, dust-stained buildings sitting on muddy streets formed the "Magic City of the Plains." Aislynn wondered what had happened to the magic.

When the locomotive exhaled its last smoky breath, the prairie wind brought new scents her way. The air filled with the smell of fried meats, boiled coffee, roasted peanuts, laboring animals and sweaty men. Passengers disembarked like soup pouring from a tureen. They spilled in every direction. Some attended to necessities during the thirty-minute stop. Others, like Aislynn, were meeting friends or family and staying a while.

The conductor returned with the wooden steps. He placed them below Aislynn and offered his hand. Simultaneously, three men, dressed in rough camp clothes and carrying packs with bedrolls, stumbled from the adjacent car. Each one stopped on the platform and gawked as Aislynn gathered her skirt to descend.

"Need some help?" The tallest man approached Aislynn.

"Get away, you ruffians!" the conductor barked as he shooed the men with his free hand. They scoffed and turned to join the rowdies with the ramp. "We have a terrible element in these parts, Mrs. Maher; they are scoundrels of the worst sort. You must beware."

"I will. Thank you for rushing to my defense."

"I hope there's someone here to meet you. You shouldn't be alone."

Aislynn surveyed the cacophonous crowd one more time before stepping down. Toward the end of the platform, she spied Orrin Sage. "Please don't worry about me. I see my escort now. If he takes care of me half as well as you have, I'll be quite fine."

The frontier had altered radically in the two years since she had last seen Sage; apparently, he was unaffected. He wore the same buckskin shirt covering shoulders wide enough to block the horizon. His hefty arms cradled his old rifle and two Colt revolvers filled the holsters hanging low on his narrow hips. Buckskin covered his muscular, saddle-honed thighs. Knee-high boots with an enormous hunting knife strapped to his right calf completed the outfit. With an expression that could sour milk, he watched the scruffy men pulling a cannon down the ramp from the boxcar. Aislynn closed her eyes and took a deep breath. *He's all you've got,* she told herself. *You have to make the best of it.*

Quick to feel her gaze, Sage flashed his gray eyes to hers. He nodded and made his way through the bustle. Reaching her, he removed his hat and bowed his head. Aislynn, standing on the platform with a carpetbag in her hands, bobbed a quick curtsy. He scanned her and grinned. "You're lookin' good, not so scrawny." His words rolled out in a slow, rumbling bass.

"And you, sir, haven't changed a bit," she said, with a dismissive shake of her head. His sandy hair still hung down to his shoulders. His bushy beard and long, thick moustache remained rooted on his face. A hint of bay rum reached her nose. She thought, *At least he bathed.* The conductor surveyed Sage's guns and looked at Aislynn with fear in his eyes. She smiled and said, "He's not as bad as he looks." They said their goodbyes as Sage frowned over them.

"Friend of yours?" he asked with a critical tone.

"He's a very sweet man, and so are you when you come out from under your arsenal. Are you trying to scare me?"

"That'd take more than three guns," he stated without a grin. "I booked you a room at the Ford House. Let's get you settled and a bite to eat." Sage stuffed one bag under his arm and lifted the other two by their handles with his huge paw. He leaned his rifle on his right shoulder and told Aislynn to "grab hold." As they started to proceed, the scruffy men dragged the cannon into their path. Sage shot them an angry look.

"Are we at war?" Aislynn asked.

"They're fixin' to start one."

"With whom?"

"Sioux and Cheyenne."

"I thought that war was over."

"For them men, as long as there's Injuns, there's cause for war."

Aislynn sighed and said, "Pity."

"It ain't your business." He cocked his head toward the street and added, "Let's go."

Just as their path cleared, the argument between the two women developed into a violent fistfight. "Stop them!" Aislynn cried.

4

"Ain't my jurisdiction. I'm a deputy federal marshal. Right now, they're the sheriff's job. When they kill each other, it's my job."

He pulled her along through the depot. The street was perfect pandemonium. Dozens of freight wagons teamed with dozens of horses, mules or oxen jockeyed for positions. Ruts carved in the thick mud corrugated the road. Puddles and piles dropped by the draft animals fouled the way and the air. Rotting, fly-covered garbage increased the stench. Pieces of wire, bottles and trash impeded their path. Long boards, laid as a bridge across the mucky moat, were nearly submerged in the mire. Sage barked over the din of shouting men and braying animals. "You'll have to lift your skirt." Aislynn bundled her carpetbag beneath her arm and gathered her dress in her hand. She grasped Sage's arm with her free hand. Together they navigated the perilous roadway.

They stepped up on the boardwalk into a knot of men loitering in front of a saloon. The men stopped speaking when they spied Aislynn's ankles. Flushed with embarrassment, she dropped her skirt and defensively smoothed the wrinkles. Sage's eyes burned over the men. They doffed their hats, bowed their heads and cleared a passage.

Aislynn stayed tethered to Sage as they negotiated the boardwalk along Eddy Street. The heart of the town seemed to be packed in a six-square-block area north of the station. With a few glances, Aislynn could see Cheyenne still held the rawness of a town recently raised from the dust. Despite its young age, the town wore a weary face. Frigid winters, blazing summers and abrasive winds can scar even the best of man's efforts. A scattering of two-storied stone buildings stood among false-fronted, frame structures tilting and sagging under peeling paint. Farther down the side streets, small homes dotted the way until the settlement faded into the endless prairie.

Sage and Aislynn shared the street with businessmen dressed in baggy sackcloth suits, roughs wearing tall hats and low hanging guns and dusty cowboys in chaps and spurs. The first women they encountered wore bright frills, store-bought faces and unnaturally colored hair. Aislynn wanted to peer into the windows and faces, but matching Sage's long strides took all her effort.

A few blocks on, they stepped into the dimly lit hotel lobby. Feelings of sadness and regret caught in Aislynn's throat. Peeking into the dining room, she could almost see Johnny sitting at the table they had occupied a mere two years ago. Through her reverie, she heard Sage's voice. "This here's Mrs. Maher." Aislynn turned toward the reception desk.

"Good afternoon, Mrs. Maher. I'm Barney Ford. I own this place. I have reserved my best room for you. I'll get my wife to take you upstairs." Ford turned and called into the kitchen, "Julia, Mrs. Maher is here."

A small, dark-skinned woman emerged and introduced herself. "You must be wantin' to freshen up. You come with me, and I'll get you settled."

Aislynn turned to Sage. He handed her a bag and gave the other two to Mrs. Ford. "Go on. I'll be waitin' in the dinin' room."

She listened to Mrs. Ford as they climbed the stairs to the second floor. "You're way back here. We think it's the best bed, and it's the quietest room."

"I'm sure it will be fine."

"So you're here to visit with Mr. Sage? Can't say he's ever had a visitor before." Mrs. Ford dropped the bags to unlock the door. "Here you go." She opened the door and waved Aislynn inside. "I left the window closed to keep out any dust and noise. I put fresh water in the ewer and there's a new bar of soap. If you get cold, you'll find an extra blanket on the chair."

"You're very kind to have gone to such trouble."

"It ain't trouble. No, not for you; you're Mr. Sage's *friend*." She winked and placed the valises on the floor.

"Thank you." Aislynn put her carpetbags down and waited for Julia to leave.

"How is it you know Mr. Sage?"

Aislynn sensed Mrs. Ford suspected a romantic relationship between her and Sage. She searched for a way to quash her misconception immediately. "My dear husband, Johnny, and I met Mr. Sage when we passed through Cheyenne on our trip from New York City to the Utah Territory. In fact, we stayed here at your hotel. Mr. Sage helped us a great deal. He is simply a good friend."

Mrs. Ford studied Aislynn for a moment. "Of course." Doubt dripped from her tone. "If you need anything, just let us know," she offered as she left the room.

Aislynn assessed the spartan room. Blue stripes and red roses faded on the walls. The scrolled iron bed wore a quilt stitched from remnants of calico. Between the dirt-streaked windows, a whitewashed vanity table supported a mirror spotted with silver rot. A washbasin and pitcher sat on the vanity and a chamber pot hid under the bed. Aislynn fell on the hard mattress. Running her hands over the coverlet, she wondered about its cleanliness. Aislynn sighed and reminded herself the room came cheap. In her current circumstances, she had to conserve her money.

Lying there, Aislynn could see the sky through the dingy window. She studied the unbroken blue until tears blurred her sight. Closing her eyes, she prayed, "Bless me, Father, for I have sinned."

Aislynn paused at the dining room door. Back in April 1868, she and her fiancé, Johnny, had arrived in Cheyenne, the terminus of the transcontinental railroad. They were hungry and tired. They found the Ford House and checked in. Here, in this dining room, they got their first real view of the Wild West. Seated at a corner table, four hard-looking men drank and gambled. Menacing six-shooters rested at each man's fingertips. The gambler in her view possessed pale eyes, frozen in a permanent squint. A huge moustache and bushy beard clung to his face. His long blond hair hung down to his shoulders. His hands were large and strong with veins protruding through the dark, weathered skin. He held cards in one hand, while the fingers on his other twitched against the table. Aislynn thought him alarming and terrifying until he became her friend.

She sat on the edge of the stiff chair across the table from Sage. As always, his threatening Colts rested on the table between his ever-ready hand and a glass of whiskey. Scanning the room, Aislynn did not see anything new. The porch roof shaded the windows facing the street, making the room gloomy despite the fair afternoon. All five of the empty tables scattered around the space sat under unlit kerosene lamps. The only bright spot was their corner table, dressed in a white cloth and glowing under the orange light of the burning lamp.

He greeted her with, "You hungry?"

"A sandwich and a cup of coffee would be lovely." Aislynn tried to present a buoyant, positive attitude.

"Julia," Sage called without leaving his seat. Julia immediately burst into the room and took the order, leading Aislynn to assume she had been waiting and listening behind the kitchen door.

Sage silently sipped his drink, studying Aislynn. His scrutiny made her uncomfortable. "Well, Cheyenne has become quite a town," she said without conviction.

He shrugged. "We got all the makin's of a town: stores, restaurants, a school, churches, even a museum."

His description brightened Aislynn's expectations. "How wonderful. I am tired of life confined to a mining camp. For a full two years, I barely left Treasure Mountain. I simply went from my home to my restaurant. I found no polite society or amusement."

Leaning over the table, Sage's eyes met hers. "Cheyenne ain't all that polite or amusin'."

"Why not?"

Sage shook his head. "You just said you've been west for two full years." His tone indicated his statement answered her question.

Frustrated, Aislynn pushed on. "So?"

"Most men here ain't no different than the ones in your camp. They're varmints seekin' fortune and pleasure and don't want to abide by no rules. It's still a place favorin' the strong and the violent."

Aislynn listened with growing unease.

"Them fellows just do what they want no matter who gets stomped on. We're tryin' to make a town," he continued, "a place with laws and rules, a place where a man who breaks them laws faces judgment." Sage shook his head. "Right now the law ain't big enough."

Aislynn sank back in her chair, her stature and hopes shrinking.

"We got a full measure of drinkin', gamblin' and whorin' men. There's shootin's every night and sometimes durin' the day. Now, we got that nuisance, the Bighorn Expedition. You seen them men with the cannon? Ne'er-do-wells of every stripe. Four hundred of them are here, Injun haters all and more comin' every day."

"Why are they coming here?"

Sage steamed on, "They're a bunch of miners, ex-soldiers and speculators. They know there's gold in the Black Hills, Red Cloud's Black Hills. While they're spendin' money and makin' businessmen rich and happy, they're also skirmishin' with any braves they come across. They're draggin' us back into the bad old days. Last week, Injuns attacked two families settled just north of here, killed everyone, even the children." Sage took a breath. "And soon, the cattle drives will hit town. All hell's gonna break loose with them dry, lonely cowboys carousin'."

Julia appeared with Aislynn's meal. Bending over her sandwich, Aislynn weighed Sage's news while she watched him from under her lashes. One hand held his drink while the other beat a nervous tattoo next to his guns. Sage's gray eyes scanned the room. She remembered his heightened senses: his eyes were like spyglasses, his ears could hear a spider crawling on the wall and his nose rivaled any dog's. But his hands cemented his reputation. Those browned, lined, blue-veined hands wielded knives and guns fast and accurately. Aislynn knew he was a man to be feared, but he was also a man she could trust. She did not doubt his assessment of Cheyenne. But, Aislynn was searching for a place to make a home. As bad as Cheyenne might be, it made no difference; she had nowhere else to go.

"Is there any hope?" Aislynn asked, thinking more of herself than Cheyenne.

Sage's eyes returned to hers. "Well, we got laws and courts."

"So what's the problem?"

"They ain't workin'."

Aislynn's aggravation and fear expanded. "Can't someone fix them?"

"Yes."

Aislynn took a sip of coffee and quieted her eagerness. She knew the information would come, but Sage required patience.

"The federal government is replacin' our U.S. marshal. In two days, there's a hearin' to decide who gets it."

"You?" Aislynn brightened.

"That's the idea."

"How wonderful for you." *And for me.*

"Me and Justice Howe got an idea how to turn things around."

Curious, Aislynn rested her elbows on the table and cradled her chin in her hands. "Tell me."

"Women," he stated and drew on his whiskey.

Again, she waited for an explanation.

He relaxed back in his chair, keeping his hands on the table. "The problem is we arrest them outlaws and bring them to court, but nothin' happens. Lawyers are drunk and more shiftless than the criminals. Justice Howe already sent two of them lawyers to jail for thirty days. The jurors have no respect for the law. They don't want to convict men for the same crimes they're committin'." Both of Sage's hands began tapping the table. "When it's murder, the jury says, 'One man's dead, why kill another?' That's why we need women."

Aislynn cocked her head and wrinkled her nose; expressing her bewilderment plainly on her face.

"Women." He repeated the word and lifted his hand in emphasis. "Justice Howe says, 'Women are a civilizin' influence.' Him and Justice Kingman got Governor Campbell to sign a law lettin' women vote. That law even lets them hold a government office. In Wyoming, married women get to own their own property." Sage nodded with conviction, his pride showing. "We even got a law that says women teachers get paid like men. It's called nondiscrimination. We got ourselves three women teachers in Cheyenne."

"How revolutionary." Aislynn's excitement rose.

"Most important, they can sit on juries. Governor Campbell says, 'Women will conquer the Wild West.' We just gotta get them here. We're thinkin' givin' them rights will help."

"Having more rights appeals to me."

Sage's brows rose. "You a suffragette?"

Jerking her chin at him, she said, "Proud of it. I even voted in a camp election."

"But you ain't 21."

Aislynn thought for a moment and grinned. "Prove it."

Sage chuckled. "Got me there." His demeanor altered, replaced with an accusatory tone. "A handful of rights ain't why you're here."

"No, but they're another reason to stay."

CHAPTER 2

BELLS clanged as Sage pushed open the door of Avery's Grocery. Aislynn entered to find a multitude of merchandise. Colorful cans, bottles and boxes crammed ten-foot-high shelves that ran up three walls. In front of the shelves, glass display cases supported wooden counters holding piles of fresh vegetables, breads and crates of eggs, bringing a farm-fresh smell to the store. Barrels of grains and nails rose from the dark floor, while brooms, picks and shovels leaned in the corners. An array of furniture lined the broad windows facing the street.

Behind the center display case, an older couple assisted a woman wearing a tight bun and a long black cloak. Two young girls, one plump and fair, the other dark and slight, rolled bolts of fabric. In front of the unlit stove, a stocky, balding man sat scribbling on a pad. A large, heavy-haired, black dog snoozed at his feet. Aislynn entered to no one's particular notice. When Sage's heavy boots clomped through the door, all twelve eyes turned toward him. They saw Aislynn take his arm, and the room fell silent.

"Cat got your tongues?" Sage asked in his brusque manner.

"She's a woman!" the fair girl exclaimed in a high-pitched voice.

"Good eyes, Emmie."

"You said a friend was coming, not a woman."

"Can't a woman be a friend?" he barked.

The woman behind the counter spoke, "Forgive our rudeness, ma'am." She nodded toward Aislynn and turned to Sage. "We are sorry, Mr. Sage." She stepped out and approached Aislynn. With a short curtsy, the sturdy, gray-haired woman introduced herself, "I'm Maggie Avery and this is my husband, Paul. We own this store. That's our daughter, Emmie, and her friend, Molly. And may I introduce Miss Joan Petty? She is one of our most esteemed teachers."

"It's lovely to meet all of you," Aislynn said as she turned to greet each person. "I'm Mrs. Aislynn Maher."

A gruff voice piped up. "I know I'm half-blind, but I ain't invisible. Come over here, gal." The scribbler struggled to his feet. His twisted left arm hung at his side. He extended his good hand. Aislynn offered hers and he clasped it. "I'm Cap. He's Smokey." He pointed to the husky mutt.

Sage stood behind her. "This here's Captain Elliot Walker, one of the best Injun fighters and scouts who ever walked the plains."

The old man squeezed her hand. "You're a dainty little thing, ain't you? Can't be more than five feet. I can see your black hair, but can't make out the color of your eyes in this light." He placed a hand on her cheek.

"You know they're green, you old coot," Sage snapped at Cap. "He sees fine," he said to Aislynn. "He just pretends he's blind so he can touch every woman who comes near enough."

"Why a sweet, young thing like you'd be friends with such a coldhearted brute like him, I'd like to know.

"If he's so bad, why are you friends with him?"

"Sharp mind. I like that in a woman. I've been his friend for more years than I can count, but I had to 'cause no one else would have him." Cap grinned at Sage.

"I'm his friend, too." Emmie sprang from behind her workstation. With a pretty smile, Emmie curtsied. She launched into a stream of questions. "Where are you from? How long are you staying? How did you meet Mr. Sage?"

"Emmie," her mother reprimanded, "don't pry." Facing Aislynn, she added, "I'm sorry, she doesn't mean to offend. She's excited to see Mr. Sage has a friend."

Aislynn recognized the meaning in the term *friend*. She explained, "My late husband, Johnny, and I met Mr. Sage on our trip west from New York City two years ago."

"You're a widow." Emmie stated the obvious.

"That's quite enough, Emmie." Maggie's sweet timbre turned angry.

"Sorry for your loss, Mrs. Maher. You're awful young to be a widow," Cap said gently.

"Is anyone ever old enough?" Aislynn asked.

An uncomfortable quiet filled the room. In an accent hinting of a formal education and a wealthy, eastern upbringing, Miss Petty pulled them out of the awkwardness. "Welcome to Cheyenne, Mrs. Maher. It will be nice to have another seemingly educated woman in town." She turned to Paul. "Now, perhaps we can return to my order."

Maggie asked Aislynn if she needed to purchase anything. Aislynn knew from experience the best way to sway a western man to your will without compromising yourself was to fill his stomach. Men who lived on the three Bs—biscuits, bacon and beans—became quite malleable after a good meal.

"I'd like to prepare a nice meal for Mr. Sage."

"Have you seen his lodgings?"

"No."

Maggie shook her head and announced to Sage, "You talk to Cap while I help Mrs. Maher."

She took Aislynn's arm and whispered, "It's behind the jail. It was a cell; the metal bars are still on the window. I think it's the first real roof he's ever had over his head, poor thing." Maggie sighed. "He has a potbelly stove, a coffee pot, skillet and one plate. Tell me what you're planning to cook, and I'll make up a box of everything you need."

"I'm thinking of chicken and dumplings in a cream sauce with carrots and peas."

"My, you must be quite a cook."

"I own a restaurant in Utah and do all the cooking."

"Well, that must be exciting. I can give you everything but the cream. You can get that at the dairy."

"I forgot dessert. May I have a jar of peaches, too? I can dress them up by pouring some cream over the top," Aislynn explained.

Maggie dashed through the store calling to Sage, "Do you have flour? Salt? Sugar? Baking soda?"

Sage turned toward the woman with frustration. "I do cook you know."

Maggie shook her head at Sage's demeanor, while she presented Aislynn with a wooden box brimming with all her necessities. "I'll put this on his account." She smiled tolerantly. "He has his good points; you just have to dig deep enough." Shrugging her shoulders, she added, "Should I include a shovel to this order?"

"No, thank you," Aislynn responded, "I think this is all I'll need." *At least I hope so.*

"If you start the fire and get some water, I'll fix dinner." As Sage exited, Aislynn inspected his compact home. The only light sifted through the barred window. It painted dark stripes down the opposite wall and across the long, narrow bed. A stove huddled in a corner next to a table and a straight-backed chair. For a man who had carried all his possessions in a saddlebag, these belongings demonstrated Sage's rising status. A kerosene lamp and two leather-bound books rested on the table. Aislynn ran her finger over the embossed titles, *A Discourse on the Study of the Law* and *The Practice in Civil Actions and Proceedings at Law.* A few sheets of paper scratched with small, broken letters stared up at her. His efforts brought a sympathetic smile as she recalled Sage's pitiful childhood. His father died before his birth. When his mother passed a mere four years later, soldiers at Fort John adopted him. They provided Sage with a meager education in the three Rs. However, more importantly, they taught him how to survive in the unforgiving West. Sage honed those skills into a reputation reaching beyond the plains.

Sage walked in while she snooped. Caught, she felt impelled to explain, "I'm admiring your books."

He nodded. "They're Justice Howe's. I'm tryin' to make up for what I lack."

"This knowledge will help make you a better marshal."

"If I get appointed."

"Why wouldn't you?"

"There's a banker in town who fancies the job. Can't even shoot straight."

Aislynn huffed. "No one would pick a banker over you. You have experience. Besides everyone knows you can shoot straight." Aislynn waved her hand over the imaginary people in the room who agreed with her. "You have nothing to worry about. Now you go do whatever it is you do in the jail, and I'll make you a sumptuous dinner." She gently guided him out of the confined space. "Be back in a half an hour and bring another chair."

Sage pushed himself away from the table. "Gal, you ain't much, but you're a good cook."

Trying to be the perfect lady, Aislynn accepted his back-handed compliment with grace. "Thank you. You light the lamp and rest a minute while I clear up." She reached under the table and brought out a bottle. "I found this. May I pour you a drink?"

Sage bobbed his head with a satisfied grin. "That would be right nice."

He stretched out in his chair with his long legs crossed at the ankles and his glass balanced on his lap. Aislynn washed and repacked Maggie's cookware. When the clanging of pots and plates ceased, Sage asked her to join him for a drink.

Aislynn never drank whiskey but surmised relaxing with a drink would give her an opportunity to ask for his help. She settled into her chair. The darkened room smelled like warm cream, and the kerosene lamp held them in its golden glow. Her first, small sip made her gag. "It's awful."

"Toss it back quick."

Aislynn took a breath and brought the quavering amber fluid to her lips. She closed her eyes, filled her mouth and threw her head back. She shuddered and felt the whiskey burn all the way to her stomach. She sat up straight and gasped. "That was worse."

Sage leaned over and poured her another two fingers. "It'll grow on you." He reclined and crossed his arms over his chest. "Why you leavin' the cool hills of Utah to come here for the hot summer?"

"It's not the weather," she began. "I couldn't stay in that dreadful mining camp another minute. It holds too much sorrow."

"That loss has been sittin' on you for awhile. Why now?"

"Well, you know what it's like to lose your spouse and your child."

Sage's deep voice plunged into a growl. "I didn't lose no one. I killed them."

Aislynn slapped her hands on the table and bent toward him. "Don't say such a thing! You did not kill them!"

"Good as." Sage's hands strangled his glass.

Aislynn knew to never touch a boiling pot. Leaning away from the potential explosion, she studied him from the corner of her eye and waited for his anger to subside.

Aislynn and Johnny had ended the first leg of their trip from New York City to Utah when they arrived in Cheyenne. Ahead lay a 436-mile trail and one full month in a covered wagon. Once they made Sage's acquaintance, he generously shared his extensive knowledge. For one lesson, he marched her out to the prairie with two handguns and a rifle. The physical intimacy of shooting gave birth to an emotional bond between them, one primed for shameful confessions.

Despite her engagement to Johnny, Aislynn disclosed the true reason she wanted to go west: her seventeen-year-old self believed she was in love with the handsome, bookish Tim. She harbored a devious desire to be with Tim and wanted to follow him to Utah. "I can't help what I feel."

"Yes, you can," Sage replied. "It's all in how you choose to look at someone. Sometimes young'uns get ideas, and they get bigger than what's real." He shook his head. "Just be careful. Mistakes can't always be corrected."

He spoke from experience. "One day this pretty, blonde gal pulled into Fort Laramie. Her family stayed four days to rest and resupply. When it come time to go, I wouldn't let her leave. I just held on to her. Her folks left. After a time, she had a child."

He sat stone still, his long blond hair blowing under his hat in the stiff wind. He unclenched his teeth and continued, "The baby looked like an Injun. Black hair, black eyes, deep skin. She swore 'twas mine, but I couldn't make no sense of it, neither could no one else. There was plenty of Injuns about the fort, on the trail. I'd left her alone some to go scoutin', huntin', but she seemed such a good gal. I just couldn't believe she'd done it, but there it was atauntin' me. I believed the worst, and told her to go. She took that baby, walked out onto that prairie and never looked back."

He finished his confession with a tragic discovery. "A few years later, an old Osage woman come into the fort with a bunch of Injuns. She heard my name and said, 'Your pa was my brother. He took a white wife and that Christian name.' Ain't no one never told me I was half-breed, no one 'cept that ol' Injun woman . . . and that baby."

When Sage placed his glass on the table, Aislynn returned her attention to him. Their eyes met and he wordlessly gave her approval to speak.

"You were nineteen. You made a mistake," she whispered. "We all make mistakes. You're young enough to start another family—"

Sage jumped on her words. "Stakes are too high. A woman needs lots of lookin' after; a baby needs even more. I showed I ain't no good at either one."

"You can't punish yourself forever."

He stared into his whiskey. The muscles in his face appeared ready to snap. His taut lips parted and he whispered, "Just till I die."

While she waited with sealed lips for him to calm himself, a question rose in Aislynn's mind. *Do you chase outlaws and Indians hoping to be killed?*

He dipped his head and looked at her from under his heavy brows. "What is it brings you here? Ain't your fiancé in Utah?"

"Liam?" Aislynn queried.

"Yes, Liam Moran. You wrote you was gettin' hitched."

"No."

"No, he ain't in Utah or no, you ain't gettin' hitched?"

"Both." She took another sip and rested her head on her hand.

Sage refilled her glass and shook his head slowly, his eyes burning on hers.

"He's gone and he's not coming back." Aislynn pulled away and chewed her lower lip.

"What'd you do?"

She huffed and asked, "Why do you think I did something?"

Sage narrowed his eyes and twisted his mouth into an accusation.

Confusion filled her head. She planned to ask him for help, not confess her sins. "Well, Tim—"

"No, not Tim!" Sage fell back in his chair.

"You've never understood about Tim. He's like my brother. After my mother died, he raised me." Aislynn thought on this for a moment. "He's my *anam cara.*"

"Huh?"

"Oh, you don't know." She waved a dismissive hand. "In Irish, it means my soul friend, a friend for life."

"Two years ago you wanted him to be a lot more than a friend."

"Yes, I remember." She moaned. "But you were right. As soon as I gave Johnny the chance, he showed me there are different kinds of love. He filled my heart." Aislynn stopped, closed her eyes and stifled her grief. "Besides, Tim had a girl and wanted to return to New York City. I wanted him to go. I wanted him to know the joy I had with Johnny." Tears were brimming and Aislynn paused to catch her breath. "Then, I lost Johnny and our baby." Aislynn crossed her arms and curled into herself. Her eyes focused outside the ring of light as if she could find them there.

Sage pushed her glass at her. Aislynn blinked away her tears, straightened and took a sip.

"Tim wouldn't leave me. Just like a good brother, he felt obligated to take care of me. But I got some money together and sent Tim home to Emma." Aislynn sniffed and wiped her nose. "Poor Emma was such a frail thing. He lost her and their baby five months later."

"And you wanted to run to Tim's side and Moran said no."

Aislynn dipped her head and brushed away her tears. "I told him I'd return. I asked him to come with me. He flew into a jealous fury. He walked out and said he wouldn't be back."

"A man of his word."

She slumped in her chair and leaned her cheek into her hand.

"And?" he asked.

"And what?"

"There's more."

Aislynn shook her head, which made her a bit dizzy. She closed her eyes and rubbed her temples. When she looked,

Sage seemed bigger and more censorious. Indignation filled her. She folded her arms, rested them on the table and faced him. "So I went, but I returned to Utah."

"And?"

"And I waited five weeks." Aislynn spread her fingers and held up her hand. "Five weeks! I sent Liam two telegrams and two long apologetic letters, but I received nothing in return."

The room grew darker and the shadows expanded. She covered her face with her hands while Sage watched and waited. Her humiliation burned across her cheeks. The words rising in her throat tasted worse than the whiskey. In a voice thick with tears, she said, "I was lonely and grieving for my lost husband and child. Like a fool, I trusted Liam. He said he loved me. He promised marriage and . . . children." She parted her hands and her eyes met Sage's. "Liam has to know it's a possibility." She covered her face again. "I couldn't bear to stay and be called Moran's whore and have my baby labeled a bastard. We'd be cast out of all decent society. I'd be ostracized and no one would associate with me. The child would be ridiculed and abused. It would face so many obstacles in life. I had to leave."

"You ain't a whore," Sage started. "You're just young and stupid. All you know about men you learned from the boy you was married to." He sipped his drink and continued, "It ain't your fault to fall prey to a vulture. They find the helpless and wounded. They land, do their damage and fly away." Aislynn wiped her eyes, trying to recover her dignity. Sage studied her for a moment. "I'm sure he's had lots of practice. Ain't he an older man?"

"He's thirty-five."

Sage studied her for a moment, clearly pondering something. "Didn't think you'd be interested in an older man."

"Frankly, I never thought about his age."

"Hmm, he's even older than me." This information startled her. Sage looked much older than Liam. The lines on Sage's face and hands reflected a life on the rough in brutal winters and blistering summers. Liam had made his money early and lived a life of ease. "Well, he might be a snake, but he should be told; he is the father."

"No!" Roused from her humiliation, she bolted upright in anger. "You're a man. You don't understand. Try thinking like a woman, Sage. I waited five weeks for him to come back to me." Aislynn looked away. "Can't you see?" The words choked her. "He doesn't love me enough to return. How can I ever trust him?" Aislynn wrapped her arms around her belly. "I know Liam. I know if he discovered my condition, if he thought I had something, anything belonging to him, he would swoop in here and claim it. Liam has limitless money, he could drag me into court, and I'd have no recourse. No judge would say I'm a fit mother." Her voice fell into a whisper. "I had relations with a man outside of marriage." Aislynn could feel her whole body burn red with shame. "Even if he married me, he could divorce me and just take my child. In fact, he could have me committed to an asylum, and I'd have no way out." Aislynn shook her head slowly. "You're so proud of what Wyoming promises women. The reality is women have no rights. He'd own my child." She pointed to her heart. "My child!"

Sage studied her for a few long moments. He moved closer and asked, "Do you love him?"

"I thought I did. He's like a force of nature." A hint of wistfulness tinged her voice, but it quickly shifted to resentment. "He can be controlling and demanding. He wanted me to change, to be who he wanted me to be." Aislynn's whole body slumped in the chair. "I wasn't happy with him. But I went back for the baby's sake. I would have tried to be a good wife, maybe not a happy wife, but a good wife and mother."

Sage rested back in his seat, nodding and crossing his arms. "What you need is a good man. Cheyenne's just the place. We got six men to every woman."

The idea nearly sobered her. She leaned across the table. "The last thing I need or want is a man. In my opinion, I've had one too many already." Aislynn paused and considered her predicament. "Besides," she said in a hushed tone, not wanting to hear her own admission, "I'm damaged goods."

"You ain't the first woman to be taken on a buggy ride. A good man will overlook your shortcomin's."

"Good glory!" She straightened. "If I wanted to marry a man who doesn't love me, I'd tell Liam."

Sage studied her for a moment and questioned her again. "Well, what about Tim? Why ain't you marryin' him?"

"You clearly have not understood. He's like a brother." Aislynn curled her upper lip. "You don't marry your brother." She shook her head at Sage. "Besides, I can't go back to New York City. My plan is to claim Johnny is the baby's father. In New York, everyone in my neighborhood knows Johnny died almost a year ago. Here in Cheyenne, I can hide my indiscretion. Only you know the truth, and I know we can trust each other with secrets."

Sage raised an eyebrow. With a grin, they sealed their pact.

With her sins confessed, Aislynn decided it was time to complete her mission. "When I decided I was better off alone than living my life with the wrong man, I was thinking about myself. Now, I'm responsible for someone else. I am going to do this on my own. I know I can." Aislynn hesitated a moment. "I just need a little help from you."

"Me?"

"I need a job and a place to live."

"You're in the wrong place. You seen all them men at the station. There ain't a room to be had. I only got yours at Ford's 'cause they're my friends."

"You must know people with boarding houses or vacant rooms in their homes."

"Anyone with a vacant room has rented it. I told you there's four hundred men and more comin' every day."

"What about a job?" Her question was more of a plea.

"There ain't no work for women. Who'd hire a woman when there's four hundred men hereabouts?"

"And housework? A man wouldn't clean."

"That's what Injun women do."

"Someone might want a white helper."

"They'd pay you like an Injun. You couldn't live on that."

Aislynn started to feel sick. She did not know if it was the whiskey or Sage's news. "Something has to be available."

Sage shrugged. An unsettled hush fell between them as they listened to the lamp hiss. Aislynn stared at the ceiling, vision clouded by her tears. She wiped her eyes, pulled herself up and faced him. "I'm having a child." It was the first time she made the declaration out loud. The admission emboldened her. "I will muck stalls, empty chamber pots, lie, cheat, do anything to care for my child. It's not just a job and a roof; it's our survival. Sage, I have twenty-seven dollars. That's all. If you can't help me, I will go door-to-door and beg for work. If I can't find work in town, I will walk through the prairie until I find someone who will help me." As the words slipped out she regretted them, remembering Sage's wife walked out to the prairie when she left him.

His eyes flashed and the muscles in his neck snapped straight as troops at inspection. She instantly knew the fear of men who faced the business end of his guns. She whispered, "I'm sorry," and recoiled in her chair waiting for him to recover.

When Sage cleared his throat, Aislynn looked up in anticipation. His hands were folded on the table, and his eyes were fixed on hers. "There's one job that's gone beggin', but it ain't for you. If you ask around town, someone's bound to tell you, but it ain't for you."

Like a spark in dying coals, Aislynn's hope rekindled. "What is it?"

"You ain't takin' this job."

"Tell me what it is."

"First, you promise."

"Why?"

"It's too dangerous."

Aislynn tried to appear sincere as she crossed her hands over heart and said, "I promise."

Sage nodded. "There's a group of Sioux camped at Fort Russell. Bunch of old men, women and children. They got separated from their band of Hunkpapa. They can't move till the chiefs settle the dispute about where all the tribes are gonna live, or till Sittin' Bull comes for them. You remember the Treaty of '68?"

"Yes, we were at Fort Bridger when the negotiations were just starting. All the Plains Indians were being restricted to reservations."

"But miners, settlers and that damned expedition are pushin' their way into them Injun reservations. Red Cloud, the big chief of the Oglala Sioux, Sittin' Bull and the other chiefs say the treaty's broken. President Grant says it still stands. Them Injuns still get food, clothes and everythin' while this gets sorted." Sage pointed his finger at her. "Now that's a real sore point 'cause lots of hard-workin' white folks think they're savages and don't deserve nothin'."

With her impatience surfacing, she asked, "What's the job?"

Sage's eyes rested on hers. "Treaty says the Injun kids get schooled."

Aislynn instantly saw the opportunity. "I could teach."

His eyes flew open. "No, you cannot."

"Why not?"

"This ain't Utah, Aislynn." Sage stretched over the table, so close she could feel his breath. "We got a serious Injun problem here. War's been goin' on for years. Injuns massacrin' whites; white slaughterin' Injuns. Hate on both sides festers deep. Most folks hate Injun lovers more than Injuns. Whoever takes this job is gonna look like an Injun lover."

The whiskey soaking her brain muddied her thoughts. She tried to think clearly. "I don't hate Indians. And I'd be teaching children. I love children. How dangerous could they be?"

"You ain't followin' me. The Injuns ain't gonna do nothin' to you. The whites would hurt you, maybe even kill you."

If I can't keep this child, I'll die anyway. She concentrated, building a defense. A notion passed through the fog, and she grabbed at it not fully knowing where she was going with it. "Indians are being educated all over the nation by religious groups, Quakers I think."

"Not here."

"Who's doing it here?"

"Catholics."

She grew three inches with excitement. "I'm Catholic!"

"And with child. They won't hire you."

"I'm not showing and when I am, I'll hide it."

"How you gonna do that?"

"Smocks, pinafores, aprons. Haven't you noticed? Women never make a show of their pregnancies."

"They want a man."

"Do they have a man?"

His head dipped and he glared at her. His cadence slowed and his tone threatened. "Do you remember the promise you just made?"

Aislynn waved away his question. Adrenaline pumped reason into her brain. "Sage?" Her mind whirled, developing a rationale. "Grant signed that treaty, his Peace Plan or something."

Sage cocked his head and stared. "And?"

Pointing at him with both index fingers, she said, "President Grant wants the Indian children educated, and you want Grant to appoint you federal marshal. Wouldn't it be a feather in your cap if you found him a teacher?"

He froze. She imagined the answer evolving in his head. Aislynn held her tongue, hoping for the desired response. She received it when his moustache drooped into a resigned frown. Huffing and shaking his head, Sage growled, "Gal, you are gonna be nothin' but trouble. Don't come lookin' for me when you need help."

Aislynn jumped up with excitement. Her quick movement made her head spin. She grabbed the table to steady herself. "I won't, except maybe right now. I think I'm going to be sick."

CHAPTER 3

A sound, indefinite and unidentifiable, woke Aislynn from her drunken dream. The instant she opened her eyes and raised her head, nausea washed over her. Without thinking, she reached under the narrow bed and thankfully found a chamber pot. After her expulsion, Aislynn collapsed back on the mattress and waited for her strength to return. She examined the room, puzzling over her whereabouts. Bright moonlight drifted through a small, barred window. The shadow of thick books flowed over a table.

Aislynn's eyes popped open and she bolted upright. *Sage's bed. Goodness, I'm in Sage's bed!* She took a deep breath and ran her hands over her clothes. Ties were tied and buttons were buttoned. She noticed her shoes were still clinging to her feet. Before the night lifted its dark skirt and revealed all the secrets that lay beneath, Aislynn had to act. She peeked out the door and checked for pedestrians and prying eyes. Her ears listened for the slightest human sound. She silently berated herself. *I came here to avoid being labeled a whore, and my first night I place myself in this compromising position. If someone sees me in the street at this hour, I'll be ruined.* Certain of her solitude, she made a dash out the door.

Striving for invisibility, she stepped carefully and hugged the walls along Eddy Street. At 16th, she turned and crept to the corner of Ferguson. From this vantage, she could see the

Ford House. The moon emblazoned the intersection like a theatrical stage. She studied the gloomy facade and prayed for an unlocked front door. With one quick glance in all directions, she lifted her skirt and raced diagonally across the street. Aislynn ignored the damp sounds of her feet slapping through the mud. *I can replace my shoes, but not my reputation.*

Up on the walk, she slunk along the boards until she reached the door. The knob felt cool to the touch. Like a professional safecracker, Aislynn turned it slowly until she heard the telltale click. Exercising great caution, she guided the door as it swung open, trying to stifle any squeaks. Stepping inside, she pulled off her shoes and tiptoed up the stairs. One sconce flickered. The windowless hallway stretched out ahead of her, dark and sinister. She walked a straight line to the last door and turned the knob. *Locked!* She heaved a great sigh and dropped her shoes when she remembered the key hanging behind the desk in the foyer. Aislynn skulked against the wall as she wound her way down the stairs, wincing with every creak. One lonely key hung on the board. She grabbed it, tore up the stairs and shoved it into her door lock.

Aislynn's eyes slowly opened to the sun slashing through a gap in the velvet curtains. The shadow of a headache rested behind her eyes and her mouth felt as dry as old newspaper. The morning light revealed a white ceiling spoiled by billowing, brown water marks. She stared at the damage and announced, "You're just like me, stained. Lucky for you a coat of whitewash will solve your problem. Me? I need a miracle."

She folded an arm over her eyes and replayed her conversation with Sage. Anxiety tingled through her entire body as she thought about providing for her child. "Baby," she whispered, "they won't let me be a teacher. Seven years of grade school doesn't make up for a degree from a normal teaching college. Being a student is not the same as being a teacher. Our twenty-seven dollars will give us less than two weeks of room and board here. With Johnny's mother working my restaurant, she may send some money, but who knows how much she'll be able to spare or when we'll see it." She closed her eyes and groaned. "What do we do? Go back to Utah? To Liam?"

Liam Moran had come to her parish hall in the autumn of '67 looking for hardworking men to go west. He was a right-place-at-the-right-time American success story with a ranch, a silver mine and a piece of the Central Pacific Railroad. With unemployment in post–Civil War New York City running high for returning veterans, men like Tim were eager to find work. The room overflowed with willing candidates and Aislynn. When Liam stood at the podium, she noticed he was tall, well built and attractive for a man who appeared to be twice her age. His tanned skin and black hair set off his light blue eyes, giving him an almost sinister look. He radiated confidence. Moran seemed to be a man who could make a pact with the devil, sure he could retract it at will. Scanning the crowd, his eyes found Aislynn's.

From the start, the attraction he held for her floated just below the surface of every private interaction. His innuendoes, overtures and advances felt dangerous, forbidden and exciting. With his words and his actions, Liam could turn an innocent moment into a sexually charged encounter, leaving her in a state of discomposure.

On Liam's first visit to the tiny cabin she shared with Tim and Johnny, he had found her home alone.

The close quarters and his strong masculine presence made her uncomfortable. She was relieved when he rose to leave.

"By the way," he said, looking down at her, "I suggest you button up your bodice before you go over to the restaurant. I can only hope you don't display yourself for other men."

She looked down to find her blouse open to her camisole, exposing the tops of her breasts. "Why didn't you say something?" Her anger and embarrassment flared.

"And spoil my view?" He backed out the door, but through his laughter Liam said, "I look forward to seeing more of you in the future."

Liam hurled suggestive comments and scorching looks at her whenever he knew no one else would notice. To a degree, she enjoyed the sexual tension. However, when she displayed her fluster and annoyance, Tim and Johnny presumed she harbored a strong dislike for the man. She did think him arrogant, self-centered and coarse. She longed to take him down a peg or two. But in her heart, she held a kernel of tenderness for him. Although he was a mature, experienced man, she could sense the abandoned, frightened child hiding inside him. As a newborn, he was left at a Chicago foundling home. At twelve years old, Liam ran away from an abusive foster family and went west. Aislynn believed he yearned for the same devotion and love she lavished on Johnny and Tim.

She tried to visualize her life with him. In her imagination, she saw his big house and fine furniture, luxurious carriages and thoroughbred horses, new clothes and old brandy. Extravagant parties danced in her head. She saw them walking through the foggy streets of London, exploring ruins in sunny Rome and making love in Paris. Aislynn's head swam remembering his touch.

Her thoughts shifted to the child in her womb. She covered her belly with her hands. "He could give you the best schools, books, ponies . . . ."

Liam had invited Aislynn and her friends to his Christmas party. The huge, pine-scented hall of his ranch house shimmered under flickering candles. His guests dazzled in their fine attire and expensive jewels. Aislynn stood in the doorway clad in her well-worn blouse and shabby skirt, feeling the sting of humiliation. But, Liam had anticipated her embarrassment. He had a long, embroidered, velvet jacket and two intricately carved silver combs waiting for her in his bedroom. She smiled, comparing Liam to Cinderella's fairy godmother.

Aislynn pulled the pillow over her head trying to block her confusion. She spoke into the darkness. "Of course, when Liam gives, he wants something in return. He has requirements and expects me to abide them: how I should dress, who I should speak to and write to, how frequently I should visit Johnny's and the baby's graves. He insisted I give my home and my restaurant to my mother-in-law, give away all I worked for and achieved. Why? He said being his wife meant my 'time and attention belonged' to him. He wanted me to spend my life at his ranch, isolated, four miles from my friends and family in camp." Aislynn squeezed the pillow and vented her anger. "He wanted to treat me as a possession, like his house and silver mine. Liam told me, 'I want your mind and your heart and your soul and your spirit.' He wanted control of my whole being; he wasn't leaving anything for me." Loosening her grip she confessed, "I tried to please him, until . . . until I couldn't."

Throwing the pillow off her head, she sat upright. "Baby," she said, "a man like Liam Moran could give us a great deal, but he could take even more. Years ago, my da told me a woman wasn't a real woman without a man. Now, I know he was wrong. Believe me Liam can make me feel like a woman. But, he can also make me feel like less than a person."

Aislynn pushed herself off the bed and sat at the vanity. She peered into the hazy mirror and rested her hand on her belly. "You need a mother who can take care of you and herself, a mother who can stand on her own two feet and be an example. We have to get a job and a place to live. This teaching position would be perfect, if I were just qualified."

In the looking glass, Aislynn searched the reflection of the room as if the answer lay there. Since nothing helpful appeared, she explored the vanity's drawers one by one. The right drawer housed an abandoned sock. The left held a bar of used soap. The fragrance of lavender rose up and awakened a scent memory, her only recollection of her mother. When she opened the middle drawer, an idea struck her, and a smile spread across her face.

By the time Sage banged on her door, Aislynn felt refreshed and ready to meet the men who held her fate in their hands. Aislynn had prepared for her interview with great care. A good scrubbing made her skin glow. One hundred strokes left her hair shining. She donned a clean dress with a neckline hinting at her full, young breasts. Her hat, perched on an angle, gave her a sophisticated air. Aislynn knew this was a fight for their survival, and she drew on every weapon in her arsenal. She took one last look in the mirror. The reflection pleased her and raised her confidence.

Stepping into the street, she wrapped herself head to waist in a large shawl to protect her assets against the dusty road between Cheyenne and Fort Russell. As he helped her into the buggy, Sage scanned her. He scoffed, "We ain't going to a party."

Aislynn suppressed her fears. She tossed her nose in the air. "No, but we will have something to celebrate."

The old buckboard Sage had borrowed to drive them to the fort was nothing more than a seat on springs wobbling over four wheels. It rocked and jounced as the swaybacked horse pulled them along the uneven dirt road. Sage's weight on one side tilted the seat, leaving Aislynn teetering on her edge. With every lurch, she feared flying off into the dust. They moved one block before Aislynn slid next to Sage and slipped her arm through his. "Are you trying to hit every hole?"

"This road ain't nothin' but holes. Just grab hold and stop complainin'. You are the whinin'est woman."

Aislynn gripped Sage's arm. Its firmness triggered an unexpected thought. "How different the world must look to you up there over six feet tall, with your hard muscles and your fast guns. Down here in women's world the view's a whole lot different. While you men can grab a whole loaf of life, we have to scrape along on crumbs. Gosh, I can't even imagine what my life would be like if I were a man. I surely wouldn't fear Liam Moran."

"You got no cause to fear him till he's standin' in front of you. Then, you show confidence you can beat him."

"With what? Words?"

"Well, gal, you got plenty of them." He snickered, amused with himself.

Aislynn could not argue the point, so she turned her attention to the view. A short way north of the business center, a few homesteads held on to Cheyenne's apron strings.

But within a mile, Cheyenne dissolved into the vast, empty prairie. This country held a hidden beauty revealed only to those with curiosity and imagination. In May, the brown remnants of winter gave way to a blanket of green, sprinkled with spring flowers of blue, yellow and red. Large outcroppings of solid rock, cracked by the pressure of time and sculpted by the wind, pushed up through the grass in a riot of shapes and sizes. Gusts of wind pressed down the grass and the silvery sagebrush as if they were bowing to the solid, stone carvings.

As the buggy rolled, it disturbed small, unseen creatures hiding in the tangle along the road. They scurried in protest and sent a covey of birds bursting into the limitless blue. To the west, Crow Creek curved and smiled up at the sun. Miles ahead, the white smoke from Fort Russell's numerous fires rose like threads, stitching the sky to the earth. Away from the heavy smells of the town, the air held a sweet scent. Aislynn filled her lungs and held the fragrance like a promise of good things to come.

Her wandering eyes caught Sage. His forearms rested on his thighs as he held the reins. A quiet man, he only spoke when he had something to say. Aislynn found his silence comforting, particularly his lack of comment on her indecorous behavior the previous night. Sage's buckskins, long beard and wild hair reflected his reluctance to adapt to a civilized state, like the frontier itself. She knew beneath the rough, raw exterior resided a good heart and a deep, wise soul. His quick temper and bursts of anger terrified some people, but they failed to impress her. Like a magic lamp, he could be rubbed the wrong way. But, when he stormed at Aislynn, ridiculed and derided her, she heard a caring message beneath the rumbling thunder.

About three miles from town, the road rose. The fort stood on a low plateau, laid out in the shape of a diamond, and exposed on all sides without a protective stockade. Sage drove through rows of low, solidly built houses of vertical boards and batten. "Officers' quarters are on the north side," Sage stated, nodding to his right, "and enlisted barracks are on the south. All them shacks behind the barracks are for laundresses."

Aislynn craned her neck to take a count. "Goodness, there's so many of them."

"They got over three hundred men here."

"If I don't get this teaching job, perhaps I could be a laundress."

Sage whipped around to face her, his eyes wide and mouth open. "Gal, you really don't know nothin'. They don't just wash clothes. There's three hundred men here with no women."

She winced from the sting of her ignorance. Aislynn straightened and stared ahead with a red face. "It's irrelevant. I am going to be a teacher."

Sage rolled the wagon around the parade ground and pulled up to a two-story, stone building at the top of the diamond. He sprang out, lifted her off the seat and gently placed her on the ground. As Aislynn walked up the stairs, she chewed her lips red and pinched her cheeks hoping some color would shine through.

He led her to a long room with dark wood paneling and a coffered ceiling. Six-over-six windows lined the front wall and lit the room with sun. The two men seated at a large table jumped to their feet as Aislynn entered.

Pointing at the men, Sage made the introductions. "This here's Colonel Hayes, commander of Fort Russell. He's Father Gilhooley, pastor of the Catholic church."

Aislynn curtsied deeply to both men. She knew these men held the power to save her and her baby from destitution. She tried to calm her anxious heartbeat. With a deep breath, she told herself, *Just believe.* She put on her sweetest smile and said, "It is a distinct pleasure to meet such esteemed members of the community."

The colonel, a slim man in his thirties, rushed to her side and pulled out a chair at the table for Aislynn. "Please sit, Mrs. Maher." He stood a few inches taller than her. His tiny eyes, hooked nose and thinned-lipped smile resided in a face so pale she wondered how he survived the western sun. Aislynn decided she might be able to influence him by tempting his masculine side. She locked eyes with him and slowly slipped the shawl off her head and down her back. His white skin heated into a bright red. Aislynn knew she had succeeded.

The priest's rotund body and flushed face showed his proclivities. The middle-aged man wore the customary black suit and white collar, both showing signs of wear. A nervous man, he steepled his chubby hands and beat his fingers together. Sage moved behind the men. He place one foot on the wall and leaned back, arms crossed, scrutinizing her.

Aislynn spoke first, addressing the colonel. "Thank you for seeing me. A man of your stature, responsible for such a large fort"—she waved her hand toward the windows—"must be quite busy. What a good soldier you must be to have risen through the ranks at such a young age."

The commander puffed up. "I've been lucky."

"Luck? The army promotes on hard work and initiative." She spoke in an authoritative tone based on no authority at all. Sage rolled his eyes, but Aislynn pressed on, "Where did you start your career?"

She turned his interview into hers. He revealed he hailed
from Albany and attended West Point. He served in Missis-
sippi during the Civil War and was eager to solve his problem
of the Indian children's education. "Well, I do hope I can
help you and Father Gilhooley." She turned her attention to
the cleric. "I just arrived so I haven't attended church yet,
but I am pleased to know Cheyenne has a Catholic church.
I have lived the past two years in a godless mining camp."
Leaning toward the plump priest, she continued, "I own a
restaurant, and I have been told I am a good cook. But I had
to return to civilization and the church."

"I'll be glad to see you there, very glad."

"Is this your first parish?"

"Oh no, I've had several, yes, several."

"Where did you get your start?"

Gilhooley mentioned Ireland and Aislynn jumped at the
opportunity to forge some common bonds. Sage watched
her fawn, shaking his head and frowning. When they had
exhausted the subject of the old country, the colonel inter-
vened. "Mr. Sage tells us you are interested in teaching our
Indian children."

Wide-eyed and excited, she straightened in her seat and
replied, "Oh yes, sir. I believe it is my patriotic duty. I am
familiar with the president's Peace Policy, and I understand
his mission: educating Indians to civilize them and make
them good Americans."

"Yes, that is his intent," the colonel confirmed. "While I
would prefer to simply turn them out, I have my orders."

"I'm no soldier, but when the president of the United
States issues an order, I, too, am willing to follow it," Aislynn declared with vigor.

The commander leaned over the table. "Frankly, Mrs.
Maher, I believe this position is more suitable for a man."

Fear made her heart rate soar. She knew her very exis-
tence teetered on her response. She held her breath, calculating her answer. Holding her head high, she began her
supporting argument. "Well, Colonel, many women are fine
teachers. Marshal Sage tells me Cheyenne has three female
teachers doing a marvelous job." She moved to her second rationale. "Also, I believe women and children have a special
bond. Therefore, it would be far more natural for me to take
these children under my wing and teach them. As a man,
you know men don't always have the proper temperament
to deal with difficult children. I suspect these children will
be a challenging group. I am sure I can work with them."

The colonel considered her for a moment before he asked,
"Would you please tell us about your credentials?"

"Of course." She folded her hands on the table and addressed both men. "As you know, many teachers on the
frontier educating our white students are children themselves, without any formal education. I have completed
the full course of study required by the great city of New
York at a Catholic school, the Church of the Transfiguration
School."

"Did you attend college or normal teaching school?"

"No sir, but I have had teaching experience." Aislynn saw
Sage's head rise to attention.

"Really?"

"Why, yes. I taught young children at an orphanage in
New York City. They were a challenging group, Negroes
and immigrants. But, it was rewarding. My students had
no previous experience in a classroom, yet they shined." She
paused as she reached for her purse. "In fact, I have a letter of
recommendation from the school's principal, Sister Angelica
of Mercy."

Sage's heavy brows climbed into his forehead and his jaw fell. She handed the two men the letter. They nodded and murmured to each other as they read the florid script. "I also taught Sunday school at my church. My pastor wrote this flattering letter for me." Aislynn reached across the table and handed them a second letter printed with large, block letters. Sage lurched forward to read the letter over the interviewers' shoulders. His foot slipped to the floor with a bang, startling everyone in the room. Aislynn shot him an angry look and attempted to return the men's attention to herself. "If I can successfully teach thirty students of various ages and cultures, I can assure you I can help the poor, pagan children here at Fort Russell."

The colonel's thin lips curled into a broad smile. He declared, "I think we should give her a chance. What's your opinion?" he asked, turning toward the priest.

Father Gilhooley agreed. "Yes, yes. I think she would do a fine job, fine job." Profound relief relaxed her whole body.

"She ain't comin' out here every day," Sage announced. Aislynn's heart jumped. Her eyes bore into his as she subtly shook her head. "It's too dangerous for her to be on the road alone. You'll have to bring them children into town. You've got men comin' in every day; they can escort them."

"Is it safe to bring them in?" the priest asked.

"Ain't none of it safe, but men are more apt to attack a lone woman than a bunch of kids, if you know what I mean."

Sage's remarks flustered the father. "Yes, yes, but where? Where?"

Aislynn's anxiety rose as she imagined her job slipping away.

After a few long seconds, Father Gilhooley rescued her. "They can congregate in the church's narthex. Yes, we'll put

a table, yes, a table in the narthex, the hall right inside the
front door of the building." While the men agreed, Aislynn
said a silent prayer of thanksgiving. "You'll be living in the
parochial house," the priest offered. "We have a small room
on the second floor; you'll be living upstairs. It will be very
convenient, very convenient. I live there, and so does Mrs.
McKenzie, my housekeeper."

"And, of course, you will receive a stipend of forty dollars
a month," the colonel added.

Aislynn wanted to finish the interview before Sage caused
any more trouble or her good luck ran out. She stood and
said, "Thank you for this opportunity. Shall I start on Monday?"

All eyes focused on the priest. "Yes, yes, Monday would
be fine, Monday. The town's school day runs from eight until
three o'clock, Monday through Friday; so will we, yes, so will
we."

The colonel interjected, "But the Indian children will be
schooled through the summer. No sense in giving them a
break when they have so much to learn."

Aislynn rushed to agree, totaling up the extra months of
income in her head. "That's so generous of you to grant them
additional instruction," she said with an appreciative nod.

"I'll tell Mrs. McKenzie you'll be moving in," the priest
offered.

As they drove away, Aislynn turned and sent the two men
a broad smile and a ladylike wave. As soon as they rolled out
of earshot, Sage started, "That was quite a show, Mrs. Maher.
You were almost indecent, acting like a saloon girl with all
that big-eyed flirtin' and lyin' goin' on."

Aislynn crossed her arms over her chest and huffed. "Well,
I don't have two Colt persuaders to get what I want. So I

guess we both have our methods." Sage harrumphed. Aislynn continued, "As far as decency, if you compare shooting people to flirting, I think I'd win."

"Yeah? Where'd you get them letters, Mrs. Decency?"

Aislynn equivocated. "Well . . . I may have found some paper in my room and written them myself."

"Ain't no *may* about it. That's forgery. I should lock you up for a federal offense. You better pray they don't write to Sister Angelica and Father Whoever."

"They can write all they want. They won't get a response." Sage turned and looked at her squarely. "They both died years ago."

"Don't you beat all?" Sage chuckled. "Well, you said you'd lie and cheat; I suppose that makes you kinda honest."

"Yes, it does." She wove her arm through his. "Oh Sage, I have a job and a place to live. Don't spoil my joy by being judgmental." She looked at the sky and inhaled a long, deep breath. Beaming up at him, she gushed, "Yesterday, I was so afraid. I didn't know where I was going to live or how I would care for my child. Now, I'm going to be a teacher. Me! Aislynn Denehy from Worth Street. What an honor! And thirteen children." She threw her head back and announced to the heavens, "I am going to change their lives."

"You best be careful. I told you this was dangerous." He snapped at her, "You go no farther north than that church and no farther south than 16th Street. You stay between O'Neil and Warren. You got that? And you never go out after dark without me."

Aislynn murmured, "Uh-huh."

"You abide me," Sage threatened with a stern face.

"Yes." She pouted for a moment, but her uncontainable happiness bubbled up and overshadowed his warnings.

Turning to him, she placed her hand on his arm. She whispered, "Thank you."

Aislynn rested back in her seat, but her mind whirred, turning over ideas until she struck the right one. "Sage," she announced, "now I have my perfect job; I'm going to get you yours."

CHAPTER 4

THE early morning sunlight struggled through grimy windows and a haze of cigar smoke to reveal the disorderly courtroom of Cheyenne. Around the room, men reclined on the benches. Gamblers rolled dice and played cards at the tables. Overflowing spittoons sprouted from a floor littered with discarded butts and bottles. The heavy odors of alcohol and unkempt men hung in the air. "This looks more like a saloon than a courtroom," Aislynn declared.

"We know," Sage replied.

As she walked across the floor, the loungers sprang upright and the gamblers stowed their gear. The bustle caused the three men shuffling papers at the front of the room to look up simultaneously. Their chairs scraped the floor as they all stood.

After performing their customary bows, all six eyes shifted to her companion. Sage stood with an uncomfortable stare. He wore a new, black sackcloth suit, a white shirt and a black vest. His two Colts hung beneath his jacket in black leather holsters, and his rifle rested on his back, suspended from a thick shoulder strap. He held his old hat in his hands, revealing his shorter, contemporary haircut. A thorough trimming left his eyebrows thinner, and his beard and moustache precisely carved. Aislynn allowed him one crime against current fashion: his hunting knife remained strapped to his calf.

Recognition spread visibly across the three faces. "Holy smoke, it's Orrin Sage!" exclaimed the oldest man.

The shorter one shouted, "Look at you!" The third man simply gaped. Aislynn grinned at her creation and judged him almost handsome.

Sage jerked his head at Aislynn and turned the attention away from himself. "This here's Mrs. Maher. She's come to teach the Injun children."

The shortest man introduced himself in a smooth, comforting voice. "I'm Governor John Campbell." The man appeared to be close to Sage's age. He wore an abundant moustache and beard, perhaps compensating for his receding hairline. Aislynn instantly liked his kind eyes and calm tone.

"He's the man responsible for givin' women the vote," Sage explained. Aislynn smiled her appreciation. "The Democratic legislature figured John here would veto their bill. Joke's on them, ain't it? All them women will be votin' Republican come September."

"That is our hope, Mrs. Maher," the governor asserted.

Sage turned to the other men and completed the introductions. "This here's Chief Justice John Howe," he said, pointing to a taller, older man with a long face and eyes reflecting his gravitas. "And he's Justice John Kingman." In Aislynn's opinion, the distinguished Kingman resembled Robert E. Lee: tall, attractive and stately.

"It is an honor to meet you all. Thank you for allowing me to attend this hearing," Aislynn said.

"No, ma'am. We must thank you for accepting such a big job. It shows a great deal of courage. Let me know if there's anything I can do to assist you," the governor offered. "You take a seat right in front, and we will get started."

Straight and proper, Aislynn sat with her hands folded in her lap. Sage sprawled next to her with his hands hanging between his widespread legs.

Campbell addressed the assemblage. "We are here to consider the appointment of the new federal marshal for the Wyoming Territory of the United States of America."

A commotion erupted in the back of the room. Several men and women entered and took seats. The governor waited for the ruckus to calm before he continued, "I see our other interested party has arrived. We will review each man's qualifications, allow each candidate to speak on his own behalf, then the panel will decide who to recommend to the president of the United States. I will start with James Pruitt. Mr. Pruitt hails from Pennsylvania. He is a graduate of Dickinson College. He began his career as a banker in Philadelphia. He transferred his banking skills to a position with the Union Pacific Railroad in charge of their accounts. He came to Cheyenne to work in the bank owned by an official of the UP." Campbell concluded with, "Thank you for your interest, Mr. Pruitt."

"Now for our next candidate, Orrin Sage. Mr. Sage was born in the territory. He grew up at Fort John, which is now Fort Laramie. Based there, he served as a scout and an Indian fighter. Mr. Sage has shepherded wagon trains across the Great Plains. He rode for the Pony Express. In 1860, during the Paiute War, he was commended for his bravery, when he held off a band of renegade Indians at an express station, saving the lives of five people and several horses. Mr. Sage was hired by the Pacific Telegraph Company to protect workers building the transcontinental telegraph line. With that duty completed, Sage entered the Union Army and served as a sniper under General Grant's command. He earned several honors, including the Medal of Honor, for saving the life of an officer even though he was severely injured himself." The governor paused and nodded at Sage, who vibrated with embarrassment. His nervous legs shook with such fury they rattled Aislynn's chair. She smiled at him with pride, but he concentrated on the floor, trying to ignore the whole ordeal.

Campbell added, "Mr. Sage returned to the territory and protected the payroll for the transcontinental railroad until its completion. Mr. Sage was appointed deputy marshal for the Wyoming Territory in June of 1869. He has served with distinction in this role. We thank you for your service, Mr. Sage."

With a quick scan of the room, the governor added, "We will now take comments from our candidates. You each have five minutes."

Mr. Pruitt carried a sheet of paper to the front of the room. He stood erect and stiff with his head high. He began to discredit Sage. "Firstly, I would like to point out that Mr. Sage has no formal education." Aislynn could feel a nearly imperceptible flinch from Sage. Lack of education was not exceptional in the West nor was it a source of shame, but the words stung.

Pruitt continued, "We all know the deputy is quick with a gun, but perhaps he's too quick. We have a widow with us, Mrs. Tom Linden. Mr. Sage murdered her husband."

Sage jumped from his seat with the word *murdered*. Campbell waved Sage down, and Aislynn touched his sleeve. "Excuse me, Mr. Pruitt. Please be careful with your choice of words. We"—he acknowledged the panel—"are all familiar with the Linden case. Deputy Sage rode after Mr. Linden as he absconded with Mr. Wallace's horse. Stealing horses is a capital offense, as I hope you know if you want to be the US federal marshal. Deputy Sage and Deputy Winston pursued Mr. Linden, who refused to give up."

"He was drunk!" Linden's widow cried.

The governor dismissed the woman. "Nonetheless, he was still a horse thief. Now, let's continue."

With the matter resolved, Aislynn felt Sage's tension dissipate.

"I also feel the panel should be aware of Mr. Sage's moral character," Pruitt began again. "He is a fornicator. He passed the night with that woman." Pruitt pointed at Aislynn.

Sage's hands circled the man's throat before anyone else could move. Howe and Kingman wrenched the two men apart, allowing the purple-faced Pruitt to catch his breath. Before he could utter any additional slanderous words, Sage shouted, "I should put a bullet in your head!"

Culpability flooded through Aislynn, forcing her to act. She moaned with force, placed the back of her hand on her forehead and swooned ever so slowly. Sage dashed to her side in time for her to collapse in his arms. She lolled her head on his chest and pinched her eyes closed.

"You blasted . . . Look what you did," Sage seethed.

Aislynn could hear moving and scurrying. "Get back." It was Campbell's calming voice. "Give her some air. Let's get her a drink."

"Here's some water," Kingman offered.

She heard the sloshing water and decided to avoid the deluge. Aislynn blinked several times. Her eyes swooped over the four men huddled around her. Her hand rushed to her throat. "Goodness, I'm sorry." She gasped and sat upright. Fighting tears, she said, "I didn't mean to cause such a fuss. I seem to be making a habit of fainting lately." She dabbed at her eyes with her hankie. "You see, I've recently suffered a great loss." She glanced into each man's eyes. "The other night, after I prepared dinner to thank Mr. Sage for all of his help, I felt faint. He gallantly allowed me to rest on his cot. When I woke in the middle of the night, he was gone. I later discovered my frailty forced him to sleep in a cell." Aislynn placed her hand over her mouth as if the words were too awful to be spoken. "A jail cell!" she cried, shaking her head. Addressing her attendants, she said, "I am deeply sorry to have caused such trouble."

Governor Campbell, balancing on one knee and patting her hand, reassured her. "No need to fret, Mrs. Maher. No damage done. Please drink this." He handed her the water. "This will refresh you."

Aislynn gave him an innocent smile, thanked him and took a sip.

The governor stood and addressed the assemblage. "I think we've heard quite enough. The panel and I will make our decision. Mr. Pruitt, you and your cronies may leave. Court will begin as soon as Mrs. Maher recovers."

Pruitt started to object, but Sage telegraphed a visual death threat. The man grumbled as he stomped out the door.

Campbell said, "Excuse me, Mrs. Maher." He stepped back toward the table where the other men were returning to their seats. In the time it took Sage to inquire if Aislynn were able to walk, the governor returned.

"We'll submit your name to the president today."

Aislynn steepled her hands and whispered a thank you to the panel. All three smiled and nodded. She struggled to her feet and declared herself to be recovered.

Howe spoke. "Wonderful. You are welcome to stay and witness our court proceedings if you feel up to it. I would appreciate your opinion."

The governor jumped into the conversation. "If you aren't feeling strong, I can take you safely back to your hotel. A governor is in a totally separate branch of government. I am not required to participate in the court."

The man's offer seemed innocent and kind; however, Aislynn and every man in the room could hear the meaning hidden inside the words *I can take you*. Two years in the male-dominated West taught Aislynn that women were commodities to be claimed and owned. Single women were accosted the instant they arrived in a town. Widows received no reprieve to mourn. Advances and proposals came days after a husband's passing. Maintaining one's standing as a good, decent woman took serious thought and deliberate action. And a woman with a devastating secret had to be extra vigilant.

Campbell's request forced Aislynn to make an unwelcome declaration. "Thank you for your lovely offer, but I will defer to Mr. Sage's wishes." She recognized all of Cheyenne would link them romantically, and that suited her. She and Sage shared a mutual understanding; she knew he did not believe he deserved another woman, and he knew she did not want another man.

"I understand," the governor replied. The two words sealed an agreement among all the men in the courtroom. Campbell winked congratulations to Sage and bade farewell to the judges. Turning back to Aislynn, he said, "It was a pleasure to meet you, Mrs. Maher. If I can be of service to you or your students, let me know."

"Deputy, we can wait a few minutes, if you'd like to accompany Mrs. Maher back to her room," Justice Howe offered with an approving smile.

When they reached her door, Aislynn looked up at Sage and glowed with relief. "After so much worry, we've achieved a great deal in two days." She clasped her hands and pinched her shoulders with excitement. "I got a job and a place to live, and you're going to be the United States marshal."

Sage peered down at her in the dim light. Without his wild hair and furry face, he seemed to be a different person. The dark clothes and slicked hair made him seem somber and wise. His deep bass rolled like distant thunder warning of a storm. "Now comes the really hard part."

"Well, Marshal Sage, nothing worthwhile is ever easy."

CHAPTER 5

THE Parochial House matched the church: small, white and wooden. They occupied a large lot on the corner of O'Neil and 21st Streets. The housekeeper, Mrs. McKenzie, guided Aislynn to the attic. "Father Gilhooley said to put you up here. I've tidied up but if you have any complaints you can tell him. I do my best but there's too much work. Now I have you to do for."

"I'm sure I'll be no trouble." Aislynn tried to appease the testy woman.

"You'll do your own cleaning and washing. You'll take your meals here," she said, pointing to the bare table. "Father and I eat together in the kitchen." With brassy hair, sharp features and a strong body, Mrs. McKenzie's looks reflected her attitude. Aislynn decided to keep her distance from the prickly woman.

A low peaked attic afforded a small area where Aislynn could stand erect. As in her hotel room, the basic necessities filled the space. The drayman, who brought her trunk from the depot, struggled to carry it up the narrow stairs. He pushed it to the center of the room and wheezed his way back down the stairs.

Aislynn opened the windows in the gables and started to work. After much maneuvering, the trunk stood next to the bed, now dressed in Aislynn's own sheets and quilts. She covered the naked table with an embroidered cloth and spread a lace runner on the dresser under the ewer and washbowl. The oil lamp traveled from the dresser to the table until it landed on the trunk. Sitting in the wooden chair, Aislynn surveyed her new home. The roof looked tight but the absence of a stove gave her pause. Winters bore down on the plains like conquering hordes. She decided to avoid Mrs. McKenzie and ask Father Gilhooley to remedy the situation.

The familiar smells of sweaty children, chalk dust and well-worn books greeted Aislynn as she entered Miss Petty's classroom in search of help. The teacher stood with her back to Aislynn, washing the blackboard. She wore a gray dress and a gray snood over her low, dark bun. When she turned and noticed Aislynn, her dark eyes squinted and her lips parted, revealing an overbite and an abundance of gum in her long, pale face.

"Mrs. Maher, if I recall correctly."

"Yes, I hope I'm not interrupting, Miss Petty."

"This is the hour I plan tomorrow's lesson, but I can spare a few minutes."

Aislynn thanked her and began her request. "I have recently accepted a position with St. John the Baptist Church to teach the Indian children from Fort Russell."

Miss Petty took a seat behind her desk and pointed Aislynn into one of the children's benches. "I suppose you need something," she stated with a superior edge to her authoritative voice.

"Yes, I am seeking some advice."

"Have you taught in the past?"

Aislynn explained her inauthentic credentials. "My concern is teaching a group of varied ages."

"Yes, it does take some finesse. My advice is to be regimented and strict. Children learn better when there's routine and predictability. Make your rules clear and enforce them, especially with the older boys. Those fourteen-year-olds are truly a handful. Keep your ruler within reach and display it often."

"My children are ages five through thirteen, all in one classroom."

"You'll have to break them into blocks of grades. They'll all be at different levels. Use the older children to teach the younger ones. Give the little ones something to occupy their time and teach the older ones. Then give the older ones an assignment to do with the younger ones while you teach the middle group. Rotate all day. I have everyone work on the same subject at the same time. It makes it easier to keep track."

"Sounds like I have to do a great deal of planning."

"It will occupy your off hours. You also have to get to school early to open your classroom, bring in drinking water and the dipper and keep your stove fired. School starts at eight o'clock, and it can be a ten-hour day."

Aislynn felt small in a child's seat with a teacher telling her what to do. Miss Petty studied her for a moment. In a softer tone, she said, "It's nothing you can't handle. I teach grades one through three. Come by tomorrow and spend the day. Observation is the best teacher. I always tell my students, 'If you're not looking, you're not listening. If you're not listening, you're not learning.' "

Under the morning sun, the children circled the flagpole. Their high-pitched, juvenile voices sang out "The Flag of Our Union" as an older boy raised Old Glory. In unison, the children bowed their heads and Miss Petty prayed loudly. They marched into the building and filed into their seats without uttering a word. Aislynn stood in the doorway waiting for the orders she knew would come.

"Children, we have a guest. Her name is Mrs. Maher. Today we are going to show her how a proper classroom works."

The children sat with their hands folded and their eyes on Aislynn.

"What do we say to Mrs. Maher?"

They answered, "Good morning, Mrs. Maher."

"Eileen and Marjorie." The girls stiffened at the sound of their names. "Slide over and make room for Mrs. Maher."

Aislynn nodded to the two girls and glided into the last-row bench. A familiar terror rolled through her body as her mind flashed back to her third grade and the terrifying Sister Alma Delores. Aislynn folded her hands and looked straight ahead.

"We will start our day with a reading from the Scriptures."

Miss Petty read the story of the Good Samaritan. She enunciated the last words, "Go and do thou likewise," as her eyes searched the room. "Herbert, tell me the meaning of this story."

A tall, thin, redheaded boy stood and explained, "The story means we should help our neighbors."

"Very good. Why did we read this story today, Ann Marie?"

A tiny girl with a large bow rising from her blonde hair stood and hesitated.

"You read the story because . . . we should be nice to our neighbors."

"Yes, but why did I read it today?" Miss Petty's hand rested on the menacing ruler.

Aislynn silently prayed, *Please don't let that child get hit because of me.* Ann Marie's fear rippled through the classroom. Aislynn coughed and said, "Excuse me."

"Mrs. Maher!" burst from Ann Marie's mouth. "We're helping Mrs. Maher." Miss Petty aimed a stern look at her guest.

"Our first subject today is reading. We have three Bibles. William, please distribute them." A pretty, dark-haired girl wearing a starched white blouse raised her hand. The teacher frowned and said, "Yes, Betty, I know; only you can touch your family's Bible. Share with Nancy." Looking down at Nancy, she continued, "Try not to touch the book." With the curriculum's emphasis on virtue and high morals, the Bible provided perfect reading material. Some affluent families trusted their older children to bring the precious books to school. Miss Petty announced, "Group Three will be reading Luke 10:38 through Luke 11:13 aloud." She turned. "Group Two, get the level one *McGuffey's*. I want you to help your Group One partners read lesson number 57, page 81."

Aislynn watched the children move into their groups. The girls with the prettiest dresses squeezed together on one bench. Those in faded fabrics with worn cuffs and collars fell into the row behind. Boys sat haphazardly, quietly bumping each other when Miss Petty's eyes were diverted. *Some things never change.*

Reading was followed by orthography, the study of spelling. "Group One, take out your copy books and give them to your Group Three partners. They will read a word, and you will write it on your slate. Then, they will help you with the definitions. Group Two, we will work on new words."

Aislynn roamed among the groups listening to the spelling lessons and studying Miss Petty. In less than a week, Aislynn had to transform into a teacher. She decided to accomplish this feat by following Miss Petty's axiom of looking, listening and learning today and doing a great deal of imitating on Monday.

Recess arrived and Miss Petty organized a game of Red Rover. Aislynn watched from the school steps. Observing the pecking order, Aislynn felt herself regress. Those bygone feelings of inferiority and rejection churned in her stomach as she remembered the girls who ruled her playground. Mary Alice Ahearn's father owned a grocery, and Grace Cleary's mother had a dress shop. They had beautiful clothes and full lunch pails with treats they meanly displayed. As third graders, they had a loyal following. A few years later, priorities shifted. Aislynn smiled remembering how no amount of candy or clothes could compensate for budding breasts and the attention of boys.

The sound of scuffing in the dirt caught Aislynn's attention. Turning, she found a small girl with dark unruly hair, sad eyes and a toothless smile.

"Why can't you play?" she asked Aislynn.

"I'm too old."

"How old are you?"

"Older than you. Why aren't you playing?"

"I'm lame," she replied matter-of-factly. "Can I sit with you?"

Aislynn tried not to stare at the child's leg. She patted the step. "I'd be happy for the company."

Joy lit up the little round face. "Do you have friends?"

"Some."

The child shook her head and looked at her foot. "I don't," she whispered with a shrug.

Her words pierced Aislynn's heart. "I could always use a few more. I was hoping to find a little girl, preferably one with dark, curly hair."

"Like me?" The sad eyes glistened.

Aislynn scrutinized her up and down. "Yes, I think you'd be perfect."

"I'm Amy."

"I'm Mrs. Maher."

"I know," Amy stated as she scooted closer to Aislynn and took her hand. "Where do you live?" she asked.

"I live in the house next to the Catholic church, just about a block north of here. Where do you live?"

"Far away, on 14th Street."

"That's a long walk."

"If I had a sister, she'd walk with me."

"Do you have a brother?"

"No, just me. Mama said she doesn't want another cripple," the child replied with impassive acceptance.

Aislynn blinked away her anger. "I don't think you're crippled. I think you're different. You know everyone has something about them that makes them different from everyone else. You have an ailing foot, yet you walk six blocks to come to school. That shows you're strong and determined."

Amy beamed. "You're going to be my bestest friend."

After lunch, as the children played in the school yard, Miss Petty and Aislynn remained in the classroom. While they discussed the morning's lessons, Miss Petty asked Aislynn to call her Joan and Aislynn reciprocated. The relaxing of formalities prompted Aislynn to ask, "What brought you here?"

Joan rested back in her chair and let strict conversational conventions fade. "Look at me. I'm twenty-six and unmarried. My choices were growing old in an upstairs room at my father's house in New Jersey or coming west. Not that I came here looking for a man. I have no use for men." She scowled. "Wyoming has laws that respect women. Here I have the chance to be more than an old maid."

"It does seem this territory is progressive."

"Although, I have to say, I was surprised they didn't hire a man to teach the savages."

The word *savages* bit into Aislynn. She rushed to defend her still unknown charges. "They're children." She started softly, not wanting to offend her hostess. "We were all children once. We were ignorant until someone took the trouble to teach us. Our president wants to give these children a chance to learn, and I feel privileged to be their teacher."

"You're certainly approaching this challenging assignment with a positive attitude."

"When my husband and I crossed from New York City, we met Indians, Bannocks, right here in Wyoming. They were meeting with several generals at Fort Bridger to work out the exact treaty the president is trying to enforce. The chiefs were dignified men. They pleaded their cases to save their homes, their sacred lands, with logic and reason."

"You were a witness to history," Joan said in a lofty tone.

Aislynn nodded and leaned closer to her new friend, "Are you Irish, Joan?"

"Yes. My family hails from County Cork."

"Catholic, then?"

"Aye, so we are." Joan affected an Irish lilt.

"My father and his family, like all Catholics in Ireland, starved because the English took their land and forced them to live on tiny plots where they couldn't grow a decent crop. The English believed the Irish were godless heathens who needed to be ruled with an iron fist."

Joan sat a bit straighter and tightened her lips.

"At Fort Bridger, I witnessed Americans taking the Indians' wide open lands and forcing them to live on small, arid pieces under the heavy hand of the United States military. We've taken almost everything from them." Aislynn looked Joan squarely in the eyes. "We're just like the English." She sat back and finished. "My da told me, 'They can take your home, your land, your tongue, even your eyes, but they can't take what's in your heart or your head.' " Aislynn tapped her temple. "I believe the least we can do is give them an education."

Resting her elbows on her desk and cupping her chin in her hands Joan slowly smiled. "Aislynn, I predict you're going to be a very effective teacher."

At the end of the school day, Aislynn found Amy sitting on the steps. "I waited for you."

"Thank you, but isn't your mother going to miss you?" Aislynn asked.

"My mama works. She won't be home till morning."

Aislynn rolled the statement around in her mind. "You put yourself to bed?"

"Yes, ma'am. Mama says I am independent."

"That's another thing that makes you a very special little girl."

"Can I go to your house?"

"I'm actually going to the church to set up my classroom. Would you like to help me?"

A gaping smile answered Aislynn's question. As they walked to the church, Aislynn pulled an apple from her pocket. "Are you hungry?"

"Yes, ma'am." Amy tore into the fruit with her tiny bicuspids.

"Did you have lunch?"

Amy shook her head.

Aislynn's frustration with Amy's mother deepened. She decided to remedy the situation. "You come to see me before school whenever you need lunch. I'll give you some jam and bread to take with you."

Through a mouthful of fruit, Amy said, "I will."

The narthex extended across the front of the church, long but narrow. The sun spilled through windows stretching up the side walls, and provided the only light. She found the supplies for her students stacked in crates: slates, chalk, pencils and lesson books. An eight-foot-long table flanked by benches claimed one side of the space. Aislynn planned to get a chair and position herself at the head. The children would have to squeeze together on the benches.

Aislynn pried open the boxes. In her mind, the scent of fresh ink from the books symbolized her exciting new adventure. She handed Amy a slate and a piece of chalk. "You write your spelling words and practice your penmanship, while I unpack." They worked silently. Aislynn inventoried as Amy scratched and erased and scratched and erased.

The door swung open with a bang. Amy sprang up from the table, hid against Aislynn's back and covered her head with her hands. Aislynn pulled her forward and surrounded the terrified child with her arms. "There's nothing to be afraid of." Aislynn pinched her mouth and burned her eyes into Sage's. He shrugged and offered his open hands. "He's

Marshal Sage. If you are ever afraid or need help, you go straight to Marshal Sage."

"Who might this little lady be?" he asked softly, trying to make amends.

Amy peeked at him but returned to Aislynn's arms. "This is my new friend, Amy. I met her at school today. She came here to help me set up my classroom."

"That was right nice of you, missy." Sage squatted on his haunches. "I am sorry I scared you. I do that to some people, but you ain't got no call to be afraid of me."

"Amy, we don't want to hurt the marshal's feelings. Please tell him you're happy to meet him."

The child unburied her head and studied his face for a moment with wide eyes. Still holding Aislynn's skirt, she gave him a little curtsy. "I'm pleased to meet you." As Sage stood, Amy ran her eyes up his body. "You sure are big."

"I've been told that."

Her fear thawing, Amy asked, "Want to see what my friend gave me?"

"Sure."

Amy grabbed the slate. She presented it with such pride Aislynn could not tell her it had been a loan. She sighed and resigned herself to using her meager funds to replace it.

"That's right nice, Amy. Why don't you draw me a picture?" As soon as Amy took a step, Sage's eyes caught to her shortest leg and twisted foot. With a slight nod, he turned to Aislynn. "I've been lookin' for you."

"I've been in school." Aislynn recounted her day.

"I got somethin' to show you." He turned to Amy. "Missy, ain't it time you got home?"

She lifted her head. "It's not dark yet."

Sage's brows stitched. "Where's your ma?"

With her head down, Amy furiously chalked up the slate. "She's not home."

"Hmmm. You come on now; we're gonna walk you home."

"I haven't finished my picture."

"You can work on it tonight and show it to me tomorrow."

"Will I see you tomorrow?"

"Sure."

"Are you my friend, too?"

"Course I am."

Amy shoved the chalk in the pocket of her weary dress and hugged the dusty slate to her chest. She grabbed Aislynn's hand. Looking up, she whispered, "I have another friend."

Aislynn smiled at Sage. "Yes, sweetheart, you have another friend."

Fourteenth Street lay on the south side of the tracks. They made their way down a foul trail passing through the rail yards to Amy's neighborhood. To Aislynn, it looked like Hell on Wheels, the itinerant collection of tents and portable wooden buildings that followed the construction of the transcontinental railroad. It provided every manner of sin. She surmised it rolled into Cheyenne during 1867 and never moved on.

This was the jittery, sinister part of town. The collection of saloons, gambling dens and sporting houses wore signs that blared their unsavory purposes. The flimsy, wooden shacks looked as if they would take flight in a gusty wind. The wet smell of bad whiskey, stale beer, animal and human waste washed over them as they followed Amy deeper into the filthy slum. It was late afternoon, the time of day when the wretched inhabitants crawled out of their sodden slumber to curse, shout and restart their orgies of excess.

The child opened the door to a tiny shack with a metal roof patched with flattened tin cans. Wads of newspaper filled gaps in the walls. Debris cluttered the floor. A rumpled cot filled most of the space.

They squeezed through the door. Sage spied two dresses hanging lifelessly on the wall. "Where's your pa?"

"He's getting us gold," Amy replied with pride.

Aislynn noticed a small skillet sitting on the cold stove and a bowl covered with a filthy napkin resting on a shelf. She lifted the napkin and found a thin soup of potatoes and onions. "Goodness, we should tidy up this awful mess and get her a decent meal."

Sage grabbed Aislynn's arm tightly and pushed her out to the street. He stepped out behind her. He called to Amy, "You eat your supper and get yourself to bed, missy. We'll see you tomorrow."

He dragged Aislynn away from the shack and glowered at her. "Don't you do that," he reprimanded. "Don't you talk down her mama in front of her. Your New York standards ain't got no place here. You don't know what it's like to have a selfish man leave you with a child. Her mama may be a whore, but she's givin' that child a roof and food and she is payin' the fee for her to go to that school."

Angry, embarrassed and chastened, Aislynn twisted out of his hold. She lifted her skirt and stomped away to the sounds of her shoes smacking through the mire. Safe on 16th Street, she stopped and turned. She waited for Sage with her eyes flared and her jaw set. Sage crossed his arms and peered down at her with an indulgent grin.

Aislynn squared off and spoke slowly in a harsh whisper. "As you know, thanks to Liam, I am learning what it's like to have a selfish man leave me with a child." Aislynn took a breath and calmed her tone. "I never meant to disparage her mother. My only concern is for Amy." She looked down and continued, "I will never mention her mother again, but I will give her comfort." Aislynn turned and started to walk away from Sage with her nose in the air. "And bread and jam when she's hungry."

He stood for moment then stomped up beside her. "You puttin' that bread and jam on my account?" he demanded.

She looked up and shrugged. "It's possible."

Sage shook his head muttering, "Nothin' but trouble." He took her arm and said, "Come on. I got somethin' to show you."

CHAPTER 6

O N the corner of 20ᵗʰ and O'Neil, a one-story, yellow house, iced with white trim, glowed in the late afternoon sun. Sage stopped at the path linking the house to the street. Aislynn's eyes flitted from the house to Sage, back to the house, until they rested on Sage. He stood with his feet apart and his arms crossed high on his chest, nodding as he assessed the property with a tight grin.

"What's this?" Aislynn asked.

Sage's grin fell into his perpetual frown. "It's a house," he replied, stating the obvious. He directed his attention back to the house. His grin returned.

Aislynn tilted her head. "Whose house?"

"Mine."

"You bought a house?" The question exploded from her lips. Recognizing her inappropriate volume, her hand rushed to cover her mouth.

"I gotta have a place to live, ain't I?" he snapped.

"Yes, I'm sorry. It's just . . ." Her hand waved over the surprise. "It's a whole house."

Sage looked down on her with frustration steaming from his eyes. "They come whole." Aislynn rolled her eyes. Sage continued, "Caufield, the guy who owns my stable, lost his ma. He's so broke up, he's leavin' town. He just wanted to get rid of it."

Aislynn recovered from her shock. "Can we go inside?"
"Sure." Sage presented the key with a proud flourish.

The door opened to another unexpected sight. Bloated
furniture of heavy, dark wood and dreary fabrics crammed
the space. "Caufield said she liked buyin' stuff," Sage explained. They squeezed in and negotiated the narrow path-
ways carved through the tangle.

The east wall held a stone fireplace, but the west wall beck-
oned to Aislynn. A cast iron stove with six burners, a large
gray firebox and two ovens drew her like a magnet. Shiny tin
trimmed the corners and feet. Iron filigree climbed the stack
and supported a handy shelf. Aislynn caressed the gleaming
damper spindles hanging like silver earrings on the flue pipe.

Sage interrupted her trance. "There's two bedrooms." He
pushed open a door on an austere room with bare walls, a
bed, dresser and washstand. "Must be Caufield's room. The
old lady must have died over here." He squeezed toward another door. "This one's chock full."

Aislynn stroked the stove. "What are you going to do with
all this stuff?"

"That's what I'm askin' you."

"Me?"

"Even I know it's a mess. I figured you'd be good at settin'
it right."

Aislynn threw her hands on her hips. Her anger made
her rise up on her toes and sputter, "Me? This?" Her voice
quaked. "Orrin Sage, I have been cleaning, cooking and
washing for men since I was eight years old. This is the first
time in all my memory I have to take care of me, only me!"
She pounded her breast. "I am not cleaning or doing for
you!"

Sage pointed a finger at her and raised his deep voice. "I
got you a job."

"I got you a job!" she yelled back.

Sage moved closer and hovered over her holding an accusation in his eyes. "You almost lost me that job."

Aislynn puffed up to object but deflated when she realized his point of view trumped her perspective. When her shoulders slumped, he knew he had won. "You can clean it tomorrow."

Arms akimbo, Aislynn studied the room for a quiet moment. She peered up at him and said, "These are my terms. You get two strong men to move everything out of here first thing in the morning. I'll sell everything that doesn't fit, and we split the profits."

"You mean fifty-fifty?"

"Exactly."

Sage's fingers drummed against his holsters as he scanned his treasures. "I gotta pay the men, too?"

Aislynn foot tapped loudly. "I'm not paying them."

"You got a deal."

"That's not all. I want you to hire Molly and Emmie for the day. Once all the furniture is removed, this place will need a good cleaning. Most likely there are mice, bugs and all manner of creatures nesting here. Curtains need washing, rugs need beating. You can't see through the windows."

"You can't do it yourself?"

Aislynn shook her head and released a loud groan. "You have no idea how much work it takes to clean a house." *Have you ever lived in a house? Goodness, have you ever been in a house?* Aislynn's compassion began to kindle.

"They work in the store," he declared.

"I'm sure Maggie could suffer a day without them once she knows the circumstances."

"Pfft!" He expressed his annoyance. He looked around the messy room. "Agreed."

Sage's eyes fell to the floor. She watched him slowly stroking his moustache, waiting for another request to fall off his tongue. "One more thing, if you could see your way clear to havin' a meal on that table tomorrow night, I'd be much obliged."

Aislynn's eyes popped open. A choleric response formed on the edge of her mind. Before it made its way to her lips, his wistful tone touched her heart. *Oh, what this house must mean to you: status, permanence, the symbol of a new chapter in your life.* Her eyes drifted to the stove. "I'll try."

In the dim light of early morning, Aislynn stood on Sage's porch, directing the men to separate the abundant treasures into *save* and *sell* piles. While the men hefted the large pieces out the door, Aislynn fired up the stove to heat water for the washing.

When Emmie and Molly arrived, the three women stripped the curtains from the windows and the linens from the beds. They stirred them in hot water laced with ash lye soap. Aislynn handed each girl a carpet whip. She told them to drape the rugs and mattresses over the sturdy, backyard clotheslines and "beat them until they scream."

Inside, Aislynn started at the top. With a long-handled broom, she swept the cobwebs and dust from the ceilings and the walls. She took vinegar and hot water to the windows. When the girls finished beating, they washed the woodwork and doors. Together, they all scrubbed the filthy wood floors and rinsed them with water laced with cayenne pepper to discourage mice.

The women took a rest on the front porch, sipping cold water and occasionally haggling with customers. Aislynn promised to share her half of the profits with the girls. Emmie wanted the green felt hat sitting in the milliner's window. To increase their earnings, she embellished her negotiations with fantastic stories of each piece's provenance. "This chair belonged to the prince regent of Peru." "Andrew Jackson drank from these goblets." Her shameless lies brought such high prices Aislynn and Molly hid their amusement and held their tongues. They returned to work, leaving Emmie in the front yard drawing a crowd of curious buyers.

Aislynn and Molly rinsed and wrung out the curtains. They slipped them back on their rods while Aislynn explained to a dubious Molly, "It's a time-saver. They'll dry with some wrinkles, but Sage will never notice." Together, they twisted and squeezed the water from the sheets and towels. Once hung on the line, they whipped and snapped in the warm, dry wind.

Molly covered her nose with a cloth and began pushing the mouse-deterring cayenne powder into the cracks of the woodwork and walls. Aislynn wiped the bedsteads with kerosene to kill bedbugs. With those chores finished, they were ready to heave the mattresses into place.

In the front yard, Emmie helped them beat the upholstered furniture and polish the wood pieces Aislynn had decided to keep. Slowly they started to arrange them throughout the house. A round table with six chairs and a carved hutch found their way to the dining area. A dry sink and a tin table with drawers lined up on one side of the stove. A maple cupboard and jelly safe, still full of canned fruits and vegetables, filled the space on the opposite side.

A tufted settee and an old trunk packed with extra linens faced the fireplace. Thinking Sage's old friend Cap would be a frequent visitor, Aislynn set a rocker next to the hearth. A deep, plush armchair with a matching ottoman upholstered with a tapestry of a hunting scene came to rest across from Cap's rocker. End tables and lamps slid into place on both sides.

"Perfect," she announced to the girls, "not even Sage could find fault with this."

They filled the hutch with china and glassware. Pots, pans and cooking and cleaning tools found homes in the kitchen area.

Aislynn heated the kettle. The three young women sipped tea at the table while they polished lamps, cleaned chimneys and changed wicks.

Leaning back in her chair, Emmie brought her cup to her mouth and giggled into her tea. "Mr. Sage won't be needing Sheila now that you're here."

"Emmie!" Molly stepped out of character and reprimanded her friend. "That's not nice." She turned to Aislynn. "She doesn't know what she's saying."

Her curiosity piqued, Aislynn asked, "Who is Sheila?"

Molly shot a stern look at Emmie, who was hanging her head.

"She's a whore," Emmie replied in a soft voice.

Outraged, Aislynn asked, "You think I'm his whore?"

Emmie jumped. "No, but you're going to marry him, and married men don't need whores," she prattled.

Aislynn shook her head, not knowing where to start to set Emmie straight. "First off, ladies don't discuss that kind of woman. Second, I am not marrying Mr. Sage. I don't know where you got such an idea."

"Marshal Sage changed completely for you. He even bought this house," Emmie observed.

"He did those things for himself."

"But you're together all the time. He's nice to you, and he can even be funny."

Aislynn's eyes widened and her jaw fell. "That's not why you marry a man, Emmie!"

"Why do you?"

Aislynn took a breath and thought for a moment. "Because you trust him. You know he'll be at your side no matter what kind of trouble or heartbreak comes your way, no matter how sick or unattractive or wrong you can be." The words were catching in her throat.

"That's what love is?" Emmie asked.

"That's how it looks."

"How does it feel?"

"Emmie, stop," Molly interjected. "You're upsetting her."

Aislynn sat quietly for a moment, studying the girls. "You feel . . . you feel empty when he leaves the room, like something is missing, and you don't feel whole again until he returns."

Emmie straightened, crossed her hands over her heart and sighed deeply. "Oh, Aislynn, it must be tragically heartbreaking for you to know Johnny won't be back. How will you ever heal?"

The young girl's pose and tone were so amusingly melodramatic, they brought out Aislynn's sense of humor. "Well, I know how you don't fill the gap." She was thinking of Moran, but she used the Sage situation to make her point. Leaning toward Emmie with her brows lowered and her finger wagging, she said, "You don't marry the first man who is nice and funny."

With a sheepish grin, Emmie asked, "Would you tell us about Johnny and New York City?" Her excitement rose with every word.

"My mind is so crowded with memories of him. How do I start? I don't remember a time I didn't know him. We lived in the same neighborhood, went to the same church and school. New York City is so different from Cheyenne. People like us don't live in houses. We live in apartment buildings. They are four, five, even six stories tall. Streets are cobbled. They're crammed with horses, wagons and people. There are so many people from different parts of the world, speaking different languages. It's almost like music to hear them. There are vendors from places as far away as China and Italy on every street selling food with rich aromas." Aislynn took a deep breath of remembered scents. "But you would love the stores. The shopping is marvelous. You'll find anything you could ever want in the New York City stores."

"Why did you leave?" Emmie asked.

"A few years ago, one of our friends, Tim, went west to find work. He was a dear friend, and I missed him terribly. Johnny understood. So we packed up and went west together to find him."

"And he was in the mining camp in Utah?" Emmie stated with authority.

"Word travels fast around here."

"You're a novelty," Emmie said with a tilt of her head.

"In 1868, we railroaded through Chicago to Cheyenne. That was before you girls arrived. Mr. Sage befriended us. He gave us a great deal of guidance and sound advice." Aislynn put her hand to her throat. "But wagoning is no picnic. Many people die from sickness, accidents, drowning, childbirth; I almost lost Johnny to a rattler." Aislynn took a few sharp breaths remembering the fear.

Molly placed her hand on Aislynn's arm. "But he lived."

"Yes, that time. Tim worked for the mine, so we settled in the camp." A wave of anxiety passed through Aislynn
with the recollection of Liam and his mining town. "Johnny
opened a smithy, and I started a restaurant."

"Mr. Sage said you're a good cook," Emmie added.

"That's kind of him." Aislynn smiled and continued,
"Johnny and Tim were well liked. People trusted and respected them, even though they weren't much older than
me. The camp elected Tim to the council. Johnny was
appointed chief of the fire brigade." Aislynn paused and
took a long breath. "One night there was a big fire . . . .
Johnny entered a building . . . ." Aislynn stopped talking.
She looked deep into her teacup. She could see everything
clearly in the dark brew.

*The alarm had sounded in the middle of the night. A great
blaze was glowing at the bottom of Main Street. When they arrived, Johnny said, "My men are either half asleep or full drunk.
It would be a help if you brewed some strong coffee." A stab of
fear struck her; she didn't want to leave. "Now show these men
what a good, lovin' wife you are." Johnny kissed her, patted her
behind and sent her to the restaurant.*

*She stood at her stove. The door opened. Moran appeared.
His singed hair and beard, the charred ruffles on his shirt and
his hands wrapped in bloody handkerchiefs telegraphed the devastating news. Without a word, he shattered the life she was
living.*

"Get out!" she screamed.

*He reached his arms out to her. "I'm sorry." His voice was
thick with sorrow. "There was nothing . . . ." The tragedy
lodged in his throat.*

*Her bones turned to liquid; she flowed to the floor. She curled
into a heap, and her hands clutched at her hair.*

Liam's hand caressed her back. "I'll take you home."
"I have to get him; I have to help Johnny."
"No one can help him. We tried. The roof collapsed. Let me take you home."
He calmed her with a drink laced with laudanum and carried her to bed. When she awoke the next morning, Moran was still watching over her and all Johnny's arrangements were complete.

The cup shook and her reflection trembled, bringing her back to the present.

Aislynn felt Molly patting her hand. In her tiny voice, she whispered, "I'm sorry."

"Me, too," Aislynn replied with a sad smile.

"You could marry again," she suggested.

"When you've had a love as unconditional, as unselfish as Johnny's"—she paused and shook her head—"it's impossible to replace him."

Molly and Emmie sighed in pity. "That's just beautiful," Emmie uttered.

Aislynn blinked her tears away and saw the two girls with rivulets of tears running down their faces. "Goodness," she said, "we have beds to make, and I have to prepare dinner. So let's get going." She clapped her hands, punctuating the only end to her story she wanted to reveal.

The lamps glowed and the stew simmered. Aislynn rested in the big chair with her legs stretched across the ottoman. In the comfy chair, with the smell of dinner on the stove, she closed her eyes and imagined being back in her home in Utah, in the house Johnny designed and built for her, and for their child.

For months after she had lost Johnny, she had stayed close to home. But that day, a sunny September day, Aislynn and her friend had hitched a wagon and driven off to Moran's ranch. He had an extra side of beef, and she wanted it for her customers.

Halfway there, two outlaws sprang into the road. One held a knife. He sliced Aislynn's arm and stabbed deep into her thigh. She woke to find herself in Liam's bed: weak, helpless and in burning pain. Darkness had fallen and a storm had rolled in. Through the flashes of lightning, she saw Liam keeping watch over her.

The following morning, the stress from the attack and the loss of blood started the contractions. Her water broke. Pee Yeh, Moran's housekeeper, arrived with every necessity except the three months her child still needed to develop. She begged, "Please save my baby." The delivery was quick. Pee Yeh wrapped the tiny, purple body in a towel. A few hour-long seconds passed while Aislynn listened for a cry. Her son did not draw a single breath.

Without Johnny and their baby, she wanted to die. She stayed in Liam's bed for several days, alone in the darkened room, thinking of ways to end her life; she just couldn't find the means.

On the day Pee Yeh bathed her and washed her hair, Liam peeked around the door and found her struggling to unsnarl the tangles. He sat behind her on the bed and began gently pulling the brush through the matted mess and smoothing her hair with his hand. Tears came to her eyes. "You have to excuse me," she said, "I've been crying a lot."

"You've plenty to cry about."

"I feel like I was at the bottom of the mine without a candle, and just when I thought I was moving toward the light, I fell back into the pit."

"I've been thinking about something to say, something to make you feel better."

She sniffed and wiped the tears off her cheeks. "I appreciate that, but there aren't any words. I learned that when Johnny died."

"I've been feeling rather useless," he confessed.

"Useless? You saved my life, gave me your bed, nursed me to health, and I know you brought a priest from California to . . ." she pushed the words out, "bury my baby. I thank you for that."

Aislynn sighed and wiped her eyes. *I did have reasons to care for Liam, even love him.*

Aislynn woke when the door squeaked open and Sage stepped inside. She feigned sleep and watched him through narrowed eyes. His gaze slipped over her as he trod softly to the center of the room. Turning slowly, he studied the table set with a lace cloth, china and a crystal goblet. His eyes glided over the kitchen and came to rest on the parlor side. He perched on the edge of the ottoman and nudged Aislynn's legs. She fluttered her eyes open.

"You done good," he said, jerking his head toward the rest of the room.

"I'm glad you like it."

"You tired?"

"It's been a long day."

"Didn't know it was so big." Disbelief colored his tone.

"Before I forget, this is for you." Aislynn fished a roll of bills out of her apron pocket.

Sage counted them. "Sixty dollars? How'd you make so much money?"

"Ask Emmie," she said, struggling out of the deep chair. Sage pulled her up.

"I'll get dinner on the table before I collapse from exhaustion." Aislynn walked to the table and pulled out the chair. "Would you take a seat, Mr. Sage?" she asked, sweeping her hand like a maître d'.

She placed a bowl of stew on the china plate in front of him.

"Ain't you eatin'?"

"I wasn't invited."

Sage pointed to the chair. With a mouthful of stew, he mumbled, "Take a seat."

"That's not the way a gentleman homeowner invites a lady to dinner, sir."

He looked up at her. "Get a plate," he ordered.

Aislynn stood at the stove with her arms crossed, studying the ceiling.

He pushed his chair off the rug with a thud. It scraped the wooden floor. Standing over her, he twisted up his mouth in anger. She simpered and batted her eyelashes.

"Would you sit down and eat?" he growled.

Aislynn frowned and tapped her cheek with her index finger.

"Please!"

Aislynn curtsied. "Thank you, sir. I'd love to."

She set a place and filled her plate. Sitting next to him, she raised her glass of water and repeated an Irish blessing:

"May you always have walls for the wind,
a roof for the rain,
tea beside the fire,
laughter to cheer you,
those you love near you

and all your heart might desire."

His cynical eyes met her wide, bright smile. "You can get all that with a house?"

"They're all my wishes for you." She took a sip, closed her eyes and made a wish of her own.

CHAPTER 7

A ISLYNN sat at her little table sipping the thin porridge Mrs. McKenzie considered a suitable breakfast. At seven in the morning, the attic room started to gather heat. She reached for the window sash. It shook and rattled as she pushed it open. Movement in the churchyard caught her attention. She watched as Tommy Two Hawks, the young Indian man who worked at Sage's livery, slipped through the narrow opening between the barn's bay doors. Aislynn thought it odd that Tommy would be attending the priest's animals. With only one horse and a cow, Father Gilhooley cared for them himself.

A few moments later, Aislynn spied Molly sneaking through the same opening in the barn doors. *Ah, love.* Aislynn's body sighed as melancholy settled on her. A tiny fleck of doubt fell into her consciousness. *Did I make a mistake and judge Liam too harshly? If I had told him, would a man who never had a mother be so cruel as to separate me from my baby? Could I have been more patient, more understanding, more trusting? After all, marriage is compromise.* Aislynn saw the barn door close. She shook her head. *If only Liam knew how to compromise . . . .*

Parishioners packed the pews shoulder to shoulder. The large congregation surprised Aislynn. Though she knew

Cheyenne had five churches, she perceived its lawlessness as godlessness.

Aislynn closed her eyes and allowed the scent of burning incense and candles to bring her to a familiar, unambiguous place. Here, in her church, she always said and did the right things. Mass offered an hour of peace from her doubts and fears.

She opened her eyes and surveyed the church's bare-beamed frame. Two rows of pews flanked a center aisle. At its head, two tables covered with white cloths awaited the priest. One served as the altar, and the other held the tabernacle.

The colorful crowd sat according to their status in life. Matrons in fashionable dresses and elaborate hats sat up front with stiff men in starched, white collars and well-behaved children. Next in line, families wearing frayed fabrics and weary, overworked faces filled the pews. Bleary-eyed roughs followed. Clean shaven from their Saturday baths and trips to the barbers, they hung their heads and prayed for relief from their hangovers. Outcast women and converted Indians huddled in the back. Hiding her shame under the veneer of good manners and proper dress, Aislynn edged herself into a forward pew.

Tiny brass bells tinkled. Father Gilhooley began. "*In nomine Patris, et Filii, et Spiritus Sancti.*" The congregation responded, "Amen." The words brought her to a mysterious, holy place, a place where sins were absolved and salvation was possible. Aislynn wanted to believe in God, but secretly her devotion inched away with every loss: her father, Johnny and their baby. She envied those who accepted without question. Sitting in church, with the sacred words filling her ears, her faith rekindled.

Up and down, they all knew the steps of the dance. *Deo gratias* signaled dismissal. The assemblage rose and drifted out. Aislynn remained on her knees. Unable to confess her sins to Father Gilhooley, Aislynn begged God for his understanding and forgiveness. In the solitude of the sanctuary, she looked toward the heavens, "Please God, I beg forgiveness for my sins and protection from Liam. If you could allow us to live this new life, I know I can care for myself and my child." Behind her, the sound of hard-soled shoes walking deliberately up the aisle echoed in the emptiness. Aislynn froze. A sick feeling rose from her stomach. The man passed her and started to clear the altar. In a hasty murmur, she said, "And please help me become a real teacher tomorrow." Flashing the sign of the cross, Aislynn rushed out the door.

The wagon creaked and clattered up to the church with Aislynn's thirteen silent, frightened students huddled in its bed. A grizzled private with a bulging belly protruding between the straps of his suspenders struggled down from the seat and opened the tailgate. "Come on you little beasts," he growled as he pulled the first child out.

"Be gentle." Aislynn read the name embroidered on his shirt. "They're children, Private Foster."

The older boys and girls jumped down. They lifted the little ones and placed them on the ground. Aislynn surveyed her charges cowering together. They wore western clothes with intricately beaded moccasins. The boys' and girls' glossy black hair hung in braids around their gaunt, hollow-eyed faces.

Aislynn approached them with a soft smile hiding her own ever-expanding anxiety. "Welcome to your new school. Won't you come with me?" She walked toward the church.

No sound of shuffling feet followed. She turned. Rooted in place, the children faced her with questioning stares. "Please." Aislynn gestured toward the door. "Come this way."

Her pupils exchanged bewildered looks. All her apprehension bloomed into a terror that pressed down so hard she felt herself sinking into the ground. "Do you speak English?" she asked the group in a panicked voice.

"I speak," a tall, chisel-faced girl offered.

"Thank goodness."

"Hello, goodbye, yes, no."

"Please don't tell me that's all you know."

"Hello, goodbye, yes, no."

She told herself to be calm and think. She took the girl's hand and pulled her toward the door, waving the others to follow. Once inside, she pointed to the benches and said, "Sit." They did not move. "Please, sit," she begged. Understanding crept into Aislynn's consciousness. She realized the children did not recognize their surroundings. In a voice rising with panic, she said, "You've never been to school. Good glory, you've never sat at a table, have you? Have you ever seen a table?"

Their limitations became clear. Her mumbling prompted whispering. Aislynn bit her lip hard. Regret rose in her heart for all her lies, her presumptions and her ignorance. *How could I have not realized they've had no schooling?* Aislynn covered her eyes with her hand and lamented, *All my planning for naught.* Her thoughts swirled. *I've been a teacher for two minutes and already I feel like I'm being pulled down in a whirlpool of failure.* The possible consequences raced through her mind. *I'll lose my job and my home. I won't be able to care for my child. I'm letting everyone down: Sage, Father Gilhooley and good God, even the president of the United States.*

Her stomach churned. She rubbed her temples and told herself to take a deep breath. She looked at the children. Their eyes brimmed with worry and fear. Her heart opened to them. "I know you're afraid." She held up her open hands. "I won't hurt you."

Crossing her hands over her heart, she said, "You don't want to be Americans any more than my father wanted to be English." She asked herself, *What would Da have wanted?* She could hear his response, *Respect who I am, respect my customs and beliefs.* Aislynn decided she could not remake them into the government's ideal; she would simply try to give them the skills and knowledge they needed to exist in the new world being thrust upon them.

Aislynn made a grand descent into the bench. "Sit." She rose and took the English speaker's hand. Her skin was rough, her nails broken. Aislynn guided her onto the seat. "Sit," Aislynn repeated. She pushed the girl down the bench and motioned to the boy closest to her. "Sit," she ordered. The children learned quickly and filed into their places.

Once everyone was gathered at the table, Aislynn tackled names. Pointing to herself, and said, "Mrs. Maher." She pointed to herself again, "Mrs. Maher." She addressed the English speaking girl by pointing her finger. The girl said, "Kimimela."

"Good!" Aislynn clapped her hands. Her excitement drew timid smiles. She wrote their names on her pad phonetically and added notes on each one's distinctive features so she could identify them correctly.

One of the youngest boys started to squirm and whimper. He grabbed his crotch. Aislynn opened the door and pointed

SUSAN DENNING

to the privy. The child hurried to the door and started to lift the flap on the front of his pants. "No!" she shouted. "Goodness, you have to be taught everything."

Aislynn dragged the boy outside and waved all the other children to follow her. She pulled open the door to the outhouse and pushed the boy into the dark, malodorous cabinet. He started to cry and struggle. Aislynn pointed to the seat and the hole. The child shook his head. She clapped her hands to get everyone's attention. Again, she pointed to the seat and the hole. With a demonstration that defied every rule of decorum, she pointed to the boys and held her imaginary penis over the hole. "In here," she commanded as she pointed. The children giggled. She lifted the small boy and perched him on the edge of the seat. He tried to escape, but Aislynn held him fast. She pointed at the girls. "Sit," she instructed. An old copy of a farmer's guide hung nearby on the wall. Aislynn ripped out one sheet, wiped the front and the back of her skirt with it and threw it into the latrine.

She shooed the children away from the door and left the little boy in the privy. After a few seconds the door opened, and he emerged triumphantly into the light. Aislynn poked her head in to evaluate his success. She held the door open and made a grand gesture toward the latrine. Aislynn smiled at her students and patted the boy's head. She took his hand and led him to the well, motioning to her class to follow.

Aislynn pumped the handle and placed her hands into the stream. "Water." She removed her hands and placed them back into the flow. "Water." She grabbed the soap that lay on the ground and lathered her hands. "Wash." Holding up her soapy hands, she repeated, "Wash." After rinsing her hands, Aislynn grabbed the towel hanging on the pump. Flourishing it like a matador's cape, she dried her hands, saying "dry."

88

After the class watched the little boy repeat her performance, they each took a turn at the pump.

Since they were outside, Aislynn decided to allow the children a recess and give herself a few moments to think and develop a new plan of action. She demonstrated the game of tag, organized them and let them run.

Lunchtime arrived and another problem presented itself: the children did not have any food. Aislynn presumed Foster must have driven away with their lunches in the wagon bed. The loaf of bread and jar of jam Aislynn reserved for Amy sat on the kitchen hutch in the parochial house. Leaving the children alone in the classroom for a moment, Aislynn gathered the bread, jam and a knife.

A thin slice of bread spread with a thin coat of bright orange, apricot jam sat before each child. They looked at their lunch, but didn't touch it. Aislynn picked up a slice of bread. "Food," she said. She brought it to her mouth. "Eat." She repeated the words again. When the children tasted the bread and the jam, their faces brightened at the sweetness. Their enjoyment brought smiles to their faces and Aislynn's. She decided the careless driver would get an earful when he returned.

Her plans to teach spelling and geography drifted into the distant future. She introduced the children to their slates and pieces of chalk. Slowly, she drew a sun on the big blackboard. Pointing up, she said, "Sun." She drew a second sun. "Sun." She pointed to the children. They repeated the word. "Draw." She wiggled the chalk over one of the children's slates. "Draw." Their adeptness with the chalk surprised her. Aislynn remembered seeing symbols painted on their teepees and the exquisite beadwork on their dresses and shoes. "You are all naturally artistic," she announced to her audience's bewilderment. She wiped off her blackboard and drew a crescent moon. "Moon," she pronounced, pointing to the sky. Natural mimics, the children echoed her and copied her drawing.

By the end of the day, the children owned a handful of English words, and Aislynn knew she needed to learn Sioux.

CHAPTER 8

Aislynn dropped into the chair in front of Sage's orderly desk. It displayed papers stacked in neat piles, wanted posters collected in two metal rings, folders standing in dividers and his ever-ready Colts. His rifle leaned against the desk.

She rested on her elbows and cradled her head in her hands. The scent of his bay rum reached her nose, and she grinned at his continuing efforts to be civilized. Sage stopped scribbling and looked up from his papers.

"What's the problem?" He rolled his pencil between his fingers.

"Why do you think I have a problem?"

"You wouldn't be here if you didn't."

She wagged her head. "You think you know everything."

Sage put down his pencil, crossed his arms and waited.

"I need a favor."

"How could I have shot so far off the mark?" he teased.

"It's the children. They don't speak English."

"Course they don't. They're Injuns."

"Why didn't you tell me?"

"You ain't stupid. What'd you think they spoke, French?" He chuckled, clearly amusing himself.

"How can you be so insensitive?"

"Just comes natural, I guess."

"They are very sweet, and they are trying so hard to cooperate, but we can't communicate."

Sage shrugged and remained silent.

"Don't you care?"

"I told you not to take this job." He pointed an accusatory finger at her. "This is your first problem; there's gonna be lots more, and you're gonna deal with them yourself."

Aislynn reined in her frustration and changed her tactic. "Would you like a home-cooked dinner tonight?"

"Course. I get hungry every night. Have a nice, hot meal ready around seven." He picked up his pencil and put his head down.

"And you'll teach me to speak some Sioux after we eat?" she coaxed.

"I didn't say that." He replied without looking up. "If you're gonna be quid pro quoin', you've got to establish the terms before you enter into an agreement. Mrs. Maher, we have no such agreement." Sage was clearly practicing his legal terms on her.

Aislynn leaned over the desk. "But you will," she said in her most coquettish manner.

He bent closer to his page, concealing his grin. "It'll depend on how good the dinner is."

In an attempt to gain the upper hand, she started toward the door. Halting, she suggested, "Maybe I should just ask your friend Cap. He's been very sweet to me."

Sage did not flinch. "You best get out of here before I make you sorry you ever walked in," he snapped.

Aislynn grabbed her skirt and flounced out the door, sure she would get what she wanted. As the door swung closed, she heard Sage mumbling, "Nothin' but trouble."

The lamp burning over the dining table hummed and wrapped them in its soft light. The curtains yawned wide, allowing prying eyes to verify no impropriety between them. Sage mentioned their new arrangement to Emmie, thus everyone in town would soon know Aislynn was cooking in exchange for language lessons.

Sage swallowed his last bite and pushed his plate to the center of the table. Leaning forward, he said, "I'm ready to deal."

"You want to play cards?"

"No," he crabbed, "for a smart girl you can be mighty stupid."

Honest and direct, Sage eschewed tact, flattery and equivocation. Like the Nolan boys, those unpolished gems who helped raise her, he railed against injustice, bad behavior and just about everything he disliked. Anger flowed fast and easily. Caring, kindness and vulnerability lay too deep to float to the surface. Aislynn had long ago learned to hear the true emotions behind the bluster.

She leaned on the table, looking at him from under her brows. "If you spoke in plain English—"

He cut her off. "That's what I want. The deal is you teach me English, and I'll teach you Sioux."

"You speak English."

"Not your English."

To the untrained ear, his request sounded gruff and irritated, but Aislynn heard much more in the simple statement: the shame and humiliation of recognizing his inadequacies, the fear of exposing them and the courage to ask for help. She often marveled at their relationship. It seemed they formed an instant bond of trust, something she had never truly developed with Liam. "Agreed."

Aislynn had come equipped with a list of words for him to translate.

"Let's start with hello," she suggested.

"*Hau.*"

Aislynn noted the word phonetically.

"Come?"

"*Hiyu.*"

"Go?"

"*Iyaya.*"

"Sit?"

"*Iyotake.*"

"Run?"

"*Iyagke.*"

They worked through her list. "There ain't no word for *read* or *write*," he said.

"I understand. That's one of the things that makes my job so difficult. They have no concept of a written language." Aislynn put down her pencil and folded her paper. "This is a good start. I'll memorize these words tonight and start using them tomorrow."

They sat across from each other in silent anticipation. Never one to suffer quiet for long, Aislynn spoke first. "Where do you want to start?"

Sage's brow furrowed. "You're the teacher."

"What do you want to know?"

His eyes strafed the room as if looking for eavesdroppers. "I told you," he grumbled.

"I know you want to learn to speak my English." She shook her head. "You know I'm not really a teacher. I can only tell you what I hear. I think you have three problems."

He leaned closer, intent on listening. Aislynn continued speaking. "First—double negatives."

"Sounds serious."

"It's not. I think it's the easiest to fix."

"Keep talkin'."

Aislynn bumped her chair closer to Sage's and picked up his writing tablet. "Let me show you." She wrote *You ain't got nothing* on the page. "There are negative words like *not, nothing, none, no*. When you say, 'You ain't got *nothing*,' you are actually saying, 'You do *not* have *nothing*.'" She wrote the words and underlined the negatives. "See? There are two negatives, *not* and *nothing*."

"What should I say?"

She crossed off *nothing* and wrote *anything*. "You say, 'You do *not* have *anything*.' See?"

"Give me another."

Deciding not to fight a war against the ubiquitous word *ain't*, she explained, "You say, 'You *ain't* going *nowhere*.' You should say, 'You *ain't* going *anywhere*.' 'You do *not* know *nothing*,' should be 'you do not know *anything*.' "

"I can do that. Gotta remember the *any*s.

"The second and third things are a bit more difficult."

Sage's jaw clenched.

"Let's look at pronouns. There aren't that many to learn, but you have to know how to use them. They have to agree with the antecedent, the noun that comes before."

"What the heck are you talkin' about?"

"Pronouns have to agree in number with nouns. You know nouns are singular or plural, like *gun* and *guns*, *hand* and *hands*."

"Yes," Sage fumed.

Aislynn put her hand on his. "Just calm down and I'll explain." She opened her bag and pull out one of her student's textbooks. "Here are some pronouns that can be used with nouns. Let's look at *this* and *these*. You can say, 'Give me *this plate*'; *plate* is singular. Or you can say, 'Give me *these plates*;' *plates* is plural. You match the singular pronoun with the singular noun and the plural with the plural."

"That's as clear as mud," he grumbled.

"I know it sounds a bit difficult." She patted the book. "Study this. It will be a better teacher than I, and I'm sure you will understand it. Let me give you one more example. You can say, 'Give me *them*,' but you never say, 'Give me *them* plates.' That's a rule."

"No *them* men or *them* horses."

"Correct. See, you are a quick learner. Now let's talk about irregular verbs."

"What?"

"Verbs, words that show action, like to *bake*, to *cook*. Some are complicated like to *go*, to *be*, to *sing*." She turned the pages of the textbook and reviewed verb tenses for some of the most difficult conjugations. "If you learn these three lessons, your English will improve greatly. It will take time, but it will be worth it."

Sage nodded. "You clean up and I'll start learnin'."

After washing the dinner dishes, Aislynn spotted a dirty glass next to Sage's big chair. Collecting it, she noticed the law book sitting on the end table. She opened the top volume and skimmed the page. Peeking over at Sage, with his huge hands gripping the children's book, Aislynn decided he needed one more thing.

The bookstore sat two blocks outside the perimeter Sage had established for Aislynn. Its raw wood and watery glass windows indicated a low-end store. Low-end meant low prices, one of Aislynn's favorite things. A light jingling of bells announced Aislynn's entrance. A tall, thin man with thick glasses stood behind a counter peering over an open ledger. Tables arranged in rows around the room held stacks of books in precise piles.

"Good afternoon, miss."

Aislynn bobbed a short curtsy. Calculating a "miss" had a better chance of negotiating a good price than a "missus," she did not correct him.

"Please feel free to browse."

"Thank you, I will." Aislynn tried to look sophisticated. She glided her fingers over bindings, crinkled her nose at some volumes and feigned interest in others.

"Is there anything in particular you are looking for?"

"In fact, there is. I am looking for a dictionary," she said in a haughty manner.

"I have an exquisite work right here. It's leather bound and gold embossed."

"Goodness no, that would never do. You see it's for my students. Perhaps you have one that has seen better days."

"In fact, I have one in the back. It's water damaged. I actually use it for my own reference."

With a coy smile, Aislynn asked, "Would you consider parting with it?"

"I might consider it," he said in a suggestive tone.

Aislynn sent him a sideways glance. "May I see it?"

The shopkeeper brought it to his counter. The warped cover revealed curled pages.

Trying to devalue the book, Aislynn gave him a troubled look. "It's in terrible shape. Is the print legible?"

"Yes, but the children might need to follow each line with a finger."

"Is the binding strong?" She flipped the cover, hoping for a loud creak that did not come. "Hmmm, I wonder if the parents would be offended if I had something this worn in my classroom."

"I would think they'd be happy if their children were learning new words."

With an exasperated air, Aislynn said, "One never knows with parents. Some can be so demanding." She pulled her lip between her teeth and fondled the cover of the book. "How much is it?" she asked, holding his gaze.

"Half price, six dollars?"

Aislynn's eyes widened. She wanted the book, but it was beyond her means. She stroked the binding. With a heaving breast, she said, "That's quite high. I could ask the school board, but I am afraid they'd never authorize such a large expense."

The shopkeeper's eyes rested on her chest.

"I'm sorry," she said, "I see now it's probably not a good idea. Thank you for your time."

"Please, don't leave," the bookseller pleaded and reached for her arm. Aislynn flinched from his brazen overture. His face reddened. Trying to recover from his misstep, he dipped his head and apologized. "Perhaps I could lower the price. Would they consider five dollars?"

"No."

"Four dollars?"

"No."

"Three?"

"I think two dollars would be acceptable."

Before they began their lesson, Aislynn placed her package on the table in front of Sage. "Open it," she commanded.

"What is it?" Sage glowered.

"You'll find out when you open it." Aislynn beamed as he examined the book. "It's a bit worn, but serviceable. Any word you don't know or don't understand can be found in this book. It will tell you the meaning and how to pronounce it."

"It's gonna talk to me?" he replied, trying to humor her.

Aislynn ignored his remark. She hurried to the end table and returned with a law book. "Find a word you don't know."

Sage opened to the page where his marker rested and pointed to *excoriate*.

"Let's find the *E*s." Aislynn flipped through and found the first *E* words. She pointed to the words at the top of the pages. "Then the *EX*s and the *EXC*s." Sliding her finger down the page, she stopped at *excoriate*. "Here's the definition—*Ex-co-ri-ate*—*verb, to censure or criticize severely.*"

Aislynn held her tongue, anticipating a sarcastic response. Sage stared at the book in stunned silence. "Hmm, would you look at that?" Wonder filled his deep voice.

Relieved, Aislynn flipped to the front of the book. "This is the key for pronunciation and information about grammar. There's a lot to look at and learn in this section."

Sage drew his lips into a tight line. "I can't take this."

"Why not?"

"You're a woman."

"What does that have to do with a dictionary?"

"It's a gift. A woman can't give a man a gift, and a man can't take it. Just ain't proper."

"Don't be silly. We don't think of each other that way. I don't view you as a man, and you don't think of me as a woman. We're friends. Friends do things for one another. You need this book for your education. I got it for you. You're keeping it."

"You gotta watch your reputation. Bad enough you're teachin' them . . . those Injun kids."

"No one will know unless you tell them. It's just another secret we'll share."

"I ain't got nothin' . . . anythin' for you."

"And you better not get me anything. That would be an insult."

"I'm beholden." He scowled.

Amused, Aislynn said, "Cheer up, Marshal. Maybe, someday, I'll need something from you."

Sage slowly turned the dictionary pages, grumbling into the book, "Ain't no . . . any maybe about that."

CHAPTER 9

"I'LL be right back; just wait," Aislynn called over her shoulder to Private Foster. She ran to the jail and burst into Sage's office. "I can't make dinner tonight. I'm going to the Indian camp."

Sage shook his head. "No, you ain't."

Poised to run out the door, she explained, "Today, I tried an experiment with my listless students. I bought a loaf of bread, some butter and thirteen apples. At noon, I gave each child a slice of buttered bread and an apple. Every single child perked up this afternoon." She shook her head. "They are not getting enough to eat, and I'm going to find out why."

"Aislynn, that ain't any of your business." His volume increased with his anger.

"They can't learn if they can't stay awake." She turned to leave.

"Don't you go out there," Sage commanded.

"Excuse me?" She pivoted and aimed her eyes at his. "Let me remind you one more time, you're not my father, my husband, or my guardian. You can't order me about."

The cloud of anger covering his face grew darker. "You're gonna cause trouble for them and yourself. When are you gonna understand, you teach them; you don't meddle in the army's business? That fort is dangerous; the road is dangerous. Remember, a lot of people ain't happy about those kids gettin' schooled."

"They're starving! I'm the only one who cares enough to find out why. So I'll risk it." Her hand reached for the door-knob.

"How you gettin' there?"

"On their wagon." She pulled the door open.

"How are you gettin' back?"

"I'm sure Colonel Hayes will furnish me with a wagon. If not, I'll walk." She closed the door on the end of her sentence and ran.

The rickety old wagon provided by the army rattled and cracked as it rolled to the fort. Sitting next to Private Foster as they bounced and swayed, Aislynn clenched the wagon seat and wedged her legs against the floorboards. She hoped they would arrive without throwing a wheel or breaking an axle.

They approached a ring of white teepees, shining like sails on the prairie ocean. Dogs barked, announcing their arrival. The women gathered together on the road. Seeing Aislynn sent them into a feverish conversation. When the wagon stopped, the children jumped out and paired up with their mothers. Foster gave Aislynn his hand and helped her climb down. As she approached the women, he whipped the horses. They charged away.

The group eyed her with suspicion. Attempting to use their language, Aislynn said, "*Hau*, I am Mrs. Maher." Aislynn pointed to herself. "Mrs. Maher." Gesturing to the children, she said, "*Wicicala* and *hoksila* are *lila waste*, your girls and boys are very good." Aislynn bowed to the mothers. "Thank you, *pilamayaye*."

A woman with a ring of red and yellow beads adorning the neckline of her dress directed Aislynn into the teepee ring. The smell of buffalo hides and sagebrush smoke could not mask the stench floating in from the open pit latrine festering beyond the teepees. Old men, weathered and worn, huddled in the sparse shade of the tallest teepee. Elderly women toddled over to see the spectacle that was Aislynn.

The tallest mother spoke to Kimimela. The girl told Aislynn to sit. Aislynn gathered her skirt, kneeled on the ground and sat back on her heels. The women formed a circle. The mother with the beaded dress brought a bucket of water with a gourd ladle and placed it in front of Aislynn. She took a sip of the tepid water. With eyes wide, shoulders raised and a bewildered look, Aislynn silently asked which direction to pass the bucket. The women laughed and motioned to Aislynn's right. "Thank you, *pilamayaye*." Standing behind their mothers, the children watched with a mixture of curiosity and confusion on their young faces.

Studying the women, Aislynn noticed their complexions varied in tone from dark copper to light brown. While each looked different, they all shared high, widespread cheekbones. Like the children's, their black hair hung in long, shiny braids. Aislynn envied their comfortable clothes, no corsets or layers, just simple, doeskin dresses without shoes.

Aislynn wanted to see the Indians' rations before Foster reported her to the colonel and literally called the cavalry. Like most Americans, Aislynn knew each Indian on a reservation received one set of clothes every year plus a weekly ration of one pound of meat and one pound of flour. Newspapers decried the injustice of hardworking whites feeding and clothing lazy Indians. They ignored the fact those meager provisions were in exchange for the Sioux relinquishing most of their land and their way of life. However, these Indians were not on a reservation and were clearly underfed.

Pointing to her eyes, Aislynn stated, "I want to see your food." She pretended to pick up food and place it in her mouth. The women wore expressions ranging from offended to bewildered. Hesitant to use her feeble, broken Sioux, Aislynn pointed to her imaginary meal and then she pointed to her eyes. She scanned the camp as if looking for the food. She decided to supplement her pantomime. "*Wayaka*, look for food, *woyute*." Then, she walked among the women searching.

One of the older women understood Aislynn's request. She led her to a small tent and threw open the flaps. The sun poured through the opening and seeped through the surrounding canvas, revealing three barrels and four bulging muslin sacks. Aislynn removed the top from a previously opened barrel and found blue-green meat floating in brine. The rancid smell filled the tent and made her gag. She slammed it closed. An empty sack lay on the floor. Aislynn lifted it and remnants of flour puffed through the weave. Four large bags sat on a wood pallet against one side of the tent. Each had a small tear in the top. Aislynn reached in and found two full of milled rice while the others contained dried macaroni. She grabbed a handful of the noodles and displayed it to Kimimela. Aislynn brought a piece to her mouth.

"Eat, *wote*?"

Kimimela shook her head. She picked up a piece, took a bite and held her tummy and moaned.

Aislynn studied her for a moment, wondering why macaroni would give Indians bellyaches. She asked herself, *If they can digest flour, why not rice and macaroni?* Aislynn looked at the noodles in her hand and reasoned, *They may have eaten too much, or too fast on empty stomachs.* She rolled a few grains of rice between her fingers. *I'm sure it's all infested with bugs. Perhaps they don't cook it long enough . . . or not at all!* The

Sioux knew meat: buffalo, deer and rabbit. They ate corn, squash, potatoes and flour but not rice or macaroni. "Let's get some pots and water, and we'll learn something other than reading, writing and arithmetic," Aislynn said, with no one comprehending.

She gathered two pails and signed to the older boys to fill them with water. The younger children were tasked with collecting wood for a fire. She scavenged for bowls and motioned to the women to get the gourd ladles.

Aislynn waited at the supply tent. With all her equipment at the ready, she ladled rice into some bowls and macaroni into the others. Like a general leading a charge, she raised her hand and sliced the air toward the camp, and her tiny army followed. She found two empty pots sitting near a teepee and set them on the fire. Counting out one, two, three, four ladles of water into the first pot, she held up the proper number of fingers for each portion. In the second pot, she counted another four ladlefuls. Aislynn took a bowl of rice and added some water. She stirred the rice with her hand, rinsing it and picking out any gravel or hard, dark grains. She poured off the bugs floating on the surface. Once the rice was clean, Aislynn filled two gourds and spilled the grains into the first pot.

When the rice water started to boil, Aislynn motioned for the women to look into the pot. "Bub, bub, bub." She imitated the sound of boiling rice. Holding the pot with her skirt, she moved it to a cooler part of the fire. To indicate it must sit and simmer, she contrasted her "bub, bub, bub" with "siss, siss, siss."

They turned their attention to the other pot. A column of steam rose from the water. When it reached a boil, Aislynn repeated, "Bub, bub, bub." She measured a ladle of macaroni and dropped it in. The wait began. Aislynn tried to convey cooking time by pointing to the sun and moving her hand slowly. Periodically, she shared a taste of the rice and noodles with the women. She shook her head and spit out the uncooked morsels.

The dogs began barking. The sound of galloping horses reached Aislynn's ears. Colonel Hayes and two soldiers dismounted outside the tepee circle. The ring of women around the fire broke apart. They rushed to shield their wide-eyed children. Everyone, even the elderly, stood stiff and alert.

The soldiers removed their hats. "Mrs. Maher," the colonel began in an annoyed tone. For the first time, Aislynn realized Sage's warnings were not simply about the physical dangers she faced; she could lose her job. In her mind, she berated herself for failing to consider that Hayes gave her this job, and he could take it away.

She faced her fear and the man with her most effective weapon, femininity. With a tilt of her head and a blazing smile, Aislynn jumped on his words. "Colonel Hayes," she said oozing abundant pleasure, "how nice to see you." She held his eyes just long enough to unsettle him.

"It's lovely to see you, Mrs. Maher." His demeanor softened. "I rode over to tell you, to ask you, well, when you want to visit the fort, you must inform my office."

Pretending to be contrite, Aislynn raised her hand to her throat and apologized, "Please forgive my ignorance." She smiled as her eyes scanned him. "I am sorry, but this is not a social visit. An educated man like you knows learning does not stop at the schoolroom door." She turned to the women and played to his sentiment. "The army has generously supplied these people with food, but in their ignorance, they don't know how to prepare it." She swept her hand over the pots. "This is a cooking class."

The colonel's eyes scanned the fires. "Well, that's thoughtful, ma'am. Carry on. Next time, please let me know when you want to visit the fort, so I can service you." His misspoken words sent his pale skin into a burning blush. One of the soldiers snickered with amusement. "I mean be of service to you."

Feeling her power over the man, she decided to use it. "In fact, there is something you can do for me. May I have a private word? This is a delicate matter." She brazenly slipped her hand in his and led him aside. "These people must learn about proper hygiene. I am afraid we are not setting a good example."

The colonel drew back; his eyes blinked with embarrassment. Aislynn whispered, "I'm sure you have no idea about this situation." Clicking her tongue, Aislynn pointed at the latrine. "It's a disgrace and must be corrected. They must have privies, and they must be maintained." She leaned closer to his ear. "After all, these are grown women." Aislynn stepped back, leveled her eyes at his and crossed her arms. "Besides, it could cause illness. I don't know how it happens, but I know it can cause cholera and other diseases. Now, wouldn't it be a tragic irony if these Indians brought disease to our heroes here at the fort and to all those good souls in Cheyenne." She crossed her worried hands to her heart. "These women and children could kill hundreds of whites without shooting an arrow."

The man's facial expressions tumbled from incomprehension to understanding to fear. "I'll get some men on that right away, Mrs. Maher. Thank you for alerting me to the situation. I was not aware. I rarely get to this part of the fort."

"Thank you for your understanding. I know this camp is a challenge, but you're just the man to handle it." Aislynn glanced over her shoulder at the women. "Oh dear, I must get back to the rice." With one last smile, she dismissed him. "It was nice to see you, Colonel."

The rice was thick and sticky but cooked. Aislynn dramatically removed the pot from the fire and gave each woman a taste. Feeling the softness in their mouths, recognition washed across their faces. Aislynn turned her attention to the macaroni. With a gourd ladle, she fished the macaroni out of the water and placed it in a bowl. Without a colander, she placed a knife on the lip of the bowl and tilted it until most of the water drained out.

The dog alarm sounded again. Aislynn looked up to find Sage riding into the camp. He wore his buckskins and his habitual scowl. He greeted the Sioux women in their own language.

"I could have used you an hour ago," Aislynn said with frustration clinging to her words.

Sage grumbled, "I'm here now. What are you doin'?"

"It's a cooking class. Want to join?"

"No, thanks. I recently got me a cook," he replied, peering into the bowl resting in her hands.

Aislynn turned to the women and motioned for them to taste the pasta.

"What is that?" he asked with more disapproval than curiosity.

"It's macaroni."

"Never seen it."

"They have bags of it and rice in their supply tent. The army must give them their leftovers. Now they know how to cook it, so they shouldn't go hungry."

Sage's eyes widened a bit and his frown nearly disappeared. He nodded a reluctant approval.

"Want to taste it?" She held up a noodle.

"Where is it from?"

"Europe. Italy, I think."

"No, I mean where'd it come from? Is it a vegetable?"

"It's basically flour and water formed into this shape and dried. Try some."

"I like real food," he said.

Aislynn shook her head. "Your new cook may prepare some new foods."

"She better get to town and get started," he ordered.

Turning her back on him, Aislynn returned to the women. She pantomimed. "You do this and eat."

"Want some help?" Sage offered.

"We're doing just fine without you."

Aislynn said her goodbyes to the women and the children. Turning to Sage, she gasped. "I forgot to ask the colonel for a wagon."

"You don't need one." Sage said something to the women and jerked his head at Aislynn. He led her to his horse and a mule.

Understanding dawned. "You want me to ride a pack mule. I am not baggage!"

"No, but you're both so stubborn and contrary I thought you two would get along." Sage pursed his lips, trying to hide his amusement, but his eyes crinkled and shined.

"I'll walk."

"It's three miles."

"No, thank you." Aislynn turned and marched down the road swinging her arms in a crisp, angry rhythm. The sun burned high and hot. With every step, she kicked up dust. Her tight, damp corset chafed. Gravity tugged at her legs. With pregnancy, she discovered her legs grew heavy in the late afternoon. *Maybe I am stubborn,* she thought, *but a mule! He could have borrowed a wagon. He's just punishing me for not obeying him.*

Her steaming anger propelled her for a half a mile as the mounted Sage trailed behind with the mule in tow. She stopped in the center of the road, braced her hands on her knees, and tried to catch her breath.

Sage jumped down and handed her his canteen. She looked up at him, shading her eyes with her hand. "Whiskey?" she asked with sarcasm.

"Drink it, you little fool." Aislynn took a sip and handed it back. "Gal, you are so stupid it hurts my brain to think of it. You know there are hundreds of men hereabouts dying to get their hands on a white woman. How'd you get it in your head it's safe for you to be on this road alone?"

"Men have always been respectful of me."

" 'Cause Johnny and Tim had your back. They ain't here and I ain't got the time to watch you every minute," he snapped.

"I have my gun." She patted her apron. A small, two-shot revolver, one of the few things her father bequeathed her, lived in her pocket.

"You're so small a midget could wrestle that away from you." Aislynn fumed as his rant continued. "You're so afraid of Liam findin' out about that baby and comin' to get you, but you come out here alone and give another man the opportunity to claim you." Sage pointed a finger. "What'd you do then?"

His words struck home. "I'm sorry. I just want to do a good job teaching those children, but I can't teach them if they can't stay awake."

"That's all well and good. But you gotta learn when a man tells you to do somethin', you do it."

"Any man, every man?" she challenged.

Sage stopped in midspew, considering his answer. With a smile in his eyes, he said, "Just me, I know what's best for you."

Aislynn knew his anger resided in his concern for her safety. Accepting his tirade, she offered, "I'm truly sorry. I was wrong." Turning away, she started back down the road.

"Damn, would you get on this mule?"

"No."

"You are so mulish. You're probably related. Now, mount up."

Feeling embarrassed and inept, she hung her head.

"You afraid?"

"No!"

"Then, mount up."

"No!"

"Nothin' but trouble, why not?"

Furious, Aislynn threw her hands on her hips and screamed, "I can't ride!"

A short laugh burst from Sage's mouth. "Can't ride? How's that?"

"I never learned. In New York, it would cost a small fortune to buy a horse and feed it. And where would I board it? You can't just trot it up the stairs to your apartment, you know."

"What about out here?"

Aislynn stared at the ground and revealed her true, very personal fear. "Johnny didn't think it was . . . safe for a . . . married woman."

Sage studied her for a moment with his face twisted into a question until it softened with understanding. "You don't exactly ride a mule. It's more like sittin' and holdin' on."

He lowered the volume of his deep voice. Bending close to her ear, his words rolled out like warm honey. "You and the baby will be fine." Sage's large hands encircled her waist. He lifted her slowly and gently placed her on the mule's back. He handed her a hank of mane. "Hold this and try to stay on."

After a mile or so, Sage shouted back at her, "You're cookin' dinner, ain't you?"

Aislynn decided it was her turn to be smug. "Is that why you rescued me?"

Sage was silent.

"I swear you men will do anything to get women to cook and . . . well, never you mind."

He turned fully around in his saddle, his eyes laughing at her. "You offerin' to never you mind?"

"You know full well I'm not offering you anything."

"Woman, you gotta learn your role in life," he said behind a smirk.

"I know my role! I am an independent woman. As I recall, in Wyoming women have rights."

"Yeah, you got rights as long as men want you to have them."

"Are you implying they could be rescinded?"

"Course. If they ain't workin' the way we want, you'll lose those rights in a flash."

Her entire body slumped, and she nearly slipped off the mule. *Those laws are going to protect me and my child from Liam.* Righting herself, she tightened her grip and rode on, praying Sage was wrong.

CHAPTER 10

Dance hall girls, gamblers and drunken toughs bumped and elbowed the refined citizens of Cheyenne as they crowded the stifling stairwell up to the courtroom. They ascended slowly, pushed through the door and shuffled into the rows of benches parading up the hall. They all assembled to see the historic spectacle of women serving on a jury.

Many of the spectators came to see a freak show with beards growing and breasts shriveling as women turned into men. They claimed there would be convulsions, collapsing and crying as female jurors fled the courtroom. Predictions and questions flew like snowflakes in a blizzard. "Can they bear to face the accused?" "Will they be able to absorb all the necessary information?" "Everyone knows women aren't as strong as men. The pressure and the stress will be too much for them."

Cap, Aislynn, Joan and Maggie listened to the banter, shaking their heads and rolling their eyes. "They are God-fearing, Christian women who will be honest and fair," Maggie said. "They will behave as they always do, in a responsible and dignified manner."

"I don't know where these people get such ideas. I've done a man's work many times. I've driven a mule team, felled trees, carried boulders for the foundation of my cabin, and I'm still a woman," Aislynn pronounced.

Joan looked over her shoulder and gave Aislynn an admiring glance. "You sound like Sojourner Truth when she said, 'I have plowed and planted and gathered into barns. And ain't I a woman?' "

"That's right," Maggie said, nodding.

"Sojourner said, 'If the first woman God ever made was strong enough to turn the world upside down all alone, women together ought to be able to turn it back and get it right side up again.' If her words are correct, I think we may see these women get Cheyenne right side up," Joan claimed.

Sage hammered the gavel and announced, "The Honorable Chief Justice Howe and Associate Justice Kingman." Both men were well respected in the community. While most Cheyenne residents knew the courts struggled to enforce the law in the territory, they also knew these men were diligent in their attempts to rectify the situation. The throng fell silent as the judges took their seats.

Six male and six female jurors entered the courtroom, with two women concealing their identities under veils. Shouts of insults and encouragement exploded in the courtroom as two deputy marshals shepherded the jury to their box.

As she watched the women file in, Aislynn decided the West was the perfect place for this experiment. Western women were tough; they had to be. Most of the good women of Wyoming rolled in on rough wagons or crude trains. They plowed and harvested crops. They hunted and dressed meat. They chopped wood and toted water. They faced wild animals, outlaws and Indians. Men could leave home for weeks or months selling wares or searching for gold. Women stayed to care for children, livestock and the homestead. They endured blistering sun, roaring blizzards and a constant wind that could drive one to madness.

While Aislynn and her friends were able to observe the proceedings without any direct repercussions, they knew each female juror could face devastating consequences. The women summoned to sit in judgment of their peers would be judged themselves. Changes in customs and laws never came easily.

The women jurors could face retribution if they sat in front of the whole town behaving like men. They risked ostracism and being labeled *loose* and *immoral*. Within their homes, husbands could punish them for bringing shame or economic hardship on their families. Once people doubted their morality, employed jurors and their husbands might lose their jobs. Family-owned businesses could lose customers. Mortgages and loans might be withheld, as well. Being the *Wild West*, violence against those who broke with custom was never out of the question.

However, Aislynn believed western women would embrace this opportunity. These women broke barriers. They knew the reward for all these risks was a more civil society, which would benefit themselves, their families and all the citizens of the territory. Selfishly, Aislynn hoped the change would be immediate, just in case she ever found herself seated in the witness chair.

Justice Howe addressed the courtroom. "It is a novelty to see, as we do today, ladies summoned as jurors. The extension of political rights and franchise to women is a subject that is agitating the whole country. I have long seen that woman was a victim of vices, crimes and immorality and with no power to protect or defend herself from these evils." His eyes fell on the ladies of the jury. "I have long felt that such power of protection should be conferred upon women, and it has fallen on our lot here to act as pioneers of this movement and to test the questions. I shall be glad of your assistance in accomplishing this objective. The eyes of the world are today fixed upon this jury." He turned to his colleague. "Justice Kingman would like to add a few words."

"You ladies know well how our courts have been utterly unable to enforce criminal law. We believe the remedy would be found if the intelligent and moral woman would come forward and help us by exercising the new powers, now, for the first time put into your hands. You are more deeply interested in sustaining the honest and vigorous enforcement of the laws than any other class of citizens. We implore you to aid us as judges and to protect yourselves and our young society, now just organizing itself. The time has come to choose." Kingman leaned toward the jurors. He closed his address with one single word: "Ladies?"

The crowd held its breath. A loud silence buzzed through the room. The only noise came from the shifting of bodies, straining to view the women enduring a trial of their own. Despite the pressing heat, Howe and Kingman sat frozen in place at the head of the room, their eyes focused on the history being made.

The ladies subtly glanced at each other. Collectively, they turned to face the judges. No one rose to leave. Each woman remained solidly committed to her position and her duty.

A gasp of surprise and awe flowed through the room. When the crowd exhaled, it blew away the old disregard and disrespect for the law. The change showed instantaneously. The attorneys took their heels off the tables, stopped chewing and expectorated their tobacco. They sat upright and straightened their clothes. Justice Howe hid his satisfaction behind a stern face, but Aislynn saw his eyes smiling.

Once the real work of the court began, the disappointed drifted away. But for most of the room's occupants, including Aislynn, the procedures of a courtroom remained a mystery. They stayed for the show; and like a play, the story of a trial unfolded.

The two attorneys rose. "Excuse me, young men." One of the female jurors spoke out. "Aren't you going to start with a prayer?"

Justice Howe and Kingman exchanged satisfied grins that said to the assemblage, *We did the right thing*.

A minister's wife, the lady stood and recited a prayer. "Our loving God, grant we women the strength to do our duty to God and country. Let our moral, Christian faith shine forth. May we enter these proceedings with the profound respect they deserve. May You guide us on our journey. In Christ, our Goodness, Amen."

The attorneys stood before the jury. The district attorney, Joseph Carey, asked the members if they knew the defendant, a man named Grayson. Caleb Horne, the defense attorney, explained that his client lived on the south side of town, but warned the good citizens in the jury box not to assume he was guilty because he resided with people who had a reputation for lawlessness. In Aislynn's mind, she heard Tim teaching her, *everyone is innocent until proven guilty*.

Sage escorted the shackled Grayson into the courtroom. The young, dark-haired man tried to shake the marshal's hand off his arm. With one strong swing, Sage sent Grayson into the chair next to his defense attorney. With great boldness, the accused glared at the women in the box. One of the ladies pulled back into her seat with wide eyes and an open mouth. The others held their heads high and stared back at the ruffian.

Carey asked Dr. Hamilton to take the stand. Sage brought a Bible to the doctor and asked him, "In the presence of God, will you tell the truth?"

Hamilton answered, "Yes."

The doctor began, "I was called by the victim's wife. She came to my home around 11:00 PM. She said Horace Collins was delirious, trembling and screaming with pain. We went to their shack, and he was, in fact, demonstrating all those symptoms. I examined him. He had cuts and bumps on the back of his head." The doctor pointed to the spot. "His right eye was dilated. I concluded the blow to his head caused hemorrhaging. I couldn't save him."

A brightly dressed, slatternly woman, sitting near the front, began to wail. All eyes turned toward her cries. The doctor said, "He died before I left." The woman howled.

Justice Howe banged his gavel. "Quiet or you will be removed."

Carey asked if there were any other marks on the body. "I examined him and found nothing."

"Was the room askew?"

"Yes, but that may be its normal state."

"Did you see signs of a struggle?"

"My eye is untrained; I couldn't make a judgment."

Carey called another witness, who claimed to have seen Grayson in front of Collins's house. George Price testified, "I don't know if he did it, but I did see him there. But we all know Horace was a bad sort with all kinds of gambling debts, stealing—"

"That's enough," Howe interrupted. "Mr. Collins is dead, allegedly murdered."

"But he should've expected it."

"Simply answer the questions or Marshal Sage will put you in a cell." Howe turned to the jury. "Ladies and gentlemen, I'm sorry you had to hear that. Please disregard Mr. Price's comments. His opinion is not relevant. Any further digression will not be tolerated."

Sage stood and asked Mrs. Collins to take the stand. The weepy woman rose and walked to the chair. Her hair glowed in an unnatural shade of yellow. The woman's huge breasts, riding high in a gaudy, plaid dress with a low décolletage, reminded Aislynn of two large loaves of unbaked bread.

Mrs. Collins looked up at Sage, down at the Bible and back to Sage. "I ain't really Mrs. Collins," she said, audibly ashamed to display her loose morals.

Sage glanced at the judges, and his eyes swept the jurors. He shrugged and slowly shook his head. "If it didn't make a difference to you, doesn't make a difference to me."

An awkward silence hung in the air until some in the audience started twittering. Aislynn clapped her hand over her mouth to muffle an indecorous giggle. Howe's gavel hit its mark and the room quieted. The witness raised her head and pulled her ponderous breasts high, trying to gain some semblance of respectability. She swung her abundant hips into the chair.

"So what's your name?" Sage asked.

"Ina Goodbody."

Laughter rolled through the courtroom. Aislynn pulled her lips between her teeth as her body shook with amusement. The dour Sage stared up at the ceiling for a few seconds and swallowed. He pushed the Bible at her. "Just say, 'I will.' "

Ina admitted Horace Collins had debts, and Grayson had come around looking for payment. She claimed the last time he had appeared, he had threatened Horace and promised to be back.

A next-door neighbor testified to Horace's screams around 9:30. Ina's employer confirmed she had not left the saloon until 10:30.

Grayson's attorney summarized his defense with the conclusion that there were no witnesses to the murder, and all the evidence was circumstantial. The prosecutor countered with his opinion that the deputies' investigations confirmed Grayson's threats and his record of violence. Finally, Grayson had no alibi for the time Collins died.

Sage led the jury to another room. In the courtroom, knots of citizens debated the facts. The heat in the room seemed high enough to melt the paint off the walls. The sky darkened and a heavy rain began to fall. The longer they waited, the more the temperature and the sound rose. Howe called for quiet, explaining the jurors needed to deliberate in peace.

After three hours, the jurors filed into their box. A tense silence dropped like a curtain. Everyone knew Grayson's life rested in the hands of the six men and six women.

The male foreman rose and spoke to the judge. "Justice, these women gave close attention to every detail in this case." He shook his head and expressed his exasperation. "I never heard so many questions. After a thorough discussion of every word said at this trial, we came up with a guilty verdict."

A roar rose in the courtroom. Those for Grayson booed and those against him cheered. Justice Howe again called for order.

Before the jurors were discharged, Justice Howe praised the brave women. "You exerted a refining and humanizing influence. You were careful, painstaking, intelligent and conscientious. Your presence marks a new and improved epoch in the administration of justice. I am proud to be a witness to this seminal event in human history."

The magnitude of the day made the three women giddy. They gushed excitedly about possibilities. "Maybe women on the council, or in Congress, or president," Joan offered.

Cap interjected, "Ain't you aimin' a bit high?"

Aislynn's eyes brightened. "Women could be lawyers or judges."

"It's a proud day for Cheyenne," Cap agreed.

As they stood, Joan said, "How blessed we are to have witnessed such an historic display of female citizenship."

"I wish Emmie had been here. Her head is so full of boys; I can't get her to think of much else."

"It's her age," Aislynn observed. "I'm sorry Molly missed it, too. But we witnessed it, and we'll be able to tell our grandchildren about this milestone."

"It's been an amazing day. I feel such pride, and I didn't do anything but watch." Maggie smiled at her friends. "But, it's late and I better get back to the store and relieve Paul."

Cap said, "I have to check on Smokey."

Joan looked wistful. "I'd like to stay and drink in the triumph, but I have lessons to plan. Are you coming, Aislynn?"

"I'll stay and wait for Sage. I'd like to thank Justice Howe. I think he and Justice Kingman have given us a real chance to have our side of the story heard, if we ever need our side to be heard." She tried to sound hypothetical.

As Aislynn watched the crowd clear, she heard a male voice, high-pitched and bitter, behind her. "There's that Injun teacher. Hey you, teacher. I know you. You steer clear of my girl, Molly. I don't want none of your Injun filth on her."

Aislynn refused to honor him with her attention. Spying Sage, she stood tall and swanned toward him.

She gave Sage a quick curtsy and praised him. "You acquitted yourself well today, Marshal. You were quite professional."

Sage bobbed his head. "Thank you kindly."

"How you ever controlled yourself with Miss Goodbody, I'll never know. I thought I would burst."

One side of Sage's mouth rose in a half smile. He looked straight into Aislynn's eyes. "I'm gettin' a lot of practice with self-control."

Aislynn recognized he was referring to her and chose to redirect the conversation. "Do you think I could thank Justice Howe for what he did for women today?"

"He's right there." Sage's head tilted toward Howe.

When the justice was alone, Aislynn approached. She curtsied. "Thank you for allowing women to serve on this jury."

"I think I'm the one who should be doing the thanking."

"I truly appreciate what you've done." Trying to be nonchalant, she maneuvered her concern into their conversation. "The marshal and I sometimes discuss the law." Howe gave her a puzzled look. She pushed on. "It's an interesting topic, although extremely complex. I always have unanswered questions. One particular issue has me puzzled. With Wyoming's Married Women's Property Act, are children considered a woman's property or do they still belong to the man?"

"That, Mrs. Maher, is a very good question. We have a long-standing precedent granting ownership to men. However, when new laws are passed, it's up to the courts to interpret them. Laws are subjective. We have juries so a group of reasonable people can decide what they mean. If you asked a man, you might get a different answer than the one you would receive from a woman. That's why it's important for women serve. Do you understand?"

"Oh yes, sir. It's very clear to me."

CHAPTER 11

CLOUDS of dust puffed through town announcing the arrival of cattle and cowboys. Considered the scourge of the civilized towns, they rode in lonely, thirsty and flush with hard-earned cash. Mostly young, impressionable and untamed, they created immeasurable trouble.

In Cheyenne, they camped south of the rail line at prairie ranches or makeshift stock pens. With its settled community and a new inclination toward law and order, the cowboys caroused in Cheyenne's seamier part of town. When they entered the business district, the merchants saw their antics through dollar signs. They simply turned a blind eye to the boyish behavior. Aislynn's neighborhood, with its churches, houses and quiet industry, rarely received visits from cowboys.

Therefore, Amy and Aislynn were surprised to find three young boys lounging on the church steps. They scrambled to their feet and whisked their hats off their heads as the two approached. Aislynn's eyes raced over them: hats brushed, faces scrubbed, clothes washed, boots polished. The scent of strong cologne sailed past her nose. She judged they were fresh off a drive.

"Good afternoon," Aislynn greeted them.

The boys nodded. They repeated her "good afternoon" but added "ma'am." They stared at the ground until Aislynn asked, "Can I help you with something?"

"Yes, ma'am." The tallest boy looked up. He surveyed his companions. Following another uneasy silence, he asked, "Are you the lady who teaches the savages?"

Aware of the possibility of danger, Aislynn's free hand dipped into her pocket, and her fingers curled around her tiny pistol. "My students are Indians."

"Yes, ma'am. Sorry, ma'am. No disrespect, ma'am. You see, ma'am, we wondered, we thought maybe if you taught Injuns, you'd teach us, too."

"Do you go to school at home?"

"No, ma'am, we don't have no school."

"No pastor to teach you to read the Bible?"

The boys laughed. "He can't read. He says he can, but my mama asked him to read a letter once, and he said it would be a sin to touch something that had traveled so far. Said it could be bewitched."

The middle-sized boy added, "He pretends to read the Bible, but he just shouts about the Lord and the devil." He shrugged. "But he's all we've got."

"Where is your home?"

The tall one answered, "The New Mexico Territory."

"We drove five hundred head," the smallest one added with abundant pride.

Aislynn looked at the child. "How old are you?"

"Thirteen."

"He's almost eleven," the middle boy corrected, elbowing the fibber. "But I was joining on, and I couldn't leave him behind."

"How old are you two?"

"I'm fifteen and he's thirteen," the tallest replied.

"How long are you in town?"

"The trail boss is headin' back in two weeks, and we have to ride along if we want to get home."

"You want to learn to read?" Three pairs of eyes pleaded with Aislynn.

The tall boy interjected, "And to write if you'd be obligin'."

"I truly don't know how much we can accomplish in two weeks." She ticked off her responsibilities. "I teach all day, and you cannot trespass on my students' lessons. After school, I have to clean my classroom and write my lesson plans for the next day. Then, I have to make dinner." She hesitated. "I suppose if I boil and fry for two weeks . . . "

"I could teach them," Amy offered.

Offended, the oldest said, "You're a baby."

Amy lifted her face and took three faltering steps forward. She threw her fists on her hips and stated, "I can read and write."

The boy looked at Amy's leg. "Yeah but . . . " Feeling Aislynn's disapproving eyes, he swallowed his words.

Aislynn acquiesced. "If you boys help me clean every day after school, perhaps we can get you started with some basic skills. I can't promise much but we can try."

The boys whooped and slapped their hats on their thighs.

"I suppose we should introduce ourselves. I am Mrs. Maher. This is my assistant, Amy."

With a flourish, the oldest boy waved a hat emblazoned with three gaudy, silver medallions and bowed. "I'm Jimmy Snyderly. This here is Jorge Gonzalez and his little brother, Roberto, but we call him Puny. They're Mexican."

"We're as American as you." Jorge's voice rose in anger. "My parents were born here just like yours."

"We will not be disparaging each other in my classroom. I expect you boys to be respectful and considerate of each other and us. Now, let's get to work."

After sweeping the floors, wiping the blackboard, rinsing the water bucket and cleaning the outhouse, the boys took their seats. Aislynn wrote each boy's name on the board. "These are letters and they spell your names." She ran her finger under each name. "*Jimmy, Roberto* and *Jorge.*" Aislynn pointed to the alphabet posted on the wall next to the table. "There are twenty-six letters. Each has its own distinct sound. *A*—ah, *B*—ba, *C*—ca." She touched each one. "When you put them all together they form words: *J-I-M-M-Y. Jimmy. J-O-R-G-E. Jorge. R-O-B-E-R-T-O. Roberto.* We'll start our lessons learning letters. I'm sure you know the different brands marked on the cattle. This is the same idea. Just like a brand represents a ranch owner, each letter stands for a sound. Amy will point to each letter while she teaches you a song which will help you remember all twenty-six."

"We can sing it to the cattle while we're on our watch tonight," Roberto suggested.

"I'll write out the alphabet on pieces of paper. Each of you can take one. Study it and we'll see how much you learn for our next lesson."

A shadow fell over the room. Aislynn looked up to see Sage blocking the light in the doorway.

"What's this?" His deep voice bordered on anger.

"This is a class," Aislynn said.

"They're cowboys. I warned you not to mix with cowboys." He turned and addressed the boys. "You stand when an elder enters a room." The boys jumped to attention. Their eyes searched Aislynn's for an explanation.

She rose and walked to Sage. "Marshal Sage, I'd like to introduce Roberto and Jorge Gonzalez." The wide-eyed boys nodded at the man glowering at them. "And this is Jimmy Snyderly."

Sage squinted. "Where're you boys from?"

Roberto and Jorge waited for Jimmy to answer. Jimmy, withering under Sage's stare, remained silent. Roberto looked from Jimmy to Aislynn to Sage. "Bentbone, New Mexico Territory."

Sage's eyes hardened. "You got a brother, Jimmy?"

The stoic boy held his tongue; his eyes focused on the floor. Roberto nudged him. "Yes, sir," Jimmy mumbled.

"You know where he is?"

"No, sir."

"You wouldn't tell me if you knew."

Jimmy shifted his weight and kept his head down.

"You boys do what Mrs. Maher tells you. I'll drop by every now and again to see how things are goin'." Sage jerked his head toward the door, indicating Aislynn should follow him. Leaning so far over her he blocked the sun, Sage asked, "Do you look for trouble, or does it just find you?"

"Trouble?" Aislynn head fell back in exasperation. "They're little boys. Roberto is ten years old." She stood as tall as she could stretch. "My da said, 'Education is the greatest gift you can give a child.' " She rested a finger on her chest. "I choose to give it to them."

"They're still cowboys with bad habits, indecent inclinations and outlaw relatives." Sage's fingers drummed on his holsters. "Jimmy's brother is a rustler and a thief. Probably a murderer. You watch them close. You notice anyone hangin' around, grab Amy and hightail it to my office." He started to walk away. "I forgot. I'm goin' out to the fort. You got the night off."

Aislynn reentered the classroom to the sound of Amy, Jorge and Roberto's voices. She stood behind Jimmy, placed her hands on his shoulders and whispered, "You are not your brother. Now, get back to your lesson." She stood behind him until he started to sing.

With her Sioux lesson canceled, she worked with the boys until six o'clock. Before they left, she handed each one a piece of paper with the alphabet, the numbers one through ten and instructions to buy a copybook, pencils and a *McGuffey's 1st Eclectic Reader.*

Their second lesson focused on the sounds each letter makes. On the third day, they learned to hold a pencil and began forming letters. Their eagerness made them apt pupils. Once they were able to shape letters, it was time to start reading. "Let's open our books to page number six. You'll find a picture of a rat and the first lesson, *A, and, cat, rat.* She stood behind the boys and ran her finger under the words. "Jimmy, try to read this word." She pointed to the *C.* "Ca," he replied. He read the *A* and the *T.* "Ah ta."

"Very good. Put the sounds together."

They waited for Jimmy to read the full word. He sat in silence.

"Cat," Roberto shouted, "it's cat!"

Jimmy swung his elbow at the trespasser. "Shut up. Give me a chance."

Aislynn raised her voice, "Stop. We'll have no fighting. Jorge, you read next." She ran her finger under the word *rat,* and the boy pronounced the word perfectly. A beaming Roberto read the first full line. "A cat and a rat."

Jimmy's turn to read came again. He pronounced the sounds of each letter but struggled to join them into words. Embarrassed and angry, he rose to storm out.

"Wait," Aislynn ordered. "Amy, you continue with the boys." Taking Jimmy's arm, she wheeled him into the church and pointed to the first pew. "Please, sit." She slid in next to him. "Reading is a difficult process."

"Those dunderheads can do it."

"Some things come easier to some people. Please don't give up; you haven't even started. You're a smart boy. You picked up the alphabet and numbers quickly. You write them beautifully. You'll read as well, but you have to take the time to try."

They reentered the room. Lesson two was in progress with *Nat, hat, fan and can.* As Jimmy struggled, Aislynn's frustration and guilt surged.

Sitting in Joan's room, Aislynn let her feelings flow. "I just don't know what to do with one of my cowboys. I'm failing him. I feel so guilty. You know I don't have a teaching degree and barely any experience. I'm simply out of my depth." She explained Jimmy's issue.

"Are you sure he doesn't have a hearing or sight problem?"

"He has no obvious impairment. He sees the board. He can copy the letters. He hears everything I say."

Joan leaned on her head in her hand. "I've had a couple of students with similar problems. They were bright and creative. They were able do many things. However, one could not master numbers. He could read and write but failed with numbers. He stayed in school. The other could not identify the sounds of letters. No matter how hard I tried I could not teach her to read. She was removed from school. I don't know what happened to her." Joan shrugged and sighed. "She was my one great failure."

"I can't let Jimmy fail. He's a responsible and mature boy. I think reading would change his life. He could be more than a trail hand."

"I don't have a definitive answer. You can try going slowly with him. Read alone with him where there are no other sounds. In school, we were taught people learn with all five senses. He can't taste or smell the words, but he can hear, see and touch them. Perhaps he can trace each letter while he sounds them out. That way he'll have one more sense working. I don't know if it will help, but it can't hurt."

"Today, Jimmy and I are going to work in the church. Amy will do lessons four through six with you."

"She's a baby," Jorge protested.

"Yeah, she's a baby," Roberto agreed.

"I'm six," Amy shouted back.

"Stop, all of you." Aislynn moved between the two boys. "Roberto, Jorge, may I ask a favor of you?" The boys nodded. "I don't know how to ride a horse. Do you think you can teach me?"

Jorge's face lit with a smile. "Of course. We'd be honored." His little echo agreed.

"But you're much younger than I. How can you teach me to ride?"

"Because we know how and you don't." Jorge slumped. His head fell to the side, and his face dimmed into recognition. Aislynn patted his head and walked Jimmy into the church. She closed the door behind them.

Despite the July heat, the chapel stood cool and quiet. After a full hour, the *Nat, hat, can and fan* of lesson three still eluded Jimmy. He banged his forehead with his palm. "I'm thick, thick." Anger and shame burned his cheeks and disappointment pooled in his eyes.

"You're not thick. It's a new skill, just like riding and roping. Could you just mount up and ride when you were learning?"

"Yes."

She placed her hand on his shoulder. "Well, I know I couldn't. Understand, Jimmy, we all have different talents."

"It takes me too long."

"It seems that way, but it takes years to learn to read well."

"They're doin' it."

"Yes, but how many people can't even read *cat* or *rat*? You're starting slowly but you will be able to do it." Aislynn tried to lighten his dark mood. "You already can read more words than your pastor."

"They're gonna ride me."

"Hmm, I'm sure you'll remind them you're bigger and stronger. Tomorrow is Saturday. Meet me here and we'll work an extra hour."

Even working alone with Aislynn, Jimmy could not get past lesson four. With his patience and self-esteem depleted, Jimmy shot out of his seat and pulled on his medallioned hat. "You've been real kind, Mrs. Maher." He puffed up his upper lip and held his breath for a moment. "You can't make me smart. I got no hope of readin'." His voice cracked. "I'll make my way without book learnin'."

With encouragement and positive reinforcement failing, she searched for a way to change his mind. She decided desperate times called for desperate measures; she turned to guilt and manipulation. "If you fail, I fail. You don't want to make me feel bad, do you?"

Jimmy's face fell with acceptance. He picked up his books and said, "I'll see you Monday."

Sage swallowed his steak and said, "You ain't eatin'."

"No. I'm so disappointed." Aislynn settled her cheek on her hand. "Jimmy didn't come to class today. He's gone."

"Did he say where he was goin'?"

"No. The boys said he just rode off. He told them to say thanks and goodbye to me."

"He's gonna find his brother."

"The outlaw? No, he's a good boy."

The creases in Sage's forehead deepened. "Gal, you don't know anythin' about boys."

Aislynn jerked her chin at him. "And you know everything because you're a man."

Sage pulled his shoulders back. "Finally, you're catchin' on." He leveled his eyes at her. "Right now, he's ridin' alone with his anger and it's growin'. It'll keep on festerin' till it's all built up like steam in a closed kettle. When he finds his brother, they'll find a way to let it out."

"You think everyone has evil lurking deep inside."

"Give it time; you'll learn everybody does."

CHAPTER 12

A ISLYNN was sitting at the table, worrying over a sheet of paper with her hands in her hair when the door opened. Sage hung his hat and holsters on the rack and turned toward her.

"Dinner ready?" A hopeful tone permeated his question.

"Yes." She set a plate before him and returned to her former posture.

He studied her as he chewed. "Bad news?"

"Mr. and Mrs. Spittlehouse and their children are moving to Pennsylvania."

"Hmm." He returned to his meal.

"I don't know what I'm going to do."

"Is Pennsylvania that bad?"

"Pennsylvania isn't the problem."

Sage bobbed his head and returned to his meal. Aislynn's foot beat a tattoo against the table leg.

"It might not be Pennsylvania, but somethin' ain't settin' well with you."

"They're passing through Cheyenne this weekend and want to visit with me," she explained with wide eyes. She stood up. "I'm afraid they might see this." She pointed to her belly.

Sage looked at her tightening waistband. "Are they blind?"

Bewildered, she replied, "No."

"Then, there ain't no might about it."

Looking down, she cried, "Do people know?" The fear of losing her job and home sprang into her mind.

He shook his head. "Stop squawkin'. Cheyenne folks don't know that's not your normal size."

"I'd better start covering up with a pretty pinafore. I don't want anyone in town to suspect anything. And God forbid the Spittlehouses find out I'm with child, they'll report right back to Liam." Aislynn groaned. "I have got to get out of town."

"Can't you just stay in your room for two days?"

"They'll ask around and find out where I live. Mrs. McKenzie will say, 'Oh, she's upstairs; I'll go get her.' She'd never lie for me. No, I have to get out of Cheyenne. I just need to find somewhere to go and someone to go with."

"I'd love to get out of Cheyenne!" Joan said. Her excitement expanded with each word. "My cousin Virginia lives in a Colorado mining town called Fork Lick, not far from the new Denver rail line that's opening this Friday. We could be among the first people to ride it!" She clasped her hands. "I'd love to see her. She owns a boardinghouse. Her husband died a couple of years ago, and I haven't heard from her recently."

"Colorado sounds like fun." Aislynn knew she would have agreed to go to the moon if Joan had suggested it.

"It's a lively town. They give a tour of the mansion houses owned by the wealthy mine owners. There's an opera house and a music hall, a full measure of diversions."

The dingy boarding house stood on the back side of Main Street. Its dirty windows looked out on shabby homes. The paint showed wear. The stairs tilted. In the yard, debris blew over last year's leaves.

Joan and Aislynn walked in and found Cousin Virginia and a man standing in the foyer. The man glowered at the women. "Who are they?"

"These are my cousins, Carmen and Yolanda. They're from Utah."

"They don't look related."

A trembling Virginia lied again. "They have different mothers."

Aislynn's eyes jumped from Joan to the couple, processing the dishonesty and pondering the reason behind it.

"I don't care who they are; they're paying like anyone else."

"They'll share my bed."

"They eatin' here?"

"Yes."

"Then, they pay a dollar a day, each!"

He walked into a room and slammed the door. Virginia became the gracious hostess. "Please follow me to the kitchen," she said a bit too loudly as she hobbled toward the back of the house. The warm kitchen shone in the morning light. The smell of pie floated through the air. A small boy played on the spotless floor with a battered doll.

Virginia closed the door and her mood altered. The tiny, frail woman covered her face with her hands and collapsed into a dining chair, weeping silently.

Joan rushed to her side. Kneeling, she placed an arm around the distressed woman. "What on earth is going on?"

In a voice just above a whisper, Virginia spun out her story. "My life is in ruins. I couldn't write to tell you, because I don't have the money to buy a stamp. Mr. Brett won't give me a penny. He checks all the accounts. If I purchase anything without his approval, he hits me or Daniel."

"Who is he?"

The distressed woman kneaded her bony hands. "I don't even know where to start." The story and her tears streamed out. "He was a boarder, a normal boarder. One evening, he sat in my late husband's chair at the head of the table. I had so many men at the time, I allowed it. I didn't realize the other men would see this as my anointing him head of my household. They began giving their board money to Mr. Brett. When I protested, he told them he was head of the house, my house." She beat her breast. "He started bossing me and limiting my movements. He only allows me to go to stores where he has developed agreements and accounts. He keeps Daniel with him whenever I step out to ensure I'll return."

Virginia stopped, wiped her nose and took a sip of cold coffee. "I went to the sheriff and filed a complaint. He said he'd investigate. When he asked the other boarders, they confirmed Brett's story and swore I was his woman, which is not at all true." Her voice filled with anger and disgust. "I have never allowed that man touch me." She shivered and continued her tale. "I borrowed money from some women friends to hire an attorney and took Brett to court. I wanted him removed; I wanted to regain control of my house. The judge decided the house belonged to that interloper and gave him the right to rule his house as he saw fit."

As Virginia sobbed for a few seconds, a vision of Moran appeared in Aislynn's mind. A flush of fear heated her entire body. She could see his determined face and hear him ordering her to give away her home and her business as if they were his to control. When Virginia recovered her ability to talk, Aislynn pushed Moran into the dark space where he belonged.

"Brett makes me work like a slave. He hits me; he even knocked me down the stairs. That's why I limp. The worst is—" She broke down again. Continuing in a voice thick with distress, she uttered, "It's Daniel. He locks him alone in the attic at night. He's only four years old. The child is afraid of everything. Mr. Brett beats him and threatens him with terrible tortures. One night, he slammed Daniel so hard his ear bled. I begged him to call the doctor, but he wouldn't. Now, Daniel can't hear in his left ear." Tears rolled down Virginia's face.

"Why haven't you run?"

"How can I run? He watches every move I make. I can't leave the house with Daniel, and I will not abandon my boy. When Brett leaves, he locks my baby in the attic. But even if we could get out, and believe me I plan an escape every day, I don't have a penny to buy a stamp to write to you. How would I go anywhere? I have no one left to help me."

"We'll help you," Joan said with conviction.

Seated in the park, Joan assessed the situation. "She has aged years since I last saw her. I always envied her: petite, pretty and lively. Now she's thin and drawn. We have to free her from that tyrant."

"How?"

"You have a gun."

"You can't shoot him. What would we do with the body?" Aislynn joked.

"I'm serious."

"So am I." Aislynn turned and looked at Joan with her mouth open and her eyebrows reaching toward her hairline. "We can't shoot him. We'd hang!"

Joan chewed her thumbnail. "We have to keep him away from the house long enough to get them out."

"Once they're out, where will they go?"

"Virginia was smart not to give our names or let him know where we live. He'll think we're going to Utah, but we'll get off the train in Cheyenne."

"He'll tell the marshal or the sheriff. They'll wire every lawman on the route to Utah. They'll pull her off at the first stop and send her back."

"We could rent a carriage. Get Daniel out of the attic and drive up the rail line to Evans. We can catch the train there."

"How would you return the horse and wagon or are you stealing them? And before you answer, remember, horse thieves hang, too."

"We have to think of something."

"Just make sure that something is not going to land you in jail or worse."

"Won't you help?"

"Joan, I am sorry for Virginia, but I have to consider my own child." Aislynn recognized her mistake and recovered quickly. "I mean my own children, my students. Who would teach them?"

Aislynn and Joan refused to eat at the same table with Mr. Brett. Offended beyond reason, he stormed into the kitchen. He grabbed Daniel's collar. The child screamed. Brett held him fast. He brandished the back of his hand inches from the boy's face. Daniel held his breath, waiting.

Brett's arm arced up. "Let him go! We'll come," Aislynn shouted. Her eyes burned into the strong, sinewy, sinister hand, and she remembered something she should have never forgotten.

Aislynn had finished the breakfast shift and headed home. Passing the woodpile, she heard rustling and mewling. Hidden in the stacks was a young girl. Her skin told Aislynn she was a Negro and her gown said "whore." She had a gash across her neck and blood streaming down her dress. Aislynn nursed her numerous, unspeakable wounds, helped her bathe and put her to bed.

When Aislynn returned to the restaurant for the dinner rush, she discovered the entire camp had been searching for a dead whore.

"She's not dead; she's asleep," Aislynn stated.

Tim spoke up, "Aislynn, Mr. Moran has been looking for that girl all day."

"No one asked me." She shrugged. Dismissing their concerns, she said, "I'm tired and I'm going home."

When she reached the house, Moran stood behind her. Aislynn faced him. "What do you want?"

He started in his superior tone, "She's going back to the whorehouse. She owes Stella money."

"She can't. Those men torture her. There should to be limits, some rules."

Liam chuckled. "There are rules; the first one is when a man's paying, he does what he wants."

She looked up at him and declared, "Liam, she's a human being. She has a right not to be burned or bitten or sliced or scarred." She could hear herself becoming shrill. "You go tell Stella that Carrie is not coming back." She marched up the front steps and put the key in the door.

She heard him kick the dirt and stomp up behind her.

As she stepped inside, he called, "Don't shut me out!"

She slammed the door behind her. It flew open and crashed against the wall. Shaken, she backed into the hall. "I didn't invite you in."

Like an overwound spring, he seemed ready to snap. "Too late." His breath came short and hard. Aislynn stood her ground as he hovered over her. She felt his heat as he hissed, "I want that girl."

For an instant, she thought she saw into him, into a place where he kept his secrets, his pain. He caught her looking, and anger flared in his eyes. She lifted her face to his and shook her head. She whispered, "You can't have her."

"Aislynn," he shouted with enough force to push her back two steps, "she owes money and she's going back."

"So, it's money you want, Mr. Moran." Aislynn wheeled, opened the closet door and stooped. Out of the dark, quiet space, she produced a glass jar full of coins and a few greenbacks. She held the jar out at arm's length. "Here, Liam, the most important thing in the world."

He brandished the back of his hand. It arced up. Her eyes followed the strong, sinewy, sinister hand. She felt the breeze as it swept inches from her face. The jar shattered. Glass flew. Coins pinged. Bills floated to the floor.

Aislynn left Liam in the past when she heard Brett ordering her to take the seat next to him. She watched the other men as she lowered herself in the chair. Joan dropped down next to her.

A forward miner asked, "Where you gals from?"

Joan gave him a chilly response. "Excuse me, sir, we do not speak to strange men. We will eat in silence."

"Not at this table." Brett made his authority known. "You women do what you're told."

Aislynn and Joan sat stone-faced, nibbling at their food while Virginia rushed in and out of the dining room. The other men recognized their disdain and ate in silence. Brett pushed on. "Harlon asked you a question. Where you from?"

"Utah," Joan answered with a bite in her voice.

"We know that, where in Utah?"

Aislynn knew she should answer the Utah questions. Her eyes rose to the ceiling. "Salt Lake City."

"What do you do there?"

"I teach."

"You both teachers?"

"Yes," Joan groaned.

"You Mormons?"

"No." Aislynn took a turn.

"Your husband a Mormon?" he asked Aislynn.

"No."

"How long you a widow?"

"Since March."

"You miss havin' a man?" Brett asked with lust in his voice.

Aislynn fumed and pulled her lips taut.

"If you need anythin' while you're here, I could oblige." He leered at her.

She threw down her fork and stomped into the kitchen. Joan joined her. Aislynn seethed. "That man is disgusting and despicable."

The three women cleaned up and sat at the kitchen table trying to chat cordially. Brett stomped into the kitchen. Daniel scrambled to his mother. He wailed and threw his arms around her. Brett seized the child's arm until the little boy's strength gave out. Brett dragged the screaming child across the floor.

"What in the world are you doing?" Joan blocked the kitchen door.

"He sleeps in the attic." Brett twisted the child's arm. Daniel yelped.

"Let him loose." Joan stood nearly as tall and wide as Brett.

"This is my house and everyone abides by my rules."

"Do your rules include abusing a child?"

"Abuse? This is discipline."

"There's no need to discipline a child who has done nothing wrong. If you don't unhand that child, I'll go to the sheriff. You can intimidate her, but it won't work with me."

"Go get the sheriff. But he won't do nothin'; he never does." He turned a scornful eye at Virginia. "Right?" Virginia stood and raised her chin to him. Pulling Daniel along, he approached Virginia. He brought his fist up to her face. She fell back in her seat and looked at the floor in defeat.

Brett pushed past Joan. The three women listened to the child's sobbing until it faded up the two flights of stairs to the attic.

As they lay in bed, the normal house noises subsided. Through the quiet, they could hear a tiny voice calling from the floor above Virginia's bedroom, "Mama, Mama." Aislynn pulled her pillow over her head. Her thoughts whirled. *We women are a pitiful lot, oppressed by so many rules and constraints. We are kept ignorant of men and sex and the power of both. We just blunder through life never sure when to say "yes" and when to say "no." One mistake and our lives change forever. God help me; I made one such mistake. Now I'm paying with everything I valued: my family and friends, my home, my livelihood; just like Virginia.*

She tore the pillow off her head. Resolute, Aislynn nudged Joan. "I'll do whatever you want."

On Saturday morning, Aislynn and Joan entered the Majestic Inn armed with a plan. Joan, an avid reader of dime novel romances, believed one such story provided a strategy that would work. Doubtful and nervous, Aislynn gathered her courage and agreed to her role.

"I want a room with a large, comfortable bed, please." Joan started their first maneuver.

"I have a suite available. Would you like to see it?"

"Yes, thank you."

The suite possessed a front parlor and a back bedroom with a large, four-poster bed. Situated next to the back stairs, the room provided exactly what they needed.

"Perfect," Joan declared. "May we have it for tomorrow night?"

"Certainly, you can check in anytime; it's vacant."

Joan sent the man a smile full of teeth and gum. "Nine o'clock tomorrow morning would work well for us."

Following the inspection, Joan headed to the hardware store and the locksmith. Aislynn visited the druggist and the clothiers.

Saturday night dinner repeated Friday's fiasco. Brett's brazen innuendos flew. Joan deflected most of them. Aislynn's job required her to appear sweet and submissive. When Brett's knee touched hers, Aislynn bowed her head meekly. Inside, her fury rose and fed her newfound resolve.

After Sunday breakfast, they moved to the Majestic. They took their bags and two of Virginia's. Aislynn left an envelope behind. It held a key and an invitation. Joan left a lockpick.

With the curtains drawn and candles lit, the parlor adopted a romantic air. Two glasses, one full, the other empty, waited on the table next to an adulterated bottle of whiskey. Aislynn sat in the dimness, biding her time by swirling her drink and checking the little pistol resting in her pocket.

At precisely 9:30, she heard a key in the lock. Brett strode through the door. "Aren't you the dark horse?"

Aislynn took a deep breath and drew him in. She raised her glass and said, "I'm sorry I started without you. I've only done this with my husband, and I'm a bit nervous."

She poured him a drink. In his rough way, he jerked the chair out and slammed himself into it. He grabbed the glass and drained it. "Well, it ain't my first time; you just let me take the lead." He reached under the table and grabbed her knee. Aislynn fought her revulsion with a deceptive smile.

Stalling for time, Aislynn asked, "Won't you tell me about yourself?"

"I didn't come here to talk."

"Please, it would make it much easier if we could drink a few and relax."

Brett tossed back the second glass. He ran his hand up her thigh. Aislynn swallowed the disgust rising in her throat. "I'm a man who likes women, even a ripe one like you." He squeezed her leg. "I like them unused and unsure."

Aislynn refilled his glass. "Where are you from?" she asked, praying he would keep talking and drinking.

"Don't matter. What matters is where I'm goin'." Brett tried to reach between her legs.

She squealed and pretended to swoon. She tried to disguise her nervousness as breathlessness. "Oh, Mr. Brett, why don't you toss that down?" In a stilted, well-rehearsed voice, Aislynn repeated the horrid line Joan had stolen from the dime novel. "If you undress and lie down, you can watch while I undress for you."

Brett stripped quickly while Aislynn averted her eyes. When he was lying on the bed naked, she rose and brandished her revolver. Joan rolled out from under the bed.

"What is this?" Brett sat up quickly. His hand raced to his head, evidence the whiskey and laudanum brew was taking effect.

"Be quiet or I'll shoot."

"You wouldn't shoot me."

Her disgust burned brightly. "Pulling this trigger takes very little effort. Watch." Aislynn cocked the hammer.

"The whole house will hear and come runnin'."

"Yes, but you'll be dead and naked."

Joan stuffed one of Aislynn's camisoles in his mouth. His eyes grew wild, and he tried to struggle.

Aislynn moved closer. "Behave," she suggested and aimed between his legs.

Joan tied his hands and feet to the four posts as tight as her strength would allow. Brett's eyes were fluttering. "Sleepy?" Joan mocked him. "You'll be out for a good four hours, and with any luck, no one will find you until tomorrow morning."

Aislynn dumped the tainted whiskey in the dirty slop jar and blew out the candles. Joan sacrificed a pair of her underdrawers and laid them over his eyes. She stuffed his clothes in her valise. They checked the hallway and hung a handwritten sign on the door that said *Sleeping—do not bother me*. Grabbing the bags, they locked the door and slipped down the back steps.

The Denver train pulled into Fork Lick at 10:45. It stopped to pick up a woman draped in thick, black mourning veils. She held the hand of a small child wearing a long dress and bonnet that covered the neck and shoulders. Behind them, Joan and Aislynn, hunched in their upturned collars and low-brimmed hats, sprang up the stairs. All held transfer tickets to the Utah Territory. Fifteen minutes before the eastbound to New York rumbled in for its thirty-minute stop, the quartet's train slipped into Cheyenne.

Virginia hugged her long, black veils as she descended the steps. She took care of her necessities and retreated to a seat in a corner of the station. Aislynn pressed Daniel's bonnet around his face. They raced to buy food, drinks and two tickets to New York City. Joan sprinted to her room for cash and jewelry. When the eastbound train arrived, Virginia entered the third car. Aislynn and Daniel followed. She handed Virginia a sheet of paper. "His name is Tim Nolan. This is his address. Tell him your whole story, and he'll help you disappear." Aislynn rushed past Joan. She gave her a reassuring nod and returned to her room.

After school on Monday, Aislynn stopped at the Western Union. Her cryptic telegram to Tim read: *My friends arrive on Friday. I'm sure you will take good care of them.* She listened until the operator stopped tapping. Relieved, she paid the three dollars and left.

Sage put down his fork. "That was mighty fine."

Aislynn cleared the table for their lessons. She took her seat next to him, opened her notebook and poised her pencil. Sage rocked back in his chair and asked, "Where'd you say you went this weekend?"

"A big mining town."

"What's the name of this town?"

His curiosity roused her suspicion. Aislynn mumbled, "Fork Lick."

"That's what I thought." He removed a sheet of paper from his breast pocket and spread it on the table. Aislynn read the title. *Official Notice to Marshal Sage, Cheyenne, Wyoming Territory.* Her eyes stretched open.

Sage continued. "This came in on the train today. *MISS-ING: Female, runaway wife, twenty-seven years old, five feet* two inches tall, brown hair, brown eyes. Male, child, four years old, about forty inches tall, brown hair, brown eyes."

Aislynn cringed. "It says, *Two accomplices.*" His words frosted the room. She shivered and perspired at the same time. "*Female, about twenty years old, five feet tall, black hair, green eyes. Female, about twenty-five years old, five feet eight inches tall, brown hair, brown eyes, buckteeth. May be armed and dangerous. Believed bound for Utah Territory from Fork Lick. Signed, Barry Andrews, Marshal, Colorado Territory.*" Aislynn's pencil tapped the table with fury. "There's a hand-written note attached. *Complainant found naked, tied to bed. Appears two professionals got the best of him. He just wants the wife and kid back. Barry.* Ain't that interestin'?"

Her hand rushed to the mouth as her meal rose in her throat. She concentrated on swallowing it down.

"You need some water?" His voice sounded far away.

Aislynn felt lightheaded with fear. She nodded and took a long, calming sip.

"Aislynn? Kinda coincidental, huh?"

She focused on the notice, took a few deep breaths and collected herself. "No, it's distressing."

"I can see that," he replied.

Anger drove a rod of strength up her spine. She faced him and raised her chin. "Can you? Can you picture a poor, young mother who needed to run away? I . . . I imagine she must have good reasons. I'd say she was fortunate to have assistance from two very courageous, but very scared women."

"The ones who are armed and dangerous?"

"I'm sure they were more terrified than dangerous. Maybe he deserved it. Perhaps—" She hesitated to consider her words. "Perhaps, he stole that widow's home, and held her and her child hostage. He may have beaten them so badly he crippled the mother and actually deafened the child." Her volume rose. "Perhaps he locked that child alone in a dark attic every night. I think a man like that should not just be humiliated; he should be shot."

"Aislynn." He leaned toward her and spoke in a low, stern voice. "Those women have to stick to teachin' and let lawmen deal with criminals."

Her eyes burned as she moved her face closer to his. "What if the lawmen sided with the criminal? What if the good, male judge gave that man her home, all her money and left her and that child to be abused under his control every day?" Aislynn calmed her voice and slowed her cadence. "I want you to imagine something. I want you to close your eyes and pretend you are lying in bed. It's dark and quiet. In the attic above you a four-year-old child is locked in the terrifying gloom crying for his mother. I know you can imagine a four-year-old, alone and crying for his mother." She let her words trigger his own memory. "For two straight nights, all you hear is that baby weeping for his mother." She imitated a child's cries. "Mama, Mama." She challenged him. "Now, what would you do about it?"

Sage leaned back and studied her. He clenched his jaw. The muscles in his face tightened until they vibrated with anger. When his trigger finger began twitching, Aislynn knew he understood.

He blinked and released a long, frustrated breath. Sage shook his head in defeat. "I reckon I'll write back and say if they were bound for Utah, they'd be there by now."

Her anger subsided and her face softened. "That would be a splendid idea."

With a raised eyebrow and smirk, he said, "Although I am mighty curious to know how you got that man naked, don't tell me." He held up his hand. "And do not ever tell me where she and that boy have got to." He sent her a sour look and grabbed her chin. "Aislynn, I know sometimes you do the wrong thing for the right reason, but you gotta stop. Don't go messin' in the business of men again. You got a problem, you come to me. You hear?"

She saluted him. "Yes, sir."

CHAPTER 13

"WHAT in blazes is goin' on in here?"

Sage's house bustled as Aislynn and her friends prepared for their Fourth of July celebration. "We're cooking," she answered.

"Doesn't smell like my dinner," Sage said with suspicion in his voice.

Aislynn brushed her hands on her apron and walked toward him with a cookie. She held it in front of his mouth. He grabbed it. Aislynn said, "Your dinner is roasting in the little oven."

Swallowing the tasty snack, he asked, "What's all this?" He passed a hand over the cluttered dining table.

"They're treats for my children."

"You ain't got any children."

"That's right, you ain't got *any* children," she enunciated slowly, "but I do."

His eyes widened and he pulled himself up to his full height. He dipped his head toward her. "Did I pay for all this?"

Aislynn crossed her hands on her chest and leaned in his direction. As if she were assuring God she would atone for a sin, she said sweetly, "I'm going to pay you back."

Sage mimicked her sweet tone. "You don't have any money."

Aislynn pulled away and push her hands down on her hips. "I will when I get paid." She rebuked him and turned back to her work.

His masculine bulk changed the dynamic in the room. He scanned the tables. "What's all this for?"

"We're having a Fourth of July celebration for my children. They've been excluded from the town's party, so we're having one of our own."

He frowned his disapproval. "Do you try to stir things up?"

"I'm teaching them about an important American holiday."

The other ladies listened to the exchange silently. Molly and Emmie put their heads to their tasks, while Joan looked down at Amy and swung her head in dismay.

Aislynn took his arm and pulled him into the small bedroom. Her excitement burst forth. "See? We're going to have games. These are sacks for races and embroidery hoops for ring toss. We made beanbags; the children will throw them at stacked cans. This is rope for the three-legged race."

"What do they win?"

"It's not about winning something; it's about having fun."

"No, it's always about winnin'," he said with certainty.

"You're such a man."

"Yes, I know," he replied with sarcasm. She pushed past him on her way out of the bedroom.

Aislynn returned to mixing cookie dough at the table where Molly and Emily were dipping apples into caramel. Joan worked at the dry sink, placing handfuls of sweetened popcorn on small squares of cut newspaper. Amy drew up the corners and held them together as Joan tied the little packages with strings.

Sage surveyed the dozens of cookies cooling on the hutch, cupboard and tin table. "How many folks am I feedin'?"

"I have thirteen children. I'm hoping the women and old men from the camp will come."

Sage threw his hands in the air. "Why don't you just invite the whole damn town?"

"I tried." Aislynn faced him with a wide, exaggerated smile. "They won't mix with the Indians."

"Look at this place." Flags and bunting covered the settee, rocker and armchair. Boxes waited on the floor to carry food. "You do know this ain't your house?" he questioned.

Emmie could not contain her laughter. Once she started, Molly joined in. Amy caught the germ and giggled. Joan and Aislynn could not control themselves, either.

Sage's angry eyes swept over each of them. When they rested on Aislynn, he pointed at her and leveled a stern look. "You're like damn fleas. Let one woman in your house and they multiply."

As if rehearsed, the door swung open and Maggie walked in. "Evening," she called. All five females looked at Maggie. They turned to Sage. In stunned silence, his jaw dropped. The disbelief racing across his face sent the cooking crew into hysterics. Sage stormed to the door, grabbed his hat off the rack and pointed his outrage at Aislynn. "I will deal with you later," he shouted. Each woman caught her breath and closed her mouth. He slapped his hat on his head and grabbed his rifle. His wooden heels clomped down the porch steps. When silence returned, they all looked at Aislynn. She placed her hands on the side of her face and mouthed, "Oh no!" The hilarity returned.

At three in the morning, the town awoke to gunfire. The rowdies started their celebrations early. In her mind's eye,

Aislynn could see Sage jumping out of bed and racing toward the commotion.

The annual Cheyenne Fourth of July parade began at ten o'clock. It marched down Eddy Street under a gray morning sky. The great Sioux chief, Red Cloud, kicked off the procession surrounded by twenty braves. They were followed closely by a regiment of the Wyoming Militia in full regalia. The Fort Russell Band played marching tunes. At their heels, schoolchildren waved flags. The fire companies ended the procession, flaunting their shiny equipment.

Three hundred of the town's finest people assembled for luncheon under a large tent donated by Mr. McDaniel, owner of the museum and various other town establishments. Governor Campbell presided over the ceremony honoring the two qualities westerners valued most: freedom and independence. Justice Howe gave an oration.

Aislynn's teaching position made her too controversial for an invitation. She walked a fine line in the community. Some citizens believed she was an angel for civilizing the pitiful natives. Others reviled her as an Indian lover coddling the red hellhounds. However, her exclusion from the meal allowed her to stage her own event.

Aislynn and her little, curly-haired assistant returned to the churchyard and prepared for their celebration. They hung flags and strips of bunting on the church and the house to billow patriotically in the ever-present wind. When Maggie, Joan, Emmie and Molly joined the crew, they brought out the games from Aislynn's room and lugged her teaching table to the churchyard. Maggie mixed the lemonade while the other ladies arranged the treats. Everything was covered with towels to protect them against dust and flies.

Around one o'clock, the army wagon arrived with the Indian children and their families. Aislynn's excited students pulled their hesitant relatives into the celebration. Aislynn greeted them with her limited Sioux. "Welcome. *Tanyanyahipi.*"

The children had practiced the games at recess and were eager to display their skills for their families. Aislynn started the sack races with the youngest children. When the older boys stood at the starting line anxious to hop, Aislynn raised her flag. She looked toward the spectators and saw Red Cloud and his warriors trooping into the churchyard behind Sage. The boys dropped their sacks, clearly embarrassed before the great chief and his braves.

Aislynn looked at the buckskin-clad Sage with a plea in her eyes that said, *Don't let him ruin our day.*

With the slightest tilting of his head and narrowing of his eyes, Sage told her to behave. She ordered the boys to join their families and glided toward her unexpected guests with a bright smile.

They presented a gorgeous spectacle. Red Cloud wore a full-feathered war bonnet, a bib of painted quills and a soft doeskin shirt trimmed on the shoulders and arms with brightly colored beads. The braves were decked out in smaller headdresses and equally flamboyant clothes.

"Mrs. Maher, let me introduce Red Cloud, Yellow Robe, Tells the Truth and Thunder Man." Sage said each name in English and repeated it in Lakota.

Aislynn curtsied deeply. "*Hau*, hello. *Tanyanyahipi*, welcome."

Sage invited the guests to sit and watch the games. The headmen settled on the ground, and the younger braves stood behind.

Aislynn asked the boys to pull up their sacks, and she dropped the flag. The crowd cheered and laughed at the youngsters' antics. When they continued to the ring toss and beanbag competitions, the chiefs shouted instructions. Seeing one six-year-old boy struggling with his rings, Yellow Robe rose and gave the terrified child a tutorial.

With the games behind them, the children sat with their families. Aislynn took a tray of cookies and approached the headmen. She searched Sage's face for a clue to the proper etiquette. When his eyes went to Red Cloud, so did Aislynn. She handed him a cookie and waited. Red Cloud chewed and nodded his approval. Aislynn pointed at Sage with her free hand. In her elementary Sioux, she said, "You thank Sage for food." She pointed at the cookies. "Sage give to all." She beamed at the marshal. His face showed no expression. Aislynn gave Red Cloud a second cookie and followed Sage's eyes as he designated the chiefs' order of importance. Once each brave had a cookie, Emmie and Molly handed out the apples and popped corn to each child. Joan and Maggie served cookies and lemonade to the children and their families.

With the cookies consumed, Aislynn offered the games to the young braves. When the competition between the young men grew heated, Sage stepped in. He bowed to Aislynn. The Indians acknowledged their gratitude, and Sage led them away without a word.

After the children and their families were safely on their way back to the fort, Aislynn and her friends began packing games, flags and bunting. A scruffy man in worn, filthy clothes staggered into the yard. He opened his mouth, exposing brown teeth, and bellowed, "Molly!"

Aislynn and her friends turned in the direction of the gruff voice. Molly froze. "Oh dear," Maggie fretted. "Mr. Fawcett, please—"

"Shut your lyin' mouth," he shouted.

Fawcett grabbed a handful of Molly's hair and yanked her to his side. He pointed his finger at Aislynn. "You Injun lover! You stay away from my girl." He stumbled away, dragging the weeping Molly behind.

Aislynn's eyes searched Maggie's for an explanation. "He's a vicious drunk. She'll show up at work tomorrow bruised and battered. The sheriff just says, 'She's his daughter.' He claims he has no right to interfere in family matters. He won't tell that man to spare the rod."

"Isn't there any recourse?" Aislynn asked.

"I've tried." Maggie grew tearful and Emmie sobbed.

Joan looked at Aislynn. "You could get Sage to do something."

"He's a federal marshal. He'll say it's not his jurisdiction. She'd have to be dead or close to it for him to get involved."

For the citizens of Cheyenne, a baseball game between the Fort Russell team and the Eclipse Club filled the drizzly, late afternoon. Aislynn and Amy used the time for a well-earned nap. In the evening, Aislynn served punch at the community dance. Women in mourning could only appear at a dance to assist, never to venture out on the floor. She stood against a wall, behind a table covered with refreshments. She ladled for two hours until Joan appeared and offered to take her place. Aislynn found a chair and rested.

As soon as she started to relax, Sage appeared in the doorway. She watched him stride across the floor and drop himself into the chair next to hers. He stretched out his long legs and folded his arms. Aislynn decided to keep the incident with Molly's father to herself. Exhausted from the day's activities, she did not have the energy to endure Sage's harangue. "Did Red Cloud enjoy the celebration?"

He glanced sideways and gave her a quick bob.

"He must be impressed by your generosity, especially for the benefit of my poor Indian children."

He turned his head and gave her a withering look. "You're still payin' me."

"Hmph."

"And you know they ain't your children. They gotta go to the reservation sometime real soon."

His remark made her sit up straight. She faced him. "When?"

"Before autumn. Red Cloud is lettin' Sittin' Bull know some of his people are at the fort."

"Can't he just leave them alone?"

"It's the law."

"What about their education?"

Sage shrugged.

"I could go with—"

"No."

"But, I—"

"No."

"You haven't let me say anything."

"It doesn't matter, the answer's still gonna be *no*."

Aislynn crossed her arms and fell back into her chair. Sage silently lounged next to her. "I don't understand why I couldn't go with them."

"That's a man's job."

"Why?"

"It's rough livin', down on the ground livin'."

"We could keep them . . ."

Sage sat up and turned to her. "They belong with their own tribe." His irritation showed. "Don't you see they want to be settled with their own people? They don't want to live with the army. Besides, in a few months you'll have a child of your own to care for. That'll be enough till you find other work."

Silence settled between them. As they watched, the dancers picked up a reel. Aislynn, staring straight ahead, started at him again. "You know you are exceptionally bossy for a man with no authority over me." Impassive, Sage listened. "You declare time and time again that I am not your responsibility, yet you have no reservations about telling me what I can and cannot do." Aislynn sulked and Sage sat unmoved. "And you're extraordinarily ornery." She raised her crossed arms and slammed them down on her chest to punctuate her criticism. In the corner of her eye, she caught him grinning. She turned to him with raised brows and a questioning look.

"Everyone's got to be good at somethin'." His grin widened as he amused himself.

"Well, you're perfecting it!" Aislynn turned away in exasperation.

"I heard about Fawcett draggin' Molly away."

"Do you have informers stationed everywhere?" Surprise filled her voice.

"Watch out for that man. He's one of those Injun haters I told you about."

"Poor Molly, she's so embarrassed." Aislynn's mind rushed to thoughts of Tommy Two Hawks, and how Molly's father would react if he knew.

"Just be advised," Sage warned.

Widow Stern strolled by and said a good evening to Sage with a gap-toothed smile and a swing of her wide hips. She took a breath and addressed Aislynn in a tolerant tone. "Mrs. Maher."

Sage rose and bowed slightly. Aislynn gave the woman an artificial smile. The tall, gangly blonde leaned toward Sage with a glint in her eye. "You're not dancing, Marshal?"

"No, ma'am, just came to make sure Mrs. Maher gets home safely."

With an "oh!" and a look that could cut Aislynn in half, she walked away. Sage returned to his chair and rested his hands on his thighs. Aislynn turned to Sage with an amused smile. "Well, would you look at this? The great gunslinger and Indian fighter is hiding behind my petticoats." She laughed.

"You gotta admit she would scare a cow dry. You seen them . . . those teeth?"

"You could be sociable."

"Ain't no sociable with a woman like that. She'd cling to a man like a tick. There's only two things a man wants from a woman. I got you for one of them and sure don't need her for the other."

Aislynn was shocked by his comment. She wished the rules of decorum allowed her to ask if Sheila provided the other. Unlike men who could say such things and do such things without consequences, women were condemned, ostracized and, as she knew, left with the results. A shadow of jealousy passed over her. She wondered if it was because he had those privileges or was exercising them.

Aislynn pushed the thought away. "You should dance."

"You ain't dancin'."

"I'm still in mourning."

Sage studied her for a moment and asked, "How long does that last?"

Aislynn watched the couples twirl past, searching each other's eyes for their futures, while her mind returned to the past. "Grief changes and moves." Her hand raced between her head and her chest. "I know it needs to settle somewhere within my heart and my mind." Aislynn swallowed the catch in her throat. "I've lost so much." She shrugged. "Sometimes, I feel I'll be mourning forever."

When the music died, the crowd drifted away into the stormy night. Aislynn helped clean the plates and the punch bowls. The men began collecting the chairs. The band packed their instruments. With her work completed, Aislynn searched the room for her escort. Across the dance floor, Molly's tipsy father swayed in a dim doorway. He formed a gun with his hand and pointed it at Aislynn. His mouth formed the word *bang*.

CHAPTER 14

THE attic baked each day in the relentless August sun. The small windows in the gables provided scant relief. When Aislynn retired to her room at night, the air felt like an oversized coat: bulky, heavy and burdensome. The heat made the beams sweat a clear, sharp-smelling sap. She rolled in her bed, searching for a nonexistent cool patch of sheet.

The shouting seemed to come from a loud dream. "Injun whore, it's all your fault. You're both Injun whores. You'll pay for this, you Injun whore!"

Aislynn rose and crept to the window. Fearing a hail of gun fire, she stood to the side and peeked out the tiny opening. A dense darkness soaked the churchyard. A rectangle of light appeared from the kitchen door and stretched out into the pitch. Father Gilhooley called, "What do you think you're doing? You're . . . you're disturbing the peace of this sanctuary."

"You're no better. I should shoot all of you." Molly's father stepped into the glow. Aislynn heard the door slam. "It's your fault, all your fault." The drunken slurring diminished until it faded into the thick, black night.

Aislynn's mind tossed thoughts like tumbleweed. *Why is Mr. Fawcett yelling at me? What's my fault? Drunken fool. Probably had no idea what he was doing or saying.* Scanning her memory revealed a new possibility. *He may know about Tommy Two Hawks.*

The heat and worry kept Aislynn awake. She ran a wet rag over her entire body hoping for relief. It didn't come. Sitting at the window, she waited. As white light quivered on the horizon and began turning off the dimmest stars, a shadowy Tommy slipped into the barn. Aislynn pulled on her dress and slipped her feet into her shoes. She returned to the window and scanned the yard. *Empty.* She started toward the door. Apprehension stopped her. Her little revolver lay on the trunk. Stuffing the weapon in her pocket, she tiptoed down the stairs.

The barn door stood ajar. The small opening gave Aislynn enough room to squeeze through sideways. The barn's thick, moist animal smell surrounded her. Pale light slipped through the gaps in the roof. She carefully picked her way around the animal droppings and puddles of urine dappling the floor. Through the near darkness, she whispered, "Tommy? Tommy?" A rustle came from the loft. "It's Aislynn. Come down."

Dressed all in black, he seemed almost invisible. "I thought you were Molly. Why are you here?"

"Her father visited me last night. He stood in the yard shouting, 'It's all your fault.' "

"What is?"

"I hoped you knew. He was shouting about Injun whores. I presumed he meant me and Molly."

"You think he knows about us?"

Aislynn shrugged. "Maybe you should stay away from her for a while, until this blows over."

"I can't leave Molly now, not now." His distress vibrated through the dark space between them, telegraphing his meaning.

"Oh, no, she's pregnant." The blunt reference to a very private matter fell unfiltered from Aislynn's lips. She regretted her forthrightness. However, in her mix of fatigue and fear, she thought, *It doesn't matter what I call it. It's trouble, serious trouble.*

Tommy ran his hands through his hair. "What will we do?"

Aislynn folded her hands. "Good glory, could her father know that?"

Tommy winced. "Maybe she's showing?"

Aislynn threw her head back. Her eyes searched the ceiling as if an answer were posted there. "I, of all people, should have noticed." With her hands on her hips, she asked, "Did you give this possibility any consideration? What are you going to do?"

Tommy's head hung. "We love each other."

Aislynn huffed. "You have to make yourself scarce. Is there somewhere you can go, somewhere you can be safe? I'll try to get word to you after I speak to Molly."

"There's a shack about two miles out of town. It's an old brown hut just east of here, right off the rails."

Aislynn could hear Sage saying, *Stay out of this.* She nodded. "Yes, that's good. I'll watch for Molly. When she comes, I'll tell her our plan. I'll get word to you as soon as I can. In the meantime, think about where you two can go. There has to be a place somewhere. Now, scoot."

With a quick nod, Tommy bolted to the door. He stopped and turned. "Tell Molly I love her."

Aislynn walked back to the house, wondering if love was the solution or the problem. She watched out her window until the sun blazed. Molly never appeared.

Aislynn arrived at the store and greeted Cap. "Good morning." Aislynn touched his shoulder and bent to pet Smokey.

"How are you this morning, Mrs. Maher?" he asked.

"I'm not sure." Aislynn turned her attention to Maggie.

"Is something wrong?" Maggie inquired.

"I'll tell you in a minute. May I speak to Molly?"

"Molly isn't here."

"But she works on Saturdays."

"Yes, it's a bit peculiar," Maggie explained. "It's not like Molly to miss a day's work or be late, but she hasn't arrived."

The tiny embers of anxiety smoldering in Aislynn's belly since Mr. Fawcett's visit burst into flames. "Excuse me, I have to find Sage."

Aislynn stood before Sage's desk. "I need your help."

Without looking up, he said, "Ain't that a surprise."

Aislynn explained Molly's absence. Sage leaned back and rolled his pencil between his fingers. "You think Molly's father is keepin' her home so she can't see Tommy Two Hawks?"

"Yes."

"Ain't that his right? He's her father."

"Yes, I know, but I have a feeling, a very bad feeling that he has hurt her. He came to the parish house last night. He raved like a maniac. I think he's discovered their relationship, and in his warped mind, he thinks I'm responsible. He threatened to shoot us all: Father Gilhooley, Mrs. McKenzie and me. Do you think he arrived home and simply said, 'Molly, you're a bad little girl. You can't go out today'?"

Sage tried to dismiss her. "Even if he beat her, she's his kid."

"No, you cannot be that cavalier. He's a violent man in a drunken rage. He may have hurt her very badly."

"And maybe he didn't."

"Sage, she didn't meet Tommy, and she didn't go to work."

"I can't go checkin' on everyone who misses a day's work."

"You told me to come to you. Here I am. If you don't help, I'll go out there and see for myself." Aislynn turned.

"Aislynn," he called with an edge in his voice, "Molly's shack isn't in your territory."

Aislynn squared her shoulders and grabbed the doorknob. "I'm not your kid and you can't make me stay home." She pulled the door and scurried out.

Before she reached the street, Sage clamped a hand around her arm. "You're lookin' for trouble."

"We need a wagon in case Molly needs to come back with us."

Sage mumbled his frustration under his breath as pulled her along toward his stable.

Molly lived in a collapsing shack on a muddy, garbage-strewn lot a mile west of town. As they rolled in, several dogs growled and barked a loud unwelcome.

"Stay here. Fawcett may be inside," Sage ordered.

"He's got a gun."

With exasperation in his voice, he said, "Everyone's got a gun. Get yours out."

Sage descended into a small pack of dogs. With one kick, they all scattered. Aislynn tried to watch the house while Sage searched inside, but her eyes wandered the yard, watching for Fawcett to sneak up and shoot her.

"Aislynn!" Sage's deep voice rumbled into the yard. "Get in here!"

She jumped into the mud and ran through the shack's door. Broken furniture, splintered glass and debris strewn across the floor choked her path as she tried to reach Sage.

"In here!" His voice pulled her into a narrow, slant-ceiling bedroom.

It appeared as though a cyclone whirled its way through the small space. A dresser, with a fractured frame and a shattered mirror, stood against one wall. Clothes, shredded and torn, littered the floor. Molly lay on a collapsed bed. Blood stained her swollen face. Bruises blossomed on her calves. A gory mess pooled between her thighs.

"Oh, good Lord!" Aislynn cried.

Sage held a piece of the broken mirror under Molly's nose and over her mouth. "She's breathin'."

Snatching a scrap of a cloth off the floor Aislynn gently wiped Molly's face. "Molly? Molly? It's me, Aislynn. Wake up, Molly, please."

The battered girl's eyes fluttered. She looked at Aislynn and down at the bed. "My baby," she mumbled in a distraught tone, "he killed it." Heartbreak distorted Molly's face. Several tears moistened the blood on her cheeks.

"Yes, Molly, I know. Oh, sweetheart, I know."

"Molly, can you move?" Sage asked.

Molly twisted slowly.

He turned to Aislynn. "See if you can make that wagon comfortable."

Aislynn pulled the flimsy blanket off the bed in the main room and shouldered the mattress. She draped them over the tailgate and climbed up. Once she arranged everything in place, she returned to the shack. "You can bring her out. I have a blanket to cover her."

"Molly, I'm gonna lift you up and lay you in the wagon. We're goin' to bring you to the doctor. He'll fix you up."

Molly whimpered as Sage lifted her. Aislynn's eyes fell on the bloody mess soaking the mattress. The sight and the smell overcame her. She ran from the room gagging and vomited in the dirt. Once Sage settled Molly in the bed, Aislynn climbed in and covered her with the blanket. Molly moaned as they bounced and bumped. A half a mile toward town, she fainted.

As the doctor treated Molly for her wounds and miscarriage, Sage and Aislynn stood in the waiting room. A tragic sadness held her in its grip. Her mind raced from Molly to her own lost baby and arrived at Tommy. She looked up at Sage. "Someone has to let Tommy know."

Sage nodded. "I'll ride out there once Molly is settled. Doc will keep her overnight, but then where's she gonna go?"

"Maggie and Paul sleep in the parlor. Emmie only has a small cot in that tiny room. Joan lives with a family and has to share her bed with one of the daughters. We can't put any of them in danger." Aislynn looked up at Sage. "You have an extra bedroom."

"Which is gonna stay empty."

Aislynn took a deep breath and thought out loud. "We could sneak her into my room. Mrs. McKenzie is hard of hearing and never goes into my room. As long as Molly is quiet while I'm at school, she'll never know." She looked up at him and spun out a plan. "Vespers is at three o'clock. They'll be in church. We can carry her while they're gone."

Sage stood with his legs wide and his arms crossed, looking down at her with disapproving eyes. "It's a bit troublesome to see how fast you can spin out a scheme."

Dismissing his criticism with a scowl, Aislynn added, "They know how dangerous Molly's father is. Even if they discover her, they may keep quiet. They know her father could come back and kill us all."

Sage bent his head inches from hers. "You gotta be extra careful till we find Fawcett and lock him up."

Aislynn crossed her hands over her heart. "I won't leave the churchyard. Promise."

On Wednesday, Sage decided to call a meeting with Father Gilhooley and Mrs. McKenzie. When they were seated around the worn kitchen table, he appealed to their Christian spirit to allow Molly to stay in the attic with Aislynn. "She needs to heal, and she needs to do it in secret."

"You could have just asked me," Mrs. McKenzie said, aiming her anger at Aislynn.

"I'm sorry; I was trying to keep her and us safe."

"He might come back," Mrs. McKenzie added.

Father Gilhooley steepled his fingers and brought them to his lips. "God bless that poor child and protect us."

Mrs. McKenzie considered the situation and softened. "I have no objections, but she takes care of herself. I don't do laundry or cleaning up there."

The startled Molly sat up as they came through the door. "Marshal! Did Mrs. McKenzie see you?"

Sage settled himself on the trunk next to the bed. He bent toward Molly with his hands clasped between his knees. "Yes, she and Father Gilhooley agreed to let you stay. Now you don't have to worry about gettin' caught." Sage pointed to the bed. "Sit down, Aislynn." He turned his attention back to Molly. "Gal, I got a question for you. Did your father wear a gold ring?"

Molly's eyes flitted between Sage and Aislynn. "Yes."

"Engraved with an *F*?"

"Yes."

"What hand?"

"His left."

"We think we found your pa. I can't say for certain, but we found a man, same build as your pa, dead on the south side. The body's burned bad. Looks like his guns and knife were took . . . taken. We know he gambled and owed lots of people. I'm thinkin' someone bashed his head, stole his weapons and set him on fire. Guess they couldn't pull the ring off." He opened his hand and displayed the evidence to Molly.

Aislynn sat biting her lip and holding Molly's hand, waiting for the breakdown.

Molly straightened. Her face grew hard. "God forgive me, but it's a relief." Her swollen eyes filled and her lips trembled. "He terrorized my mother, drove her to her grave. Then he turned on me." Tears lined her bruised cheeks. "God's finally punished him for his sins."

Molly's sobbing caused Sage to fidget. "Sorry, gal," he muttered. Molly nodded and looked at Aislynn. Through a thick, tear-choked voice, Molly said, "We're safe." Sniffing and forcing a smile, she repeated, "We're safe."

CHAPTER 15

B URSTS of dry, hot wind whipped the dust into sporadic furies. In the searing morning sun, Aislynn and Father Gilhooley waited for her students to arrive. Behind them, a volley of gunshots rang out. Someone shouted, "There's the Injun whore." Aislynn and the priest whipped around. Molly's father strode forward with two grubby men, one burly and the other lanky. All three discharged their revolvers into the blazing sky.

"Grab her," Fawcett ordered.

They sprang toward Aislynn. Father Gilhooley shielded her. The stubby ruffian swung his meaty fist. The priest fell. Aislynn bolted, searching her pocket for her pistol. The thin man pounced. She stumbled, dropping her gun. Aislynn scrambled through the dust. The man snatched her leg.

Thrashing, she slammed her heel into his nose. Stunned for a moment, he froze as blood gushed over his mouth and chin. Aislynn rolled and tried to stand. The stocky man yanked her arm. She toppled on her side. Her first assailant recovered. He seized her free, flailing arm.

"Haul her into the barn," Fawcett yelled.

Terror, as dark as a grave, tore through her mind. *My baby, they'll hurt my baby.*

Aislynn heard Mrs. McKenzie screaming, "Leave them alone!" Another round of gunfire forced her back into the house.

The two men pulled Aislynn across the churchyard. She dug her heels into the dirt trying to slow their pace. Father Gilhooley recovered and lunged at the largest assailant. With a kick, he flattened the priest into the dust.

The barn doors opened with a low moan. They dragged her through heaps of cow and horse manure piled on the urine-steeped ground. She could taste the stench of the animals and the beer-soaked men.

Fawcett shoved the doors closed, leaving a small shard of light. Slivers of sun sliced through gaps in the roof like shiny daggers. They dumped her in the muck. Fawcett stood liked a shadowy specter between Aislynn and the splinter of daylight slipping between the doors.

He dropped his gun. He unbuttoned his pants. Aislynn panicked. She kicked, screamed and twisted out of her captors' hands.

The scrawny man on her left cracked the barrel of his gun against the side of her head. The stout one kicked her in the ribs. Dazed, she heard Fawcett command them to "hold her down." The stocky attacker stomped her hand into the filth. He bent over her, tore her dress open and with a squeeze, he twisted her breast. "You like that, you Injun whore?"

"You're in my way, back off," Fawcett ordered. "Hold her still."

The assailant on her left jerked her arm. Her shoulder popped. Fire radiated from the joint.

Molly's father pushed up Aislynn's skirt. He tore at her underdrawers. Aislynn pulled her legs back and thrust both feet into his face. Fawcett fell backwards. A trickle of blood ran from his lip. He fumbled for his gun. "I'm gonna kill you." He pointed the gun.

The skinny man kicked at Fawcett's hand, knocking the revolver to the ground. "No, we won't have no fun," he said. He returned his foot to her useless arm and loosened his pants.

Fawcett caught Aislynn's flying feet. He wrenched her left leg; Aislynn felt a snap in her thigh. She screamed in pain. "Shut her up; she's screamin' too much," Fawcett complained.

Both men drew their guns. The thin man placed his Colt at Aislynn's head. "Stop! Stop screamin'! And stop strugglin'! Let's make this quick. Go on, Jake. Poke her. Poke her hard."

Aislynn stopped screaming. "Kill me!" She shouted. "Just kill me!"

Fawcett kneeled on her calves. His filthy hand reached between her legs. The searing contact made Aislynn buck and twist. Her right leg escaped. "Damn you. Hold her down," Fawcett demanded. The burly man kicked her side for a second time, knocking the breath from her lungs. She fought to stay conscious. Before her eyes, a blaze of light appeared. As it expanded, she thought, *Go to the light.*

The scrawny man turned toward the door and uttered, "Marshal." Aislynn saw a flash and heard a blast. The man flew out of view. Before she could turn her head, another loud pop rang through the barn. The fat man no longer stood on her good arm. A wispy cloud of gun smoke wafted through the swath of light and reached Aislynn's nose. Fawcett snapped back on his heels.

"You ain't gonna shoot me in the back. I ain't armed."

She lay still. Refusing to give Fawcett any advantage, she focused her eyes down toward her legs. Fawcett's right hand slowly slipped toward his boot. His fingers reached in. Aislynn saw the hilt. "Knife!" burst from her lips. Two shots flared into Fawcett's chest. Blood burst from the holes, spraying Aislynn. Fawcett disappeared from her sight.

Sage cradled Aislynn in his arms. She moaned and took hold of her left arm. Rushing her out of the barn, he called to Deputy Winston, "Send the doc to my house."

"The men?" the deputy asked.

"Let the devil deal with them. Now get!"

As Sage whisked her through the street, she heard someone screaming. After a few seconds, she realized the screams were coming from her, but she was unable to stop.

Sage pushed the door open and laid her on the table. "Aislynn." He stroked her face. "Look at me. Take a breath. Stop screamin'. I have you. You're safe," he spoke through her cries. He pressed his fingers to her lips. "You're safe now. Don't scream. The doctor's comin' in a minute." He stroked her filthy hair. "They're dead. You're safe. You understand?"

Aislynn pleaded, "My baby?"

"He's safe, too. Don't you worry."

Within minutes, the doctor threw the door open. "Let's see her."

"My baby?" Aislynn begged.

The doctor shot a look at Sage. "Baby?"

A denial rushed from Sage's lips. "Ain't mine."

The doctor pushed up her dress and pulled down her drawers. He placed the cold stethoscope on her belly, gently rounded from five months of pregnancy. Aislynn held her breath. "I hear the heart beating. It's beating. Now tell me, did they violate you?"

Aislynn looked for Sage. She found him facing the fireplace with both arms resting on the mantle. Her body burned with a deep blush. "He touched me with his hand."

"Did he penetrate you?"

She pinched her eyes closed, shook her head and whispered, "He touched me." She cringed and turned her head away.

"It could have been worse. Now, tell me where you hurt."

The doctor diagnosed bruised ribs, a possible torn ligament in the thigh and a dislocated shoulder. "Sage, I need you to hold her down while I try to slip the shoulder back. Mrs. Maher, this is going to be very painful. I will be quick. You can help by lying still. I know it's difficult, but you can do it."

Aislynn nodded. She wanted the ordeal to be over. She wanted to wash their violation from her body, to purge their stink embedded in her nostrils, to eradicate their faces from her mind.

"Hold her down," he directed Sage, "but not so hard you break something else."

An excruciating flame shot through her arm. Once the bone was back in place, her shoulder throbbed. It felt like a separate being with its own independent pulse expanding and contracting with pain.

"Aislynn!" Joan banged on the door.

Sage's eyes rolled up and his frown deepened. "You want to see her?"

"Yes." *A woman friend.* "Please."

Joan rushed to Aislynn's side. Bending over she said, "Aislynn, I'm here. I'm going to help you." She looked at the doctor. "Are you done?"

"I have to wrap her chest and her thigh."

"Is that all?"

"Yes."

"I can do that."

"You?"

Joan's eyes turned soft and full of pity as she scanned Aislynn. "Yes." She nodded with conviction. "She needs to be cleaned up." She turned her attention to Sage. "Put some water on to boil, lots of water." Sage balked at the woman giving him orders. Joan's eyes burned into Sage's. "She needs a bath. She needs to feel clean!"

Aislynn nodded.

"Let's go," Joan commanded Sage.

Sage poured the hot water into the large washtub. He carried Aislynn into the bedroom. "You step outside," Joan directed, "and I'll get her into the tub." Aislynn sat on the edge of the bed. Together, she and Joan gently eased off her clothes. Joan supported her as she hobbled to the tub and slipped into the hot water. It stung her scrapes and cuts, but Aislynn took the harsh brown soap and immediately scrubbed between her legs until Joan grabbed her arm. "You're clean now; you're clean." Joan put some soap on a washcloth. "You lean back while I soap you up. Then, I'll comb the mess out of your hair and wash it. You'll feel all clean in a few minutes."

Joan pulled Sage's robe off the back of the door. She carefully wrapped Aislynn in its warmth. "Can you walk?"

"My leg is so weak."

Joan called, "Marshal?" He appeared at the door. "Put her in bed and I'll wrap her wounds."

"In my bed?"

Joan's eyebrows rose to her hairline. "She needs to rest and get well. Are you going to send her back there?"

"Where am I gonna sleep?"

Aislynn knew she should suggest going elsewhere, but her mind could not hold the offer long enough for her to speak.

Her thoughts rolled like balls of mercury. She could not catch hold of them. They spun from the horror of the attack, to her baby, to her pain, to the attack, to the pain, to her baby. Confusion reigned.

"You have slept on the rough your whole life. Go find yourself suitable spot. Now, leave us."

"Damn, it's no wonder you ain't married. You are the starchiest woman . . . ." His voice trailed off as he left the room.

Joan poured a teaspoon of fluid from a small brown bottle. "Swallow this. It'll help with your pain."

Laudanum. Like most women, Aislynn knew the reddish-brown tincture of opium well. It seemed doctors prescribed the highly addictive drug for every female complaint. Laudanum helped her when Johnny died and again when she lost her baby. She opened her mouth, and Joan fed her like a child.

Her shoulder burned. Her thigh ached. Her head throbbed. She smelled the men, heard their words and saw their evil faces. Fear cycled through her body. Her muscles tensed, her nerves prickled and her heart pounded. Joan chattered as she bound Aislynn's arm to her chest, stabilizing the shoulder. Aislynn could hear the words of encouragement, but they did not seem to penetrate the chaos in her brain.

Molly's voice called through the house, "Aislynn!"

"In here," Joan answered as she tied the bandage.

"Aislynn, I'm so sorry. This is all my fault." The frail, wounded girl hobbled into the room and fell on her knees at the side of the bed. "Please, forgive me."

Aislynn collapsed into the pillows. She tried to speak, but no words came. She placed her sore hand on Molly's head.

Molly sat on the bed and stroked Aislynn's arm, saying, "I'm going to take care of you day and night until you're better. I promise."

Maggie and Emmie crowded into the room. Emmie wept, while Maggie asked, "What happened? Who did this?"

Molly cried, "My father!"

Maggie gasped. "He's dead."

"He is now," Joan stated in a flat, disgusted tone.

The conversation went on outside Aislynn's consciousness. In the twilight of her drug-induced sleep, she heard: *Whore. I'll kill you. Poke her hard.* She saw her attackers' hate-filled faces, smelled their repulsive odors and felt their hands on her. She curled into a tight ball, trying to protect herself and her baby. In her mind, the men were hitting her, kicking her and touching her. Tears bloomed on the pillow. She reached for the little brown bottle and took another sip.

CHAPTER 16

WITH the curtains closed, Sage's room became a warm, dark, private sanctuary. However, Aislynn felt cold, fearful and exposed. Despite the August heat, she lay with a blanket pulled up to her chin and her good arm hugging her pillow. When Aislynn opened her eyes, she found Molly sitting in a chair next to Sage's bed.

"How do you feel?" she asked.

"I'm not sure." Bewildered, Aislynn asked, "What time is it?"

"Around five o'clock."

"What day?"

"Still Friday."

"Hmm . . ." Aislynn's mind fell back in time. The ordeal played out in her head, detail by detail. *Just a few hours ago I felt so confident, safe and strong. The attack probably lasted a few minutes. Such a short time, so much damage done. It happens that way though. It took Johnny a few seconds to tell me Da died. When Johnny died, Moran didn't have to say a word. I knew instantly. And then I lost our baby . . . . How quickly life is upended.*

Aislynn's eyes skimmed the room. Once again, she noticed Molly. "I'm sorry, did you say something? I'm a bit dazed."

"I understand."

"I know Sage said they couldn't be sure, but your father's death . . ."

"Knowing my father, he killed that man and staged the whole thing to protect himself. He sickens me."

Aislynn's head swam. She covered her face with her hand and a spoke in a rasping whisper, "But to violate me, to try to kill me. I know he hated me, but such violence . . ."

"That's the only language my father spoke—violence. I wish someone had killed him before he sent my mother to her grave, murdered my baby and hurt you."

"Molly, I'm forgetting he took so much more from you. You should be resting yourself."

"No, I'm fine." Her voice faltered. "I'm the one who's sorry. If I hadn't been involved with Tommy none of this would've happened."

"And if I hadn't come to Cheyenne, if I hadn't taught those children, so many *ifs*. You can't blame yourself for his behavior. He made his own choices."

Molly limped around the bed, smoothing the blanket. "I know he's dead, and God forgive me, I'm relieved and happy, but I think I'll always be afraid of him. I'm not sure I can explain it. I think he'll always be lurking around in my mind waiting to hurt me."

Aislynn's rational side answered, "But he's dead."

Molly leaned against the bed. "As I said, I can't explain. Are you hungry?" she asked.

"No." Aislynn grimaced. "I hurt. My head throbs, and my shoulder and thigh are burning."

"I can give you more laudanum," Molly said, retrieving the bottle from the nightstand. "It'll ease your pain and let you sleep. I found it worked very well."

She drank the brown draught. Aislynn fell back on the pillow and clutched the blanket. She smelled bay rum. The word *safe* edged into her mind. She wanted to see Sage; she wanted to apologize. *He warned me, but I knew better. I'm such a fool.* "Is Sage here?"

"No, he went to his office. I think all the women made him uncomfortable."

"Women? Here?"

"Emmie, Maggie, Joan, Mrs. Howe, Mrs. Kingman, and even Mrs. McKenzie are sitting around the table."

"What are they doing?"

"Drinking tea and fomenting a revolution. Seems everyone is upset about this morning. I closed the door so they wouldn't disturb you."

Grinning, Aislynn said, "You're a good friend, Molly. I do want to rest, but you should rest, too." Aislynn patted the empty side of the bed. "Hop in. I think I'll sleep better with company." Molly pulled off her shoes. "Oh," Aislynn remembered. "Would you do me a favor? My gun . . . ."

"Mrs. McKenzie found it; it's right here." Molly picked it up from the nightstand.

Aislynn winced as she tucked it under her pillow.

Molly lay next to her and whispered, "Aislynn?"

"Hmm?"

"They're dead."

Perplexed, Aislynn turned to Molly. Recognition dawned. She smiled. "I can't explain it, either."

On Saturday morning, Father Gilhooley hovered at the end of her bed like a ghostly apparition. The priest wore his black robe, and a jute string dangling a wooden crucifix hung around his neck. "Aislynn, you poor child, poor child."

"Father Gilhooley, thank you for coming. I'm honored." Aislynn pulled the covers over her nightgown.

The nervous little man tapped his fingers together. "My blessed duty, blessed duty to minister to the infirm."

"You were injured, too."

"A mere blow, a mere blow. Do you suffer, my child?"

Aislynn shrank a bit in the big bed. "Yes, Father, more than I can explain to you."

"Should we pray? Yes, let's pray."

Aislynn joined her hands in her lap, careful to keep her shoulder still. Gilhooley inhaled a deep calming breath, "Hail Mary, full of grace . . . ." They repeated the prayer five times like a penance. Aislynn wondered if he blamed her as much as she blamed herself. "And now for our Lord's Prayer . . . ." With a sign of the cross, he blessed her, "God, we beseech thee . . . ." After the prayers, Gilhooley said, "I brought you Communion." Surprised at the offering, Aislynn humbly accepted the Sacrament.

The priest considered Aislynn for a moment. "I haven't eased your suffering."

In the dim light of Sage's bedroom, Gilhooley seemed old and worn. Aislynn's eyes searched his. Questioning a priest was not done. The nuns told her it was a sin against God. Tim would have smacked her for being disrespectful. However, she needed an answer. In a soft voice tinged with uncertainty, she asked, "Why would God punish me for helping those children? For helping Molly? How can good deeds reap such a result?"

The priest wrapped his hands around his crucifix. Aislynn wondered if he held it for divine intervention or to shield it from her affront. "My child, my child, I also struggle with that question. I can only say there's a purpose. While we don't know what it is, God does. Like his Son, his blessed Son, you don't suffer in vain. There is a purpose and a reward. I'm sure of it."

She wanted to believe reasons existed for all her losses, but they eluded her. For the first time since Sage carried her from the barn, Aislynn buried her face in her hand and cried.

Gilhooley fidgeted at the foot of the bed. Aislynn realized her tears made the jittery man uncomfortable. He glanced around the room, searching for an escape. Aislynn came to his rescue. "Thank you, Father. You've been a great help. I don't want to keep you. Thank you for coming."

With one last blessing, he started out the door. He stopped and turned. "Aislynn, I pray your faith grows stronger than your doubts."

As the door closed, the room darkened, emphasizing a shard of light slashing through the narrow gap between the curtains. When her eyes fixed on it, her fear flared, her heart raced, her wounds throbbed and her nerves sparked. She curled into a fetal position, encircling and protecting her child. She chewed her thumb, pulling the cuticle until it bled, waiting for the laudanum to do its job.

In the late afternoon, Joan arrived. Aislynn lay in bed, deep in thought. Joan fell into the seat next to the bed. With her stern teacher's face aimed at Aislynn, she commanded, "Tell me."

"I can't stop it. The memories press on my mind. I try to push them away, but they're loud and intrusive. They're stuck, repeating over and over."

"I know, believe me, I know."

Their eyes locked; a delicate question hung between them. Aislynn watched Joan make her decision, rise and push the door until the latch clicked. She locked it, returned to her seat, folded her hands in her lap and studied them. "I was thirteen, young and headstrong. I never liked being told what I could or couldn't, or should or shouldn't, do." She lifted her head and met Aislynn's eyes. "A carnival came to town." Her words halted for a moment. "My sister and I were allowed to go together. There was a maze. She refused to go through it. I was younger and wanted to show I was braver. So I went . . . alone." She pushed out the last word in a strained breath.

"There were doors throughout where workers could come and go. When I had walked halfway through the course, a door opened in front of me. A man pulled me out of the maze. He clapped his hand over my mouth and yanked me into some nearby bushes." Joan's breathing became labored. "He smelled of tobacco, whiskey and old-man sweat. He had dark brown hair and black eyes. His hands were rough and smelled of grease. The one over my mouth pressed against my nose, and I thought I would suffocate." Joan's voice cracked with fear. "I thought I would die." She covered her eyes. "He left me in the dirt, all torn and bloodied."

Joan collected herself. In a controlled voice, she said, "I straightened my clothes and hid the stains in the folds of my skirt. When I found my sister, I told her I had to go home. He's never left me, Aislynn. He's right here." Joan tapped the back of her head. "He took so much, but he left a piece of himself right here."

Stupefied, Aislynn gaped at her; no words escaped her mouth.

"Nice women didn't speak of such things. I'd heard the word . . . but the details never followed." Joan looked into Aislynn's eyes. "Now, I know what it means." Her voice quivered with anger. "When I smell tobacco or whiskey, when I see a man with dark eyes and dark hair walking toward me on the street, the memories rush back."

Aislynn gently shook her fragile head. "That's why you have no use for men."

Joan slumped in her chair. "I couldn't marry. I could never have a child. The idea of the act is revolting to me."

"I'm so sorry."

Joan's reply sounded thick and tearful. "So you see, I understand."

"Did you tell anyone?"

"No. You know I would have been blamed, shunned and labeled a fallen woman. Once, just to test her, I told my sister I had heard about a girl being abused at the carnival. She said a girl who goes off by herself deserves to be treated that way. Then she said, 'That girl could've been you.' "

Aislynn disagreed. "She was wrong, Joan. You were young; you were at a carnival. Children are supposed to go in the maze. That's why it's there." Joan reached for her handkerchief and dabbed her eyes. Aislynn continued, "It wasn't your fault. He was a predator. He planned it. He was waiting. I bet you weren't his first victim."

Joan's mouth fell agape. Her ramrod posture returned. "You think that's true?"

"Of course. He planned it just like Fawcett planned the attack on me. He knew you were coming. He knew when to open the door. He knew the bushes would conceal his crime. A man has to plan all that. You did not fall from the sky and land under him."

"That never occurred to me."

"It was not your fault."

Joan's eyes reflected bewilderment and doubt until they glowed with understanding. Her lips parted to speak but she covered her face with her hands and sobbed. Aislynn leaned on her strong arm and pulled herself close to the edge of the bed. She patted Joan's shoulder. "We know women are good jurors. My verdict is not guilty." *Now, if only I could erase my own guilt and shame.*

Wiping her eyes and nose with her hanky, Joan said, "I hope my story brings you some solace, Aislynn. You've been brutally beaten. I don't want you to think I minimize your pain, your fear or the nightmarish memories you will suffer, but I do want to stress those men did not violate you. When a woman is injured, she's a saint; when she's raped, she's a whore. No one will ever claim you were soiled. Sage rushed in and saved you from that fate." Joan paused and chuckled. "It's like all those fairy tales; you had your own knight, minus the shining armor."

Joan took a few quick breaths. "No one rescued me." Her voice trembled. "Until today, no one has ever helped me. I thank you for that, and I hope my revelations keep you from allowing this dreadful experience to rule you and ruin your life." Joan's eyes filled. "You know, perhaps we are helping each other," she said, blinking away her tears. "My goodness, Aislynn, speaking to you has done me a world of good."

Sunday afternoon brought a visit from Maggie and Emmie. They delivered a small box wrapped in paper printed with pink flowers. "These are magic. They heal all wounds and solve all problems," Emmie explained with her perpetual optimism.

With a woozy head, Aislynn struggled to sit up. "That's just what I need." Aislynn opened the box to find six chocolate-covered cherries. "What a treat!"

"I told you they were her favorites," Emmie reminded Maggie.

"We ordered them from a confectioner in Denver," Maggie added.

Aislynn took one and passed the box to Emmie.

"Mama said they were all yours."

"Then I can choose to share them with my dearest friends." Aislynn pushed the box at an eager Emmie.

Maggie and Emmie tried to cheer Aislynn with gossip, amusing anecdotes and local news. Aislynn listened and attempted to enjoy their company, but her memories crowded out their cheer. Pleading pain and exhaustion, she reached for her laudanum and laid her head on the pillow.

Alone in her room, Aislynn waited for the drug to slow the spiral of memories winding once again. This time they stopped when the doctor announced he heard the baby's heartbeat. She tried to remember the last time she felt a fluttering in her womb. In her cloudy memory, the past two days bleared like a window in a rainstorm. Thoughts flooded through her brain then cascaded out of reach. She focused and waited for the baby to move. Aislynn held her breath, lay stock-still and willed the baby to move. Time ticked away. Grief hung over her like an unlit chandelier spreading darkness and doubt. Tears slipped down her cheeks and clouds of damp billowed on the pillow until the drug stole her consciousness.

Aislynn dragged herself out of an opiate sleep. "Molly?"

"I'm afraid you're down to me." Cap limped into the room with Smokey at his heels. "Molly had to get back to work. Joan's teachin' and Paul, Maggie and Emmie are at the store. We don't want you to be alone, so that leaves me and Smokey." Cap gave her a peck on the head and eased down into the chair.

She took a sip of water and shook the dullness from her brain. "I'm pleased to see you." Aislynn reached down to pet Smokey.

"How you doin'?"

"I'm healing. I'm less dizzy when I sit up. My shoulder doesn't hurt as much, and my leg is stronger."

"I'm sorry for your troubles."

Aislynn leaned back on the pillows and closed her eyes for a moment. In a weary voice, she confided in the old man. "You don't know this, but I was attacked in Utah." Cap's smile left his face. "It was right after the completion of the transcontinental railroad. You may remember that thousands of workers found themselves stranded in Utah without money or a way to return home. It turned some of them into criminals."

Aislynn patted the bed and invited Smokey to sit with her. The hefty dog pulled himself up, circled and dropped his head on Aislynn's lap. She stroked his back with her mobile hand as she continued, "One afternoon, a friend of mine and I were out on the main road in my wagon when two men jumped us. I got off a couple of shots with this revolver." She carefully removed the gun from under the pillow.

"I hope you killed them," he growled.

Aislynn blushed. She nodded and whispered, "Let's keep that our little secret."

Cap winked in agreement.

"Before they died, one of them cut my arm and stabbed me in the thigh. It was awful! But, it didn't feel like this. This time was so personal. They wanted to kill me, they wanted to . . ." Aislynn looked away. "They wanted to punish me. I know they're dead, but I'm still afraid of them."

"You know they can't hurt you now. No such thing as haunts."

"I understand but I feel so vulnerable. There are other men who hate Injun lovers. I imagine them saying to each other, 'They didn't get her; we should try.' Makes me want to stay in this room and never go out again."

"You can't do that. That's like lettin' them varmints win. It's good to be a little scared. Keeps you alert, 'cause there are dangers aboundin'. But you got gumption. I know that. You come here to start a new life all by your lonesome. You can't let them weasels take that away from you. Now, you got a gun, and I want you to have Smokey."

"No, no!" Aislynn held up her hand.

"Yes, you need him more than me. He's a good dog. He'll keep a lookout for you. Help you feel safe."

"That's too generous."

"No, I wanna. Least I can do." Cap leaned closer. He held his lips taut and stared into her eyes. "Gal," he started, "those men shamed me. I'm sorry to say they were one of my kind. With men, it seems fightin' and killin' come natural, especially here in the West." He shook his head. "We allow men to beat the whores. If a man abuses his wife and kids, we look the other way. We need to call him out. Sage, Howe and Campbell are all countin' on women to come here and civilize us. I think we men got some work to do on ourselves."

Aislynn considered the old man. "You're an exceptional person. Your wisdom is boundless."

"Yes, I'm the quiet, brainy type; I don't usually share my great thoughts. Don't want to show off."

Aislynn smiled. "I understand."

Pointing at her, he said, "You ain't no dummy yourself. I'd venture you've learned how to see some good in a bad situation. You're young but experienced." Cap leaned on the bed. "Which is way better than being old and experienced."

Aislynn reflected for a moment. "How sad it would be if you were old and not experienced. Your life would have been very boring."

"It wasn't." Cap winked. "You know if I could see better, I'd write me a book."

"I'd pay to read that."

"It would scald your pretty eyes."

"I'd risk it."

Cap pointed his finger at her. "Do I hear some gumption comin' back?"

Aislynn looked at the brown bottle. "I am feeling better."

CHAPTER 17

THE sound of glass breaking woke the woozy Aislynn. She opened her eyes to a truculent Sage standing at the bedroom door, ready for a fight. "Time for you to get up and earn your keep!"

"Molly?"

Sage interrupted, "Molly's gone to work, and it's time you did, too."

"I can't; I'm in pain."

"I've seen women with arrows in their backs livelier than you. Get up."

Aislynn rolled to get a sip from her bottle. The nightstand stood empty. In a panic, she sat up. "Where's my bottle?"

"Gone."

"Why?"

" 'Cause you're fallin' in love with it."

"It's my medicine."

"It's snake oil. It bites you and won't let go. Now, it's gone." He pointed his chin at her. "You! Get out here!"

Mourning her loss, Aislynn struggled to the edge of the bed and dropped her legs over the side. Her feet searched for slippers. She stood. A wave of dizziness and nausea rolled through her. She reached for the chamber pot and vomited. She collapsed back on the bed and waited for the strength to stand. Her head pounded. It reminded her of her bout with whiskey. She had lain for a few minutes, when she heard Sage bark, "Aislynn, get out here!"

She rose and tucked her right arm into her robe and felt her way along the wall to the door. The distance to the kitchen stretched for miles. She leaned against the doorframe trying to catch her breath. After five days in a dark room, the kitchen's blaring sunlight nearly blinded her. The pain in her shoulder screamed and her legs wobbled. *If I could have some laudanum, I'd feel so much better.* Sage's face burned with anger.

With a few deep breaths, she crossed the room and reached the table. A cup of coffee steamed at her place. The smell gagged her. The nearby waste pail rescued her. As she bent over, she saw the brown bottle of laudanum smashed into tiny pieces. She realized she was alone with her pain and her terrible memories.

"I'll be back for lunch," Sage announced as he headed to the door.

Aislynn's fear rose. "You're leaving me alone?"

"Smokey will be here."

"But there are men out there," she pleaded. The door swung closed behind him.

Aislynn tried to concentrate, but her mind focused on the drug. She considered her options. *I could go buy some. No, I'm too afraid to go out.* The thought of leaving triggered her memory; the door stood unlocked. She rose slowly. When her brain stopped vibrating, she hobbled to the door and threw the bolt. *The windows.* Aislynn struggled around the room checking each window's lock.

She passed the mirror and froze. Purple eyes, swollen cheeks and brown scabs tattooed her face. She leaned against the wall and lifted her nightgown. In the bright light, she saw bruises like blue, yellow and green clouds puffed on her white skin. A fury burned through her. *They did all this and killed my baby, too!*

Aislynn slid to the floor. She sat for a while, fuming. *I'm sorry they're dead. That's one more thing robbed from me. What I could have done to them!* Her mind reached back to novels and newspaper articles describing torturous crimes. *Comanches eviscerated their victims. The ancients flayed their enemies.* She waffled between the two trying to decide which would be worst. Then, she decided she could have combined them.

Her musings strengthened her. Some sense of power returned. *I could have mutilated them without regret.* She had heard revenge was sweet. For a few moments, she relished the feeling. But her conscience interfered when she realized her thoughts were un-Christian and unladylike. Her eyes scanned the room for disapproving looks. Only Smokey watched her with his sweet, contented face. Aislynn scratched his head, and he flopped his muzzle on her lap. "You'd help me, wouldn't you? We might have gotten away with it, too. After all, it's the West. Having eastern sensibilities is a handicap in a land where violence for good and evil rules."

Thoughts of vanquishing her attackers energized Aislynn. Restlessness raised her off the floor. She moved slowly, balancing her shaky head and protecting her painful shoulder. Fear of Sage trumped the debilitating memories of those men. She shoved them out of her mind and got to work.

The cupboard yielded a piece of ham and some root vegetables. With her bound arm hampering her mobility, she pressed her left hip against the tin table, and used her limited left hand to steady the food while she cut it with her strong right. She prepared a meal of fried onions and potatoes with cold, sliced ham.

Sage arrived ready to eat. Aislynn took a seat opposite him, resting her head in her hand. "I haven't thanked you for saving my life."

Sage shrugged and sipped his coffee.

"I'm sorry I've caused you so much trouble." She looked down and tried to subtly wipe her misty eyes. "I know you warned me, but I believed if I tried hard enough, things would work out. Now, I've lost everything." Aislynn choked down a sob. "Even my baby."

"You lost it? How do you know?"

"It hasn't moved. I haven't felt anything, not even a tiny flutter."

"That's it? Nothin' else?"

"Isn't that enough?"

"It's probably drugged into stillness. You've been pourin' so much of that swill down your throat the poor thing can't wake up."

Aislynn clasped her hands and grabbed the bit of hope he offered. "Do you think? I'd do anything to make that true."

"Then don't take another drop, get off your rump and move around."

"Yes, of course. I'll move."

Sage shook his head. "And get your mind movin' too. You're stuck feelin' scared and sorry for yourself. You're gonna heal, your baby's gonna wake up and you gotta stop lettin' this get you down. It's over."

"But—"

"Ain't no buts, just do it."

Aislynn considered his advice. "Yes, I'll try. I can't go back to work yet, not like this." She looked over her body. When her eyes rose and met his, a shadow had fallen across his face.

A ruinous thought burst into her brain. Joan and Molly saw her naked. They may have noticed her girth and surmised her condition. *Have they confided in Maggie and Emmie?* A sinking, sick feeling of dread shortened her breaths and increased her heart rate. *If Emmie knows, all of Cheyenne will know. I'll lose my job, my home.* "Does everyone know I'm pregnant? Am I losing my job?"

"Yes and yes."

"Did Emmie tell?"

"I think it was the doc. But that ain't why you don't have a job. The children are gone."

"Because of me? Because of what happened?"

" 'Cause it wasn't safe. Those men had enough shots left to kill half those kids."

Aislynn's stomach turned; the taste of bile rose to her mouth. She covered her eyes with her hand and cried.

She peeked at Sage through her fingers. "Everyone in town must hate me for starting this whole mess. The children are gone and three men are dead. It's all my fault." She sobbed.

Sage's disapproving frown formed on his face. He hung his head and snapped at her, "Now you're just gettin' crazy. Calm down. I swear that drug has eaten away your sense."

"I have been so frightened, so ashamed; I think I'm losing my mind."

Sage walked to his chair and returned with a pile of newspapers. He laid them in front of her. In the sunlight streaming through the windows, Aislynn skimmed the pages. Next to the long column of national news, the local headlines shouted:

The Cheyenne Leader. "Angel of the Prairie Attacked for Civilizing the Heathens"

The Wyoming Tribune. "No Peace for the Peacemaker"
Our agent of peace, the young woman who labored to educate and tame the wild savages, was attacked yesterday by three miscreants who paid the ultimate price.

The Rocky Mountains News. "Can the Ruffians of Cheyenne Sink Any Lower?"
The article began:
Our untamed neighbor to the north again shows it is stuck in its wild past, while Denver is on the path to becoming the greatest city of the West. At a church school in Cheyenne, a young teacher was brutally attacked. The patriotic woman spent her days answering President Grant's call to educate and civilize the ignorant, feral Indian children. Yet, Cheyenne allowed three outlaws to beat a priest and batter the fragile lady.

Aislynn looked at Sage with disbelief in her eyes. "No one's blamin' you. And no one hates you," Sage declared. Aislynn's attention returned to the newspapers. Other headlines screamed:

The Cheyenne Leader. "Hero Marshal Saves Young Widow"
Marshal Orrin Sage shoots three men in thirty seconds to save our dedicated Indian schoolteacher.

The Wyoming Tribune. "Hero in Our Midst"
Rest easy, Wyoming, Marshal Orrin Sage is on duty and ready to draw his gun in defense of good citizens everywhere.

Rocky Mountains News. "A True American Hero Graces the West"

Aislynn marveled at the papers. "You're a hero?"

Sage snatched the papers. "I didn't tell you to read that."

"No one's angry? Not even their families?"

"They found them the way I left them. It was clear what crimes they were tryin' to commit."

The recollection of the men unbuttoning their pants rolled a wave of disgust through Aislynn. She shuttered. When the memory passed, she asked, "What about the Bighorn Expedition? They must be up in arms."

"They're gone, too."

"All of them? Where?"

"Sweetwater. Justice Howe cleared the way with the rulin' to allow the expedition to move out."

Aislynn searched Sage's eyes. "Did you ask him to do that?"

"I didn't have to." Sage spread a different copy of the *Cheyenne Leader* on the table. He turned to the "Letters to the Editor" page.

> *Dear Editor,*
>
> *We, the good women of Cheyenne, believe our fair city has come to a crossroads in its young life. Like any child, Cheyenne needs to be disciplined with a strong hand.*
>
> *When a decent, hardworking, young woman is preyed upon and severely injured, can any good woman feel safe? We should no longer fear danger every time we venture out of our homes. We believe our husbands, fathers, brothers and sons should take every action to execute their sovereign powers to protect our fair sex. Rid our city of this violent, criminal element or no longer call yourselves good Christian men.*

Signed,

Your wives, mothers, sisters and daughters.

Aislynn's hand flew to her mouth. Tears filled her eyes and the ladies' support filled her heart. "I'm so grateful. Thank you for showing me these stories. Perhaps things aren't as bad as I have imagined." She looked into Sage's eyes. "Maybe Father Gilhooley was right. Something good did come from my . . ." She waved the word away.

Sage gave her a noncommittal shrug. "There's always gonna be danger lurkin' around, but you gotta put all this behind you and move on."

Aislynn shook her head. "I don't think I can."

"Think again because you ain't holin' up here."

CHAPTER 18

WHILE Cap and Sage sipped their coffee, Molly and Aislynn conferred in the kitchen. Since Sage's prediction that her baby would move became a reality, Aislynn's secret dread slipped unnoticed into the past. The baby's lively movements gave her new hope for an uncertain future. Homeless and nearly penniless, the girls developed a plan. They linked arms, stood at the table and addressed the men.

"You're getting your wish," Aislynn announced.

"Which wish is that?" asked Sage in his skeptical voice.

They answered in unison, "We're leaving."

Sage leveled a stern look at the young women. "Where you goin'?" he demanded.

"Molly and I realize we have to give you back your home."

"I appreciate that," he responded with exaggerated gratitude.

Aislynn nodded toward Molly. "Now that we're both stronger and feeling less afraid." She grinned at Molly. "We're moving to Molly's shack tomorrow. Since everyone knows about the baby, I won't be able to find work. With the small income my mother-in-law sends from my restaurant plus Molly's pay, we think it's our best option."

"No, it ain't," Sage announced flatly, and sipped his coffee.

"We're going to clean it and patch it up a bit," Aislynn pushed on.

"You ain't livin' there."

"Why not?"

"First, it ain't in your territory. When are you gonna learn your boundaries? You are thick as a brick."

The shack's location unnerved Aislynn, but they had no other choices. True or not, Aislynn was determined to believe she and Molly would be safe. "You are sweet to be concerned, but—"

Interrupting, he added, "Second, Cap's got a better idea."

All eyes turned to Cap. "My shack ain't much, but it's in your territory." He grinned and tipped his head toward Sage. "I'm thinkin' I could settle my bones in that bedroom right there. You could make a nice little nest in my place for the three of you."

Both women were struck dumb for a moment. Aislynn recovered first. "Cap, you can't do that. It's your home."

In her timid voice, Molly interjected, "And we can't afford rent."

Cap said, "You ain't gonna pay no rent."

"We owe you both so much already," Aislynn insisted.

Sage explained, "You're gonna work for it, Aislynn. You're gonna cook, clean and do our laundry. You'll be a housekeeper, like Mrs. McKenzie. That'll make us square."

Aislynn's eyes jumped from Sage to Molly to Cap. She gasped, "Oh Cap, I do love you!" She threw her arms around his neck and kissed his cheek. "You are so good to us!"

Molly followed and gave Cap a tentative hug. She turned to Sage. With one hand touching his shoulder, she said, "Thank you, Marshal."

Aislynn replaced Molly. She draped her arm around Sage's shoulders. "You're full of surprises." She bent to kiss his cheek, but he turned slightly. Her lips grazed his mustache and touched his lips. She pulled back as if she had touched a hot spoon to her mouth. An unexpected blush bloomed on Sage's cheeks. Composing herself, she said, "Thank you for *everything*." They all knew what she meant.

"Someone's gotta keep you out of trouble," Sage replied.

The isolated, one-room shack sat on the sparsely developed end of 20th Street. Across the way, two warehouses stretched along the entire block between Hill and Ferguson. One lone house stood a few vacant lots to the east. It belonged to Mr. Bigelow. He worked odd hours for Western Union manning the telegraph. On the western side, between the shack and the Diamond Corral, Mr. and Mrs. Darnell owned a lovely home. The old couple was rarely in residence. Their son ran a ranch south of town, and they spent most of their time with him. Behind Cap's, Mr. Steiner operated a dairy. His cows and goats wandered the unobstructed prairie.

Cap generously left most of his furniture. The girls had a nice wide bed, two dressers and a nightstand. They hung a drape around the bed, creating a private sleeping alcove. A sparsely equipped kitchen occupied the space opposite the alcove. Sage, being a man who spent a great deal of thought on his stomach, arranged to move the big stove, tin table, cupboard and jelly safe to Cap's shack, explaining, "They don't do us any good."

An old rocker remained in front of the hearth, and Cap's bearskin, complete with its enormous head, stretched its paws across the floor. Amy, a daily guest, named the rug Herman. With a few extra dining chairs, a jar of flowers on the table and the warm scents rising from the stove, the shack became the place where they all gathered for comfort and friendship.

The move affected all of them. While cooking and baking were Aislynn's daily chores, she developed a new schedule to accommodate her housekeeping duties. She washed Sage's and Cap's laundry on Mondays. Washday for Molly's and her laundry filled her Tuesdays. On Wednesdays she ironed. She devoted the rest of the week to cleaning both houses.

Cap spent his time socializing at the store, acting as justice of the peace and relaxing at Aislynn's. Molly slipped in every night just in time to sit down to eat. They all knew her secret, but they all chose to remain silent on the subject.

After dinner, while Aislynn and Molly washed the dishes, Amy amused Cap. She created fantastic plays about pirates and princes. From his rocker, Cap filled all the male roles as Amy transformed herself into all the female characters. The versatile Smokey could be cast as anything from a unicorn to a dragon. At times, she enlisted Herman as a magic carpet, dungeon or deck of a ship.

The greatest change settled on Sage. He arrived with Cap for breakfast, quiet and grumpy, but his mood lifted by noontime. Most days, Sage and Deputy Winston appeared at odd hours for coffee and a taste of whatever sweet snack Aislynn saved in her cookie tin. Their visits gave her a sense of security.

Within a few days, Sage's upholstered chair, accompanied by an end table and a few books, migrated to Aislynn's hearth. During dinner, he seemed happy to be a part of the family. Although he did not participate, he listened to Cap's tidbits of gossip, Molly's reports on the antics of customers and Amy's adventures at school.

Every evening, he relaxed with his whiskey, reading and observing Amy's ever-changing dramas. A contented grin found a home on his face. In the glow of the lamps and candles, his hard lines seemed to soften. To Aislynn's eyes, he appeared almost appealing.

For Aislynn and Molly, a nightly routine helped them feel safe. They checked each door and window to make sure they were locked. Before drawing the curtains around the sleeping alcove, they placed a lamp with a low burning wick on the mantle. Smokey slept at the foot of the bed, and Aislynn's small revolver waited in the drawer of the nightstand.

Smokey's sharp barks sliced the air and woke both girls. "Someone's knocking at the door," Molly whispered.

Aislynn's heart raced. "I'll grab the gun." As they slipped on their robes, Smokey's barking dissolved into a whimper. Aislynn hooked her arm through Molly's and together they approached the door.

"Aislynn, please let me in," a small voice called.

Suspicion and fear led Aislynn to ask, "Amy? Are you alone?"

"Yes."

"No one's with you?"

"No," the child whined.

Aislynn pointed the gun, and Molly slowly opened the door.

Amy threw her arms around Aislynn's legs and wailed. "Bolt the door and turn up the lamps," Aislynn ordered Molly. She slipped the revolver into her pocket. Crouching on her tender leg, she brought Amy into a one-armed hug. "Why are you out so late?"

"Mama told me to get out."

"Why?"

"Papa came home. He gave me a slap. She told me to get. I ran till I got here."

Aislynn pulled back and assessed the child's condition. "Are you hurt?" Mud splattered her shabby nightdress.

"I think I cut myself." Amy pointed to her legs.

Aislynn lifted the child's gown. Amy displayed her filthy, wounded, shoeless feet and cut knees.

"Let's get you cleaned up." Nodding at Molly, she continued, "We'll wrap you in a big towel, you can wear my robe and we'll all get into bed and snuggle." Aislynn tried to make the situation sound like fun.

They prepared a shallow bath. After scrubbing Amy clean, they bound her feet with gauze and bandaged her knees.

"Are you hungry?" Aislynn asked.

"Just tired."

It was nearly 2:30 when they calmed the lamps and crawled into bed. Aislynn lay with something new to occupy her overwrought mind. *Why would a mother push a child out in the middle of the night?* She struggled with the question until she fell asleep.

Aislynn woke at daybreak. She rubbed her shoulder and stretched her leg. The pain remained, but her strength increased with each day.

She closed the curtain around the sleeping alcove. Quietly, she fed the stove, started a pot of coffee and filled a pan with bacon. Just as the coffee began to boil, Sage's boots hit the porch. She threw open the door while he was inserting his key and said, "You're early."

"Amy here?"

"Yes, how did you know?"

"Just a hunch." Sage hung his holsters on the back of a dining chair, leaned his rifle against the wall and pulled himself up to the table. "What did she tell you?"

Aislynn placed a cup of coffee in front of him. She repeated Amy's story. "Can you imagine a mother throwing a child out into the night alone?"

"She did good."

"Good?"

"Amy's pa rolled into town last night. Seems he figured out how her ma's been makin' her livin'. He shot her, lit the place on fire and shot himself."

Aislynn's hand rushed to her mouth. She sank into the closest chair. "Thank goodness Amy didn't witness such a horror."

Sage's arms rested on the table, and he cradled his coffee in his large hands. "She got any kin?"

"I don't know." Aislynn considered the little orphan for a moment. "She has me."

"You're about all she's got. Guess you'll be her ma till we find family."

Aislynn looked into her cup. "Do you have to look for them? What if they're strangers to her? What if she has to go away from here? She'd be terrified." Sage tilted his head and peered at her through narrowed eyes. "I know it's the law. What if you don't find anyone?" *God, please don't let him find anyone.*

"That's for the judge to decide," he said in his official voice. He leaned back and asked, "How about some grub?"

Aislynn greeted Amy with, "Good morning, sweetheart, would you like some breakfast?"

The child struggled to keep Aislynn's robe from slipping off her shoulders. "Yes, please." She looked around the table. "Morning, Marshal. Howdy, Cap," she said as she climbed into her chair between the men.

When the table was cleared, Sage pulled Amy onto his lap. "Missy, how'd you like to live with Aislynn and Molly for a while?"

"I'd have to ask my ma."

"Amy," he started in his soft, deep voice. "You know about God and heaven?"

The little girl gave Sage a somber stare and nodded.

His hand stroked her hair as he explained, "Last night, God took your ma and pa, seems He needed them in heaven. Since you have Aislynn, Molly, Cap and me, He thought you'd be just fine and cared for real good by us." Aislynn watched and listened as Sage turned into a tender giant who warmed her heart.

"Can I ask her first?"

Sage's eyes darted to Aislynn's. She stooped next to their chair. "Sweetheart, they're already in heaven. They are angels now; they're your guardian angels. If you want to talk to them, they'll fly down and sit right here." Her hands fluttered above Amy and came down on her shoulders. "You won't feel them because they are as light as a cloud. But they'll be here to listen to you and to help you in any way they can."

Amy turned and searched her shoulders. She looked at Aislynn and her entire face melted into a deep frown. Tears poured. "I want to see them." Aislynn stood and lifted Amy to her hip with her strong arm. She limped to Cap's chair. Aislynn rocked the child, stroking her hair and murmuring reassuring words. Molly sniffed and gasped as she stood at the dish tub with heaving shoulders.

Cap twisted his face in every direction to hold in his emotions. He pushed his chair back and said, "Smokey needs to go outside." He escaped through the front door. Sage stared out the front window. When the exhausted child cried herself to sleep, Aislynn put her to bed and closed the curtains.

She sat across from Sage. "What happens next?"

"Suppose we should bury them. She's gonna need a dress and some shoes."

"I have some fabric," Aislynn offered. "Molly can take her to the shoemaker."

Molly tried to agree, but Sage addressed Aislynn. "You're gonna get the shoes. You're goin' to the cobbler and gettin' her a proper fittin' pair of shoes."

She opened her mouth to express her lingering fear of walking in the street. Sage's finger in her face made her stop. "Don't you teach Amy to be afraid. Get dressed and get goin' soon as she wakes up. You take Smokey and your gun." He started for the door. He picked up his hat and pointed it at her. "Don't you show her you're scared of nothin' . . . anythin'."

The cobbler shop sat a mere three blocks southeast of Cap's house on 18th and Hill Street, but the trip terrified Aislynn. She still feared strange men. Her heart raced every time she made eye contact with a man or caught a man's eyes on her. Holding Amy's hand and knowing Smokey trotted at her side, made Aislynn feel more secure. She believed they protected her from harm, like living talismans.

Clearly an afterthought, the tiny shop appeared wedged between two taller buildings. A single cowbell suspended over the door announced their arrival. Several lamps hanging from the ceiling brought the only light into the space. Wooden shoe forms hung on the walls. Pots of glue and piles of leather covered most of the workbench and filled the air with a sharp, sour animal scent. Awls, needles and spools of thread sat in cubbyholes that climbed the wall in front of the bench. A small, dark-haired man slipped off his stool and approached.

He greeted them with a *buongiorno* that sounded like a song in his clear, tenor voice. He smiled, displaying strong, white teeth under a straight nose. Thick, dark lashes framed equally dark, alluring eyes. "May I help?" he asked in slow, halting English.

Aislynn reminded herself not to stare at the man she quickly judged to be the most beautiful human she had ever seen. "My—" Aislynn stopped, unsure of how to refer to Amy. "This lovely young lady needs shoes."

"This I can do." He motioned toward a stool. "You take the seat," he said, addressing Amy. The man's eyes rested on Amy's feet, clad in a pair of Aislynn's woolen socks.

Embarrassment heated Aislynn's cheeks to a bright red. "She seems to have lost her shoes," Aislynn offered as an excuse.

"This is fine. I make new." He crouched before Amy and asked, "May I see the foot, please?"

Amy's look asked Aislynn for assurance. "He won't hurt you. He has to measure you to fit the shoes correctly."

The cobbler examined Amy's twisted foot. He bent and craned his neck. Aislynn asked, "Can you make a shoe for her?"

"*Si, si,* a special shoe. May she sit?" He pointed to the workbench.

"Of course."

He cleared a space and lifted Amy. She sat with straightened legs. The cobbler measured and scribbled and measured and scribbled. "It's good." He helped Amy down.

Aislynn looked at him with a question in her eyes. Shoes were costly items, and Aislynn had scant savings. She chewed her lip while she framed her question. "Mr.?"

"San Marco, Tony San Marco. And you?"

"Mrs. Maher." She dipped into a quick, perfunctory curtsy. "I'm sorry to ask, but what will the shoes cost?"

San Marco's eyes brushed across the softly rounded belly under her apron and came to rest on the shoeless Amy. "I think three dollars," he said to his bench.

Aislynn thought she heard him wrong. She paid two dollars for cheap factory-made shoes. The humiliation of poverty pressed on her. Shame washed over her. Moran and all his money dashed through her mind. *How amused he would be to see me taking charity from an immigrant.* San Marco looked up and smiled. *A very good-looking immigrant.* "Thank you so much for your kindness. When can I get them? You can see she is going without shoes right now."

"I bring them to you tomorrow evening. You write where."

Sage and Cap nursed their coffee and dawdled over their pie while Molly and Aislynn cleaned the kitchen. "What are you doin', Amy?" Cap asked.

Amy was stretched out on Smokey's back lifting his ears and dropping them repeatedly. "I'm making sure his ears get exercise."

Cap threw his hands up and looked at Aislynn. "I gave you that dog to keep you safe. But now, I'm wonderin' who's gonna keep Smokey safe?" Through the laughter, Aislynn heard a knock on the door.

"*Buonasera*, Mrs. Maher. I bring shoes."

"Mr. San Marco, please come in." Turning, Aislynn addressed Amy. "Please come greet Mr. San Marco."

The child curtsied and said, "Good evening, Mr. San Marco. You have my shoes." She clapped her hands.

"*Si.*"

"Mr. San Marco, let me introduce you to everyone." Aislynn directed him toward Cap. "This is Captain Walker, but we call him Cap."

"Howdy." Cap rose to his feet.

"May I introduce Marshal Sage?"

Sage stood and looked down on the man. "Welcome," he said without conviction.

"And this is Molly." The girl bobbed a quick curtsy.

"I have shoes." The right shoe looked like any other, but the left shoe sat on a block of wood sculpted on the top to reflect the curve of Amy's twisted foot and carved on the bottom to be level with the ground. San Marco helped Amy into a chair. Everyone stood and watched as he got on one knee and tied the shoes to the child's feet. "You walk," he encouraged.

Amy eased her feet to the floor. She stood straight with level shoulders. Aislynn gasped at the miraculous transformation. She turned to the others; they all wore expressions of wonder. Amy took a step, an almost limpless step. A sob escaped Aislynn's throat. She covered her mouth to contain her emotion, but her eyes watered. A hand came down on her shoulder. She looked into Sage's eyes and leaned into him. The wooden shoe hit the floor with a thud. San Marco addressed them all. "I fix that."

Aislynn dabbed at her eyes. "Mr. San Marco, you performed a miracle. How can I ever thank you?"

Cap waived at a chair and said, "Sit and join us for dessert."

"No, no, I stranger."

"A stranger is a friend we don't know yet. Sit down, man. We owe you far more than a piece of pie and a cup of coffee."

Amy thumped to the table and squeezed in next to her new hero. "I love my shoes. Maybe I can play at recess, now."

San Marco's forehead wrinkled at the word *recess* but nodded a polite agreement.

"So pilgrim, where're you from?" Cap asked.

He told the same story as most who had crossed the Atlantic. He explained his emigration from a hill town in northern Italy. The men in his family had been cobblers for generations. His great-grandfather crafted shoes for a duke. His village was very poor and the stories of America very rich. He saved enough to pay for his fare and landed in New York. Hearing stories about gold in the West, he decided men with such wealth would want good, handmade shoes. "So here I come."

"And you settled just three blocks from us," Aislynn added.

San Marco's eyes brightened. He beamed at everyone around the table. Aislynn noticed Sage did not smile in return.

CHAPTER 19

A ISLYNN read aloud.
  September 6, 1870
The Wyoming Tribune. "A Matron's View of Women's Suffrage."

> *Dear Editor,*
>
> *I just don't believe in these new women notions. I raised six boys, four of them vote now, and the other ones will soon be old enough. Now these good-for-nothing women, who have fooled their time away and never raised a single boy, come around and want every woman to vote for herself. I don't believe in this nonsense. I have raised my six boys, and I am going to have each one of my sons vote for me. These women who go lecturing around the country instead of raising boys have no business to vote anyway. Why were they not raising boys to vote for them? I will not be cheated out of my six votes.*
>
> *All women should have their men vote for them. If women go to vote, they'll humiliate their husbands and fathers. They will lay waste to the family. Unlike men, the women of Wyoming are not capable or qualified to vote, nor should we venture to indecent*

places like the polls where drunk and disorderly vagrants could disgrace us and bring us harm. All good Christian women should behave like good Christian women and not vote.

Dear Readers,

Is the matron right or wrong? Wrong, of course. These women who intend to vote are not man haters, quite the contrary. You claim Wyoming's women are not capable of voting. Our women came here and established new lives doing yeomen work alongside their men. Yet, they continued to fulfill their roles as God intended: good Christian wives and mothers. They meet this new responsibility with dignity, which will strengthen their families' respect.

Polling places will be decent forums when populated by the virtuous Wyoming woman. We predict drunkenness and violence will cease. The paid voters shipped here from Colorado will disappear and their absence will raise up the quality of our elected officials' ethical and moral standards. If fact, we are sure our women will send the right man to Washington, DC, to represent our interests. By giving women the vote, our wise Republican governor is maintaining the true spirit of our republic—equal representation for each American—and the noble men of Wyoming stand behind him.

Yay, good matron, you may have claim to six votes for yourself, but won't you be Christian and find generosity in your heart to grant your sisters one each?

The Editor

Aislynn folded the paper and placed it in the center of the table. "Thank goodness the *Tribune* has such a reasonable and rational editor."

Sage looked up from his breakfast. "He's a man."

Aislynn winked at Molly. "Well, when they make a good strong effort, men can be as reasonable and rational as women."

Sage responded with dismissive puff of air.

"Amy, you're going to be late for school today. Do you know why?"

"No."

Trying to appear strong and in control of her fears, Aislynn said, "You, Molly and Emmie are going to watch the women of Wyoming make history. Women all around the world have fought and suffered for the right to make laws. We will be the first in the nation to vote in a national election. No other women are voting today, just us."

Bewildered, the child said, "But the marshal makes the law."

Amused, Sage said, "You are one smart girl."

"Hmph." Aislynn's mouth stretched into a straight line. "He thinks he does."

Like most women in the territory, Aislynn knew the election was more important than the voters. Unlike states that took care of themselves by voting for laws and appropriations in the House and the Senate, territories were like children with distant parents. They needed money to develop roads and irrigation ditches. They needed laws that allowed land grants and development of natural resources. However, the territories had no votes in either house. They were granted one delegate who could lobby for their causes but not vote.

Aislynn and her friends believed Wyoming needed a man in Washington with connections to the party that ruled the

White House and the Congress—the Republicans. Judge William T. Jones held the full support of the Wyoming Republicans, while the Democrats experienced a breach within their ranks. The well-respected Cheyenne resident Thomas Murren lost his party's support to a new resident from Colorado, John Wanless. This split gave faithful Republicans like Sage and Cap hope for their candidate's victory.

Both of Aislynn's men held key roles in the voting process. Cap was responsible for checking voter registrations with Justice Howe. The two ballot boxes, marked *male* and *female*, were under Sage's protection. He would ensure they were empty and padlocked when he placed them in a street-level window at the City Hall. He and County Clerk F. E. Addoms would watch the voters drop their ballots in the boxes. They would unlock them when the polls closed and the counting began.

Aislynn and Amy waited for Joan at Maggie's store. All talk centered on the election. Emmie threw her head back, pleading to the heavens. "I can't wait for this voting to be over. Then, we can get back to talking about important things like clothes and dances."

"I think it's simply a disgrace for Democrats to run a man against Mrs. Pickett for county clerk. She's a widow," Maggie declared. "And Mrs. Arnold would be perfect as a superintendent of schools. How could they be so unchivalrous?"

Paul's voice rose from behind the main counter. "If you want to vote and run for office like men, you have to expect the same treatment as men."

"Oh, who cares?" Emmie moaned.

Bells clanged as Joan burst through the door. "What a fine day for the women of Wyoming!" Joan flung her arms open to her friends.

"I'm so glad you're here. I'm getting weak-willed," said Maggie.

"If you're afraid, don't vote," Emmie suggested.

"Don't vote?" Joan's eyes popped open with defiance. She strode across the store and reprimanded Emmie. "You are a frivolous girl. Don't you realize men and women fought and died for the right to vote? After the revolution, John Adams declared we would be 'a nation of laws, not men.' Yet, even though his own wife asked him not to forget the ladies, the founders created a government of men."

Joan's agitation increased. "Do you know what women have suffered for the privilege we are being granted today? They have been humiliated, beaten and imprisoned." She placed her hand on her heart. "Today we are a part of a new revolution. Today we show the nation and the whole world the women of Wyoming can shoulder the weight of this civic responsibility. Today, we don the mantle of governing." Joan turned to Maggie with fire in her eyes. "Today, we all vote!"

Trying to absorb Joan's bravado and hide her own fears, Aislynn agreed. "Let's show the world the women of Wyoming are strong, courageous and can do anything men can."

"Only better." Molly's hands rushed to her mouth as if covering her candor.

A woman at the counter turned and faced the group. Her worn dress stretched to near splitting over her swollen belly. She had an infant balanced on one hip and three other young children exploring the store. She grabbed her basket of groceries from Paul. "Let's go," she called to her youngsters. As they trooped out the door, the mother stopped. She turned to the voters. "Let me know when you pass a law that allows women to refuse their husbands."

The women stood in silent shock at her frankness.

Joan spoke up, "Come with us and vote."

"I'm not allowed." The door slammed shut.

"You see, Emmie, that's why women need a voice." With a sweep of her shawl, Joan announced, "Let's enter the arena with our heads held high. If we look like we're brave, they'll think we're brave."

"Isn't Paul coming with us?" Molly asked with a twinge of a plea.

"I'll go later. If I go with you, who will keep the store open?" Paul explained.

"That means we're going without an escort?" Her tone expressed her fear.

"There's strength in numbers." Joan grabbed Molly's hand, and the six stepped into the street. With their skirts in their hands, they walked together. "Half a league, half a league, half a league onward," Joan quoted from "The Charge of the Light Brigade."

Emmie balked. "Didn't most of them get killed?"

Joan shot her a disapproving frown. "The point is they did their duty, and we are going to do ours."

They turned left off 18th Street onto Eddy. They paused when they saw knots of men assembled in the front of several saloons.

"Keep walking," Joan ordered.

As they approached each group of unsteady men, the tipplers stepped aside, touched their hats and bobbed their soggy heads.

"What's happening?" Emmie asked.

Maggie's head whipped back and forth, her eyes watching both sides of the street. "It might be a trap."

Aislynn caught the odor of beer and sweaty men; her pace slowed.

The women saw a thick crowd of men, perhaps one hundred masculine souls, milling about in front of City Hall a few blocks away.

"Oh, no," Molly groaned.

"Goodness, we'll be molested." Maggie's voice filled with fear.

The word chilled Aislynn's blood and her feet stopped moving. With shallow breaths, quivering lip and frantic eyes, Aislynn turned to Joan. "I can't."

"Sage is there." Joan tried to calm her.

"He's inside. He can't see all those men."

"They're drunk and dangerous. We should go back." Emmie whined in a voice thick with fear.

Their apprehension vibrated through the air, and it shook Amy. "I want to go home."

"Stop it. Stop it all of you." Joan turned to face them. "Nothing will ever change if we don't make it change." She addressed Maggie and Aislynn. "Do you want these girls to live in a world where men make all the rules? Where they can beat you? Where they can take your children?"

Joan's words shocked Aislynn. For a moment, she wondered if Joan could see inside her mind and had uncovered her fears of Liam.

"Men make all the laws. They talk about liberty and freedom and rights; yet we don't have them." Joan's eyes shined with anger. "Frederick Douglass said, 'Who would be free themselves must strike the blow.' I'm going on without you." Joan raised her skirt a bit higher and stomped over the ruts in the street. She turned back and shouted, "He also said, 'There is no change without struggle.' "

Thoughts of Molly, Virginia, Amy's mother and the woman in the store pecked at Aislynn's resolve. She heard

Sage's words repeating in her mind. *Don't teach Amy to be afraid.* Her stomach churned with dread, but she looked at Amy and saw the future. She stiffened her spine and shouted, "Wait, Joan, wait. We're coming." She grabbed her skirt in one hand and Amy's hand in the other.

At the corner of 17th Street, Mrs. Aruba P. Noteware, an 80-year-old pillar of Cheyenne society, waved at them and tottered alone toward the polls. Aislynn and her friends watched in awe. Mrs. Noteware approached the crowd with trembling steps. The men on the edges reverently removed their hats. They cleared a wide path to allow the respected lady to exercise her right to vote. Like Moses parting the Red Sea, she walked to the polls.

Joan rushed into the open aisle and the others followed. The men placed their hats over their hearts and bowed. Mrs. Noteware approached the table where Justice Howe and Cap checked their list of registered voters. Judge Nagle handed her a ballot. She made her marks quickly. When the matron arrived at the window, Aislynn could see Sage standing behind the boxes. Mrs. Noteware dropped her ballot in the box labeled *female.* Three loud hurrahs erupted from the men. Relief and pride replaced Aislynn's fear.

Emboldened, she followed Joan and greeted the judges. "It's a grand day, Mrs. Maher," Justice Howe said.

"I will admit I had my doubts about the reception we'd receive, but this . . . ." Aislynn looked around at the men. "I'm nearly speechless."

"Now that's newsworthy." Cap grinned at Howe.

The justice spoke, "We didn't know how the men would react. Perhaps they see the change that's coming to the West and know it's good for everyone. They've done themselves proud. However, so have all you women, who braved the unknown."

Aislynn moved on to Judge Nagle's table. He handed her a ballot. "This little paper is a potent weapon against oppression and wrongdoing. Use it wisely."

"Thank you." Aislynn smiled but her hand trembled under the gravity of his words. The candidates' names stared up at her: bold, block letters on an off-white background, Republicans and Democrats, men and women. She marked each line with care, not wanting to make a mistake.

Aislynn left Amy with Cap. Ahead, she saw the box marked *female* and the men lining the gauntlet. Absent were the expected insults, sneers, shoving and pawing. She closed her eyes and heard her father's dense, Irish accent.

You and your children will have American stories, and they will be better than any sorrowful Irish tales. At the end, you will be strong and independent, and no one will hold you down or deny you freedom.

She swallowed the thick emotion swelling in her throat and filling her eyes. She looked upward. *Da, I've done so many things to shame you. I hope you're proud of me today.*

Reaching the window, she bobbed a curtsy to Sage and dropped her ballot in the *female* box. When her eyes met his, he gave her a rare, wide smile.

Molly and Amy slept while Aislynn mended clothes in front of the fire, struggling to stay awake. A key in the door brought Aislynn to her feet and sent the mending to the floor. Cap grabbed Aislynn and danced her around the floor. "I presume the Republicans won, and you've had a few too many," she said.

"Governor Campbell, Justice Howe, and our own Marshal Sage are vindicated. The Republican Jones is on his way to Washington." Cap grabbed her face and planted a wet kiss on her forehead. "We're safe. There's good times ahead."

Aislynn touched her belly. Moran's shadow crossed her mind. *Oh please*, she prayed silently, *let that be true.*

CHAPTER 20

With Christmas less than one week away, baking, cooking and decorating Sage's home took Aislynn's attention away from the spurts of pain nagging at her for the past week. She believed the baby should have arrived at the end of November. The doctor dismissed her calculations with, "Women always think they know when they will deliver; however, the baby decides when it's ready." He declared the baby healthy and assuaged her fears about the pains and late date.

Despite the imminent birth and all the holiday preparations, normal household chores continued to call on a daily basis. Laundry for the ladies fell on Tuesdays. Before stepping out to meet the frigid morning air, Aislynn pulled on her coat and tied her shawl around her protruding belly. Armed with two buckets, she waddled to the corner well. Smokey kept his distance as the icy water sloshed in every direction all the way home. Gloves provided small protection from the frigid water burning her clenched hands.

When she entered the house, she wondered why the water running into her boot felt warm. She deposited the pails on the stove and pulled up her dress. Her underdrawers showed a damp stain and a small patch of blood.

"Smokey, we better get the doctor." Aislynn started for the door. An intense pain sliced her from hip to hip. She crumbled to her knees. The shock made her take short, sharp breaths. Studying the floor, she rethought the long walk to the doctor's office.

Once the pain passed, she struggled to her feet. "Maybe we can find someone in the street who will get the doctor." She looked out the door. Nothing moved. Blank warehouse walls stared at her. She knew the Darnells would not be home, so she set her sights on Mr. Bigelow's.

Aislynn held her coat closed at her neck and stepped out into the chill. She shuffled the four hundred feet, hoping the man would be home or someone braving the cold would wander by. At Bigelow's door, another pain cut through her. She doubled over and held the icy doorknob for support. "Mr. Bigelow!" she screamed. "Mr. Bigelow!" The wind blew her voice down the street. The pain passed. She pummeled the door. Silence answered her. She tottered home, trying to arrive before another pain seized her.

She made her way to the alcove; another pain struck. Aislynn slid to the floor. This time she leaned against the bed and stretched out her legs. The pain shooting through her thighs forced her to roll up on her knees. She rested her chin on the bed and her breathing slowed. With a few long, deep breaths, her body relaxed. She turned to find Smokey's head next to hers and his sad eyes commiserating with her pain.

Her birthing box waited in the bottom drawer. As soon as the pain passed, Aislynn placed the box on the bed and unpacked its contents: a square piece of canvas that had been waterproofed with beeswax, three towels, two washcloths, string, a pair of scissors, some baby diapers and two small, yellow, wool blankets. Aislynn pulled back the quilts and laid the canvas over the sheet. She spread a towel on the dresser and piled everything else next to it. She made her way to the stove where the laundry water boiled. She shoved the pails to the side, off the main flame. After dipping the scissors and cleaning them, she laid them on the towel.

Another pain ripped through her. Steadying herself on the dresser, she returned to her kneeling position. Smokey sat at her side. She draped her arms around the big dog and began a rhythmic rocking. Unconsciously she matched her breathing to the swaying, and the pairing offered some relief.

When she could stand, Aislynn shed her bulky layers of clothing and slipped into a short nightgown made for the delivery. Her robe and slippers followed. Suddenly, the urge to walk moved her feet. With short, shaky steps, she propelled herself around the room, moving from the bed, to the rocker, stopping at each piece of furniture to steady herself. The contractions repeated. *Either I'm getting tired or they're lasting longer.*

She made her way to the stove, filled a bowl with some boiled water and placed it on the dresser. Aislynn lay on the bed and reviewed the birthing pamphlet. Once she completed all the steps the book prescribed, she waited and worried.

Aislynn tried to talk herself calm, but her thoughts wandered to her mother's death in childbirth. She remembered a woman who died on the wagon train. She lay back on the bed and thought of her first child. A heavy sadness fell on her as she envisioned the tiny boy resting in her hands. With him, she had help from Moran's housekeeper.

The memory brought Liam into focus. In the deep recesses of her mind, she still clung to an impossible fantasy. She acknowledged the kind, caring Liam and imagined him tracking her down. Aislynn saw him standing at her door looking dapper and handsome, armed with apologies and promises. "I love you and miss you. Come home." With one deep kiss, all their disagreements were resolved. Then, she would say, "I have something wonderful to tell you." He would rejoice at the news, confessing he really did want a family. Then he would say something like, "Our children will go to the best boarding schools and the finest colleges."

She would reply, "I don't want to send my children away." From there the dream always deteriorated into a disagreement.

In the quiet of the shack, the sound of the clock seemed to grow louder. She listened to it, taking long, slow breaths between each tick. The baby was not waiting for help to arrive.

A loud moan resulting from another contraction brought Smokey to her side. He climbed on the bed, dropped his head on her leg and tried to comfort her. Aislynn made her decision. "Maybe the pain has stolen my sense, but you can't do anything else to help me." Aislynn struggled to the door and swung it wide. "Get Sage, Smokey. Go to the jail; get Sage." He looked up at her with a sad expression. The dog stepped into the cold and turned back. Aislynn pointed. "Sage, Sage." Smokey walked through the door, gave Aislynn another forlorn look and trotted away. She closed the door and locked it. *Sending that dog into the cold was either really smart or very cruel,* she thought.

She rubbed her forehead and asked the empty room, "Why do things always have to be so hard?" She remembered discussing babies with Moran. He insisted on a good hospital in San Francisco. "But I wanted to have my babies at home," she told no one. "I am such a fool. Well, I'm getting my wish. I'm having my baby at home without a doctor, without a husband, without a friend. I even sent my dog away." Another contraction pushed her self-flagellation to the back of her mind. She doubled over moaning, "God, please help me."

Like riding through a storm, Aislynn returned to bed as the pains continued to buffet and batter her. She writhed and moaned with each passing wave. A pressure built across her back. "That's wrong," she told the baby; "you need to move down." Aislynn got up on her knees and pressed on her belly. "Go this way," she pleaded. *Why don't women speak of childbirth? How much easier it would be if I knew what to expect.* Her whole body swam in pain. She fell forward on her hands with her belly hanging like an udder. The pressure on her back eased. Poised on all fours like an animal ready to spring, Aislynn waited for the next surprise. When the contraction came, her arms collapsed, leaving her on her elbows with her face on the bed.

The sound of a key in the lock brought Aislynn's head up. The door crashed open. Sage stood in the doorway with his guns drawn. His eyes flashed across the cabin and landed on Aislynn. "What the hell . . . ? You need the doc?"

"I don't think there's time. I'm so glad you're here. I was afraid I'd have to do this alone." Sage's face showed the slightest hint of doubt. "You have done this before." It was more of a question than statement.

He puffed up. "Sure, course. Lots of times," he announced with a bravado that did not sound convincing.

Aislynn rolled on her back. "With a human?"

"A time or two."

Her fears of losing her baby and her life filled her eyes. She looked toward heaven. She asked, "Why, God? Why?"

"Don't know why you're frettin' so," Sage said, dismissing her concern. "Squaws have babies alone on the prairie every day."

"Unfortunately, I'm not a squaw; I've had no tribe of women to prepare me for this."

"You're young and strong. You'll do just fine."

Another pain stole her words and redirected her attention. The baby began pushing down. The relief from its change of direction was short-lived. Aislynn felt her opening stretch. She reached between her legs and touched the wide gap. Aislynn lay back, unsure what to do. As the baby pressed down, it frayed her skin, setting it ablaze. "I'm burning!" she cried. "I can't do this!"

"It's too late for that!"

"I'm splitting in two!"

Sage dipped his head and studied the space between her legs. "Looks like you're holdin' up in one piece. Just a bit of blood. I see his head."

Aislynn gasped. "How do you know it's a boy if you can only see its head?"

"I don't, but if you'd do your job, we'd know pretty quick."

Aislynn whined, "Why is it my job?"

"Now you're just askin' stupid questions."

A stroke of pain made Aislynn roar. "I'm tearing apart!"

"Jeez, stop yammerin' and get on with it. He's comin'."

Remembering the pamphlet's instruction, she ordered, "Wash your hands, get a towel and grab it."

Aislynn tried to listen to the baby's signals. She pushed, clenching her teeth and screeching. She pushed and pushed again. Sage caught the baby. She struggled up on her elbows.

"Don't move," he ordered.

"I want to see."

"Stay still! His leg is twisted in the cord. I gotta slip it off." Sage moved gently and deliberately. She could feel him free the baby.

His words repeated in her mind. *"His leg." A boy? I expected a girl.*

Sage placed the baby on Aislynn's belly and covered him with the towel. When she cleaned out his mouth, he coughed. She started to rub his back. The tiny bluish boy began to turn pink as he breathed steadily. Aislynn peered down at his fluff of pale, blond hair. He fluttered his dark blue eyes. "His cheeks are spotted red."

"You'd be red, too, if you just shot out of a hole that small." Sage peeked under the towel to examine the baby. "Let me see. He's fine. Got all his parts in the right places. See if he'll take your breast."

Embarrassment rushed over her. In a blink, she recognized she had no more secrets from this man. She opened her gown. With a bit of coaxing, the baby latched onto her nipple.

"Cord stopped pulsin'. I'll tie it off now."

When the placenta began its descent, Aislynn clutched the baby to her chest. The pain from the afterbirth took her breath. The bloody mess ripped through her vagina; her insides seemed to be turning out. Its smell fouled the room. Sage offered to wrap up the canvas and burn it. "I'll get you some warm water. You clean up and get some clothes on. I'll wipe this little fella off."

Aislynn slowly dropped her legs over the side of the bed, testing their strength. She grabbed a diaper and placed it between her legs. With a damp washcloth, she wiped off the remnants of the birth. She placed the washbowl on the floor and straddled it. After dipping the diaper in the pitcher's warm water, she squeezed it gently against her raw vagina. The stinging sent a shock through her body and a moan from her mouth. Bits of blood and mucus washed away. A clean nightgown, her warm robe and another diaper resting securely between her thighs allowed Aislynn to feel rejuvenated.

Settled under the quilts, she bent her knees and rested her baby on her thighs. Sage handed her a cup of sweet tea and stood over them. "Isn't he beautiful?" she asked in a voice filled with delight.

"Yes, he's beautiful." Sage's voice took on an indulgent tone.

Excitement filled Aislynn's voice. "Do you want to sit and look at him?" She saw a question form on his face. Embarrassed, she turned back to the baby. "I'm sorry, I'm so delirious with happiness; I'm being silly." She looked up. "Thank you for helping me, yet again, but you don't have to stay." She choked on the final words. Her joy slipped into sadness and loneliness. She swallowed her self-pity as Sage walked to the door. He threw the lock. Aislynn watched with wonder as he returned.

He took the cup out of her hand and said, "Shove over."

Sage sat next to Aislynn and removed his boots. He stretched his long legs over the covers and sat with his arms crossed. "What are you gonna call him?"

"Brendan, after my father, and John, after Johnny." Her heart yearned to have those loved ones near.

"Whites just slap a name on a child. Injuns, like the Osage, got a whole ceremony. Takes a few days."

"The Catholic Church has baptism."

"This ain't anythin' like that. It's bound to nature. It ties the child between the earth and the sky." Sage huffed. "You're a city girl; you wouldn't understand."

"You could try explaining. Despite what you think, I'm not totally stupid."

He dipped his head and looked at her with doubtful, lowered brows. "The Osage lived up in the stars until the sun appeared. Then, they came to the earth to live their lives like the path of the sun." He moved slightly to face Aislynn. "It's like this; the child sits in the east, like he's sittin' now, but he looks west, like the sun does every morning." He turned Brendan to face him. Sage straightened his arm toward the east and arced it over his head. "The ceremony gives him a life path that will rise in beauty, move with brightness and go down peacefully."

"That's lovely. Thank you." Aislynn petted her boy. "I hope he takes that exact path in life. But, when does the baby get a name?"

"There's a whole lot of other chantin', prayin' and promises. In the end, parents get to pick from names the tribe gives them."

"Since Brendan and John aren't among them, I'll get him baptized, too."

"Not considerin' *Liam*?"

"No, he chose to miss a life with me and, consequently, our child. Johnny had no choice. Goodness, I can't imagine how excited he would have been." Aislynn kissed Brendan and continued, "At times I feel guilty about Liam, but then I wonder if he feels guilty about leaving me flat. He had to know Brendan was possible, but he walked out that door and never looked back."

"The man's a fool and a snake."

"It's just as well that he doesn't want us. We don't want him." Silence settled for a moment until Aislynn confided, "I have lain awake some nights worrying myself to near distraction that Liam will come and take my baby away. Now that he's here, and he's someone I can see and touch, I'm afraid I'll be even more wary."

Sage stroked Brendan's hand. The baby clutched his long finger. Sage gave the child a full smile. "Don't you worry about this boy." In a tone that could melt a man's bones Sage said, "Liam wouldn't live long enough to take Brendan."

Tiny flakes of guilt and fear floated through in her mind. Aislynn knew if Liam ever came for Brendan, she would need Sage's protection. While she no longer wanted Liam in her life, she did not want him dead. "Maybe we could just scare him enough to make him leave us alone."

"That'll be up to him."

Aislynn did not want to think about Liam or losing Brendan. She pushed Liam Moran into the crowded space in her mind labeled *Things to Forget*. She ran her finger over Brendan's tiny mouth. It twisted into a partial pout. His chubby cheeks hung down like an old man's jowls. She gave them a gentle pinch. Sage interrupted her reverie. "Guess you'll be lookin' for a man now?"

The question surprised her. "Pfft. Certainly not." Paraphrasing something Sage had once told her, she said, "There are only two things a woman wants from a man: to trust that he will be there when she needs support." She nudged him. "I have you for that, and I do not want a man for the other thing."

"Without a man, how're you gonna get the other thing?"

"Orrin Sage, I just spent over an hour in excruciating pain because of the other thing. I don't want or need that ever again."

Sage leaned toward her. "But that's how you got *him*."

"He and Amy are quite enough for a woman alone."

Sage's glance fell on the baby, and he shook the finger Brendan held. "You know you ain't alone."

"I know and I am grateful for you and all you've done for me, for us." Aislynn placed her hand on his and Brendan's. "As Amy says, you are my bestest friend."

Sage suppressed his usual dismissive response to her displays of tender emotions with a nod and a grin.

Aislynn recaptured her joy. "Everyone is going to be so excited that he's here. He's the best Christmas gift we could ever get."

"Sure thing."

"Wait until they hear about our heroic dog." She looked past Sage at Smokey sleeping by the stove. "He's going to get a very big bone once I'm up and about."

"Ain't you makin' dinner?"

"I was just going to compliment you on your performance today, but I can see that your chivalry doesn't last very long."

"What? Just look what I did."

"What you did?"

He spoke to Brendan. "If it weren't for me, you probably wouldn't be here."

"I believe I was involved, my son," she whispered. "My precious, precious son." She lifted the child to her face and took a deep breath. Aislynn offered Brendan to Sage. "Inhale. That's what love smells like."

Amy arrived home first. The little girl clambered up on the bed and touched every exposed inch of the baby. "Is he my brother?"

"I suppose he's your brother in the same way I'm your mother and Molly is your sister." Aislynn placed her hand on Amy's cheek. "Families form in many ways. Ours is growing out of love." She kissed the little girl's forehead.

Aislynn recounted the story of Smokey retrieving Sage. "If it weren't for Smokey, the baby and I might not be here."

"My dog is a hero?"

"He saved our lives," Aislynn said. Amy jumped off the bed and caught Smokey in a full-body hug.

Sage stood over Brendan and Aislynn wearing a petulant frown. "She forgot to tell you I delivered the baby."

"Uh-huh." Amy rubbed her chin on Smokey's head. "But you wouldn't have been here if Smokey hadn't found you."

"I can see I ain't gonna get any credit."

Aislynn looked up at him. "I *said* thank you."

"He's a beautiful boy, Aislynn, a fine addition to our family. I want to thank you for lettin' me be a part of it," Cap said.

"It wouldn't be much of family without you."

"We wouldn't have a family if you hadn't come here." Cap leaned close to Aislynn's ear. "I know you came here carryin' a heavy sorrow, but I hope the joy you've brought us spills over and lightens your load."

Amy met Molly at the door, bursting with the good news.

"A boy and you did it all by yourself?" Molly squeezed Aislynn's hand.

Frustrated, Sage threw his hands in the air. Aislynn repeated the story and credited Sage with his part. Satisfied, he and Cap made their excuses and left the ladies to themselves.

Molly held Brendan, rocking him slowly, and gushed over him. "I can't wait to have my own baby."

"Take your time, Molly. You're young and there's no rush."

When the men returned for the dinner Molly had prepared, they carried a surprise. Cap had stumbled upon a discarded cradle in an alley and restored it back to usefulness. They carried it in and placed it between Sage's chair and the fireplace. "He'll be warm and within reach," Cap said.

"It's beautiful." Aislynn began pushing herself up to get off the bed. Sage rushed to her side. Holding her arm, he led her to his seat. Aislynn stroked the shiny wood. Molly placed Brendan in the bed, and Sage rocked it with his foot. "Thank you," she said softly. "It's perfect."

Maggie, Paul and Emmie visited after dinner, bringing small gifts and lots of excitement. Brendan passed through everyone's arms until he reached Sage. The big man took the tiny infant and retreated to his chair. While the group chattered away at the table, Sage sat silently studying the child. An expression of wistfulness settled on his face. Aislynn thought he was back in time, in another place, with another baby.

The following day a parade of well-wishers visited Aislynn and Brendan. Mrs. Howe and Mrs. Kingman arrived together. They gave the baby a generous gift of a silver rattle. To Aislynn, their visit legitimized the child, dispelling the nasty rumors that Sage was his father. Several matrons of Cheyenne society followed them with good wishes, compliments and tokens. Their appearance cemented Aislynn's and Brendan's social standing.

Joan bustled through the door in the late afternoon. She assessed Brendan. "Like most newborns, he has a large pointy head. He's awfully pale, and his hair is like goose down. He must take after his father."

Aislynn held her tongue.

"He's also a bit splotchy."

"I was told that happens when a birth goes rapidly."

"Little more than an hour, I heard."

"Yes."

"Bravo to you for getting it done and out of the way."

"Yes, it was quick, but not easy. I was panicked thinking I would have to deliver him myself, but Sage arrived just in time."

"Again, he is your knight. At least we know he's good for something."

Aislynn dipped her head to the side wearing a contented grin. "He's good for a lot of things."

Joan straightened with alarm. "You're not getting soft on Sage?"

"Of course not," Aislynn replied with questionable conviction.

Joan became somber. "Do you feel the need for a husband now?"

"At times, I feel very alone and afraid. I have two children and no job. My only income comes from Utah, when my mother-in-law makes enough to send me some. Then I remember I have Molly, Amy, Sage and Cap helping me. So I cycle round and round. I'm like a wheel."

Joan wisely shared, "A man won't necessarily make it easier."

Aislynn nodded, thinking of Liam. "I know that."

Shortly after dinner, they heard a soft knocking on the door. Mr. San Marco called to congratulate everyone on the family's new addition. He *ooed* and *ahhed* over Brendan. "I make a gift for *bambino*." San Marco presented Aislynn with a pair of soft, white leather booties.

"They are adorable. Thank you so much."

"I wish the best," he said, bowing to Aislynn.

"Won't you join us for some coffee?"

The cobbler joined the table and the small talk. Listening to the conversation, an idea struck Aislynn. "Mr. San Marco, do you attend mass at St. John the Baptist Church?"

"*Si, si.*"

"Will you be going to mass on Sunday?"

"*Si, si.* Saturday night and Sunday morning."

"If you don't have any commitments, Mr. San Marco, perhaps you'd consider joining our Christmas celebration after church. Several other friends will be joining us as well."

"I do not belong," the cobbler explained.

"There's room for everyone," Cap announced.

Without a word, Sage rose. He took Brendan from Aislynn's arms and sat in his chair by the fire.

CHAPTER 21

CHRISTMAS in Cheyenne fell between Aislynn's experiences in New York City and Treasure Mountain. In New York City, the ornate, stone church welcomed the faithful with a billowing organ, a sonorous choir and a wispy fog of spicy incense. Extravagance prevailed. The bishop presided, wearing grand vestments embroidered with golden threads. His attendants stood beside him in bright, colorful robes. The black-and-white-clad altar boys shuffled around them like chess pieces.

At Treasure Mountain, Utah, Christians of all stripes gathered in Aislynn's simple, frame restaurant to celebrate the holiday. Here, the scents of bacon and coffee replaced the incense. Inexpensive white candles glowed on the windowsills. An evergreen stood in the corner adorned with trinkets contributed by her customers. A few tunes resembling hymns squeaked from a fiddle while Tim performed an unofficial version of the mass he had memorized while serving at the altar as a boy. A bit of bread and a sip of wine substituted for the consecrated host.

As a religious building, Cheyenne's spare, white, wooden church ranked above her restaurant but fell far below the Church of the Transfiguration. Father Gilhooley's vestments were drab and worn. However, unlike Tim, he was an ordained, legitimate priest. The parish owned a small pump organ, and an elderly parishioner, Mr. Shears, wore himself out accompanying the off-key children's choir.

Christmas mass ran longer than most. Amy tried to follow Molly's and Aislynn's movements, but the six-year-old grew bored with the rituals and begged to leave. A few stern looks quieted the child until the final *amen*.

Outside church, Aislynn met several acquaintances who congratulated her and peeked at the bundled baby. Mr. San Marco approached. After introductions and brief conversations, he offered to escort her home. Ever conscious of wagging tongues, she asked him to take Amy's hand and Molly's arm. They walked briskly through the biting cold.

Aislynn cooked all the dishes on the big stove at her house, and the men rushed them to Sage's larger space on O'Neil Street. A discarded door Cap discovered near City Hall was scrubbed and strapped on top of Sage's dining table. Paul, Maggie and Emmie brought extra chairs and squeezed them around the enlarged table. Joan arrived with a fruitcake in hand. Mr. San Marco contributed a bottle of wine. While Aislynn completed her preparations for the meal, Tommy Two Hawks slipped through the back door. At the sight of the Indian, an alarmed Mr. San Marco reached under his suit jacket. Aislynn saw the hilt of a knife. When Sage welcomed the young man, the weapon returned to its secret home.

With everyone seated, Aislynn began the procession of food. A chicken noodle soup provided a filling yet inexpensive start. Two shiny hens with a coating of fat and bursting with potato stuffing entered center stage to much applause. Applesauce, green peas and Maggie's raisin biscuits accompanied the bird. A bowl of nuts followed the entree. Coffee, Joan's fruitcake and a pie baked by Emmie completed the meal. Lively discussions, gossip and laughter punctuated the two-hour feast.

The ladies cleared and washed the dishes, while the men remained at the table puffing on cheap cigars. Cap pulled himself up from the table and produced an ornate, brown glass bottle. "I've been savin' this for years, hopin' for a reason to use it." He filled everyone's glasses with the brandy. "Now, I've got lots of reasons." As he surveyed the group with his glass held high, he said, "To my family."

With all the dishes done, the ladies rested by the fire. Aislynn withdrew to the bedroom to change Brendan. She returned to a rearranged room. The chairs stood against the walls, and the door leaned on the dining table that had been shoved to a corner. Emmie announced, "It's a dance floor."

Sage retreated to a corner and reclined in a dining chair. He reached out to Aislynn and said, "I'll take him." She handed Brendan into his arms and joined the others waiting in the center of the room.

Cap pulled out his squeezebox and shouted, "Square off!"

Paul paired with Maggie and Molly with Tommy. Emmie's enthusiasm visibly faded when Mr. San Marco took Aislynn's hand. Joan pulled Emmie into her corner. Aislynn winced and moaned as she started to lift Amy to her hip. San Marco transferred the child to his shoulders.

Cap struck a note and made a call. "Bow to your partner." He played a few more notes. "Say 'hi' to your neighbor." Everyone turned and bowed to the person on the other side. "Circle to your right." They all joined hands, with Emmie holding Amy's to make the ring complete. Cap played on. "Circle to the left."

The dancing continued until Aislynn declared her exhaustion. She took Amy from San Marco and placed her next to Joan. "Emmie, would you partner with Mr. San Marco?"

Emmie glowed. "I'd be honored."

Aislynn walked toward Sage. He was hunched over whispering to Brendan and wearing a grin. Holding the baby seemed to transform him; he appeared relaxed and content. Watching them, she realized his happiness enhanced hers. Aislynn dropped into the seat next to him with a smile illuminating her face.

Sage raised his chin toward the dance floor. "You gotta be the schemin'est woman in the world."

Her eyes followed Emmie and San Marco. "It's called planning."

"How long have you been plannin' that?"

"Emmie's been talking about that cobbler nonstop for six weeks."

Sage studied her for a moment. "I kinda thought you had an interest in him."

"Hmm, I did, for a few minutes. He is a handsome man."

"I've noticed," he replied in a flat tone.

"But I have too many wounds to heal before I wander into that territory."

"How long's that gonna take?"

Aislynn crossed her arms and leveled a stern look. "You tell me."

Sage's face turned hard. Aislynn pointed at him. "You see that? You walk around grumbling, looking all mean and making women fear you. You terrified me when we first met," she confessed, "but I gathered my courage and got to know you. Underneath all the bluster is a very caring, kind and agreeable man."

Sage scratched his head. "Must be off my feed. Don't let that get out."

"I think you are afraid."

"I don't want no one . . . anyone. I got you."

Aislynn's eyes widened with confusion. Sage recognized it. "I mean you're keepin' house."

A renegade reply raced through her mind. *I can do more than keep house.* Since Brendan's birth, inexplicable thoughts of relations with him occasionally simmered. However, her common sense, the memories of the attack and her past mistake quickly cooled those ideas.

Aislynn watched the dancing for a moment. She found San Marco and Emmie enjoying each other's company. "It's been a wonderful day."

"I don't recall ever celebratin' Christmas. It's always been just another day."

"I'm sorry I couldn't give you a gift. You've done so much for me. You've given me my home, my son, my life."

"We're square."

"How so?"

"You gave us this." Sage nodded toward the dancers. "You know *family* is Cap's favorite word. He repeats it all the day long." A hint of exasperation colored his tone.

Brendan signaled his hunger. Rising, she took the baby, placed her hand on Sage's shoulder and left a kiss on his cheek. She whispered, "Thank you." Sensing his discomfort, she redirected their conversation. "Why don't you dance with Amy?"

"You know I don't dance."

"Afraid of that, too?" As Aislynn closed the door to the bedroom, she saw Sage hoist the little girl in his arms and spin her around the floor.

Aislynn settled on the bed and opened her shirtwaist. She withdrew the small, tightly folded letter she had hidden in her camisole. With Brendan at her breast, she laid the missive on the bed and carefully smoothed it open with her free hand until all the disappointing words were visible.

CHAPTER 22

Dear Aislynn,

I am sorry to tell you we had another fire in the restaurant. The back wall is gone. The stoves are ruined and much of our china is broken. I don't imagine you will want to rebuild. A mortgage would be needed and that may be too big a burden.

I know you'll be worrying about our incomes. Please don't. Carrie and Kathleen have wonderful husbands. They and their children are getting by just fine. I will be taken care of, too. I am marrying Mr. Murphy. Now, you knew that would be happening. He's a lovely man. After all these years, my heart is warming again. Know that with his income, we will continue to pay the mortgage on your house.

I fear from your letters, you have no thought of returning. We hear nothing from Mr. Moran. He lets Mr. Murphy manage the mine's affairs. There is little chance of you seeing him, if that is what's keeping you in Cheyenne. He has never returned to Treasure Mountain.

We miss you and long to see you. May God bless you,
Your loving Mother,
Mary

Aislynn covered her eyes with her hand. Her mother-in-law's words touched her heart. She missed her family of friends, her home and her business.

He has never returned to Treasure Mountain.

As Sage said, "A man true to his word." A hard unbending man . . .

She rested against the headboard and closed her eyes. The scene unfolded vividly.

Tim had lost Emma and their baby. Aislynn knew the despair and hopelessness he suffered; her own losses haunted her still. When the telegram arrived from his father begging for her help, she knew what she had to do.

"You can't go," Liam said without giving it a moment's thought.

"Oh, Liam." She rested her hand on his shoulder. "Can't we get married in Ogden and . . . ?"

"No, I've made plans for Sacramento. People have been notified, guests. No, we can't."

"I can't say 'no,'" she tried to explain.

"Yes, you can."

Aislynn tried again. "You've never had a relationship like ours."

He crossed his arms over his chest. "What is exactly is your relationship?"

Her hand went to her hip. Anxiety grew into anger. "You know very well. He's my friend, my family. Can't you see?"

"I see you running to him as soon as that impediment Emma is out of the way."

"It's not like that!"

"You made me a promise, Aislynn. There's not a man in this territory who wouldn't agree you're already my wife."

"I know. I intend to keep my promise."

"Then you'll 'obey' me."

The word bit into her. Johnny never demanded obedience. "Aren't loving and honoring enough?"

His "no" sounded like a threat.

He seemed to grow larger as his anger expanded. She tried to reach him, but her strength and feelings were exhausted. It seemed love, that mercurial phantom, was whirling out of the room. Aislynn fell into a chair and whispered, "You want too much."

His hands rolled into fists. His face distorted with rage. "Go to New York, Aislynn." Her name slid out like a curse. "Go to hell! But I won't come after you, and I won't be waiting here when you come back!"

The door slammed; its wood split, and she stared at it wondering why she wasn't crying.

Aislynn spoke to the paper. "No, Liam's threats were never idle."

She read the letter for a third time. The news remained the same. Losing the restaurant and the meager income it generated devastated her. Keeping house for Sage and Cap provided a roof over their heads and food on their table, but meeting the daily expenses proved more difficult.

While Brendan's demands on her wallet were few for now, Amy's were great. As winter grew colder, Aislynn had to provide heavy dresses, sweaters, a coat, hat and scarf. Her long woolies became short woolies. Her socks wore through quickly from her awkward step. Aislynn had her alternate them from foot to foot, but the repeated mending rubbed Amy's heels and gave her blisters. Their household needed soap, candles, oil, firewood, coal; the list rolled on. Although her small savings were depleting, no matter what she and the children needed, Aislynn double-checked each purchase to ensure it landed in her account. She never wanted to trespass on Sage's and Cap's generosity.

Aislynn needed a job. Without the detested Expedition, one would assume jobs would be plentiful. However, without the roughs' money pouring into the economy, business slowed at restaurants, stores and hotels, places where Aislynn might find work.

Searching the *Cheyenne Daily Leader* for jobs revealed nothing suitable for a young, widowed mother. Once a week, Cap returned to the shack after he and Smokey walked Amy to school. While Cap watched Brendan, Aislynn dashed through the frigid streets looking for help wanted signs but found nothing appropriate for her needs.

As the end of February approached, so did Aislynn's 20th birthday. Her years sounded young but felt old. When she remembered the struggles, sadness and loss, her years pulled her down like an anchor. In her memory, the joys seemed rare and blurred, drifting by like a scent on the wind. The bad recollections, steeped in the folds of her brain, floated to the surface with the slightest provocation. It seemed to her the feelings of grief and fear became a part of her body. In those moments when life distracted her, she would suddenly sense their absence and futilely hope they would never return. *No,* Aislynn thought, *my birthday is nothing to celebrate.*

In anticipation of birthday wishes from Tim, Aislynn stopped at the Cheyenne post office, a low, block building on Ferguson Street. Visitors entered through a door flanked by shelves bulging with newspapers, books and stationery. The north wall displayed numbered cubbyholes and the opposite side held a window and a husky Franklin stove. At the far end, the postmaster stood behind a counter with his stamps, packages and official paraphernalia. He greeted Aislynn formally with a, "Good morning, Mrs. Maher. I have a letter for you from New York City."

"Thank you so much. I do look forward to news from home."

Aislynn moved to the window and opened her precious epistle.

> *Dearest Aislynn,*
>
> *I will start with a heartfelt happy birthday. I am sure this will be a special one, as you share it with a very special boy. I do hope one day to have the honor of meeting your son. I must admit I am bursting to tell my family, but I hold your secret sacred.*
>
> *College is progressing well. My dean asked me to consider teaching a class to first year students in the fall. He believes it would not only be a good experience for me, it would provide necessary knowledge for a man who wants to be a school administrator.*

Aislynn closed her eyes for a moment to revel in the image of Tim running a school system. A jarring whiff of cheap cologne caught Aislynn's nose, interrupting her fantasy. Her eyes caught a woman in a worn overcoat approaching the counter. She ignored the intrusion and returned to her letter.

> *Of course, this takes no consideration on my part. I am jumping at the opportunity to teach and catch up with my baby "sister."*
>
> *My brothers are well. I may have mentioned Frank and Patsy are expecting their third child. Brian and Eileen are having their second. Michael is settled in*

the old country with Bridgette. My father and Sean bemoan his departure every day. He is such a contrary fellow; I believe it may be they are missing the income more than the man.

Your friend Virginia is flourishing. As you know, the Catholic Orphan Asylum is across the street from my home at Columbia College. She has found employment at the orphanage. She and Daniel have a room there. It is small but they feel safe. We found a doctor who is treating Daniel's ear. Some of his hearing has returned, but the doctor does not believe it will ever be fully restored. We see each other frequently and attend mass together.

A loud voice pleading with the postmaster drew Aislynn away from Tim's letter.

"It must be important. They know I can't read," the woman explained.

"I told you. I deliver the mail. I don't read it."

With a glance, Aislynn concluded the woman was a whore. Earlier in her life, like most women of her station, Aislynn feared and reviled the soiled doves. Living on the frontier taught her many lessons; don't judge a woman by her clothes or her profession was one of them. She knew these fallen women were forced into their occupation to avoid starvation or death at the hands of ruthless men. No woman chose to be raped, beaten or humiliated by the ostracism that came with prostitution.

"Just this once," she begged.

"No."

Without thinking, Aislynn spoke up. "I'll read it."

"Mrs. Maher, she's a whore."

"I know, Mr. Baker, so was Mary Magdalene and our Lord helped her." Aislynn folded Tim's note and slid it into her pocket.

"Thank you, ma'am. I won't come close to you. You won't catch nothin' from me."

"I know. May I have the letter?"

"Sure thing. Thank you so much," she said with a tear-filled voice.

Aislynn unfolded the yellowed page and skimmed to the signature. "It's from Pastor Barton."

"He knows how to write," the whore offered unnecessarily.

"*Margaret*, is that you?"

"Yes, ma'am."

"*I'm writing this for your ma. She hopes you are getting rich and will be coming home soon. You . . .*" Aislynn paused and gently disclosed, "I'm sorry this is not good news."

Margaret nodded. Her eyes stretched wide.

Aislynn continued, "*Your pa died after the new year. He took a chill and coughed himself to death. We could use your help. Come home for planting season or send some of your riches soon. Your Ma.*" Aislynn handed the sadness to the weeping woman. "I'm sorry for your loss, Margaret." Aislynn reprimanded the postmaster with a disapproving stare.

"Thank you for your kindness. If there's any way I can repay you, I'd be willin' to try." Margaret tucked the letter in her bodice.

"No need." As she watched the troubled woman walk toward the door, Aislynn saw a solution to her problem. "Margaret," she called, "I'll be here at ten o'clock tomorrow morning if you would like me to write a reply to your mother."

"You'd do that?"

"Yes, if you tell your friends I'll read and write for them at a small fee."

"Thank you, ma'am. I'll do that. I'll see you tomorrow."

"Wait one minute," the postmaster protested. Margaret hesitated. "You are not filling this post office with whores and derelicts."

"It's a public building. Anyone can walk in, get mail and read it. I'll just be the one doing the reading." Aislynn turned her attention back to the whore. "Go on, Margaret, I'll see you in the morning. Just remember to tell your friends."

Aislynn strode to the counter and squared off with a proposition forming in her mind. "I'll give you ten percent of every penny I make."

The postmaster gave her a narrow-eyed look. Aislynn waited with tight lips. "Ten percent you say? How much are you charging?"

"I haven't the faintest idea."

The postmaster stroked his chin. "How about two bits for a reading and a dollar to write a one-page letter?"

"That sounds reasonable."

"I'm in, but you can't tell a soul I'm getting a cut. I'll lose my job and so would you."

"It's a deal."

Aislynn explained her new business at dinner.

"So you ain't only gonna mix with whores, but with any illiterate rough who wants a letter written?" Sage's question sounded like a reprimand.

"In essence, yes."

"I thought you were afraid of those men?"

"I was, I am, but I'll have Smokey, my gun on display and the postmaster, Mr. Baker, to protect me."

Sage chewed slowly and glared his disapproval.

"I think it's right nice of you helpin' those who can't read or write," Cap said.

Amy piped up. "I can read and write."

"And we're real proud of you, missy." Cap patted Amy's hand.

"Did you think about your reputation? What people will say? You got two children now. You thinkin' about them?" Sage shot the questions at her.

"I'm working for them. Besides it's no different than Maggie standing behind a counter in her store. I'll be standing next to Mr. Baker, behind his counter, in a building owned by the US government. How wicked can that be?"

"I don't like it," Sage declared.

"I didn't say I liked it either. I wouldn't do it if I didn't have to. We need the money." Aislynn sighed. "I'm sorry to disappoint you. However, I do have two children. I can't work in a restaurant or a store or scrub floors at a hotel with a baby on my hip. But I can spend one or two hours a day at the post office. Hopefully, I'll make enough money to get by."

"Maybe I could get a second job," Molly murmured.

Aislynn gave Molly a firm look. "No, you work six days a week already. You are not going to work on Sundays. I'll bundle him up and—"

"He'll catch his death," Sage scolded.

"I'll stay with him for two hours a day," Cap offered. "Justice of the peace ain't a demandin' job, you know. I've got plenty of time." Cap jiggled Brendan's leg. "Him and me are great friends, right, bucko?"

Aislynn's business started with just a few readings a day. She discovered the letters to the illiterate came from people who were also illiterate. They were written by clergy, doctors, lawyers or friends. Most were addressed to men and carried the weight of tragedy and troubles. The missives exposed the intimate details of people's lives: accidents, sickness, death, failed crops, empty bank accounts and empty stomachs. Rarely did a joyful birth or news of good fortune arrive in an envelope. The messages begged for answers.

Eventually most recipients returned to send responses. The whores and men in scruffy, smelly clothes brought rough, off-white paper to fold into an envelope. The cowboys liked the milled sheets with a bit of color. Those hiding their failure in sackcloth suits under bowler hats purchased a sheet of fine linen with a matching envelope to complete the illusion of success.

The replies followed a basic script. First came the apologies for whatever sadness prompted the epistle. Next, she wrote assurances of hard work, followed by promises of rewards as soon as luck smiled. They concluded with pledges of joyful reunions.

After two weeks of letter reading and writing, Aislynn decided there were two types of men on the frontier: the responsible and the irresponsible. The responsible ventured to the frontier hoping to build better lives for their families. The irresponsible left their families for adventure, independence and the freedom to behave like fools. They came to town, flopped where they found a bed, believing they would head out to the gold fields. Once unencumbered by wives and children, they drank, whored and gambled away their savings before they could buy supplies and tools. If they found jobs, they would start saving for their mining expedition again, leaving nothing but disappointment to send home to their expectant families. She felt sorry for the responsible ones and harbored a silent disdain for the fools.

By the look of him, dirty, red-nosed and ragged, Aislynn knew the letter writer fell into the category of *fool*. "Haven't got to the gold fields, yet. Tryin' hard. Hope the garden saw you and the children through the winter," he dictated.

"How many children do you have?"

"Six."

Aislynn pressed her lips together and sat poised to continue.

"I'm includin' five dollars. Had a few setbacks, so this is all I can spare until I move on."

Her brows lowered and her eyes rolled up to meet his. "Five dollars? A few setbacks?"

The man reddened and hung his head.

A question festering in her mind suddenly strained to get out. She knew it broke the bounds of propriety, but it seemed to develop a will of its own. "What made you think you were such a lucky man that you'd come out here and hit the mother lode when so many thousands of men before you never found more than a handful of dust?"

"She said I could go."

Aislynn's frustration expanded. "She's your wife. Husbands make decisions and wives have to abide. Do you have family to help care for all those children while you chase some pipe dream?"

"No."

"And you think she *wanted* to stay in Tennessee and fend for herself and six children?"

"Ain't you just supposed to write?" Aislynn's glare compelled an answer from the man. "She agreed."

"That's the big difference between men and women. A woman would never leave her children to starve."

"I haven't had my chance yet."

"Gold fever must eat away at a man's sense, because there's nothing out there but dirt and Indians."

"I'm here and I'm givin' it a try." His voice rose with anger.
"Mr.?"

"Lambert."

"Mr. Lambert, did you marry for love?" Aislynn could see a blush beneath the filth on his face.

"Yes, ma'am."

"Go home, Mr. Lambert. Go home."

"As a failure?"

"No, as a real man who knows where he's needed. A man who knows where he's loved. Your family will be so happy to see you. They won't care if your pockets are empty."

Lambert hardened. He balled his fists and stated flatly, "I can't."

Aislynn's eyes fell on his angry hands. "Do you have anything else to say?"

He shook his head. Aislynn completed the envelope and placed the letter and the five dollars inside. Lambert fished in his pocket for the eight bits he owed her. Aislynn dropped the coins in the envelope and sealed it.

Lambert objected. "I don't want your charity."

"You're not getting it." Her foot tapped the floor.

"It's your pay."

"Yes, it's mine. I can use it to help those who need it more than me." She slapped the missive on the table.

Lambert bought a stamp and handed the letter to the postmaster. Aislynn watched him approach the door. He stopped, kneading his cap between both hands.

He turned to Aislynn. "Mrs. Maher you don't understand men at all."

"I guess we're even, Mr. Lambert. You don't understand women."

Aislynn tidied her workspace and stowed her pens and ink. She wondered whether Mr. Lambert was right. When it came to men, when it came to love, she considered herself mistaken and misguided. *When I was young, I believed I couldn't live without Tim. I was convinced I would never love Johnny. Finally, my biggest mistake—Moran.* She shook her head. *You just look at a man like that and you feel a thrill. Then, it all goes wrong.*

Aislynn hunched into her coat and wrapped her scarf around her head. *Or you meet someone who seems to be the last person in the world you would ever want, and he grows on you.* When she thought back on those days on Worth Street, she cringed. She had liked Johnny. He was a good friend, but he held no attraction for her. Yet, the more time they spent together, the more he appealed to her. And one day, she realized she loved him.

Unbidden, the memory of sitting on her bed with Sage and newborn Brendan popped into her mind. The recollection of his hip moving against hers and his breath brushing her hair made her heart rate rise. The feeling unsettled her. *It's only natural to want to be loved, to feel the comfort of an embrace, the release of rapture.* She reminded herself she was hardly marriage material for a man full of interior principals and judgments. *Why would he want a woman who whored for one man and whose person was violated by three others? A woman who lies and schemes?*

Aislynn pushed Sage out of her head, pulled up her collar and bunched it under her chin. Summoning her fundamental optimism, she thought, *I have all I need: a job and a home, and my family is safe and secure.* She bent her head and stepped out into the biting wind.

CHAPTER 23

A skim of snow fluffed on Sage's porch. Aislynn bundled Brendan in his blanket and placed him in the empty laundry basket under Smokey's watchful eyes. "The washing will wait," she told the baby. "I don't want Cap slipping and falling when he gets home. You stay in the house with Smokey while I sweep the stairs."

She stepped out into the dismal day; the door swung closed behind her. The broom swished across the boards. Coatless, Aislynn hurried her way down the stairs to make short work of the job. Climbing to the porch, her eyes caught a boy peeking around the side of the house. He wore a torn coat with a hem soaked in mud. The wilting cowboy hat with its three silver medallions revealed his identity.

"Jimmy! What are you doing here? Cattle drives don't arrive for months."

"I ain't drivin' cattle, ma'am." The boy watched his boot kicking the snow. "I'm ridin' with my brother."

Aislynn's eyes scanned the front yard. "Is he with you?"

"Yes, ma'am." Jimmy shuffled to the bottom of the steps and looked up at Aislynn. "I got big trouble."

Her shoulders slumped as she remembered Sage's prediction. Studying the scrawny, sodden child, she noticed a wide leather belt secured his pants. The grip of a revolver protruded above a broad, silver buckle. "What's happened?"

The boy hesitated. "It was all a big mistake. Andy robbed the stage and by accident, he killed the driver."

"Were you there?"

His pained eyes met Aislynn's. With a grimace, he nodded.

"Why?"

"You know I'm good for nothin'."

"That's not true." Frustration filled her voice. "Why did you join up with him?"

"Ma died." Jimmy's face tightened as he held in his tears. "Andy's all I got. 'Cept, a posse caught up with him last night." Jimmy's eyes darted all around him. "Marshal's got him in the jail."

"Here? Marshal Sage's jail?"

"Yes, ma'am. I come to ask for your help."

"Me?"

"You know the marshal; you can talk to him."

Aislynn's volume rose. "Andy killed a man! There aren't enough words in the English language that could talk your brother out of jail." She saw the drapes part in the house across the street. Mrs. Kowalski studied Aislynn and Jimmy.

The boy slowly nodded. Aislynn could see his face redden in anger. He narrowed his eyes and set his jaw. He ascended to the first step and drew his gun. Her hand slipped into her apron pocket and her fingers found her tiny pistol. Inside the house, Smokey sensed danger. He lunged at the door and began barking. The noise riled Jimmy.

"Shut up!" he screamed. Smokey's body pounded the door.

Jimmy waved his gun at Aislynn. "Andy's got a plan. I take you hostage, and the marshal will turn my brother loose."

"You're a good boy," Aislynn pleaded. "Don't get into more trouble. Go to the marshal and turn yourself in."

"No, they'll hang Andy."

"Take me hostage and they'll hang both of you." Aislynn tried a bargain. "Run; I won't tell."

"I'm no traitor. I won't leave Andy."

Smokey's barking continued; he began clawing at the door. Jimmy whipped the gun toward the house and pulled the trigger. Panicked, Aislynn screamed, "Brendan!" Her revolver spit two bullets into the boy.

Jimmy dropped his gun and collapsed on the steps. Aislynn pushed at the door. Smokey rumbled out; Aislynn rushed in. She snatched Brendan from the basket and tore off his blanket. *No blood, not even a scratch.* She clutched him to her chest. The relief coursing through her sent her swaying as she rocked her startled, whimpering child.

Smokey's snarling and Jimmy's shrieking rolled through the door. Aislynn wrapped her baby. Switching him from shoulder to shoulder, she bundled into her coat and buttoned it around them. She stepped out into the cold.

Mrs. Kowalski stood over Jimmy with his gun in her hand. Smokey straddled the boy, tearing at his pants and his bloody legs. Jimmy wailed. Aislynn stomped on the top stair and called, "Smokey! Stop!" Her foot hit the porch a second time and the dog obeyed. A crowd began to build. Aislynn sat on the step next to Jimmy. Comforting her baby with one hand, she lifted the boy's head onto her thigh with her other. "Please," she said to no one in particular, "get a doctor."

Jimmy looked up at her. Through his tears, he said, "I'm sorry, Mrs. Maher. I didn't really want to hurt anyone."

"I know." She wiped his tears with her sleeve. "Where did I hit you?"

"Got me once in the shoulder."

Sage pushed through the crowd accompanied by Deputy Winston and Sheriff Preshaw. Cap limped behind.

"I saw it all," Mrs. Kowalski said. "He shot at her and hit the house. The baby and dog were inside. She winged him."

Sage's eyes raked the boy and his hat. Understanding animated his face. His lips grew taut. His nostrils flared. A black rage darkened his grey eyes.

He offered Aislynn his hand. "It was a mistake," she tried to explain.

"Sure was." Sage pulled her up. "Get in the house."

He turned to Cap. "Stay with her."

Addressing Aislynn, he ordered, "Lock that door and don't open it to anyone but me."

"Let me explain—"

"Do as you're told!" His volume blasted her backwards. Clutching Brendan, she shrank through the door.

Aislynn heard scuffling on the porch. Jimmy screamed. In her mind, she could see Sage dragging the injured, bleeding child to jail. She wanted to run to the window and protest, but she feared Sage's wrath.

Aislynn sat in Cap's rocker and held Brendan close to her heart. The events of the last few moments collided. The bullet flying toward Brendan in the house, the shots she fired, the misguided boy weeping. She dissolved into tears.

"No use frettin'," Cap advised. "There ain't a thing you can do for that boy now."

"If Sage weren't so angry, I would have explained what happened. But he's in a rage."

"He ain't mad at you. He's scared. Don't think I've ever seen him so afraid."

Aislynn faced him. Her narrowed eyes and furrowed brow asked him a question.

"You gotta know how much he cares about you and that baby. He knows he could have lost both of you with that fool wavin' his gun. Don't think that's any small matter. He ain't as hard as he pretends to be."

Cap and Aislynn drained three cups of coffee and listened to the clock strike two hours before Sage walked through the door. She rose to meet him. He took Brendan into his arms and answered her unasked question. "He'll live to hang."

She straightened and raised her chin to challenge him. "Hang? He's just a boy."

"He's sixteen and if he's man enough to point a gun, he's man enough to face a noose."

"Doesn't he get a trial?"

"Of course, but you won't be there weepin' and pleadin' for him. We've got plenty of witnesses. Besides, he confessed. He's gonna hang."

"But I shot him," she said.

"You have no say in this. He shot first. He tried to kidnap you. He chose to give himself a man's problem, and he'll have to answer like a man."

"Can I see him?"

"No."

"He's all alone."

Sage flipped his hand at Cap. "Only a woman." He took a long breath and said, "He's dangerous." Sage dropped his heavy hand on Aislynn's shoulder and stooped to look her in the eyes. "Gal, you know you're linked to me. Half the town thinks this boy is mine. We're all linked. You, Brendan, Amy, Molly, Cap and me. If Jimmy doesn't hang, others will come. They'll come and kill or kidnap one of you to get to me, just like Jimmy. You understand that?"

He waited for his words to seep into her soft heart. When her jaw quivered and her eyes filled, Sage's hand slipped down her back. His arm circled her and her head fell against his chest. As he held her and the baby, Aislynn wished they could stay in his arms, sheltered from all the evil whirling outside their walls.

* * *

On a March morning with a shrill wind blowing as harsh as a slap, Aislynn bundled Brendan in thick blankets and suffered the frigid temperatures all the way to church. Kneeling in the dark, icy chapel, she listened to the wind moan through the rafters like the echoes of unanswered prayers. In a loud whisper, she implored God's forgiveness.

Aislynn fought the picture developing in her imagination, a terrified boy wailing as he is dragged up the steps to the gallows. The thought made her empty stomach heave. She tried to calm herself with rote prayers and bits of memorized psalms. When she recited "yea, though I walk through the valley of the shadow of death," her staccato sobs reverberated over the pews. She pleaded with God to be merciful in His realm. She knew that mercy came in short supply in hers.

CHAPTER 24

DESPITE the steady rain and cold temperatures, Aislynn and Molly took their places in the Legislative Council Room to hear the arguments for and against interracial marriage. As the heaving clouds darkened the room and screened the weak afternoon light, they shivered in the soggy scent of their wool overcoats.

Governor Campbell stood at the dais. "How much we should attempt to govern social life or taste by legislative prohibitions and restrictions is not easily answered, but there can be no doubt that intermarriage between white persons and those of other races should not be prohibited. It is well known that there have been, and probably will be, more relations between Indians and whites in this territory than between persons of all other races combined."

A barrage of shouted objections volleyed through the chamber.

"Just 'cause it's happening doesn't mean we have to condone it!"

"It's against the natural order!"

"Injuns and blacks will deplete the strength of the white race!"

"Maybe Negroes and Chinese, but not Indians!"

"We'll have a nation of half-breeds!"

Molly cringed with each disparaging word. She and Aislynn knew a strong double standard existed with sex roles. Legal or not, Campbell was correct. Many men lived with nonwhite women. However, if that precious commodity, the white woman, cohabitated with an Indian, Negro or Chinese, the result could be a lynching. Molly believed the new law would help her and Tommy.

The governor presented his argument. "We must pass this bill so couples will no longer be in violation of our laws regulating cohabitation and sexual relations outside of marriage. It will legitimize the offspring of these unions and limit the terrible ostracism these children face. They must be accepted into society. I can promise you they will contribute a great deal to the future of this territory. In fact, look around; many already do."

Aislynn thought of Sage. He was fortunate to have established his name and reputation before his parentage became public knowledge. Now, his ability to move naturally between both worlds made his place on the frontier unique and valued.

Campbell's tempered voice asked, "May we call a vote?"

All thirteen members of the legislature answered, "Aye."

Aislynn and Molly held hands and waited. Democrats controlled the legislature. Their opposition to every Republican position stood strong. Just last year, Campbell tried to pass legalization for interracial marriage, but the Democrats defeated it. A few new faces in the legislature gave Molly hope that she and Tommy would be protected. She squeezed Aislynn's hand as each vote was cast.

Democrats—nine, Republicans—four.

Molly groaned and sank into herself as the bill went down in defeat. She pulled up her scarf, hiding her heartbreak and her tears.

The two young women left the chamber. Once they were in the street, Molly lamented, "What are we to do now? Are we to always live apart?"

Aislynn wove her arm through Molly's and pulled her close. Patting her hand, she offered, "There has to be a way."

No amount of probing Sage, Justice Howe or the governor yielded a legitimate solution. There was no legal way for Molly to marry Tommy Two Hawks.

Molly's sadness stole her appetite. The quiet girl grew even more withdrawn. At night, she lay wakeful, shifting positions and exhaling long, sorrowful breaths.

Aislynn turned the lamp down until the wick became a solid bright red line. Sliding under the quilts, she nestled into the mattress, relishing the chance to rest. Through the darkness, she heard soft weeping. "Molly?" she whispered.

She replied with one labored word, "Yes."

Squinting into the darkness, Aislynn pulled all Molly's symptoms together. With a brave breath, she asked, "Are you in trouble?"

Molly cried harder, shaking the bed.

"Let's sit so we don't wake Amy."

Aislynn drew the curtains around the bed and lighted the lamp over the table.

"I'm so ashamed. I didn't want to disappoint you."

Aislynn held Molly's hands. "Please believe me. I'm in no position to judge any woman. I am not disappointed." Aislynn lifted Molly's chin. "Remember I was in love once, too. I understand."

"Do you?"

"Of course." Aislynn sat back and folded her hands on the table. "Let's not dwell on what has been done; we must think about what to do."

"Tommy said there are no laws against us in Canada."

"Canada?"

"It's north of Montana," Molly clarified.

"I know where it is." Aislynn chuckled. "It's just so far. It's another country."

"Tommy said there's not just white men married to Indian women. White women can marry Indians. He says it's our only solution. I don't want to leave, but I want to be with Tommy. I want to have our child here." Molly sniffed in her tears. "But our lives together only exist in that stable loft. We just want to come out and live like everyone else. Why can't people just leave us alone?" She leaned on the table with her head between her hands.

"I know. It's so unfair, so unchristian." Aislynn rubbed her forehead. "Let's not despair. We'll ask Sage and Cap for their ideas."

A regular visitor, Tommy slipped in the back door, and Sage and Cap welcomed him. When Aislynn said, "Amy, go out on the front porch and play with Smokey. I think you both need some fresh air and exercise," Sage's eyes snapped to high alert. His brows worked down into a knot and his face fell.

Molly stood and Tommy grasped her hand. "Molly and I want to get married." Tommy nodded his head nervously. "We know it ain't legal." Shame lowered his tone. "We . . . we gotta do it."

Aislynn could see recognition wash over Cap's and Sage's faces.

"What's your plan, son?" Cap asked.

"We thought we'd ask for your advice. If you ain't got any ideas, we figure we're bound for Canada."

Molly hung her head and hid her face in her hands. Tommy circled her with his arm and pulled her to him. Aislynn's pleading eyes jumped between Cap's and Sage's.

"Canada," Sage said to Cap.

"Just so," Cap agreed.

"Canada!" The word exploded from Aislynn's mouth. "Why?"

Cap explained, "As I recall there's a settlement over the border. Very acceptin' place. They take all kinds of people: Injuns, blacks, Chinese, people of all stripes. It's a rough town, not a lot of laws tellin' people how to live. There will be white women with blacks and Injuns. Might not be the kind of people you're used to, but no one's gonna separate you or throw you in jail."

"Or hang you," Sage added.

"I don't want Molly in danger," Tommy stated.

With a hard look, Sage said. "She's in more danger here."

"If only that law had passed," Aislynn said.

Sage shook his head at her. "A law wouldn't make a bit of difference; Molly's still a white woman, and Tommy's still an Injun. You know that wouldn't set well with people in these parts."

Aislynn and the young couple exchanged crestfallen looks. Molly picked up her chin. She scanned the faces around the table until her glance rested on Tommy. "I survived my father. I suppose I can survive Canada."

Aislynn kneaded her hands and chewed her lip trying to hold in her protests. Losing the battle, she said, "They'll be so far away . . . with a baby."

"And they'll care of each other real good," Cap said to Aislynn with a scolding look.

She closed her eyes and attempted to say the right thing. "Yes, and you'll start a new life together and find some good friends."

Molly's timid voice rose. "Can we get married there?"

"It won't matter. No one's gonna care," Cap offered.

"Molly cares. It's a religious thing," Tommy explained.

"We could get Father Gilhooley to marry you. We could have a wedding right here," Aislynn suggested.

Sage sent her an eye full of rebuke.

"I was taught that in the United States we have a separation between church and state," Aislynn said with a haughty tone. "So there's church law and government law. Why can't they get married within church law?"

Sage exchanged a look with Cap. When he turned back to Aislynn, she had her hands together in prayer.

"This is serious and dangerous." His deep voice threatened, "Tommy could get murdered for violatin' a white woman. Molly could get thrown in jail for fornicatin'."

Aislynn struck a conciliatory tone. "We'll take Father Gilhooley into our confidence. He's been a good friend and I trust him. Besides, he's bound to God not to reveal secrets."

"First off"—Sage said pointing his finger at Aislynn—"do you know what *secret* means? It means just us. No Amy, no Emmie, no one can know. Promise?"

Aislynn nodded vigorously and looked at Molly and Tommy, who were nodding in unison.

"You can get the priest here to say some words with the curtains closed," Sage instructed.

In his usual fashion, Sage took command. He turned his attention to Tommy. "It's a long, tough, dangerous ride. You'll have to be careful in her condition. Be prepared. Get water, bullets and guns. But don't let anybody know what you're doin'."

Sage turned to Cap. "She'll need a strong horse. You buy it. That will throw nosy people off their tracks."

Looking at Aislynn, he listed her jobs. "You make her a pack to carry on her horse. Give her your heavy coat, long underwear and socks. Run to the store and buy her pants, a shirt, and men's boots. Find her a cap to cover her hair. Best she travels as a boy, don't you think, Cap?"

"Just so."

Sage continued, "Molly, you can pack a dress and turn into a woman when you get to the settlement." Facing Aislynn, he ordered, "Gather some tonics and medicines."

Looking at the young couple, he added, "I'll ride with you till we reach Casper. On the road, I'll teach you what I can. You'll have to travel the rest of the way yourselves. It'll take at least two months." Sage pointed at Tommy. "You gotta build a shelter right quick. Winter comes early in those parts. You'll have frost in late August."

Molly's tiny voice rose. "Tommy, do we have money for all this?"

"I'll get it; don't you worry."

"How?"

"I'll work it out."

"Don't let on." Molly fretted.

Cap broke in. "I can help. I got me a gold watch. Worth a pretty penny. It'll fetch enough to get you there and started."

"We can't take your watch," Molly protested.

"You, Aislynn, Amy and Brendan are the closest things I've ever had to a family. I could leave it to you so you'd have it when I'm gone, or I could give it to you now when you need it."

Clapping her hand over her mouth, Molly shook with tears. Tommy thanked Cap and turned to comfort her. Aislynn threw her arms around Cap's full frame and placed a loud kiss on his cheek.

Molly wiped her nose and cheeks with the back of her hands and approached Cap. "I'm so sorry. I'm so sorry."

"Ain't nothin' to be sorry about." He placed his hand on her shoulder and said, "You're a good girl, Molly, and you're gonna be a good mama. I'm proud of you." He kissed her forehead. The tiny girl fell into his lap, curled her arms around him and sobbed into his neck. Cap stroked her hair. "If you ain't worth a gold watch, I'd like you to tell me who is."

Sage interrupted the tender moment. "Now we gotta keep everyone off Molly's trail or Emmie's gonna have the entire town searchin' for her."

Molly sniffed in her tears and spoke, "Yes, she'll be beside herself with worry."

"We'll tell her something plausible," Aislynn comforted her.

As Molly slipped into the chair next to Cap, he asked, "Why'd a woman rush off without tellin' no one?"

Aislynn lived with this possibility everyday of her life. The answer jumped out of her mouth before it even registered in her brain. "A man." All their eyes jumped to her with astonishment. "Well, supposing she was afraid of him, and she got word he was coming?"

"She'd run," Cap answered.

"That ain't any good." Sage grumbled. "Then Emmie and Maggie would be roundin' up a posse. And they'd be wonderin' why you ain't leadin' the charge." He pointed his chin at Aislynn.

Cap encouraged them. "We have to think of somethin' better."

Aislynn's head dipped to the side. "What if she went willingly to the man? What if he was a man she wanted to be with? We're the only ones who know about Tommy. What if Molly was in a relationship with another man?"

Sage looked doubtful. "Who's that man? How you gonna get him to leave town?"

"What if he's not in town?" Aislynn asked. "What if he's in New York and he writes to her?"

Molly brightened. "Yes, like a mail-order bride."

"Exactly. I could say you told me he wanted you to come immediately and you just left town."

"Just like that?" Sage remained skeptical.

"Maybe he has to be married in a few days, or he'll lose an inheritance," Aislynn suggested.

Sage sent her a peeved look. "We ain't writin' a dime-novel romance."

"Maybe he's dying?" Molly proposed.

Sage rocked back in his chair and opened his hands. He questioned, "Wouldn't you come back after he's dead?"

Crestfallen, Molly's face and shoulders sagged.

"I'll agree to a man, but it's gotta be more believable. What if he's someone from her hometown, someone she's know her whole life? He writes and tells her to come on the next train or don't come at all?"

Aislynn remembered Moran and how demanding most men are. "An ultimatum from a man, now that's believable. It's interesting the suggestion came from a man." Aislynn put her hand on her hip, wagged her head and sent Sage a sassy look.

Sage dismissed her with a wave. "You write a letter to Aislynn explainin' your retreat. Say he's desperately in love.

Emmie will swallow that like sugar. He sent you a ticket, and you had to go. No time for goodbyes."

Molly nodded.

"You set it up." Sage pointed at Aislynn. "Say Molly's been real secretive about him. Then, tell Emmie and Maggie you found this letter." Sage stood. "We all got jobs to do; let's get to them." He stepped out on the porch and called to Amy, "Come on, missy. We're takin' Smokey for a walk to my house."

In the early evening darkness, they all scattered to their tasks. While Aislynn took Brendan and ran to a haberdasher, Molly rushed to the church. Cap arranged for the horse. Tommy packed up.

At 8:30, Father Gilhooley came through the back door. Aislynn checked the curtains for what seemed like the hundredth time and locked both doors. She took her place next to Cap and the priest began. "Tommy and Molly, you have come together this day so God may seal and strengthen your love." With an exchange of vows, the Lord's Prayer and a "go in peace, and serve God and each other," Tommy and Molly became husband and wife.

All through the night, lessons, advice, even recipes Aislynn wanted to share with Molly repeatedly popped into her head. Knowing Molly faced a hard ride ahead and would not see a bed for two months, she held her tongue. She lay with her mind spinning, listening for the clock to strike four times.

As planned, Sage and Cap arrived at the back door. Molly, dressed as a man, prepared to switch places with Cap. Tommy waited to join them on the road to Fort Russell.

Aislynn tucked a few loose strands of Molly's hair under the cap. She helped her into the wide, heavy coat. Forcing a smile and sucking in her fears and sadness, she buttoned Molly up against the cold April night. All her thoughts gushed out. "Stay warm. Make your birthing box. See a doctor regularly and get a midwife right away. Try to settle near other women so you have friends and support." Molly's shoulders shook as she nodded silently, with tears slipping down her cheek.

"Remember to write every week. Use an assumed name; I'll know it's you. If you need anything, just ask. Don't be afraid. You can telegraph in an emergency." Aislynn reached into her apron pocket and withdrew her little pistol. She pressed it into Molly's trembling palm. "Carry this with you always." Aislynn sniffed and stammered, "If I can't keep you safe, maybe this will."

Molly's words faltered. "But it belonged to your father."

Aislynn squeaked out, "And now belongs to my sister."

The men shuffled in discomfort as the women wept and embraced for what they knew would be the last time. Holding Molly's frail frame, Aislynn knew she had to let her go. With a few long breaths, she calmed herself, pulled away and steeled her spine. "Go, and know all our love goes with you." They turned to Sage.

His eyes met Molly's. "Let's head out before the sun shows." He touched his hat and sent Aislynn a salute.

She covered her heart with her hands and mouthed, "Safe travels."

Cap's hand fell on Aislynn's shoulder. "Sage will get them goin' and they'll find their way just fine."

Aislynn bit her lip and wiped her eyes with the back of her hands. Cap said into her ear, "You know, Aislynn, we don't always take the path we planned, but I think somehow we all wind up where we're supposed to be."

* * *

After months of checking her mail cubby every day, a small envelope, with smudges and creases showing its long journey, arrived at the Cheyenne post office in late July.

"Who do you know in Canada?" asked Mr. Baker.

"I have friends everywhere," Aislynn replied as she snatched the letter from his grip.

Sitting in Sage's office, Aislynn read the letter aloud.

> *To my dear family,*
>
> *We arrived at the Haven in June. It's a rough place, just a few houses, mostly log cabins, huts and lean-tos. Tommy built a teepee out of pine poles and the thick, needled boughs. There's enough room for us to sleep and for me to cook and do chores. Tommy knew just where to place the fire pit so the smoke goes out but the heat stays in. He knows how to do many useful things.*
>
> *He is putting up firewood and making a few pieces of furniture. I am sewing baby clothes out of the man's outfit I wore on the trail. I am also sewing up two dresses for me. I am making them wide and straight, like the squaws wear. That way I can wear them no matter how big I get.*
>
> *We miss you all very much. Most people keep to themselves. They are nice and will help out when you need something, but they don't make an effort to get close. I think they're all afraid. Once you have been on the run, I guess you never feel safe and settled.*

Aislynn paused. "It breaks my heart to think of her so far away, having a baby alone."

"You know she ain't alone. You know she's where she wants to be, with Tommy. Be thankful they're safe."

"I suppose."

He stared at Aislynn for a few seconds too long. His fingers tapped the desk and face fell into a deep frown.

A kernel of fear started to grow in her gut. "What's wrong?"

"Get Cap and meet me at your house. I got somethin' to show you two."

CHAPTER 25

THE heat of the late summer sun suffocated the cabin. Aislynn kept the windows open to let the air in, and the curtains drawn to keep the dust and swelter out.

Sage unfolded a letter under the apprehensive eyes of Aislynn and Cap.

> *Marshal Sage,*
>
> *We be Amy Franklin's kin. Her ma is our daughter. Write and tell us how we get her.*
>
> *Clayton and Eula Black*

For Aislynn, the air drained from the room. She could barely fill her lungs. Her hand clenched Sage's arm as if her grip could hold Amy in Cheyenne. "No! We can't give up Amy. You can't write back."

Cap leaned back and folded his hands on his abundant belly. "It don't seem like he's got much of a choice. If they can show her birth certificate and her mother's, they have more of a legal right than we have."

"What if they're lying?"

"That's why I wrote to the US marshal in Arkansas." Sage produced the two verifying forms.

"Can we fight them?"

"I know you can't be reasonable about this—"

"I'm being very reasonable. There has to be a way around the law. Think! Let's ask Justice Howe." Aislynn searched their stolid faces. Her words flowed out in a fretful stream. "We can't just let her go. They must be strangers to her. She said she didn't know she had any family. Now we're her family."

"I've been over this with Justice Howe. You think I want to give her up?" Sage barked. "She ain't just your kid. She's all of ours."

"This can't be happening." Anger shot from her lips and she aimed it at Sage. "This is your fault. Why do you have to be so hard and fast? You could have forgotten to post those notices everywhere. No one would have checked on you."

Sage's eyes burned. Both of his hands tapped furiously on the table. Aislynn lowered her voice to a sinister tone. "Don't reply. If they write again, burn their letters. They'll give up and leave us alone."

Sage seethed. "It's the law."

"I don't care about the law." Aislynn's voice rose and her hand hit the table.

"You care when it works in your favor," he roared. Sage stood over her with determination in his eyes. "They'll be here in a week. Start gettin' her ready to go." He stomped toward the door.

Soft and tearful, she pleaded, "Orrin . . ."

Hearing his Christian name, he turned with wounded eyes and taut lips.

Aislynn took a wet breath. "Please . . ."

He slapped his hat on his head, grabbed his rifle and walked out the door.

Aislynn picked up Brendan and fell into Sage's chair. She rubbed her cheek against his hair and stroked his back. Cap settled in his chair and rocked rhythmically. A nervous silence engulfed the shack. Aislynn's mind searched for a way to keep Amy. When nothing came, her frustration emerged and her cold eyes met his.

"Don't tell me she's going where she's supposed to be."

"I ain't a believer, which you are. You think God would steer that little girl wrong?"

"God tries me and tests me. How many people do I have to lose? A mother, a father, a husband, a baby, Molly, even Jimmy. If He takes this child, I'm afraid He's going to lose me. I've lost too much." She inhaled a long, angry breath. "Look around us, Cap. A family massacred over in Rollins. Indian children and infants slain near Sweetwater. Where is God? What's He doing that's so important He turns his back?"

"Guess that's why I ain't a believer."

They sat across from each other: hushed, brooding and scheming. The ticking clock told Aislynn she had to act.

"Cap?"

"Yeah."

"Let's go to Canada. We could join Molly and Tommy."

"You'd take an infant, a crippled child and an old man over them mountains to Canada?"

"Yes."

"You gonna leave Sage?"

Aislynn tried to say, *Yes,* but an unexpected battle erupted in her heart and her mind. *Amy or Sage?* She looked down at her lap and nodded.

"You wouldn't get out of town before he'd come after you."

Aislynn nodded again.

Cap took a sip of his coffee and ruminated for a moment. "You know this rests hard on him, too."

Aislynn's face distorted in pain. In a voice burdened with grief, she said, "He doesn't bathe her and dress her and brush her hair every day. I make sure she eats right and gets her schoolwork done." Aislynn covered her eyes with her hand. "And I'm the one who holds her and comforts her when the bad dreams come at night. She's my daughter." She wiped her tears.

Cap rocked and nodded. "You know Aislynn, when her ma died, he gave you that child. Oh, I know not like you got Brendan, of course, but he gave you Amy 'cause he cared and wanted her close. He wanted her to be a part of this family." Cap patted her knee. "We're gonna get through this. We'll get through this together. Maybe you two will come out closer and more honest on the other side."

Aislynn prepared Amy's favorite meal: a roast pork, baked apples and sauerkraut. She baked a red velvet cake for dessert. Aislynn believed good food and its warm fragrance could ease pain.

She decided to tell Amy at dinner, in front of Sage. Part of her wanted him to share in the anguish his diligence caused.

Standing behind the child, stroking her hair, Aislynn broached the subject. "Amy, would you like to take a ride on a train?"

Amy shook her head. "No, they're loud and scary."

Aislynn had forgotten how close the child had lived to the railway. "They're very nice and comfortable inside."

"Where are we going?"

Aislynn looked at Sage. He lowered his head over his plate and continued eating. "Sweetheart, do you know what grandparents are?"

"Yes."

"Well, you have two of them. Your mother's parents are coming to see you."

"I don't know them."

"Yes, but you will soon."

"May I go play with Smokey?"

Aislynn drilled her eyes into the top of Sage's head.

Squatting down to the girl's level, Aislynn tried again. "Amy, I want you to listen to me for a moment." The child sat up with wide eyes. "Your grandparents loved your mother very much, and they want to love you, too. They're coming all the way from Arkansas. You know the states; Arkansas is one of them. They want to take you home with them."

"Are you and Brendan coming?"

Aislynn hesitated, giving herself a chance to conceal her distress. "No."

"Is the marshal?"

"No."

"What about Cap and Smokey?"

"No."

The child shook her head. "Then I won't go, either."

Aislynn looked for help from Cap and Sage. Cap scratched his bald head, and Sage delivered a stern expression. She hung her head. "You go play with Smokey, and we'll talk about your trip another day."

The August sun continued to scorch the city. A spell without rain and the hot, dry wind caused dust to accumulate like snow in a blizzard. Aislynn's frantic cleaning helped the cabin look nice and allowed her to expend the nervous energy and stress building toward the impending encounter.

Feigning a festive air, Aislynn made Amy a new dress. She braided the child's hair and polished her special shoes. Trying to make the meeting warm and cordial, she set a pot of coffee on the stove to boil. She baked and let the smell of fresh berry pie fill the air. Then she arranged the chairs in a circle, so everyone could converse easily.

Sage arrived with Amy's grandparents in the late afternoon. They entered the house clearly assessing everything and everyone. Aislynn and Amy stood immobilized with apprehension. Sage performed the introductions, and they all settled into the chairs.

Draped in black mourning and sporting a crown of white hair, Mrs. Black looked like a bald eagle. She presented dark, sinister eyes, a sharp, hooked nose and brown, sparse teeth. Her husband wore a poorly tailored, rumpled suit. His pants rode high on his waist and short on his legs, exposing worn, scuffed boots. Aislynn made an effort not to stare at his twitchy eye. Mr. Black's face told the story of a violent past. He had a crooked nose, twisted mouth, absent teeth and a deeply scarred cheek.

Amy clenched Aislynn's hand.

"Come here, child," Mrs. Black ordered in a thick southern drawl.

Amy hesitated. With Aislynn's encouragement, Amy slipped off the chair and thumped across the floor.

Her grandmother pulled away. "What's wrong with you, child?"

"Why she's a cripple, Ma," Mr. Black informed his wife. He reached for Amy's skirt and pulled it up to reveal her feet. The embarrassed child scrambled away from his grasp.

Objecting to their harsh judgment, Aislynn interjected, "She's a wonderful little girl."

"Can she work a farm?" Mr. Black asked. "She's gotta work. There's feedin', milkin', plantin', hard work to be done."

"And who's gonna marry her?" Ma questioned. "She's gotta marry a man who can take care of the farm. She's gotta have kids; we need hands."

"She's seven years old," Aislynn stated. Amy ran to her and buried her face in Aislynn's skirt.

Pa interjected, "We come all this way. You should've told us she's good for nothin'. We oughtta charge you for our tickets."

Cap leaned forward in his chair sporting a curiously pleased expression. "Well now, it sounds to me like you don't want this child. Sounds like she ain't no use to you."

"Sure ain't," Pa said with indignation.

Cap sucked in some air between his teeth. "Maybe we could do some good old horse tradin'."

A sly smile crossed Ma's face and Pa said, "Keep talkin', old man."

"We're partial to Amy, and we'd like to keep her," Cap explained.

Pa's eyes gleamed. "You talkin' cash money?"

A grin slowly brightened Cap's face. "We could be," Cap offered.

"We don't want nothin' but cash. Nothin' else would do us much good," Ma announced firmly.

"How much do you want for her?" Cap asked.

"She's a child," Aislynn protested.

Sage reprimanded her. "Quiet, Aislynn; this is Cap's business." He took her arm and guided her toward the door; Amy shuffled behind. "You two stay out here." He closed the door with a loud click.

Aislynn stood on the porch sputtering with fury. *She's my child. How dare he push me out?* Amy plopped down on the top step and wept quietly. Aislynn sat and pulled the wounded child into her arms. "Don't you pay those awful people any mind."

While stroking Amy's hair, Aislynn strained to eavesdrop through the open window.

"We've grown attached to the girl," Cap said.

She heard Pa's voice. "Well, she might be worth somethin' after all."

"We gotta include our tickets and hotel in the deal," Ma demanded.

"Why don't you go back to your room, decide on a price? I'll have a man come by and you can tell him what you all want to be paid."

Ma chimed in, "That's mighty accommodatin' of you."

"Just remember," Cap added, "I'm a reasonable man, but I ain't a rich man. And you want to leave with cash."

"We'll keep that in mind."

Amy sucked in her tears and looked up at Aislynn. "I don't like them. I don't want to go with them."

Kissing the child's forehead, she said, "I don't think Cap or the marshal will let that happen."

"Three hundred dollars? Do you have that much money?" Aislynn asked with hope in her voice.

"I'll get it. Don't worry," Cap assured her.

Aislynn rushed to her dresser. She pulled the strings on a purple velvet pouch and emptied the contents into Cap's hand. "I have a silver cross and a brooch with a pearl. These earrings are gold." Aislynn looked at the gold claddagh wedding ring she wore on her left hand. With a catch in her throat, she said, "And this ring. These should fetch something."

Cap touched her cheek. "You're a good girl. I'll take care of your treasures."

"Be ready at nine o'clock," Sage instructed. "Cap will leave Amy at school, and you take Brendan to Maggie's. Come straight to my office. Don't you say one word to anyone."

Despite the tension filling the air, Sage's office glowed with the morning sun. Deputy Winston stood against one wall waiting to act as a witness. Cap, Aislynn and the Blacks settled into wooden chairs and faced Sage. His cleared desk held only his Colts, an inkwell, a pen and three sheets of paper arrayed in a line.

Sage pointed to the three documents, explaining, "This one says you're Amy's grandparents and legal guardians. With this one, you give Mrs. Maher the right to adopt Amy. This is a receipt. It states you're gettin' three hundred dollars, and there'll be no further payments made for this exchange."

Pa puffed up with bravado and said, "Before we go any further, we want to see the cash. We ain't signin' nothin' without the cash."

Sage opened his desk drawer and revealed the bills.

"I wanna count it. Not that I don't trust you. Just better to be safe than sorry. Right, Ma?"

"Right," she replied.

Black counted the bills and started to pocket the cash.

"You can leave them right here until all the papers are signed." Sage tapped the desk. "Not that I don't trust you."

Pa's eyes squinted around the office and he placed the money in the middle of Sage's desk. Accepting the pen, he carefully dipped the nib in the ink well and shook it gently. He worked the handle between his fingers until it rested in the proper place. Demonstrating his lack of practice forming letters, Pa slowly scratched the pen across the papers. Once he completed his task, his wife placed *X*s next to her name. Mr. Black announced, "Done." He held out his hand.

"Our witnesses have to sign first."

Deputy Winston stepped between the Blacks and Aislynn. He leaned over the papers and signed. Both documents were handed to Cap. Sage signed the receipt and the Blacks followed suit. With all the transactions completed, Pa grabbed the cash. He stuffed it in his pants pocket, and helped Ma to her feet.

"It's been a pleasure doing business with you." Black grinned and took his wife's arm, and they started toward the door.

Aislynn crossed her hands over her heart and exhaled a long grateful breath. Deputy Winston stepped forward and said, "Mr. and Mrs. Black, selling a child is against US and territorial law. I am arresting you for the sale of Amy Franklin."

Pa's eyes exploded. "I didn't sell her!"

"Did you asked for and accept cash in exchange for the child?" Winston asked.

Aislynn stiffened with shock. Confusion muddled her mind and her eyes darted between the Blacks and Sage. Mr. Black's mouth fell open and panic violently shook his body. "I— I— She bought her." He pointed at Aislynn.

"Mrs. Maher hasn't touched the payment nor has she signed any of these papers," Sage explained.

"I was just givin' her away. It's like a horse trade, remember?"

Cap rose and calmly blocked the door. The deputy reached for Ma's arm, and she tore away from him. She pointed at her husband. "It were his scheme."

Pa shouted, "You agreed!"

Sage stood. "Settle down!" he roared. "Give me that money."

Mr. Black exhorted Sage as he handed over the payment. "We're just old people tryin' to get by. That child is no use to us, but the money is. You gotta understand."

"Sit down!" Sage ordered as he lowered himself into his chair. His cold eyes narrowed and he started, "You two are a disgrace. You came here to take that child back to Arkansas for a life of hard labor. You thought you were gettin' a slave to bring south. A slave you'd marry off to get more slaves. Those times are over. We don't sell people anymore. We got laws against that. You two broke those laws. You can spend the rest of your lives in federal prison."

Pa's body quaked violently. Ma buried her face in her hands and sobbed. "No, we can't. We're too old for prison. Please, Marshal, have mercy. We're her kin," Ma begged.

Sage's fingers twitched on his Colt. He puckered up his face and leaned over the desk, barking, "*Kin?* You didn't act like *kin.*" Sage fell back in his seat. "But I'm a merciful man. I'm puttin' you in a cell. At 1:20 this afternoon, Deputy Winston is going to march you to your hotel. You're gonna get your tickets and belongings. At 1:40, he's gonna to put you on the eastbound train. If you ever come back to this territory, you'll go straight to prison. And I intend to notify the federal marshal in Arkansas of your crime and advise him to keep a watch on you two." Sage stood to his full height. He nodded at Winston. "Get them out of here before I put a bullet in both of them."

"Yes, sir."

Once the Blacks exited the office, Sage returned to his seat and addressed Aislynn. "You did good. First time you ever kept your mouth shut when you were told to."

Aislynn looked at Cap and Sage. "What? What just happened?"

"We couldn't let that little girl go with that trash. Sage hatched up a plan." Cap looked at him. "You old mother hen. Worked perfect."

Aislynn shook the confusion from her mind. "You orchestrated the entire ruse?"

"Ain't really a ruse. You can't buy and sell people for slave labor, especially *kin*," Sage said, imitating Mrs. Black. "We did good." He extended his hand to Cap.

"I believe we saved that child's life. Hand me that cash, and I'll bring it back to the bank." Cap turned to Aislynn and pulled a small, velvet bag from his coat pocket. "Put these somewhere safe."

Realizing she was not losing Amy, her entire body trembled with the rush of relief that washed over her. She clutched the bag and tears slipped from her eyes. "Thank you."

Cap placed his hand on Aislynn's shoulder. "Let's get Brendan and Amy, and we'll pull this family back together."

Cap started toward the door, and Aislynn rose on hesitant legs to follow him. She collected her thoughts and approached Sage. He looked up at her with his brows arched in a question. She placed her hand under his chin, softly kissed his cheek and walked out the door.

CHAPTER 26

WITH her little family intact and secure, Aislynn returned to the post office. When she arrived, Mr. Baker offered her a proposition. He would suspend his ten percent cut of her profits if she helped him when she had no customers. Always short of cash, Aislynn began sorting mail, selling stamps and stocking the stationery shelves. While Aislynn filled the cubbyholes, a cowboy sauntered into the post office. He sported a head of wet hair and a fresh shave, and he reeked of Pinaud Clubman cologne, evidence of his recent arrival and visit to the bathhouse.

A small spark of desire flashed through Aislynn when her glance raced over his strong, young body. The hope of a husband, more children and a real family life seemed to float out of reach, always muffled by memories of her past errors in judgment. *Maybe someday with a man I can trust,* she thought. She stole another glance at the cowboy and returned to the mail.

As he approached the counter, Mr. Baker asked, "May I help you?"

"Yes, sir." The boy nodded with respect. "I heard a widow woman writes letters. I'd be much obliged if she'd write one for me, sir."

"That'd be Mrs. Maher." Baker's head jerked in Aislynn's direction. "She'll help you."

The boy stared at Aislynn as if she were a curiosity in a case. His silence filled the room. Aislynn turned to Baker with a plea in her eyes.

"Boy, you want a letter or not?"

The cowboy woke from his trance and said, "Huh? Yes, sir, a letter." With hesitant steps, she moved behind the counter.

"Then give her the paper and tell her what you want it to say."

The young man produced a sheet of light blue paper. He spread it out on the counter and gently pushed it across to Aislynn.

"Thank you." Aislynn smiled at his fastidiousness. "Should we start?"

"You sure are clean lookin'."

Baker pointed his finger. "You're not here to presume upon Mrs. Maher. You dictate your words, give her the envelope and address. Then you buy your stamp and get out. Is that clear?"

"I'm sorry, ma'am. I didn't mean to take liberties."

Aislynn nodded. "I accept your apology. Now to whom are you addressing your letter?"

"My ma."

"*Dearest Ma,*" she repeated as she wrote. "Go on."

"I made it to Cheyenne. Hope you are doin' well. I am safe." His eyes watched Aislynn's hand dipping the pen and rushing over the paper. Aislynn looked up and their eyes met. The sea of blue drew her in. He gave her a brilliant, white-toothed smile. "I've made a lot of money. I will save most of it in case I meet a nice girl to bring back to Texas."

Baker stopped sorting mail. He crossed his arms and glowered at the boy.

The cowboy charged on. "I'll go to church while I'm here. Be movin' out in two weeks. Your son, Trevor Hayward." He studied Aislynn as she caught up to his words. "Can I add I really miss our beautiful Texas spread?"

"I'll make that a postscript."

"What's that?"

"It's simply a line I can add at the end."

He handed her his envelope and told her the address. Aislynn sealed the missive and handed it to him. "You can buy the stamp and pay Mr. Baker."

As the young man turned to leave, he smiled and tipped his hat to Aislynn. She watched the door close with a wistful sigh.

On her way home, Aislynn stopped at Maggie's store for vegetables and conversation. The bells clanged and the scent of Pinaud Clubman sailed past her nose. "Now that's a pretty boy," Maggie said.

"Is he tall, well built with dazzling blue eyes and a heartbreaking smile?" she asked.

"Yes, do you know him?"

"He's a customer."

"Goodness, if I were only young and single. He's like a very expensive hat: you see it, you want it, but you know you can't have it."

Aislynn's eyes popped and her mouth formed an oval. "Maggie Avery! You shock me!" They giggled like schoolgirls.

Aislynn turned to leave. The young man removed his hat and bowed deeply. "Mrs. Maher, how nice to see you again."

Aislynn bobbed. "Mr. Hayward."

She took her basket and walked out the door under his gaze. Once she started down the boardwalk, she heard steps rushing toward her.

"Mrs. Maher, may I escort you home?" He reached for her basket.

Feelings of guilt and fear overcame her. Instinctively, she pulled her basket into her chest and covered it with her arm. "No, no," she stammered, "that's not possible."

The boy's face fell. "I don't mean to keep offending you. I'm tryin' to be real nice."

Aislynn collected herself. "I know, Mr. Hayward. I appreciate your effort." Without knowing why, she added, "I am not free to walk with you."

The cowboy nodded. "I see. You got a man."

"Yes . . . no."

Hayward's face reflected his bewilderment.

"Mrs. Maher, is this boy bothering you?" Aislynn cringed hearing District Attorney Carey's angry voice.

"No, sir. He's one of my customers."

Carey addressed the cowboy. "Son, if you want to speak to Mrs. Maher, you do so at the post office. Don't let the marshal see you disrespecting her in the street."

"I'm sorry, sir." He nodded at Carey and turned to Aislynn. "Ma'am, I didn't know you belonged to the marshal."

A flurry of confusion filled Aislynn's mind. She wanted to correct Carey and explain her situation to Hayward, but she was not clear about it herself.

Hayward touched his hat and trotted away. Aislynn watched him and her brief hopes disappear in the puffs of dust.

"I'm sorry you have to suffer such impertinence. Should I escort you to the marshal's office?" Carey asked.

"No, thank you. I appreciate your kindness, but I'm going home."

Brendan lay spread-eagle on Herman, with his eyes closed, breathing through his tiny, open mouth. "Just exhausted himself crawlin' every which way," Cap explained.

"If he becomes too much trouble for you, I'll bring him to the post office with me."

"No, he can't get too far in this one room."

Aislynn poured two cups of coffee and collapsed in Sage's chair. Smokey lumbered over and dropped his head in her lap. Her predicament occupied her mind so fully she failed to acknowledge his presence.

"What's ailin' you?"

Aislynn forced a grin. "Nothing."

"It's somethin'. You look like you got some bad news."

"It's not news. Sage always tells me I'm stupid; well, sometimes the depths of my ignorance, or shall I say blindness, shock me."

"How so?"

"I'm never going to get married again."

Cap nodded in his patient way. "Hmm, how's that?"

"My whole life story just revealed itself on the street."

With a chortle, Cap said, "Didn't know the streets in Cheyenne could tell the future."

Aislynn's face twisted into a knot of frustration. "It's not the street; it's what happened in the street." She explained the incident.

"You want that boy?"

Aislynn thought for a moment. "No. I want what I saw in his eyes: attraction, attention and affection." She slumped lower in the chair. "In my current circumstance, I'm not going to have that."

"You had to know people put you two together. He's an unmarried man; you're an unmarried woman. They think of you as his woman."

While Aislynn knew what the townspeople thought, she knew the truth of their relationship; she was not Sage's woman. She remembered the day he received his appointment as marshal. She could see Campbell exchanging looks with Sage, the silent language of men, the tacit agreement. With a few random words said for convenience, she tied herself to a man who shunned marriage.

"They got good reason, too. He killed three men for you. He gave you your son and your daughter. He got you this roof over your head. He pays for the food you eat. He watches over you and keeps you outta trouble. He's here first thing in the mornin'. He's in and out all day till he goes home to sleep at night."

"You're here, too." She smiled.

"And happy to be included." He reached over and patted her knee and continued, "You know how life was out here for us. Him, an orphan at the fort."

"Were you one of the soldiers who raised him?"

"The only soldier. Most men didn't have time for a laundress's whelp."

"Laundress? At the fort? She . . . ?" Aislynn covered her mouth and checked her words. *A prostitute!* She met Cap's eyes. "I never put it all together. But he was a child; he couldn't have known."

Cap's face tightened. "They were hard men. He grew up just as hard." A sad smile appeared slowly. "His ma was a good woman, but you know as well as anyone, we all do what we gotta do to survive."

Aislynn's eyes fell. "Yes, I know."

"Till the railroad come, there was no town, not much of nothin'. After Sage lost his wife, well, we just wandered like saddle bums where any work took us. Hardly saw a white woman, nay, a good white woman. Eventually wagon trains rolled through, but we were busy scoutin' Injuns, fightin' wars. Then, the railroad come. When you and Johnny railed in, well, he said, 'Babes in the woods.' He thought it was crazy; a woman like you wagonin' west. He believed you two needed help. He said he didn't want nothin' to happen to that stupid little girl."

Her eyes rose to the ceiling as she shook her head. Cap pushed on. "I reminded him you were another man's wife. He said it weren't like that. But when you rolled out and kissed him goodbye, well, that might not have meant much to you, but I could see it didn't rest easy on him. Then you wrote," Cap said with disbelief. "That touched him."

"He never wrote back."

"Never?"

"Well, he sent one response. It said, *Thank you for the letter. I'm a reader, not a writer.* "

"But you kept writin'. Every letter said you cared about him. Don't think that didn't mean nothin'." Cap took a sip of his coffee. "He felt real sorry when Johnny and your baby died."

Aislynn bolted upright. "You know when Johnny died?"

Cap leaned closer and patted her knee while shame burned her whole body. "What I know is you're a good gal. Some men take advantage of good women."

"He was going to marry me. Then, he left and didn't come back." The words flowed like the tears pouring over her red cheeks. "I had to lie or Brendan would be labeled . . ."

"Hush, it ain't a crime or nothin' if you're protectin' yourself or someone else. It's like when a man's got you in his sights and you kill him. It ain't murder; it's self-defense. You do what's got to be done."

Cap rested back in his seat. "I don't see good, but when he walked into that store with you on his arm—" He paused to chuckle. "Well, you didn't know it and maybe he didn't know it, but even *I* could see what he wanted." Cap laughed again. "Walkin' down the street with a woman for all to see."

Placing his cup on the floor, Cap put his head down and looked at her with hooded eyes. "Aislynn, he ain't gonna to say sweet words to you; they rub too close to the bone. You gotta consider what he does, not what he says."

"But he says I'm nothing but trouble."

"You know he's a man who likes trouble." Cap smiled.

"He's always angry with me."

"For men like us anger is a natural state. But you know he ain't angry; you have to listen with your heart, not your ears. He just don't know what to do with all those feelin's he's got for you. He ain't had much experience with them."

With hesitation, she said, "He was in love once."

"He was a selfish, foolhardy boy, with no way of knowin' how to be a husband or a father," Cap said in a voice full of pain. "But now he's a man who's learned from his mistakes."

"And a man who decided to never marry or have another child."

"Aislynn," Cap started slowly, "if he didn't want a family, he wouldn't be here every day."

A feeling of self-consciousness surfaced and sent a blush to her cheeks. "I have to admit he has grown on me. I do care about him very much. I suppose there's no one I trust or depend on more."

"I can see that. You two are like schoolkids, prickin' each other, and pesterin' each other. You're just wantin' each other."

Aislynn could feel her body flash scarlet. "Captain Elliot Walker! I am shocked!"

"You know it's true."

For months, thoughts of Sage had come to her at night. She always pushed then down. While the memories of her attackers rested in the dark folds of her brain, her terrible mistake with Liam Moran haunted her relentlessly. *Besides, a man with wild ways who consorted with a whore is not only a questionable mate, he's an intimidating one.* She hesitated and considered her feelings. "I don't think I love him, not like I loved Johnny."

"You can't love him like Johnny. He ain't Johnny. But let me ask you this, how would you feel if he never walked through that door again? If he got shot dead today?"

Aislynn's body jerked. She gasped. "Good Lord, Cap! Don't say things like that. Say a prayer quickly." She mumbled a Hail Mary.

"You didn't answer the question."

Aislynn looked down at her clasped hands. Her mind rushed through memories of how he helped her, solved her problems and protected her and her children. Without looking up, she said, "Sometimes, I feel like I don't take a full breath until he walks through that door."

"Maybe you do love him some."

Aislynn covered her smile with her hand.

"I know you like him and likin' is good. Love makes people crazy. Now like, like is nice and easy and comfortable."

"You seem to have given this a lot of thought."

"Yeah, I've had a lot of time to think on it. One thing I know about women is they wait for the perfect man to ride in and solve all their problems. Then, they find he's got saddlebags full of his own. Sage ain't perfect. Heck, no one's perfect. But sometimes it's better to appreciate what you've got instead of waitin' around for what you think you want."

Cap shifted in his chair. "I had shinin' dreams once, but I let the clouds roll by till I was old and sittin' by the fire alone. You gotta make your life happen; no one's gonna do it for you."

"Maybe you're right."

"Maybe? Am I ever wrong?"

Aislynn looked into the aged eyes. "You know I came here full of fear. I felt like I was alone in a blizzard and had to find shelter from the consequences of my mistakes. I believed I could never trust a man again. I didn't know what to do or where to go, but I knew I had to start a life on my own. I was going to be independent. I would get a job, find a home and raise my child all by myself. It turns out I haven't been alone for one minute."

Brendan stirred. Aislynn rose and lifted him into her arms. She paused to kiss Cap on the forehead.

He placed a hand on her cheek. "I know you've had bad times. Just think, with every step forward, you get to leave somethin' behind. It'd be good for you to take that step."

Aislynn straightened, tapped her foot and peered down at him. "Why aren't you telling him all of this?"

Cap held up his hands. "He's too ornery. He wouldn't listen. 'Sides, women are braver than men. It don't seem so because they're all soft lookin' and show their fears and all those other feelin's men ain't got the courage to own up to. But you women, you're tough as old leather."

"I guess I have a great deal to think about."

"Gal, you gotta stop thinkin' and start doin'."

CHAPTER 27

THE early September sun blushed the sky as Sage and Cap arrived for dinner. As Aislynn put Brendan to bed, Amy regaled the group with the dramas of her day. Betty had discovered a spot of paint on her family's Bible. The tale of tears, the wringing of hands and Joan's attempt to quiet the girl entertained Amy's eager audience. She reported on her spelling test and the story she read. She was finishing her account of Martin Peaver and his encounter with a bee, when Aislynn took her seat.

"What's new in the wider world?"

"I'm goin' on a buffalo hunt," Sage announced.

"They're very big," Amy affirmed.

"Yes, missy, they are. Injuns gotta hunt them for food, clothes, and shelters."

Fear flared in Aislynn's core. "Why you? Where are you going? How long?" Anxiety made her voice rise.

"Spotted Tail and Red Cloud got permission to move off the reservation to hunt below the railroad in the Republican Valley," Sage told Cap.

"That Red Cloud and Spotted Tail are smart ones. They got themselves to Washington and told Grant they ain't warriors no more; they're peaceful politicians," Cap explained.

"President Grant and the commissioner of the Indian Bureau need an interpreter, a man they can trust to make sure the Brulé and Oglala pass in peace." He turned to Aislynn and said, "I'll be gone two or three months."

Without thinking, Aislynn's feelings left her heart and her emotions rushed past her lips. Her eyes held Sage's. "I don't want you to go."

Sage blinked his disbelief. With an uncertain tone, he said, "I don't want to go."

Her voice trembled. "It's such a long time."

He cocked his head and gave her a grin. His voice was soft and low. "If I had a choice . . ."

Aislynn's "I'll miss you" sounded like "I love you."

Her feelings filtered through and settled on him. His whole body, always tense and taut, relaxed as if a valve had been opened, releasing the pressure of his fear and doubt.

Amy studied the couple. She tugged Aislynn's sleeve. "Ma, maybe we should go with him. That way we won't miss each other. Smokey and Cap can come. It's called a vacation."

His attention shifted. "A buffalo hunt ain't a vacation, missy," Sage explained. "It's serious business. Besides, it's hundreds of miles away."

"Ann Marie went on a vacation to Denver."

Sage leaned toward Aislynn. With an evocative grin and eyes shining into hers, he suggested, "When I get back . . ."

Aislynn's cheeks flushed and her whole body warmed. "Yes." She nodded to Sage.

Cap piped up, "Well, I got to meet a man about a horse." He stood, covered Amy's hair with his hands and kissed the top of her head. "Sure wish I could take you on a vacation tonight."

"To see a man about a horse?" Amy asked in confusion.

"Forget the man with the horse. We could take Smokey and go to Kramer's Ice Cream Parlor. You could spend the night at our house. That'd be like a vacation."

Beaming at Aislynn with her little hands folded, Amy implored, "Can I please?"

Aislynn quickly realized Amy's absence would leave her alone for the night. Her eyes flew open. She looked at Cap. "I don't think that's a good idea."

Amy jumped up and down clapping her hands. "Please, please?"

Stifling a laugh, Sage said, "That is a right nice offer. Go get your duds and your schoolwork."

Aislynn's hand moved to her throat, and she clutched her blouse closed. "I didn't say yes," she protested.

Sage gave her a look that could start a fire. "But you will."

She crossed her other arm over her breasts. Amy rushed to the sleeping alcove. "Ma has a carpetbag."

"Shhh, don't wake your brother."

Like a tiny tornado, Amy spun through the cabin gathering her things. She stuffed books, clothes, a blanket, her hairbrush and a doll into the case. "I'm ready." The child stood at the door. Her coat hung askew, buttoned incorrectly. Her hat tilted over her eyes. The carpetbag, too full to close, was clutched in both of her tiny hands.

"Adios," Cap called as they shuffled out the door.

"That was fast," Aislynn said with an edge to her voice.

"Hmm, depends on how you look at it." His eyes shined with amusement.

Aislynn picked up the dishes and stacked them in the wash pan. She heard Sage's chair scrape the floor. Her heart pounded and her breathing quickened. Suddenly afraid, she thought she knew how a criminal felt before the verdict was delivered.

His hands fell on her shoulders. He whispered, "They can wait, I can't." He placed a kiss on the nape of her neck. Her blood surged from her heart to her brain, causing a wave of lightheadedness.

With a halting breath, she turned to him. Sage took her face in his hands and brushed his lips over hers.

The slight touch stirred her desire. He repeated the act. A tiny whimper escaped her throat. She parted her lips. Sage spread his hands across her back and kissed her deeply. Aislynn's whole body sighed against his.

When Sage pulled away and looked into her eyes, a tiny spark of reason ignited in Aislynn's mind. "Stop, please stop. This is not proper." Aislynn shook her head and pushed Sage away.

He looked down at her with a blank expression, Aislynn heard "hmmm . . ." as he walked away.

Sage took two glasses from the cupboard and grabbed the bottle of whiskey sitting on its bonnet. He half-filled the glasses and gave Aislynn one. She looked at the shimmering liquid and curled her nose.

"Come on." Sage pulled her to his chair by the fire. Once seated, he ordered, "Sit."

Aislynn turned toward Cap's rocker. Sage grabbed her skirt and tugged her back. "Here."

"On your lap?" she asked in a tone laced with offended dignity.

He patted his thigh. Aislynn's heart pounded; she could feel her blood pulsing through her veins. Her eyes dipped to the space between his legs. With a hand on her hip, he pulled her down. Keeping her eyes glued to his, she sat. Sage slowly looped his arm around her body until his hand came to rest on her thigh. He clinked her glass and said, "Drink."

Aislynn straightened into her proper lady posture and took a long sip. Sage watched her with an unreadable expression. Discomfort moved Aislynn to speak. "I promised myself I would not enter into a compromising situation again."

"Situation?"

"Yes, you know very well what I mean. We shouldn't even be discussing this. It is inappropriate. You and Cap cooked up this whole scheme."

Sage interrupted, "This was not my idea. I have to credit Cap. I had nothing to do with this plan, but I do merit it's a good one." He smiled broadly.

"We're not married; we're not even engaged."

"Soon as I get back we can be."

"You might not come back."

"I will be back."

"You have no way of knowing that. I am not making another mistake."

His demeanor became serious. "You think I'm a mistake?"

Aislynn overcame her reticence. She knew she could be direct with Sage. "You're not a mistake; this behavior is. I know where this is leading, and I will not be left with another child."

"I wouldn't do that."

A wave of relief washed over her. Calm set in and her heart rate slowed. She laughed at her assumption. "I'm sorry. I thought you wanted to stay the night."

Sage's head jerked back. "I do."

"I don't understand."

"You will."

Aislynn shook her head. "We should wait."

"I've been with you every day since you stepped off that train; that's a long time. Your choice; you want me or not?"

Aislynn knew there were times in life when the future can be determined by one word or one act. She gazed at his face with its questioning eyes and willing lips. Like a rush of photos depicting the ways he had shown his love, in her mind's eye he rescued her, delivered Brendan and danced with Amy. She relented. "Yes."

"Finish that. I'm ready to call it a day."

Panic spread through Aislynn like a roaring prairie fire. "But . . ."

Sage pulled the comb binding her hair. "You gotta trust me."

He placed her empty glass on the table. With a quick kiss, he said, "You get yourself into bed; I'll finish this drink."

When Aislynn reached the sleeping alcove her twin tyrants, fear and guilt, greeted her, ready to take control. In frustration, she shook her head until her entire body vibrated. Then, like a curtain parting, she saw the truth. *That's exactly what Liam wanted. He's not even here, yet I continue to give him the power to control me. As long as I'm afraid and ashamed, I'll be alone. Sage was right. I was a nineteen-year-old, "stupid," lonely widow who made one error in judgment.* She caught her reflection in the mirror and peered into her own eyes. She told herself, *Break Liam's hold. Push him out of your head and let Orrin into your heart. Have the life you always wanted with a husband, a father for your children and a loving home.*

She addressed her necessities and donned her nightgown. After checking on Brendan, she crawled under the blanket and pulled it up to her chin. As soon as the bed creaked under her weight, the lamps in the cabin went dark. Watching the light of a candle move toward the alcove, Aislynn felt a flicker of doubt. *Let it go!* Sage parted the drapes. She pinched her eyes closed, too shy and nervous to watch him undress. When the mattress sagged, it pitched her into his taut, muscular body.

"It ain't like you to be so quiet." His voice was soft and low.

Words teetered on her tongue, but they could not find their way out. He propped himself on an elbow and rested his head in his hand. "Want to change your mind?"

"No," she replied with a certainty she did not feel.

Sage filled his hand with her hair and let it slowly flow through his fingers. His lips found her forehead, and his hand descended to her hip. He started to pull at the night-gown. "You don't need this." He coaxed it over her head. She eased down next to him.

He took her hand in his. His fingers ran over the tiny bones in her wrist. "You're like a little bird. You know their bones are hollow, real fragile." He kissed her palm and said, "You say if I'm hurtin' you."

Aislynn nodded. He pulled her to him. "Your heart's beatin' as fast as a scared rabbit. You gotta trust me."

His hand found her breast. Immediately, Aislynn could feel her milk rising. "Oh, dear." She squirmed away, sat back on her heels and grabbed her abandoned nightgown. She pressed it against her breasts, trying to staunch the flow, flustered and red-faced.

"It's natural," he whispered in his deep, rolling bass. "I guess I'll have to share with Brendan for a while." He lay back with his head on his arms wearing a contented grin. "You know how long I've been waitin' on you?"

Aislynn studied him and shook her head.

"I believe I've been thinkin' about you since April 5th, 1868."

Puzzled, she recalled, "That's the day Johnny and I arrived in Cheyenne."

Sage nodded.

The memory rose vividly in her mind. "You were gambling at Ford's when we came in to eat. You noticed me?"

"Weren't many wide-eyed, white, female innocents rollin' through back then who weren't covered in sweat and dust. Every man in Cheyenne noticed a clean, decent woman." He eyed her slyly. "Difference was, I got to talk to you, got close enough to smell your scent and taste your cookin'." He ran his finger across her mouth. "I even got to feel your lips on my cheek. I got through some rough times rememberin' somethin' as fine as you lived in this sorry world."

Tears rose in her eyes. She dropped her gown and lay next to him. With her hand on his cheek, she said, "I am so sorry it took me so long to see."

His arms encircled her. "I don't think I made it easy." He gave her a long, leisurely kiss that reached to her core and erased all her fears. A yearning to be a part of him flowed through her. Aislynn pressed against him. His hands and his tongue roamed her curves and hollows. Her breathing fell into rhythm with his. When his hand slipped between her legs, she trembled. When she moaned, he entered with aching slowness. Aislynn could feel his heat as his movements increased in force and speed. Not wanting to wake Brendan, she bit her lips, stifling her cries. With his first, hard thrust, Aislynn's excitement soared. His second sent her over the edge. With his third, he pulled out and spilled his seed on her thigh and the rumpled sheets.

Sage rolled over beside her, recovering his breath. As the rapture wafted away, her mind cleared; she understood the impact of the unexpected act.

She sat up and looked down at Sage and his self-satisfied grin. "That's all it takes?"

His feathers ruffled. "It ain't as easy as I made it seem," he protested.

"Why don't women know?"

"It's a man's business."

"We're the ones left with the babies," she said with disbelief saturating her tone.

Sage shrugged. "Men make the rules."

"Can all men do that?"

"Don't know why they couldn't."

"Does it work?"

"Should."

"You don't sound very sure."

"You'll be fine."

"Why wouldn't Liam have done that?"

"Because men want to stake their claims." Sage reached up and took her chin in his hand. "When I get back, it's exactly what I'm gonna do."

Sage invited her into his arms. Aislynn rested her head on the hard knot of muscles in his shoulder. It surprised Aislynn to discover that despite the discrepancy in their sizes, her body fit perfectly against his. She gently traced the wide white scars slashed through the forest of hair on his chest. They reflected the pain he had endured his whole life. She imagined the battles he had fought with Indians, rebels and outlaws.

"Do these wounds hurt?"

"Not *now*." She could feel him smiling.

"And the ones I can't touch?"

"You can't undo what's been done, but I do believe you have the power to heal."

A swell of emotion filled her heart. She searched for huge, expressive words to tell him what she was feeling. Overcome, Aislynn simply said, "I want you to be happy."

"I am." He squeezed her thigh.

"I don't mean this."

"Me, neither." Sage brushed a light kiss on her hair.

Even in his sleep, Sage was hyperalert. He sprang out of bed and carried Brendan to Aislynn before she heard his tiny cries. She sat up and began nursing. Sage lit a candle and returned to bed. He draped an arm around her and stroked her hair. The baby's enthusiastic sucking amused Sage. "He sure makes serious work of eatin'."

Aislynn tipped her head toward him. "Men do that. This could take a while; you should sleep."

"With that racket? Besides, I'd rather watch."

"This will get rather boring," she said.

"Not to me."

Aislynn tilted her head back and stretched to kiss him.

"See? It's gettin' interestin' already."

With Brendan's appetite satiated, Sage returned him to his cradle. Aislynn moved to the dresser and wiped off her milk with a wet rag. Sage stood behind her and took the cloth from her hand. She watched in the mirror as he gently circled her breasts. He squeezed the rag and a stream of cool water trickled over her belly and ran between her legs. The cloth followed the water. Aislynn gasped, trying to catch her breath. She reached her arms around his neck to steady herself. With one quick movement, he lifted her off the floor and took her back to bed.

When Aislynn's heart rate slowed and she could form recognizable words, she leaned over Sage and said, "I am going to miss you."

"I believe I'll feel the same."

"Who's going to take care of me when you aren't hovering about?"

"You be careful while I'm gone." His returned to his usual stern tone.

"I'm always careful."

Sage *pfft*ed. "Deputy Winston will keep an eye out. You behave and stay where you belong."

"You're so bossy."

"You're supposed to mind your man."

"Ha, I would think by now you would have lowered your expectations."

"I can see I have to take you in hand." Sage grabbed her leg and urged it over him. "Mount up here and kiss me like you ain't gonna see me for months."

A sadness, like mourning, filled the space left by Sage's absence. His importance in their lives became clear. Amy crossed off every day of the hunt on the calendar. After ten days, she still asked the same question at supper. "When will he be back?"

Cap gave her the same answer, "When he gets here."

Even Brendan noticed. As Aislynn bustled to get a meal on the table, the usual sign of Sage's arrival, the baby's gaze fell on the door.

Aislynn missed the daily sparring with her favorite curmudgeon. She moved through her days waiting to hear the low grumble of his voice. At night, lying alone, she ached for his scent, his taste and his touch.

Another Tuesday and another laundry day arrived at Aislynn's house. After the soaking, washing and wringing, the sheets and towels sat ready for the line. Aislynn placed Brendan on her bed for a nap. She surrounded him with pillows and closed the curtains. The house stood hushed. Amy sat in her schoolroom. Cap attended a hearing and brought Smokey along for some exercise.

Aislynn stepped out back with her full basket. She struggled against the wind until everything danced on the line. Across the prairie, heavy storm clouds kneeled on the edge of the sky. She hoped the laundry would dry before the storm arrived.

Once inside, Aislynn heard the sound of confident steps rapping against the stairs. Heavy wooden heels crossed the porch. *Sage! He couldn't stay away!* A thrill passed through her body and a smile crossed her face. Regret that she had placed Brendan on the bed flashed through her mind. Just as quickly, she reprimanded herself for being such a loose woman. She swung the door open with uncontained joy.

She found a tall, dark man with black hair and pale blue eyes, wearing a wicked half smile.

CHAPTER 28

"L IAM!"
"You're eager to see me."

Shock stunned her. When she collected her thoughts, she realized Liam Moran stood on her porch and her precious Brendan lay hidden behind the curtain. A sick fear made every nerve ending spring to attention.

Moran's eyes raked over her body. Her blush crept up her cheeks.

Reflexively, she guarded her door with one hand clenching the knob and the other fastened on the jamb. He removed his hat and bowed dramatically. "May I come in?" Moran reached for her waist. When Aislynn instinctively stepped backwards, he pushed his way into the room. With him came the familiar scent of old bourbon and expensive cigars.

He leaned over her. "Aren't you going to kiss me?"

"No." She wanted to sound strong and forceful, but the word came out soft and vulnerable.

"Oh yes, let's close the door," he said in a suggestive tone. "I missed you." He sidled up to her and touched her hip.

Aislynn twisted away. She assessed him for a moment. He stood tall, sure, arrogant. The word *danger* shined in his eyes. *I've faced worse than you.* She threw her shoulders back and struck a confident attitude. "It's been a year and a half, Liam."

"My poor darling, you missed me, too."

Caustically, she replied, "That would be an overstatement."

Moran chose to ignore her remark. He frowned over the cabin, appraising everything with his eyes. "This is . . . quaint."

Aislynn recognized the insult. "I like it," she stated with pride.

Moran placed his hat on the rack and took a seat at the table. "Aren't you going to offer me a cup of coffee?"

Aislynn turned away and approached the stove. She told herself to stay calm and protect Brendan. She handed him the coffee flavored with cream.

"You remembered," he said with longing.

"I remember a great deal," she snapped.

"That pleases me. I hoped you hadn't forgotten." His eyes held hers. They were sure and unblinking. He patted the seat next to his.

Beware. He knows.

Stiffening her back, she lowered herself into the chair and asked formally, "What brings you to Cheyenne, Mr. Moran?"

His brow stitched at her formality, but he caught himself and grinned. "You, of course."

"Me? After all this time, you've come to see me?"

"It took me quite a while to forgive you."

"Forgive me?" she asked with disbelief.

"Yes." His eyes narrowed. "You did leave me four days before our wedding."

"I recall you walking out. In fact, I can still hear the sound of the door slamming."

"You left *me*. I had to face all of my friends and colleagues."

"I asked you to come with me. I even suggested we get married and go to New York together, but you refused. You were so jealous you couldn't understand that I had to go to Tim."

"Perhaps I did understand and had reason to be jealous."

"You know better. Tim took care of me my whole life. How could I refuse to help him after he lost Emma and the baby?"

"You were always so concerned with Tim. I cared for you. I loved you but you left me," he said with bitterness.

A tiny kernel of contrition mixed with sympathy formed. She appealed to him. "But you wouldn't listen. You could never see reason when it came to Tim. I did everything you asked of me. I asked one thing of you, to understand my feelings, but you couldn't."

"You never understood mine. When you made your decision to go to New York, did you consider how I would feel?" For a moment, they faced each other in silence. Moran continued, "You forced me to explain your absence to all our wedding guests. The memory still stings with humiliation. However, when I explained that you refused to obey me, my friends agreed calling off the wedding was the best way to deal with an obstinate woman."

Aislynn crossed her arms and slid back in her chair. *I'm sure they are all men just like you: rich, powerful and demanding.*

Moran added, "I presume things didn't work out as you hoped with Tim."

"You know I had no such hopes. I wrote to you. I sent telegrams and two letters. Why didn't you answer me?" It was more of a plea than a question.

"I took our wedding trip. I went to Europe."

"Alone?"

"Of course not. There are always other women who—"

Aislynn cut him off. "You recovered quickly." *I want to console a grieving friend, and you fly into a rage. You consort with God-only-knows how many women you aren't married to, and you brag about it to me. The breadth of the inequity is wider than the prairie.*

Moran sneered at her. "Since you were running to Tim, you should not throw stones, my dear. We were abroad for months, so it was quite a while before I saw any communication from you."

"Yet you never replied," she reminded him.

"That was rude of me, but I wanted to punish you. I wanted some revenge." He said the words slowly as if he were explaining them to a child. "I wanted you to feel the same sting of rejection." He spat the last word at her.

Punish, revenge? Aislynn held her tongue, trying to assess the purpose of his visit.

"I was drunk most of the time. When I sobered up, I decided I had ignored you long enough. At the end of July, I sent a detective after you." He turned his palm up and with a look, asked her for her hand.

Aislynn kept her distance. "You should have come yourself."

"His report said you were Sage's woman. You were cooking, cleaning and with him every night. I couldn't believe it." His eyes burned into hers. "I never imagined you would throw me over so quickly for a man you barely knew. Tim, I could understand, but Sage? I was so angry. I swear I could have broken you in two." His vicious words sounded calm and controlled.

Moran continued, "Your mother-in-law recently inform-ed me that you're not married to him. I found that bewilder-ing. You're the marrying kind. You jumped at my proposal. Yet all this time has gone by, and you're not married to him. Surely, the original report was wrong or something is keeping you from marrying him." His brows rose and his eyes shined. "I believe I know what that is."

Curious, but cautious, she asked, "You do?"

"Of course, it's obvious." Moran took her hand; his thumb stroked her palm. His affection sent her mind racing and her thoughts tumbling. Her months of fears and worries could not have been misplaced. He had to know; he wanted her son. Liam added, "It was insensitive and cruel of me to leave you pining, but I was hurt and humiliated. However, I read your letters again." He pulled two envelopes from his breast pocket. "They tell me all I need to know."

Buried in the recesses of her mind, behind a wall of fears, lay a tiny grain of hope that he would come to her, declare his love and want them to be a family. In weak, lonely mo-ments, she had thrown a great deal of creative energy into embellishing the details of their happy reunion. In saner moments, she suppressed the fantasy, knowing she did not have the remotest chance of ever making a good life with him. Doubt flashed through her mind. *Was I wrong? Did I let my fears distort reality? Did you love me?*

"You think I've been waiting all these months for you?" she asked with disbelief.

"That's what I'm saying. You didn't stay with Tim, and you haven't married Sage. What else could it be? You still love me." Expressing his magnanimity, he added, "I am will-ing to put everything behind us and take you back. I think I can finally forgive, let us say, your minor indiscretions."

In the face of his reproof, Aislynn challenged him. "What indiscretions?"

"What would you call it when a wife leaves her husband to run to another man?" His grip tightened and a whiff of anger wafted toward her.

"I am not your wife. We never signed any papers."

"You shared a bed with *me*; quite willingly, I might add. Our *consummation*"—as he said the word his eyes raced over her body—"gives me the right to claim you as my wife."

Aislynn's face burned scarlet, from the shame of her actions and the sensual memory of the acts. She regained her focus and retrieved her hand. "Your wife? Your claim?"

"You made a promise to me."

"I tried to keep that promise. I returned to Utah. You didn't."

"That doesn't change anything. Any court would agree; I never relinquished my rights."

"In Wyoming, women sit on juries. I'm sure they will consider my rights."

Moran mocked her with a soft laugh. "Aislynn, you are so naive. My charges would be heard in a Utah court where no women sit on juries and your Marshal Sage holds no sway."

Utah? Jurisdiction never occurred to her. She lived in Wyoming and assumed if it came to a court case, it would be judged in her own territory. The shock made Aislynn sit up straighter. A sense of dread roiled inside her. She searched for a defense. "This is not a matter of law. It's a matter of the heart, and my heart does not belong to you."

His grin seemed forced and indulgent. "We had one real disagreement. We can overcome that."

"Liam, you don't understand. I didn't leave simply to help Tim. I wasn't happy." She huffed with frustration. "You had this idea of me, an image you conjured. You tried to mold me into that image, and I tried to be that woman." Aislynn shook her head. "I couldn't then; I certainly can't now."

"But you love me." He tapped the forlorn letters.

Aislynn touched his arm. A tiny bit of regret touched her. "That was months ago. I'm not that scared, insecure girl anymore."

"The woman I see is even more beautiful and exciting."

Aislynn lent him a tolerant smile. "I thank you for the compliment but it's too late. I've made a life here." She scanned the cabin, darkening under the approaching clouds.

His eyes roamed the room. "I can see what you have here." His faced turned sour, and he shook his head.

"You have no idea what I have." She thought of Sage.

"This isn't your life, Aislynn." His eyes narrowed and frustration dusted his words. "Your life is with me."

Aislynn tried to reason with him. "I'm sure you're earnest, but we are so wrong for each other." She touched his cheek. In a soft voice, she asked for understanding. "We had some inexplicable attraction, but it wasn't love. Truth be told, we never trusted each other. Without trust, you cannot have love. I genuinely want you to find someone to love, someone who will make you happy. I am not that woman."

Moran's tone hinted of anger. "Aislynn, I will not be humiliated a second time. I want you to come home to Utah with me."

"Liam, you cannot make me go with you."

He relaxed in the chair, rested both arms on the table and asked, "Who's going to stop me?"

Understanding hit Aislynn like a slap. "Is that why you're here now?" Her head fell back and she spoke to the ceiling. "Spotted Tail's buffalo hunt, the story was in the national columns of all the newspapers." Aislynn shook her head. "You've been waiting for Sage to leave town."

"He's a murderer."

"He's a lawman; he only kills when he has to."

"Hmm, would he mind if I took you home?"

"Of course he'd mind." Anger rose in her voice.

"Good thing he's not here." He glowed with confidence.

Fear bubbled up in her belly and formed a knot in her throat. A terrible awareness settled over her. All her worst imaginings were coming true. She admonished herself for her foolishness. For those two years at Treasure Mountain, she viewed his overtures and innuendo as exciting and sensual. The danger he radiated seemed magnetic and intoxicating. However, those feelings were actually an alarm she never heard. She allowed herself to be drawn into a web where he held all the power and control.

His plan started to unfold in her mind. Aislynn remembered Moran never gambled carelessly. He would not be here if he did not hold all the cards. Moran knew Deputy Winston had no jurisdiction and calculated the Democratic sheriff would not help her. *Don't show your fear.*

"Liam, you're being absurd." Aislynn tried to sound dismissive. "Why would you even think of taking me to Utah? No, don't tell me," she scoffed, "more punishment and revenge."

"I don't like losing, Aislynn. You see, in my version, I walked out when you disobeyed me. Now, you have learned your lesson, and you've come crawling back, meek as a lamb." He threw his arms up in celebration. "I win." His contemptuous smile chilled her.

Aislynn faced him squarely. "When have I ever been meek?"

He grabbed her chin in his hand. "I've always enjoyed your independent streak."

Aislynn jerked her head free. "What will you do when you get bored with it? Walk out again?"

"That's a man's prerogative. I'll have no lack of company, whereas you'll be alone at the ranch until I decide to return."

"My friends and family will keep me company. They may even help me leave." She sat back and crossed her arms.

"Not if I order their husbands to forbid contact with you. Don't forget, they all work for me."

A vision of Virginia appeared in her mind. Aislynn searched her brain for a threat of her own. Leaning closer, she hurled a damning option at him. "There will always be those lonesome ranch hands."

Moran's hand flew up, but he held it back. "No, Aislynn, that's not you."

She drummed up her bravado. In a menacing tone, she said, "Liam, you have no idea what a woman will do when she's alone and desperate."

"I'd kill you."

She tipped her head to the side and shrugged. "Then, we'd both lose."

Moran stared at her for a long moment. When his eyes softened, she knew he was changing his tactic. Moran placed his hand on her cheek. "You're a woman of great passion." His eyes rested on her mouth. "It belongs to me and I want it back," he declared with the certainty of a man who always gets what he wants.

"No!" her voice rose. She looked at Moran and saw Mr. Brett. She pushed her chair back and stood. "I want you to leave!"

Moran leaned back with his legs spread wide and his hands behind his head. "I have a carriage waiting. I'll give you a few minutes to gather the things you value. I want to make the 1:10 train."

I'll kick and scream. In her head, she could see the scene in the street developing. Deputy Winston, Sheriff Preshaw, the accumulating onlookers. "She's my wife," Liam would shout and the crowd would gasp. "I never married him," she would protest. Liam would declare he knew her intimately. She visualized the shock on Winston's face and felt Sage's humiliation when he returned and heard the sorry tale of her public disgrace. Aislynn's heart raced and her temperature rose. Fear dampened her skin. Defeat stared her in the face. She closed her eyes and willed it away. She blinked but it remained unmoved. *Better to leave quietly than disgrace Sage publically.* Carrying a crushing loneliness, Aislynn dragged herself to the alcove.

It's over. All my plans with Sage are over. Aislynn swallowed the lump in her throat and brushed away her tears. *Amy? I have to get her. Dear God, what will he do with her?* She gently woke Brendan, straightened his clothes and combed his flaxen hair with her fingers. Another more horrifying thought entered her frantic mind. *Oh good Lord, he'll take you.* A terror worse than what she felt lying in the muck of that barn made her feel truly faint for the first time in her life. She steadied herself against the bed. In a frenzy, she searched the alcove. *No door, no window, no tiny revolver. I could run out the back door with Brendan but to where? Absent neighbors? The prairie? He'd chase me down. Another scene.* She took a few long, deep breaths. Squeezing her eyes closed, Aislynn prayed, "Blessed Mother Mary, please help me." On unsteady legs, she faced Liam.

She stood before him with their child; panic silenced her voice. Moran's brows rose and his eyes searched hers. Aislynn had rehearsed this moment hundreds, maybe thousands of times. What they would say; what they wouldn't. It made her head spin to remember all the dreadful outcomes she had imagined.

"What's that?" he demanded.

"This is Brendan."

As Moran studied the baby, his expression grew darker. His eyes narrowed and his lips tightened as he leaned over the table. "How old is he?"

The blood pounding through her veins buzzed in her ears. She fell into the seat opposite him. "Almost nine months," tumbled from her dry mouth.

Moran's eyes focused on the child's fair hair and pale complexion. She could see his fingers moving counting off the months. His face turned into a black scowl. "Is this how you comforted your golden-haired Tim?"

The question baffled her. He stopped for a moment. "Sage is a blond, but I can't believe you would have jumped into his bed that easily . . . or maybe you did." He calculated again. "Did you stop here to seek comfort with him after Tim rejected you?" The furious, vitriolic thoughts streamed unfiltered from his mouth. His meaning blossomed in her mind. "Ha!" he derided. "He's not sure! That's why you're not married to Sage." His mocking stopped. His eyes wandered to the wide bed. Moran's jaw dropped and his hand rushed to his throat. "Is this what a woman does when she's alone and desperate?" His eyes widened and his voice descended into a growl. "How have you supported yourself?"

Aislynn pulled away from him. His words fell like physical blows. She pressed the sleepy baby's head between her breasts and curled her arms around him. Her mouth opened, but no sound escaped. His words stunned her; they were too offensive, too outlandish to comprehend. Never, in all her conjuring, had she imagined he would deny his own child. For so long, her fears of losing Brendan grew with a fevered intensity that blinded her; she could not see around it. She lost sight of a man's perspective, of Moran's perspective. Perhaps she neglected to consider it at all. Aislynn broke an age-old rule of female behavior and fornicated with a man outside of marriage. She took Moran into her bed. Of course, he assumed she would do it again with others.

With each of his angry breaths, she could see their value diminishing. Moran demanded the best of everything. His imagination made Brendan's paternity questionable and rendered them undesirable. The instantaneous sting of rejection and urge to defend herself and her precious child was replaced with a release that staggered her. *You don't want us!* Like a lamp out of oil, the fears she had harbored for so many months sputtered away. His significance in their lives vanished.

Suddenly, Moran's tone changed. His face burned red. He looked at her with uncertainty. "He's not mine; we couldn't make such a fair child." It sounded more like a question than a statement. He vibrated with suspicious fury. "Tell me! Who is his father?"

The abrupt alteration confounded her.

His eyes scorched hers. "Tell me the truth, Aislynn." His hands coiled into fists.

Recovering her equilibrium, her confidence rose and a surprising calmness settled over her. "You have already declared he's not yours."

"Aislynn, if he belongs to me—" His face contorted with anger, and he slammed his hand on the table.

The sharp noise jolted Brendan and he began crying. Aislynn rocked and petted her baby.

"You should have told me you were with child."

"And whose child should I have said I was carrying? Tim's? Sage's? Yours?" Sarcasm permeated her questions.

"Don't toy with me! Tell me the truth!" Moran stood. He seemed to grow larger, filling the room with his rage.

"Would you take the word of a whore?" she sassed. "If I said *yes*, would you think I wanted your money, your influence, your power for my child?" She tossed her head. "If I said *yes*, would you take us back to Utah? Would you raise a child you weren't sure was your own?" Aislynn narrowed her eyes and sneered at him. "I know you, Liam. You don't trust anyone; you never have. I could assure you and promise you this boy was yours, but we both know you would spend the rest of your life scrutinizing him. Is he bookish like Tim? Is he strong and muscular like Sage? Maybe, beneath his tow-head, he has your aptitude for figures. You have painted this picture puzzle with you, Sage and Tim. Whose could he be? I'll be honest with you, Liam." She erupted with force. "He's my son!"

Moran's fingers closed around her arm. Sensing danger, Brendan wailed. Her instinct to protect her child flared. Aislynn tore away. She pressed one of Brendan's ears against her breast and covered the other with her hand.

Relentless, he continued, "You don't know, do you? If my friends and associates ever find out what a slut you are . . . You are not making a fool of me!"

You've done a fine job of that without my help, you sad, angry, misguided man. Aislynn rocked Brendan and cooed in his ear. Calm and content, Aislynn stated, "I think it's time for you to leave."

With a jolt, he grabbed a chair and flung it across the floor. It scraped along the wood like fingernails on a chalkboard until it came to rest against the wall. He stood over her breathing fire. "You disgust me."

She looked up at him and said, "And men think women are fickle."

Moran stamped toward the door. He retrieved his hat. Turning to her, he maligned her child. "You know Aislynn, without a father your boy is a bastard."

Aislynn smiled. "As I recall, Liam, so are you."

Sharp steps on the porch distracted Aislynn. *Sage!* Panic rose again. This time she was not sure if it was for herself or Liam. The hard knocking filled her with relief. She rushed between Liam and the door. When she threw it open, she found Deputy Winston.

He touched his hat. "Mornin' Mrs. Maher. Barney Ford reported a strange man askin' after you." The deputy peered into the cabin. His eyes found Moran and the upended chair. "Marshal asked me to check on you to make sure you're gettin' on."

"Thank you so much. That is very kind if you. Everything is fine. In fact, Mr. Moran was just leaving." Aislynn stepped away from the deputy. She swept her hand in the direction of the door. Her words flowed like sweet syrup. "Thank you for coming by, Mr. Moran. I am so happy we have an understanding. Now, there's no reason for us to ever see each other again. Goodbye."

CHAPTER 29

THE front lock rattled and the door squeaked open. Aislynn sprang out of bed. In the watery light of the early November dawn, she saw Sage. For days, he had debriefed and deloused at Fort Russell while she waited. He dropped his bundle and opened his arms.

A long kiss ended when he pulled back. "Let me hang my things, and we can get reacquainted," he said with a smile and raised brows.

"I'll get my robe and slippers."

Sage's hand shot out behind him and grabbed her arm. "No need for that." He turned and pulled her close again.

"Amy and Brendan are in the bed."

"Hmmm, well, ma'am, I brought you a gift."

He untied the large bundle and unfurled a buffalo skin. "My reward for helpin' the Spotted Tail and Red Cloud."

Aislynn turned up her nose. "It smells quite gamy."

He tilted his head and opened his hands. "It came from a buffalo. It's a real honor."

"I'll air it out for a few days."

"Why don't you give it a try? Take a seat." She looked at the pelt and back at Sage. "Go on," he coaxed.

With sour face, she knelt on the fur and sat back on her heels.

Sage crouched with his hands on his knees and framed her between his thighs. "You could lie down . . . ."

"Orrin Sage, I will not lie with you on a buffalo skin on the floor," she whispered with certainty.

In a low voice, he said, "Gal, I've been wantin' you for over two months. Thinkin' about you day and night. I expected a warmer welcome." He ran a finger along her chin and down her neck.

She studied his disappointment and surveyed the fragrant mattress.

"Sixty-four long, cold, lonely nights," he coaxed. With a wide smile, his finger traveled down the opening of her gown.

Aislynn laughed at his dramatic entreaty. She drew herself up, puckered her lips and kissed him. As she pulled away, she reconsidered. She leaned in, opened her mouth and tried again. Sage circled her tongue with his. Aislynn took a breath and murmured, "Aren't you a bit overdressed, Marshal?"

Sage rolled on his back and wove his arms around Aislynn. She snuggled into the hollow of his shoulder. When the afterglow faded, she said, "I should get dressed and make some breakfast."

"Fine idea, I'm hungry. Cap is bringin' Joan here at 7:30. Winston will be comin', too. We can get this thing done."

"You truly are a romantic."

"You and Cap will have all day to switch homes. Get those children in their own beds, in their own room by tonight."

Aislynn cleared the table and sat next to Sage, sipping her coffee. His fingers drummed on the cloth. "I hear you had a visitor."

"Did Winston ride out to the fort to give you a report?"

"Yes."

Aislynn recounted Moran's short and tumultuous visit. "He didn't think we could have made such a fair, blond child."

Sage entwined his fingers in hers. His voice filled with sorrow. "Guess he made the same foolish mistake as me. Makes me feel kinda sorry for him."

With a nod and a forgiving hand on his cheek, Aislynn echoed words he had said to her. "You were young and stupid. All you knew about women you learned from those Indian-hating soldiers at that fort." She slipped her hand under his chin. "Orrin, if we forgive each other and ourselves for our sins, we can build a good life together." Sage placed a soft kiss on her hand. Aislynn continued, "I realized something while I was face-to-face with him. A father isn't the man who plants the seed. A father is a man who provides for a child, a man who will do anything to protect a child. A father never walks away when things get tough or disagreeable or when they seem out of his control." Aislynn rose and stood in front of Sage. He pulled her into his lap. With her arms around his neck, she said, "You truly are Brendan and Amy's father."

With a kiss, he said, "I aim to take care of the three of you. Although I have to credit you did good with Moran all by yourself."

"I believe I may have had some help." Aislynn looked up at the ceiling.

Sage gave her a puzzled look.

"It was a miracle. I prayed to the Virgin Mary for help and poof—he was gone."

"Just like that?" He snapped his fingers.

"With a bit of yelling and name calling." She laughed. "But true or not, I'm labeling it a miracle." Aislynn placed a quick kiss on his nose.

"No such thing as miracles."

She jerked her chin at him. "Really? I'm marrying you in a few minutes."

"Gal, you succumbed to my charms."

She took his face in her hands and gave him a pitiful shake of her head. "I think it's more realistic to believe in miracles."

When the clock struck 7:30, Aislynn and Sage stood before Cap. Between them, Amy held Brendan's hands as he wobbled on unsteady legs. Joan and Winston flanked the bride and groom.

"I got just a few lines you need to say. 'I, Orrin Sage, take Aislynn . . . I, Aislynn Maher, take Orrin Sage . . .' " Cap looked at Winston. "Got the ring?"

Winston handed the groom a tiny gold band. Sage lifted Aislynn's hand and discovered Johnny's claddagh ring occupying the intended space. An awkward silence fell as all eyes settled on the little gold heart.

Sage's voice rose softly. "The past is always gonna be with us, Aislynn. Why don't you wear that on your right hand? I think Johnny'd appreciate it."

Aislynn touched his cheek and rose to kiss him.

"Hold it gal. I ain't finished," Cap objected.

With the rings in place, Cap announced, "Now, you can kiss him."

She tried to give him a quick peck, but Sage had another idea. He pulled her close and bent her backwards with a kiss.

Amy pulled on Brendan's arms, making him dance. She rejoiced, "We got a da." Sage placed Brendan on one hip and scooped Amy up onto the other. Her arms circled his neck, and she kissed his cheek.

Joan interrupted the excited child. "I'm sorry to marry and run, but it's time for us to go to school. Where do I sign?"

Cap spread the certificate of marriage on the table. After gathering all four signatures, he said, "I'll go file this." He turned to address Aislynn. "I'll be by with a wagon, and we can pack up your things and move you to Sage's. A man will be by for the stove and the heavy pieces."

As Cap headed out the door, Sage said, "I best get to work myself." He handed Brendan to his mother. Bending to her ear, he whispered, "I'll be lookin' forward to seein' you tonight."

Aislynn's shoulders slouched and a pout spread over her face. She nodded and looked away.

Sage put his hand on her cheek and redirected her eyes to his. "What's eatin' you?"

She sighed. "Nothing."

"I can see it's somethin'. You changin' your mind already?"

"No, we're married," she said.

"That's what it says on the paper."

"It wasn't much of a wedding." She sulked.

"It got it done."

Aislynn frowned. "You might as well go to work."

"Aislynn, if you want to go around again, I'd be happy to oblige but Brendan will be watchin'."

She admonished him with a stern face. "Is that all you think about? You absolutely don't understand."

"It'd be easier if you tell me the problem."

Shifting Brendan to her hip, she moved close to him. She looked into his eyes and parted her lips but hesitated. Lowering her eyes, she laid her hand on his chest and spread her fingers. She said, "Weddings should take place in church."

Sage lifted her chin and slowly shook his head. "You know I ain't a Bible thumper."

Her finger circled the button on his shirt. "Orrin," she started with an airy voice that held a promise. "Our children should be brought up in the church."

Sage ran his hand up her side. "We've been married five minutes, and you're tryin' to change me?"

With a sly grin, she said, "I believe I started that eighteen months ago."

His eyes rolled up and he took a long breath. "Gal, you ain't nothin' but trouble."

She reached up for a kiss. "I love you, too."

EPILOGUE

MARCH 1, 1875
The Legislative Council Room overflowed with guests who spanned all levels of Cheyenne society. Sage stood at the podium between Justice Howe and outgoing Governor Campbell. He smiled down at Aislynn.

Amy sat next to her mother in a starched dress, balancing a large bow on her head. A perfect little lady, she perched on the edge of her seat with her ankles crossed and her hands folded in her lap. Brendan, in short pants and a jacket identical to his father's, slipped in and out of his chair next to Captain Elliot Walker. Cap held his namesake, the two-year-old Ellie, on his knees, while baby Orrin napped in Aislynn's arms.

Behind her sat the new superintendent of the Wyoming Territorial Schools. Tim Nolan, accompanied by his wife, Virginia, their son, Daniel and daughter, Mary, watched his lifelong friend become the first lady of the territory. Paul and Maggie Avery, Tony and Emmie San Marco and Miss Joan Petty occupied the same row.

It was difficult for Aislynn to believe the man placing his hand on the Bible was Orrin Sage. Sometimes, the fact he was her husband seemed even more incredible. Her thoughts reeled back to 1868. She could see herself and Johnny sitting in the dim dining room at Ford House. In the corner, four men gambled. The man with the pale eyes, long blond hair and penetrating stare terrified her. A genuine frontiersman, dressed in buckskin, he appeared rough, raw and dangerous.

Sage epitomized all those frontiersmen who lived by their wits and their guns. Those rugged individuals, without roots or bonds, who climbed the mountains, roamed the prairies and forded the rivers. They fought Indians and outlaws. They built forts, railroads and towns. They ruled the West, until the women arrived.

The petticoat pioneers were tested by poverty, physical hardship and danger. Many were lost to overwork, illness and childbirth. Some were driven mad by the ceaseless wind and the isolation. But those gentle tamers who survived wrestled the wildness out of the West and replaced it with homes, schools, churches and civic order. A memory pushed to the front of her mind. The first day of her return to Cheyenne, in that same dining room, Sage said, "Governor Campbell says women will conquer the West." Aislynn's eyes scanned the civilized crowd and came to rest on Sage in his tailored suit and slicked-down hair. *We certainly did.*

HISTORICAL NOTES AND RESOURCES

WHEN Aislynn arrives in Cheyenne, it is in the exact state Sage describes in the first few pages. The town was out of control and residents wanted change. Outlaws roamed the streets. The Bighorn Expedition wanted Indian land. Indians' rights were ignored. Interracial marriage continued to be illegal. Illiteracy and lack of schooling remained commonplace. Women and children were abused and overworked. (I found Virginia's troubles mentioned in a few paragraphs of a book I read while researching *Far Away Home*.) Laudanum, an opiate, was over-the-counter and overprescribed, particularly to women.

However, change came and it came in the form of women like Joan, Maggie, Molly, Emmie and, of course, Aislynn. For all her naïveté, faults and mistakes, she is ever compassionate, resourceful, determined and strong. As one *Far Away Home* reviewer wrote:

"She's feisty and stubborn, but she's generous and caring. In other words—she's interesting and someone worth knowing. Aislynn is like so many women who took chances, challenged traditions and laid the groundwork for the freedoms women have today." Nancy Finch posted on Amazon June 21, 2011.

Some passages in this novel were quoted or paraphrased from newspapers or reference material. Below, I have included those sources and some additional information of interest.

Chapters 1 and 11: Sage's description of the criminal justice system and its impact on Cheyenne in Chapter 1 and the details about the introduction of female jurors in Chapter 11 are explained in the volume listed below. Although the first trial to include women jurors actually took place in Laramie, the venue and speeches were adapted for fiction.

Thomson, Rebecca W. Logan, James K. ed. "Chapter IV —Wyoming: The Territorial and District Courts." *History of the Federal Judiciary. The Federal Courts of the Tenth Circuit: A History.* Denver. US Court of Appeals for the Tenth Circuit, 1992.

Chapters 5 and 13: In Aislynn's time, *McGuffey's Eclectic Readers* were textbooks widely used by school children. Some editions are available to view for free online at Project Gutenberg.

Chapter 8, 9 and 13: For translations into the Lakota language, I used the websites:

Lakota Lexicon, www.barefootsworld.net/lakotalexicon.html and

Omniglot, www.omniglot.com/language/phrases/lakota.php

Chapter 9: This chapter addresses the scarcity of food among Native Americans who were confined to reservations and dependent on the Bureau of Indian Affairs and the military for sustenance. For those who question the presence of macaroni and processed rice in the 1870s or who are just curious about what people ate in Aislynn's time, a wonderful cookbook is available to view online: *Handbook of Practical Cookery for Ladies and Professional Cooks. Containing the Whole Science and Art of Preparing Human Food.* Pierre Blot, Professor of Gastronomy, and Founder of the New York Cooking Academy. New York: D. Appleton and Co., 1868.

Chapter 12: There is a description of Cheyenne's 4th of July celebration in the July 9,1870, edition of the *Wyoming Tribune.* For the sake of the story, I included Red Cloud in the parade. The great chief had just returned to Cheyenne on the train from Washington, DC. While Native Americans participated in parades in other communities, they were not present in Cheyenne's.

Chapter 19: Details about the election, including Mrs. Noteware's appearance, can be found in the September 17, 1870, edition of the *Wyoming Tribune.* The paraphrased Matron's letter is in the May 14, 1870 edition. By granting women the right to vote in 1869, the Wyoming Territory took a great leap forward. Women like Aislynn cast their first votes in 1870. It was not until 1919 that the US Congress passed the amendment to allow women to vote. In 1920, the 19th amendment was ratified by the 36 states needed to make it part of the US Constitution.

Chapter 20: When Brendan is born, Sage briefly describes an Osage naming ceremony. An extensive explanation can be found in *The Osage Tribe: Two Versions of the Child Naming Rite,* by Francis La Flesche. Forty-third Annual Report of the Bureau of American Ethnology to the Secretary of the Smithsonian Institution, 1925–1926, Government Printing Office, Washington, 1928, pages 23–164.

Chapter 24: Governor Campbell's attempts to pass legislation legalizing interracial marriage is on page 76 of *History of Wyoming, Second Edition.* 1990 by T.A. Larson. I found this effort quite surprising. While most of the states and territories passed laws to make miscegenation illegal, Campbell proposed the opposite. In 1967, almost 100 years later, the US Supreme Court unanimously ruled in *Loving v Virginia* that the Constitution prohibited state laws against interracial marriage.

Chapter 26: The cowboy, Trevor Hayward, says, "You sure are clean lookin'." During my research, I came across this reference several times. Women who toiled on ranches and farms when families were large, sanitation facilities were rare, water had to be hauled and soap had to be made or purchased with money that was scarce did not have the time or the means to be *clean*. Cowboys like Hayward arriving in a settled town may have never seen *city* women who had the means and the time to regularly wash clothes and keep themselves clean in the more urban fashion. In Chapter 27, Sage says, "Weren't many wide-eyed, white, female innocents rollin' through back then who weren't covered in sweat and dust. Every man in Cheyenne noticed a clean, decent woman." In 1868, when Aislynn and Johnny arrived in Cheyenne, it was just rising from the dust itself. Most women arrived after months of wagoning or days on the train with minimal or nonexistent toilet facilities. Aislynn was fortunate and exceptional to have had the benefit of stopping at boarding houses each night of her trip. They provided her with ewers of water and soap, and a chance to brush the dust, smoke and soot off her clothes.

Chapter 27: The land allocated to the Sioux in the 1868 treaty did not provide them with access to enough buffalos for the tribes to survive. In the summer of 1871, six thousand Sioux were on the move to hunt below the rail line in the Republican River Valley. This was big news and was noted in newspapers across the US. Extensive details about the issues of land allocation, reservations, treaties and Indian rights can be found in *The Nebraska Sand Hills: The Human Landscape*, by Charles Barron McIntosh, University of Nebraska Press, Lincoln and London. 1996. Reference to the hunt is on page 84.

Thank you so much for reading *EMBRACE THE WIND*. If you enjoyed this novel, please look for the first book in the series, *Far Away Home-Aislynn's Story, Book I*. You can find it on Amazon or go to www.nolimitpress.com.

At Amazon.com, readers are offered the opportunity to review *EMBRACE THE WIND*. You can also share your comments on Goodreads, Instagram, Twitter and Facebook. If you liked Aislynn's story, I would greatly appreciate you taking a few moments to let other readers know.

With deepest gratitude,
Susan

CPSIA information can be obtained
at www.ICGtesting.com
Printed in the USA
LVHW100100210722
723934LV00006B/217